Stonewall Inn M

Ke

Sunday's Child
by Edward Phillips
Sherlock Holmes and the Mysterious Friend of Oscar Wilde by Russell A. Brown
A Simple Suburban Murder by Mark Richard Zubro
A Body to Dye For
by Grant Michaels
Why Isn't Becky Twitchell Dead?
by Mark Richard Zubro
Sorry Now?
by Mark Richard Zubro
Love You to Death
by Grant Michaels
Third Man Out
by Richard Stevenson
Principal Cause of Death
by Mark Richard Zubro
Political Poison
by Mark Richard Zubro
Brotherly Love
by Randye Lordon
Dead on Your Feet
by Grant Michaels
On the Other Hand, Death
by Richard Stevenson
A Queer Kind of Love
by George Baxt
An Echo of Death
by Mark Richard Zubro
Ice Blues by Richard Stevenson
Mask for a Diva
by Grant Michaels
Sist
by
Another Dead Teenager
by Mark Richard Zubro
Shock to the System
by Richard Stevenson
Let's Get Criminal
by Lev Raphael
Rust on the Razor
by Mark Richard Zubro
Time to Check Out
by Grant Michaels
Chain of Fools
by Richard Stevenson
Government Gay by Fred Hunter
The Truth Can Get You Killed
by Mark Richard Zubro
The Edith Wharton Murders
by Lev Raphael
Federal Fag by Fred Hunter
Are You Nuts?
by Mark Richard Zubro
Dead as a Doornail
by Grant Michaels
Strachey's Folly
by Richard Stevenson
The Death of a Constant Lover
by Lev Raphael
Capital Queers by Fred Hunter
Drop Dead
by Mark Richard Zubro
Name Games by Michael Craft
One Dead Drag Queen
by Mark Richard Zurbo

By Michael Craft

Rehearsing

The Mark Manning Series

Flight Dreams
Eye Contact
Body Language
Name Games
Boy Toy

www.michaelcraft.com

NAME GAMES

A Mark Manning Mystery

Michael Craft

ST. MARTIN'S PRESS
NEW YORK

www.stonewallinn.com

Library of Congress Cataloging-in-Publication Data

Craft, Michael.
Name Games / by Michael Craft.
p. cm.
"A Mark Manning mystery"—Cover.
ISBN 0-312-24552-1 (hc)
ISBN 0-312-27079-8 (pbk)
1. Manning, Mark (Fictitious character)—Fiction. 2. Miniature objects—Collectors and collecting—Fiction. 3. Newspaper publishing—Fiction. 4. Journalists—Fiction. 5. Wisconsin—Fiction. 6. Gay men—Fiction. I. Title.
PS3553.R215 N3 2000
813'54—dc21
00-024865
CIP

First Stonewall Inn Edition: May 2001

10 9 8 7 6 5 4 3 2 1

À qui d'autre
que Léon?

Acknowledgments

The author extends apologies to the "small world" of miniature interiors, whose devotees are subjected to a bit of ribbing in this story. Further, he thanks Paul Boyer, Ray Cebula, Will Clark, Steve Culberson, Mari Higgins-Frost, Eric Olson, Leon Pascucci, Randy Price, and Paul Spottswood for their generous assistance with various plot details. Special notes of gratitude are offered to John Scognamiglio, who taught this writer to write mysteries, and to Mitchell Waters and Keith Kahla, whose efforts have advanced this series in print.

Contents

PART ONE

Small World

'ROYAL' VISIT PLANNED

Local shopkeeper announces a big event in her miniature world

By GLEE SAVAGE
Trends Editor, Dumont Daily Register

Sept. 14, DUMONT WI—Grace Lord, proprietor of The Nook, a local shop specializing in lilliputian furniture and accessories for dollhouses, announced yesterday that her store will host the annual regional exhibition of the Midwest Miniatures Society.

The show opens next weekend, on Saturday, September 23, in a large unused storefront on Tyner Avenue adjacent to The Nook. More than 100 renowned artisans and exhibitors will draw thousands of enthusiasts from Wisconsin and beyond.

Plans for the show have been under way for months, Lord (64) told the *Register,* but she learned just last week that Mr. Carrol Cantrell, the reigning "king of miniatures," has unexpectedly accepted her invitation to judge the show's main event, a roombox competition.

"Roomboxes," she explained, "are the preferred medium of most serious artisans and collectors. A single room is constructed in exacting detail, minus its fourth wall, resembling a model for a stage setting." She added that these rooms are typically built at one-twelfth scale, depicting a particular theme or design period. Figures of people are rarely used, so the finished roombox bears little resemblance to the common notion of a "dollhouse."

Carrol Cantrell (50), described by Lord as "a very big man in a very small world," is founder of the Hall of Miniatures, a large Los Angeles–based museum and store known as mecca to the miniatures crowd. Lord added, "Everyone in the field refers to him simply as Carrol, a name that is as readily understood as Barbra or Jackie."

Grace Lord modestly concedes that she accomplished no less than a professional coup in convincing Cantrell to judge the regional show at The Nook. "For one glorious weekend," she told this reporter with a wistful sigh, "Dumont, Wisconsin, will be the center of the universe—at least within *our* little world." ❑

Thursday, September 14

What's in a name?

Any journalist knows that the first order of business is to nail down the facts—the who, what, where, when, why, and how. The first of these, the who, the name of the subject, generally leads the story. The rest merely explains why that person warrants ink. An oversimplification? Maybe. But the fact remains that almost every story is about people. And we come to know people first by their names.

My name is Mark Manning. I'm forty-two, a writer by training who left his career with the *Chicago Journal* late last year, moving north to take over the reins of the *Dumont Daily Register*. My move was greeted with a measure of dismay by city friends, who insisted that my investigative-reporting skills would be wasted "up there on the tundra." I chose to refocus my career in central Wisconsin because my family roots are here, in a clean, prosperous, generally quiet little town named Dumont (the place bears no resemblance to a tundra). A sizable inheritance from my mother's family allowed me to buy the *Register*. I now serve as both its publisher and its editor.

My features editor is a woman named Glee Savage—how's *that* for a handle? On a Thursday morning in mid-September, she ran a story in our "Trends" section announcing that a local shopkeeper, Grace Lord, had secured the services of one Carrol Cantrell as judge of a miniatures show that would soon open. I had never met Grace Lord, though I recognized the family name as having something of a pedigree in Dumont. I had never heard of Carrol Cantrell, despite his stature among the dollhouse demimonde; indeed, this whole business of slaving over bitsy box-sized rooms was entirely unknown to me. Chatting with Glee in a corner of the newsroom, I complimented her on the bizarre story, but couldn't resist asking, "Are these people nuts, or just eccentric?"

"Neither!" she assured me, feigning umbrage at my comment, stretching her big red lips into a sneer. Some ten years older than I, she peered at me over her half-frame reading glasses, lecturing, "The mini world is serious business, not just some frivolous hobby." She grinned. "The 'king' is arriving this morning to take up residence for the week in Grace Lord's coach house. She invited me over to meet him—he sounds like quite a character, a good subject for a follow-up feature. Why don't you tag along?"

It was a slow morning, and my curiosity was piqued, so I did tag along—in fact, I drove. No question, my big black Bavarian V-8 would be apt to make a far loftier impression on King Carrol than would Glee's fuchsia hatchback, so we pulled away from the *Register*'s offices in style. Turning off First Avenue, Dumont's main street, I left the downtown area and drove several blocks along Park Street, crossing Wisconsin and Vincennes Avenues, toward Prairie Street. There, in what is arguably the town's nicest old residential neighborhood, I live with my lover of three years, Neil Waite, and my nephew, Thad Quatrain.

"Hey, boss," said Glee, sitting next to me in the car, "don't miss our turn. Tyner Avenue is next."

Braking hard, I swerved at the quiet intersection, apologizing for the rough ride. I had never been on that particular street before, even though it was only a few blocks from my house. The new surroundings reminded me that even though my family had deep roots in Dumont, the town was still largely unfamiliar to me. It did not yet feel like home.

Glee pointed. "The Nook is just ahead on the left. Grace Lord's house is next door."

The leafy neighborhood mixed nicer, older houses with a few tidy shops, their awnings shading the sidewalk from a benign September sun. Grace Lord's miniatures store, The Nook, already had banners hung from its eaves, announcing the exhibition of the Midwest Miniatures Society and welcoming the "king of miniatures," Carrol

Cantrell. Adjacent to the shop was a larger, vacant store, its windows soaped from within, its red-brick facade marred by rusty bolt holes where long-forgotten signage had been removed. To the opposite side of the shop, but well distanced from the street, the Lord family home sat serenely among the trees—the rolling, expansive lawn seemed the better part of an acre.

"It's huge," I told Glee, slowing the car as I approached the house.

"This area used to be the outskirts of town," Glee explained, rummaging for something in her enormous flat carpetbag of a purse. "The Lords were always well-off, and a sizable family at that, so they needed the space. But the older generation is gone now, and the others have scattered, so Grace lives here alone." Glee wagged a hand toward the drive—"You can pull all the way in, back by the coach house."

The "coach house," which soon came into view behind the main house, was a big, old two-story garage that looked like a former barn or stable. Like the house, it had walls of white clapboard, but without the Victorian trim. The ground floor still had a sliding barn door, which was closed; the upstairs, under a traditional gambrel roof, appeared to be a nicely finished living quarters, windows adorned with lacy tieback curtains. An open wooden stairway—with treads and banister freshly painted an oily green—rose along the side of the building to a covered porch that protected the door. Potted geraniums marched up the stairs and formed a riotous red hedge beneath the porch railing.

Glee and I got out of the car, closing its doors with a double thud that momentarily silenced birds in the canopy of trees. Glee walked around the car and headed for the back of the house, explaining, "The front door is never used."

I had noticed, in fact, while driving along the side of the house, that there was no walkway from the front porch to the street. Dimples in the lawn suggested that a flagstone path had once led from the porch to the driveway, now overgrown by encroaching grass and the passing of years. In contrast, the lawn behind the house was crisscrossed by well-trimmed brick walkways. One led from the driveway to the back porch. Another led from the porch to the coach-house stairs. Still another stretched across the yard to a back entrance to The Nook and continued behind the adjacent vacant building where the exhibition would be held, suggesting that both stores were part of the same property.

As Glee and I clomped up the stairs to the back of the house, we heard a yoo-hoo from the upstairs porch of the coach house. Turning, I saw a short, older woman—presumably Grace Lord—waving to us from the edge of the porch among the geraniums and the lower branches of the trees. "Thank God," she tittered with the birds. "I heard the car and thought it might be Carrol. Needless to say, I'm not ready!" She laughed at herself, as she wore a faded denim work shirt and something wrapped around her hair like a makeshift turban. She hefted a yellow plastic cleaning bucket loaded with rags, rubber gloves, and various spray bottles. Piled near her feet were odds and ends she'd removed from the guest quarters. She attempted to gather this all together so she could carry it downstairs in one load.

"Wait!" both Glee and I shouted to her. Scampering over the path and climbing the stairs to meet her, I offered, "We'll give you a hand with that," as Glee told her, "Be careful, Grace."

Grace put her things down. Through an exasperated laugh, she told us, "I guess I *could* use some help."

When Glee and I reached the landing of the stairs, she paused to tell Grace, "I don't think you've met my boss yet—the *Register*'s new publisher, Mark Manning."

I climbed the last few stairs and extended my hand. "It's a pleasure, Miss Lord." Stepping onto the porch where she waited for us, I noticed that she stood at least a head shorter than I, barely taller than five feet.

When she realized who I was, she whisked the turban off her head and wiped imagined grime from her palms before reaching to shake my hand. "*Another* distinguished visitor," she chortled, "and *me* looking like hell."

"Hardly, Miss Lord," I assured her. And indeed, her pleasant looks matched her amiable manner. Though dressed in jeans for housework, she had seemingly spent some time primping and grooming that morning, and the tight-set curls of her steely gray hair looked fresh from the corner beauty parlor. Her homey, self-deprecating humor, her diminutive stature, and her occupation as a dollhouse shopkeeper brought to mind a one-word description of the woman: impish.

She confirmed her neighborly nature by insisting, "Please, Mark, it's *Grace*. 'Miss Lord' is just a tad unbecoming at my age." And again she laughed, dismissing the bugbears of spinsterhood.

Endeared by her disarming candor, I simply told her, "Here, let me help you." And I gathered up what I could of the items she was removing from the coach house. There was a stack of linens, a wastebasket, a framed picture, and a box of junk that might have been cleaned out of desk drawers—scraps of paper, an old phone book, pencil stubs, tangled paper clips, a knot of dusty rubber bands.

Glee reached up, offering to take the cleaning supplies. Juxtaposed with the oversize tiger-stripe purse carried in her other hand, the yellow plastic bucket became an absurd addition to Glee's carefully coordinated, if over-the-edge, ensemble. I couldn't help laughing as she led us down the stairs, her leopard-spot heels pecking at the slick green-painted planks.

Oblivious to this, Grace yammered, "It really is a blessing that you arrived when you did. Carrol should be here any minute, and I was running behind getting his room in order." She added, as a note of explanation for the odd assortment of things that I carried, "I just didn't think that Carrol Cantrell, king of miniatures, would appreciate spending a week pondering the Lord family's sentimental old bric-a-brac."

As she said this, I glanced at the contents of the box, then at the photo in the frame I carried. The picture caught my eye—and how!—and I fumbled to carry it at an angle that would allow me to see it more clearly. Enshrined by the fancy carved giltwork of the frame was an old photo, an enlarged, faded snapshot of a beautiful young man at play with a Frisbee and a big friendly dog, a collie, a dead ringer for Lassie. The photo sucked me into the scene it depicted, frozen sometime in the past, somewhere in a setting of trees and rolling lawn. The man was perhaps twenty—a grown boy, really—dressed for summer in cutoffs and T-shirt. Romping with the dog, he flashed a perfect smile, flexed a perfect body.

"Most of the exhibitors have real-world jobs, so they'll be rushing up this weekend to claim spaces and set up their booths," Grace was telling Glee as we reached the bottom of the stairs, but I had lost all interest in their dialogue. Sensing my distraction, Grace explained, "That's Ward and Rascal."

I glanced up from the photo. Assuming that the latter name applied to the collie, I asked, "Who's Ward?"

"My nephew," she answered, beaming proudly. It was clear that she doted on him—who wouldn't?—but there was also a pensive edge to her smile, as if the frolicsome photo had triggered memories of happier times. She was younger back then, I realized, and perhaps the reality of her sixty-four years hadn't measured up to the promises of youth.

And I wondered about Ward. How old was he now? Where was he? What did he do? I asked, "Ward is your . . . sister's son?" I had no idea if Grace even had a sister—I was lamely fishing for any information she'd offer.

"No, my brother's." Pausing, she looked out across the vast backyard. "We've lost a tree or two since then, but otherwise, the place hasn't changed much."

Following her gaze, I realized that the photo had been snapped right there, a Frisbee toss from where we stood. I wanted more information, but feared that digging deeper might appear lecherous. What *was*, in fact, my interest in the kid whose picture I carried? Glee, who knew me too well, was already watching me with a smug grin, so I changed the subject, asking Grace, "Where should we put this stuff?"

"Here in the garage," she told us, leading the way around the corner of the building to the driveway, where she struggled to open the barn door. It inched slowly on a corroded track, and I thought I should offer to help, but my arms were full. As if reading my mind, Grace assured me, "I can get it—it just needs a little coaxing." With a grunt, she managed to slide it open wide enough for us to enter.

As the three of us stepped inside the garage, the warble of birds was snuffed with the daylight, and my senses adjusted to the dark interior space, the whiff of gasoline, the taste of dust. The shaft of light from the doorway, another from a gritty window, began to define the surroundings. As I set down the things I had carried from upstairs, Grace's car took shape—something unremarkable, a late-model Taurus, white. The rest of the space was filled with clutter, the stored debris of a lifetime, the accumulated things once treasured that would one day be the bane of griping heirs, forced to pay someone to haul it all away.

Grace flipped a switch, and several bare bulbs hanging from the rafters cast the contents of the garage into stark relief. The junk stored there, I realized, was not nearly so random a collection of miscellany as I had first presumed. No, there was a theme to this collection of remnants, a common thread to their now-defunct purpose. There were oak file cabinets, sealed cartons, and open boxes bulging with receipts and record books. Crude shelving against the wooden walls of the garage held rows of apothecary jars, both glass and ceramic varieties, their yellowed labels still whispering Latin. A marble-topped soda fountain stood upended from floor to ceiling; ice-cream tables and their wire-backed chairs were stacked for posterity in a nearby corner. A refrigerator, an old Kelvinator, still running, had a padlock affixed to its chipped chrome handle. Wedged between the refrigerator and the wall was an oblong metal sign: LORD'S REXALL. Orange streaks of rust trailed from each of its empty bolt-holes.

Grace watched as I absorbed all this. She explained, "I keep the fridge locked so little kids won't play in it." Shuddering, she added, "Can't be too safe . . ."

But it wasn't the Kelvinator that intrigued me. "That sign," I said. "Did it once hang on the vacant store next to The Nook?"

"Sure did." Grace wagged her head. "For over forty years, Lord's was Dumont's most popular drugstore. My grandfather opened it long before I was born, and my father ran it while I was in college—I studied to be a pharmacist too. But then the Walgreens chain moved into town, and Lord's Rexall was doomed. Dad and I shut it down the year after I graduated."

Although her story was succinct, told without emotion, her tone had a wistfulness that made me wonder if this broken dream of her lost career was somehow triggered by the fragment of the past captured in her nephew's photo.

Glee told us, "I remember Lord's. It was our favorite hangout—nobody made a better black cow than Grace's brother. The store closed about the time I started high school. I cried."

"So did I," Grace reminded her.

This bit of Dumont lore was interesting enough, and the sentiments of both women were touching, but I was more intrigued by Glee's mention of Grace's brother. Was Glee's pet soda jerk in fact the father of Grace's nephew Ward? Or were there other Lord brothers who might have sown the seed that produced that beautiful young man? Ward Lord—what a name—how perfectly it captured the virile energy that survived the years and still radiated from the grainy snapshot that rested near my feet in the garage that morning.

Grace waved her arms at the drugstore paraphernalia that surrounded us, telling Glee, "I finally decided it was time to confront all this and quit my grieving. My grandpa's pharmacy has been closed for nearly as long as it was open. What's done is done, and there's nothing I can do to bring it back. *Except*"—her eyes actually twinkled in the dim light of the garage—"this backlog of family tradition makes excellent raw material for a roombox project."

"Oh?" Glee's brows arched with interest. She fished a notepad from her purse.

Grace continued, "I've never really tried my hand at model-making—I've approached the shop all these years simply as a business—but I've had these unresolved feelings about the drugstore. Then, last year, I hit upon an idea that seemed both obvious and challenging. I've been toiling for months now on a miniature reproduction of Lord's Rexall. I've still got a bit of work to do on it, but my little store should be ready to unveil when the roombox competition opens next weekend." She planted her hands on her hips, a pose of easy self-satisfaction, signaling that she had very nearly vanquished the emotional baggage represented by a garageful of junk.

Glee returned her smile. "Good luck in the contest, Grace."

I added, "Hope you take first prize."

She flapped her hands, dismissing the notion. "It's probably not good enough to win—this is my first crack at a roombox, and most of the other entrants have been at this for *years*. Plus, as host of the show, I feel I should remove myself from the running. It wouldn't seem right to make Carrol Cantrell feel he was under any obligation to me when he judges the entries. So I'll enter my roombox for exhibition only."

"I'd love to see it," I told Grace. Glee nodded her enthusiasm as well.

"And I'd love to *show* it to you"—Grace moved toward the garage door, snapping out the lights—"but there's no time to dally, not now. Carrol should be arriving soon, and I've got to get into some decent clothes."

We followed her out of the garage into the bright, late morning, Glee asking, "How's Mr. Cantrell getting here?"

Grace led the way toward the back porch of the house, explaining, "He's flying into Green Bay. One of his colleagues arrived in Dumont yesterday, and he offered to pick Carrol up at the airport."

A gracious offer, I thought, as the drive to Green Bay would take an hour.

Glee flipped through the pages of her notebook as we climbed the porch stairs. She told Grace, "I didn't realize the onslaught had already begun. Who's the early arrival?"

Reaching to open the screen door, Grace turned and answered, "Bruno Hérisson." She spoke the last name with a French accent: air-ee-*soh*(*n*).

"Oh?" Glee seemed impressed, reading from her notes, "He's 'one of the world's most renowned craftsmen of miniature period furniture.' " To me, she added, "He's worth a separate feature of his own, Mark."

Lowering her voice, Grace told us in a confidential tone, "I think Bruno was a little miffed that I didn't offer *him* the coach house, but I'd already promised it to Carrol. Bruno came all the way from Paris yesterday, arriving in Milwaukee. He rented a car and found his way here on his own—it's nearly a three-hour drive. I'd have gladly picked him up, but I wasn't expecting him so early. Good thing he's here, though. I needed all the help I could get this morning. And I guess it worked out pretty well for Bruno too. He said he needed to discuss something in the car with Carrol." She checked her watch. "God, they should be here by now. If you folks want to get comfortable in the kitchen, help yourselves to lemonade—there's a fresh pitcher in the fridge—while I dash upstairs to change."

Grace opened the door wide for us and began stepping over the threshold, but it was too late. The whir of an engine, the crunch of tires on gravel, signaled that the king of miniatures was being delivered at that very moment. "Oh, Lord . . . ," Grace muttered, stepping to the edge of the porch. The door closed behind her, slapped shut by its brittle spring. Reflexively, her hands fluttered to her head, trying to do something with her hair, which looked just fine. She brushed her denim work clothes with her palms while stepping down to the driveway. Glee and I followed.

Bruno Hérisson's rented car, a no-frills compact, hurtled up the drive, swerving perilously near the house, barely missing my own car—I cringed at the thought of the damage that, by mere chance, was avoided. The car's windows were open, and its two occupants were yelling at each other. Their words were unintelligible, so I couldn't tell if the passenger was merely upset with the driver's questionable skills or if it was some ongoing argument that suddenly ended as the car lurched to a standstill within inches of where we stood.

"Jee-sus *Christ!*" barked the passenger as he swung his door open and bounded to his feet, escaping the vehicle as if he feared it would explode. "Insane Frenchman—" Then, seeing us, his tone changed and he forced a laugh, a piercing, well-practiced look-at-me laugh.

This was apparently Carrol Cantrell. In that morning's interview in the *Register,* Grace had called him "a very big man in a very small world," a description that proved to be literal as well as figurative. King Carrol stood bigger than life, at least six feet four, and I wondered how he'd endured an hour's ride in that tiny car. Though I knew his age to be fifty, his features were skillfully frozen at thirty-nine. Everything about the man—his too white teeth, his streaked-blond hairdo, his exaggerated movements and flamboyant manner—gave the monarch of miniatures an air that was decidedly queenly.

Then the driver's door opened. With considerable difficulty, Bruno Hérisson, a beast of a man, extricated himself from behind the wheel with a sputtering of oaths that, to my uncertain ear, sounded more aggressively Teutonic than charmingly Gallic. Heaving himself from the car, he told the heavens, "Ah, Cantrell! I am so blessed—the honor of hauling his precious majesty to and fro. I am but your humble handmaiden, Cantrell!" and he dipped on one knee in an absurd curtsy. His accent was thick with throaty *r*'s and aspirate *h*'s, spoken through a French pucker, but his command of English was otherwise solid, and his meaning was clear: he and Carrol Cantrell didn't get along.

With a smirk, Cantrell dismissed the antics of his colleague and whisked past him to introduce himself to us, insisting that all of us simply call him Carrol. He was especially deferential to Grace Lord, his hostess, and studiously polite to Glee and me, "the press." Engaged in conversation with us (his vivacious patter was likable enough, if phony), he ignored Bruno, who unloaded Carrol's luggage from both the backseat and the trunk of the car, muttering at the task.

An odder couple could not have blown into Dumont that morning. Carrol was almost freakishly tall and lanky, affectedly glib, obviously gay, stylishly dressed for travel in a sleek Armani suit, its jacket worn over a T-shirt—very California. By contrast, Bruno was a burly man, an unlikely figure in the tiny, fragile world of miniature furniture—the proverbial bull in a china shop. His clothes were wrinkled, and the sleeves of his corduroy jacket rode halfway up his forearms as he grunted and struggled with Carrol's luggage, heaping it into a mound next to the car. Bruno's sole affectation (or was it just that he was French?) was the richly patterned silk scarf knotted around his neck, its ends fluttering from the open collar of his shirt. He was sweating now, but Carrol looked cool and utterly unruffled by their argument in the car.

"I can't begin to tell you," Grace was telling Carrol, still primping, "how honored we are that you've consented to judge the roombox competition. The Midwest Miniatures Society is *abuzz!*"

"The honor is mine, of course," he assured her, patting her head. His stature was gigantic compared to her tiny frame.

"It's not just the fact that you own the Hall of Miniatures," Grace bubbled onward, "but the fact that you represent all of the world's major artisans—including, of course, the esteemed Mr. Hérisson."

Bruno mumbled something in French. The words were unintelligible, but his tone carried unmistakable sarcasm.

Glee entered the conversation, telling Carrol, "Grace has been working on a roombox of her own."

Grace quickly added a good-natured rebuff: "But it's not finished—you'll all see it in due time."

I told Carrol, "Don't feel slighted—she wouldn't show *us* either." It was the first time I'd addressed him since being introduced.

He spun to look at me. "Oh, really?" He smiled while eyeing me—those teeth really were too white—bleached, capped, who knows? His gaze gave me a quick once-over, sizing me up. I wore my usual workday "uniform"—khaki slacks, navy blazer, button-down shirt, striped tie—nothing fashion-forward, by any stretch. Perhaps he found me refreshingly wholesome, because his inquisitive look mutated into an eat-me leer. "What would it take to persuade her?" he asked me, his voice subdued to a purr.

"I think she just needs a little more time." Our small talk had grown meaningless, as my mind was absorbed by his come-on. Not that I was interested. I was happily attached to Neil, and more to the point, I wasn't at all attracted to Carrol. Still, it felt good to be cruised by another gay man—a rare commodity in Dumont.

"Mark, has anyone ever told you, you have the most arrestingly green eyes?"

Bruno interrupted this exchange. "If you gentlemen have finished with your chitchat"—he pronounced it more like *shit-shot*—"perhaps we could all assist his majesty in conveying his *matériel* up to the royal quarters." He flipped the tail of his gold-toned cravat over one shoulder. "Then I must leave."

Glee and I stole a glimpse of each other and, though tempted, suppressed the urge to snicker. What, I wondered, was the background of this sparring between Bruno and Carrol—professional rivalry, or something more personal?

We all exchanged a shrug of resignation, then set about the task of hauling Carrol's things toward the coach-house stairs. By my calculation, the king of miniatures would be staying in Dumont no more than ten days, but from the look of his luggage, you'd have thought he was staying for good. Indeed, I was amazed that Bruno had managed to get all of it into his car. There was a matched set of suitcases, Vuitton, of course. Added to this were an array of garment bags, duffels, leather briefcase, computer case—even a hatbox.

As Carrol leaned to lift a couple of his bags from the ground, the sleeves of his jacket rode up his arms, and I noticed that he wore jewelry on both hands—too much, in my opinion, even for a gay man. There were several rings, bracelets, and a diamond-studded watch, all of it the highly refined craft of top designers, with a single exception. Conspicuously, one of his baubles was not polished gold, but scuffed nickel—a utilitarian chain around his wrist held a medallion with a worn enamel symbol on it. Though I couldn't read it from where I stood, it appeared to be a Medic Alert bracelet.

Also inconsistent with Carrol's fastidious attire was a fat pen of inelegant design that was clipped to his inside breast pocket. I have always had an affection for fountain pens—my own pet pen, an antique Montblanc, is a civilized luxury in an age of throwaway ballpoints and felt-tips. So while I admired the man for taking a stand against the pervasive Bic culture, I was dismayed by his particular choice of writing instrument, which was, in a word, butt ugly (okay, two words).

"Hey!" a voice interrupted us as we began our ungainly procession up the stairs to the coach house. "Let me help!" Trotting up the driveway alongside the house was Douglas Pierce, sheriff of Dumont County. Stopping at the foot of the stairs, he explained, "I saw your car, Mark, and wondered what was up."

Carrol now took note of the Bavarian V-8 and told me as an aside, winking, "Tasty wheels, Mark."

Pierce's arrival necessitated introductions to both Carrol and Bruno, so we all took a moment to set down our loads while performing these courtesies. It wasn't easy conveying to Bruno the nature of Pierce's job, none of us knowing if there was a French counterpart to an American sheriff. Avoiding allusions to Hollywood or the Wild West, I explained, "The city of Dumont is part of Dumont County, and the county maintains our police force. Doug is chief of the county police."

Bruno nodded, but still seemed muddled. Tentatively, he asked Pierce, "This is how you . . . dress?"

Pierce laughed. "I'm an elected administrator. I don't wear a uniform."

Bruno's confusion was understandable. I'd first met Doug Pierce during the week I moved to Dumont. Arriving from the big bad city, I harbored the jaded view that the local constabulary would be straight out of Mayberry, but Pierce didn't fit that stereotype at all. To begin with, he did *not* wear a uniform—no badge, no six-shooter, no cop trappings. In fact, he was a natty dresser, far nattier than I, and I never saw him wear the same thing two days running. There was some trouble back then, and Pierce proved himself a dedicated professional, a new friend, and an important news source in my work at the *Register*. I'm truly glad to know him.

But I wish I knew him better. Though I see him nearly every day—he often stops by the paper to visit, and he frequently joins us at the house for breakfast after his morning workout—there's a sector of his private life that's strictly off-limits. At forty-five, he has never married, claiming to be wed to his career. Perhaps it's just my mind-set, but naturally I suspect he's gay, and he has never said anything to dissuade me from this notion. Someday, I keep telling myself, when the time is right, I'll simply ask him about this, point-blank.

"My," cooed Carrol Cantrell, "you're certainly an accommodating public servant, Sheriff." He was giving Pierce the same once-over he had given me only minutes before.

Pierce obligingly swept up several of Carrol's bags, including the hatbox. "I need to foster all the goodwill I can—I'm up for reelection this November." Pierce laughed again, and I suddenly got the impression that he was actually *enjoying* Carrol's come-on.

As we all began plodding up the stairs together, Carrol paused to finger the lapel of Pierce's sport coat. "Beautiful jacket, Sheriff. Ralph Lauren?"

Puh-leez.

Pierce answered, "Nah. Brooks Brothers." He may have blushed.

Watching this exchange, I realized that in the year I'd known him, I'd come to take Pierce's good looks for granted. For a middle-aged man, he was perfectly fit and ruggedly handsome, an image that was complemented by his knack for dressing well. Carrol was right: Pierce *was* wearing a beautiful jacket, rusty tweed, exactly right for the in-between weather of that autumn morning. His gray flannel slacks, double-pleated with razor-sharp creases, found a dead match in the darker tones of the tweed jacket. He *deserved* Carrol's compliments.

Continuing up the stairs, Carrol chattered vacuously about something as we, his retinue, prepared to ensconce him in Grace Lord's coach house.

To the fanfare of his own ringing laughter, the king, indeed, had arrived.

Friday, September 15

Domesticity had never played much of a role in my life. During my younger years, as a bachelor reporter, building a career at the *Chicago Journal*, I had little time for nest-feathering and not much interest in it either. But two events—turning points, really—would effect a profound change in my indifference to house and home.

First, I met Neil. I had never been truly in love before, and then, at thirty-nine, I found it—with a man (egads) who happened to be an architect. This resolved a particular identity crisis that had long gnawed at me (I could no longer brush aside the suspicion that I might be gay), and just as certainly, it imbued in me a new appreciation for the great indoors. I had bought a condominium loft in Chicago's trendy Near North neighborhood, but it was Neil who moved from Phoenix to live with me, setting his talents to designing and rebuilding the space. When we'd finished the project, we had carved out a magazine-perfect showplace; we'd also built a "home."

Then, less than a year ago, within a week of my move north to Dumont, Thad Quatrain's life merged with mine. It was an inauspicious melding, to say the least. My nephew (technically, a second cousin) was an absolute snot toward Neil and me, with all the charm and lovability of a juvenile homophobic bigot, which in fact he was on the day when he met us. Imagine his dismay when, that very afternoon, his mother died young and I was named in her will to look after him. Imagine *his* dismay? Imagine *mine*.

Having grown comfortable in the role of a "gay urban professional," I had never given a moment's thought to the possibility of rearing a child, but there I was, suddenly faced with that unlikely task. Adapting to the day-to-day weirdness of life with a teenager would be challenging enough; far more daunting was the forced change of mind-set, the identity crisis. How was I to think of my *self?* Did my vocabulary even possess the words that might name this new *me?* Gay dad, Uncle Mark, Neil's lover, Thad's father . . .

But we managed to pull together—Thad and I, and Neil too. While Neil taught me how to become half of a couple, Thad has taught me to be part of a family. Domesticity now plays a large role in my life. As a result, the focus of my days has changed.

There was a time, not so long ago, when the evening cocktail hour embodied my notion of the day's ultimate reward—a brief, civilized period of repose, refreshment, and conversation, replete with its own comforting rituals—the polishing of crystal to perfect cleanliness, the clink of ice, the skoal, the first shared sip. Neil and I declared an ingenuous concoction to be "our" drink on the night we met, and every evening since (every evening, that is, when we have been together), we have poured Japanese vodka over ice, garnishing it with orange peel while leaving the day's travails behind.

Now this routine has been interrupted and refocused. The interruption was my own doing, the result of moving north to Wisconsin to try my hand as a publisher. Neil's architectural practice would keep him anchored to Chicago, so he agreed to a plan of alternating weekend visits with me, taking turns at the four-hour drive. Our "arrangement" had barely begun when that unexpected death in the Quatrain family left me executor of a huge estate that includes Quatro Press, Dumont's largest industry. Because I now serve on Quatro's board of directors, I had no trouble securing for Neil a contract to design a major expansion of the printing plant. The project has kept him in Dumont full-time for several months, and we feel like a couple again, sharing the same bed nightly. Once again, our evenings are a time when we can regularly, predictably share the simple adult pleasure of cocktails at home.

But now "home" has a new meaning for us. There is a sixteen-year-old living under our roof, and that roof represents *his* home as well. Even though Neil and I still enjoy our drink before dinner, this is not a ritual that can include Thad. He is, of course, too young to booze with us, and even if we'd permit it, he could not fully grasp the pleasure, meaning, and responsibility of the cocktail hour. In time, he'll learn these things. Not yet though.

So the focus of my days has shifted from seven in the evening to seven in the morning. Breakfast—who'd have thought it?—has become the central event in our shared life as a family. We know there will be no other activities to rob us of each other's company at that hour. We can use that time to stay in touch. We can talk.

"We need peanut butter," said Thad, clanging a knife within the nearly empty jar, scooping out the last of the beige goo, spreading it on a piece of hot toast. He wore one of those long, baggy sweaters that hang a foot below the waist.

"It's on the list," Neil told him, looking up from the "Trends" section of that Friday's edition of the *Dumont Daily Register*. "I'll shop tomorrow morning."

"*That* bites." Thad sat at the kitchen table between Neil and me—we faced each other from opposite sides, dressed for work, me in a tie, Neil in a soft but tight turtleneck that displayed a buffed upper torso he'd be foolish to hide. Across from Thad, a fourth place was set with a napkin and an empty mug, should Sheriff Pierce join us, as was his habit.

It was a homey scene, in spite of its not-so-typical cast of characters. The setting too had an atypical edge. The house, built by my late uncle, my mother's brother, had been designed by a student of Frank Lloyd Wright at Taliesin. It was vintage Prairie School, a style that, while distinctly American, is a rarity in its purest execution. The kitchen had been updated before I moved into the house, but it was a thoughtful renovation, sensitive to Wright's style, leaving no doubt that we occupied a "significant" home. Walls of elongated horizontal brick intersected elegantly vertical cabinets of pale wood. A row of high windows punctured the outside wall, framing rectangles of a perfect September sky. The back door stood open to a cool morning breeze that huffed through the screen and whorled with the smell of hot coffee.

Thad chomped his toast, gulped his milk. Peering at him over the front section of the paper, I asked, "*What* bites?"

Thad cast a sympathetic glance toward Neil, telling me, "Shopping on Saturday." Thad shuddered at the thought of the crowded supermarket, the wasted weekend morning. "Hazel always shopped during the week."

I reminded him, "Hazel's somewhere in Florida." We were speaking of Hazel Healy, the unlikely name of the Quatrain family's longtime housekeeper, now retired. All of us were still busy adjusting to our new life together in the house on Prairie Street, so we'd put off the search for live-in help. The prospect of bringing a stranger into our home had little appeal for any of us, though we all recognized the logistical advantages that would be reaped from finding Hazel's successor.

"I don't mind," Neil told us, referring to the shopping. "Really." He was gracious if not sincere—the thought of slogging through those crammed aisles with a clattering, banged-up wire cart was enough to knot my stomach.

Changing the subject, I asked Thad, "Two weeks into it, how does it feel to be an upperclassman?" He had just started his junior year.

"Okay, I guess. I like most of my classes, but chemistry's a drag."

Neil winced, remembering something painful. "I never got the hang of chemistry either. I kept telling myself that it was something like cooking—that the chemical equations were just 'recipes'—but one afternoon during lab, my experimental dash of ammonia in Clorox turned the brew in my beaker sufficiently toxic to evacuate an entire wing of the school. The mixture had produced chloramine gas, a particularly noxious agent." He laughed lamely.

Thad's laughter was hearty. "So *then* what happened?"

"My counselor finally bought my argument that chemistry was of no use to an aspiring architect, and he let me transfer directly into physics. The lab sessions were considerably less hazardous, but it was still no fun."

Thad thought for a moment. "Neil? What *did* you do for fun?"

Neil glanced at me. The night before, in bed, we'd aired our concern that while Thad seemed committed enough to his classes, he had no apparent outside interests. Sports did nothing for him, in spite of our gentle prodding to make a runner out of him, an activity that both Neil and I still enjoyed together; we'd have happily included him. The dating bug had not yet bitten, though it was surely only a matter of time. As for clubs or band or whatever, he just wasn't involved. And though he never spoke of it, we assumed he was still in repressed mourning over the loss of his mother. Neil and I agreed that it was important for Thad to find *something*, or his boredom might lead to trouble.

So Neil answered, "I ran cross-country. And I got into extracurricular art projects—set-decorating for school plays. I was even *in* a play or two." He could also have mentioned chairing the decorating committee for his prom, but he must have decided Thad would judge his experience with tinsel and chicken wire a tad fruity.

Thad's face wrinkled in thought as he wiped peanut butter from the corner of his mouth. He asked me, "How 'bout you, Mark? What'd *you* do in school—I mean, besides 'school.' "

I set the newspaper on the table and folded it. "Well, I ran cross-country and track. And I worked on the yearbook and the school paper."

Thad nodded, thinking. Then, turning again to Neil, he said, "There's going to be a play at school. But first you need to know about acting and stuff, right?"

"*No*," Neil and I said in unison, leaning toward the boy.

Neil told him, "You have to start somewhere, and that's what school is for."

I added, "It's worth a try. When are auditions?"

Neil asked, "What's the play?"

Thad's head wagged between us as we questioned him. With a half-laugh, he told us, "I'm not sure. But I'll ask around."

I suggested, "Your English teacher should know all about it."

"I'll ask," he repeated, signaling that we shouldn't push further, not today. He got up from the table, crossed to the refrigerator, and poured himself another glass of milk. Before returning, he offered, "More coffee?"

"Sure," we answered. "Thanks."

As Thad poured Neil's coffee, he looked over Neil's shoulder at the "Trends" section, which displayed another feature by Glee Savage. Headlined THE KING HAS ARRIVED, it detailed our visit to Grace Lord the previous morning, when Glee and I had met Carrol Cantrell, the king of miniatures. Skimming the story, Thad nearly spilled the coffee. "Oops. Sorry." He set the pot on the table. "These people sound a little weird."

Though I agreed with his assessment, I explained diplomatically, "Let's just say they have a somewhat eccentric obsession." I grinned, reaching for the coffee.

"Not at all," said Neil, putting down the paper. His reproachful tone conveyed surprise at my attitude. "The art of model-making has an illustrious history that's long been intertwined with my own field. Miniatures have always played a role in the design of big architectural projects. I've built a few models myself and have nothing but respect for the true masters of the craft."

Neil stood to continue—he was on a roll now. "Consider the Thorne Rooms at the Art Institute of Chicago. Commissioned by Mrs. James Ward Thorne and built by the master miniaturist Eugene Kupjack, mostly in the 1930s, that series of sixty-eight shadow boxes traces four centuries of European and American interior design—all in the space of a darkened hallway. They're magnificent."

"They are," I agreed. I'd forgotten about the Thorne Rooms, but as soon as Neil mentioned them, I recalled being awed by them as a child. I told Thad, "Sometime soon, let's spend a weekend down at our loft in the city. We'll take you to the Art Institute, and you can see the Thorne Rooms for yourself—they're really worth the visit."

"Cool." His tone was flat, not quite enthusiastic, but at least he didn't react with that dreaded adolescent smirk. He was making a genuine effort to show some interest in our shared lives. While I assumed he had little interest in the Thorne Rooms, I knew that he'd enjoy a trip to the city on any pretext.

I reminded Neil, "That display represents the height of the craft. Somehow, I doubt if Grace Lord's roombox competition will be in the same league."

He laughed while crossing to the sink with his cup and a plate of crumbs. "Don't be so sure. With both Carrol Cantrell and Bruno Hérisson here, the stakes have been raised considerably."

I noticed that Neil had pronounced *Hérisson* flawlessly. "You've *heard* of these guys?"

"They're . . . 'names' to me." He sloshed the remainder of his coffee down the sink and opened the dishwasher, depositing the cup and the plate. Thad brought his own dishes over and added them to the load.

Checking my watch, I downed my coffee. "Looks like Doug isn't joining us."

Thad wondered, "Where *is* Sheriff Pierce? He hasn't missed breakfast all week." Then he grabbed his pile of books from the counter. "I've gotta go—need to review an assignment before class." He gave each of us a shoulder hug. "Bye, guys. See you tonight."

We wished him a good day at school and watched as he bounded out the back door. I was about to mention to Neil that I was beginning to feel content in our new, offbeat role as parents when the thought was interrupted by Thad's voice. "Morning, Sheriff," he said from the driveway. "They're waiting for you."

And moments later, Doug Pierce rapped on the screen door. "Any coffee left?" he asked while walking in. Responding to our curious grins, he said with a shrug, "Just running late today. Didn't even have time to work out."

As he approached the kitchen table, I noticed that he hadn't even had time to shave that morning, leaving him with an ungroomed look that was not his style at all. What's more, he wore the same rusty tweed jacket I'd seen the day before, and the pleats of his gray flannel slacks had lost their sharp creases. It was enough to make me think he hadn't gone home overnight. Clearly, though, nothing was wrong—there was an uncharacteristic bounce to his step as he pulled out a chair and sat next to me. He grabbed the empty cup that had been set for him across the table and repeated the question, "Any coffee left?" Big smile.

I wanted to ask, Where were *you* last night? You and Carrol Cantrell . . . ? But I didn't feel I should confront him, and besides, it was none of my business. "You're in luck," I told him, hefting the pot and pouring. "We were about to toss it."

Neil circled back to the table, reading my mind. Prepared for a delicious story, he perched on his chair and leaned forward on his elbows, waiting.

If Pierce knew what we were thinking, he didn't let on. "Thad was chipper this morning," he told us. "He seems to be adjusting to . . . everything."

By "everything," Pierce was referring not only to Thad's loss of his mother, but to his new life with two gay dads. I told Pierce, "We're all learning to deal with it. Even though Thad resented my very existence at first, he quickly concluded that life with Uncle Mark and Uncle Neil would be vastly preferable to life with that addled 'feminazi.' " I laughed in spite of the bitter encounters I'd had with Miriam Westerman—that harridan, that shrew, that burned-out hippie—founder of the local (and only) chapter of the Feminist Society for the New Age of Cosmological Holism, or FSNACH, known as Fem-Snach among its detractors, which certainly included the three of us in the kitchen that morning.

"Miriam never stood a chance," Pierce assured me. With one hand, he lifted his coffee and slurped; with the other, he dismissed Miriam's failed efforts to convince the courts to grant her custody of Thad.

In the early days of the Society, Thad's unmarried mother, Suzanne Quatrain, had been a sympathizer with Miriam's militant feminist movement. When Suzanne gave birth, Miriam claimed the baby as a communal child of the Society, naming him Ariel. That was all too much for Suzanne, and she broke from the movement, raising Thad on her own—there was certainly no financial burden, as she became principal heir to the huge printing company Quatro Press. Then, when Suzanne died last year, Miriam renewed her efforts to get control of Thad, claiming I was unfit to raise him. But sanity reigned.

"Watch your step," Neil warned me, joking. "Ms. Fem-Snach is still pissed."

"So am I," I reminded him. Rising from the table, I asked Pierce, "Can I get you a doughnut or something?" He nodded, so I crossed to the counter and searched a cupboard or two for some pastry that Neil had put away.

"Fortunately," said Pierce, picking up the conversation, "Miriam has her hands full right now with the opening of her new school—I'm amazed she ever got it off the ground. She's way too busy to dwell on past battles, let alone lost ones."

"Don't forget"—I turned to him—"she hasn't been too busy to dwell on her old antiporn battle. She just might throw a wrench into your reelection."

Before Pierce could respond, Neil asked, "What's up with *that?*" His tone was vexed. "Most feminists are liberal to the core. What's her beef?"

Pierce drummed his fingers, grinning. "Miriam contends that pornography is 'violence against women.' End of argument."

"Unfortunately," I added, "she managed to recruit Harley Kaiser, our esteemed district attorney, in her efforts to bully the county board into passing a so-called 'obscenity ordinance' a while back. Now she wants stricter enforcement of it, hoping to shut down a few adult bookstores—porn shops—on the edge of town."

Neil blinked. "But I've always sort of . . . *enjoyed* pornography, an occasional video," he said innocently.

"Too bad," I told him. "Miriam is pro-choice to the hilt, but not when it comes to *your* viewing or reading habits." Then, setting a plate of Danish on the table in front of Pierce, I asked him, "Didn't you go to school with these folks?"

"Yup. Miriam and Harley and I all grew up together; we're the same age, forty-five. Miriam's always been an ideologue, never happy unless she's in the heat of a crusade, so her antismut mission is predictable. That's just Miriam. But Harley Kaiser is altogether different. He's practical, intelligent, a politician. Though he's a family man, he's never struck me as a family-values type. He simply sniffed political pay dirt in Miriam's obscenity campaign, so he hopped on the bandwagon. They're an odd alliance."

"Strange bedfellows." Sitting at the table again, I laughed at the image conjured by my metaphor.

Neil said to Pierce, "I assume you have no taste for this censorship campaign."

"None whatever"—Pierce shook his head decisively—"but as the county's chief law-enforcement officer, my leeway is limited. If the DA wants deputies to collect 'evidence'—adult videos—it falls to my department to do it. Harley's brought a few cases to trial already, but he hasn't had much luck convincing juries as to exactly what's 'obscene.' "

"Ah," I interjected, "the plebeian wisdom of the common man."

"Exactly. But now Harley is preparing to bring another obscenity case to trial. He's really done his homework this time, and he's planning to bring in a busload of expert witnesses. From his perspective, it's a must-win situation. Funding is about to expire for the assistant prosecutor hired to staff these cases, and the county board is losing patience. Without a win, they'll pull the plug—and Kaiser will lose staff, budget, and political luster."

"According to Rox, he's a hot dog." Neil was speaking of Roxanne Exner, a Chicago attorney who had come up to Dumont to help me with Thad's custody matters. She was also the friend who, three years earlier, had introduced Neil and me.

"She's right," Pierce agreed, adding, "but you didn't hear it from me. I'm up for reelection in less than eight weeks, and Miriam already feels betrayed by my foot-dragging on Harley's porn raids. If I antagonize him too, then I *am* in trouble."

I nodded. "Enter Deputy Dan."

"Who?" asked Neil.

Pierce explained, "Dan Kerr, one of my deputies, decided he needs a promotion, so he's running for my job. There really aren't any significant issues to argue, so he's been making noise about stricter enforcement of the county's obscenity laws. Needless to say, Miriam is behind him all the way—for whatever *that's* worth. But I think the DA is in Kerr's camp as well. If Harley were to openly endorse him, I'd be in for a tough fight."

I reached to give Pierce a reassuring pat on the shoulder. "Don't worry. I have no idea whether Harley Kaiser will be offering any endorsements, but I'm certain that the *Dumont Daily Register* will. And I'll say this: Deputy Dan lacks credibility."

"Agreed." Pierce nodded. Then he looked me in the eye. "But Dr. Tenelli has heaps of it."

Now it was my turn to ask, "Who?"

"Dr. Benjamin Tenelli, chairman of the County Plan Commission, is preparing to announce his panel's assessment of the obscenity issue in terms of its *economic* impact on Dumont."

"That's a new angle," I admitted, "but who *is* he?"

"A retired obstetrician, he delivered nearly every baby in town for some forty years. To call Dr. Tenelli a beloved and respected figure is an understatement. Now nearly seventy, he devotes much of his time to public service."

While Pierce extolled the good doctor's impeccable reputation and civic altruism, I reached into the inside pocket of my blazer, which hung on the back of my chair. Names—it seemed I was awash with names that morning, and their unfamiliarity served to remind me that I was still an outsider in Dumont. Though now performing the duties of a newspaper publisher, I could never shake my roots as a reporter, and I still kept always within reach two essential tools. Extracting the notepad and pen from my jacket, I uncapped the Montblanc and scrawled a few pertinent facts regarding Dr. Tenelli.

Pierce concluded, "He's one of the few men I know without an enemy in the world. If he decides that it's good for Dumont County to crack down on porn—on moral grounds, economic grounds, or any other—you can bet that the public will elect as sheriff the candidate who's taken a tough stand on smut. On a gray Wednesday morning in November, Dan Kerr could plant his ass behind my desk."

He swirled the last of the coffee in his mug, paused, checked his watch. "Speaking of my desk, I'd better get moving—I'm late already." He rose.

Rising with him, I quipped, "Shouldn't you shave first?"

He scratched his chin, allowing, "I keep a razor down at the department."

Neil stood. "Want some coffee 'to go'?"

"Nah." Pierce walked to the door. "Thanks, guys. See you later."

"Bye, Doug," we told him. And he was gone.

Neil gathered some last few things from the table, carried them to the sink, and loaded the dishwasher. "I need to get going myself. Busy day today."

I walked up behind him and wrapped my arms around his waist. "We have the house to ourselves for once. No kids, no cops—"

"No sale," he interrupted, turning to me with a laugh. "There's just no time. Besides, we're both washed and dressed for the day."

"You're so practical," I observed dryly.

"I thought that's why you found me attractive."

"It's an asset. But there's a great deal more." And I kissed him.

It was a leisurely kiss, longer than a casual peck, but not long enough to qualify as foreplay. Sometimes I think that these are my happiest moments with him, when we share the simple intimacy of a kiss. I love everything about it, everything about him—the plumpness of his lips, the slick feel of his teeth on my tongue, even the smell of coffee on his breath.

It doesn't make sense. There's nothing rational about it.

It must be pheromonal.

By midmorning, the buzz of activity in the *Register*'s second-floor newsroom had risen to its weekly high. The daily deadline wouldn't pass till evening, but Fridays were hectic all day, with weekend features and Sunday sections being put to bed in advance. In days gone by, the hubbub would have been overlaid by the tatter of typewriters and the pounding of Teletype machines, but now, of course, words destined for print are processed by the silent whir of electronics. Some things haven't changed though: phones still jangle, editors still shout from desk to desk, writers still dash to their stories.

Glee Savage dashed past the glass wall of my outer office, catching my eye as I glanced up from my desk. She wore a wide-brimmed hat, but didn't carry one of her outlandish carpetbag purses, so I knew she wasn't leaving the building. A minute or two later she returned—with none other than Bruno Hérisson in tow. A big, beefy man, he panted from the exertion of climbing the stairs from the first-floor lobby.

"Look who's here, Mark," Glee called from the doorway to my office.

I strode from my desk to greet Bruno in the outer office. The space was meant for a secretary, but unlike the previous publisher, Barret Logan, I simply depended on the receptionist at the main switchboard, so the extra room served as an impromptu conference area. The decorating was tasteful if quotidian, and I wondered once more what these quarters might look like if I were to turn Neil loose with his talents—but he had other priorities just then, as did I. Shifting my attention to Bruno, curious about the purpose of his visit, I invited him and Glee to be seated. Closing the door to the newsroom, I joined them.

As we settled into the upholstered chairs around a low table, I said, "This is an unexpected pleasure, Mr. Hérisson," mangling his last name, which came out like "Harrison" with a misplaced accent. Graciously, he invited both Glee and me to use his first name, a familiarity rarely extended by the French, which suggested that he had already spent considerable time in America. We of course reciprocated.

"Bruno phoned earlier," Glee told me, "saying he needed to 'talk.' Needless to say, my antenna shot up." Indeed, she already had a steno pad at the ready, folded open atop a stack of papers and magazines she had carried into the room. Turning to the Frenchman, she clicked her pen. "If you don't mind, let's run through some background details first. The name is Hérisson, acute accent on the *e*, correct?"

"Accent *aigu*"—he jotted the mark in the air with his finger. "Correct."

"And your permanent residence is in France?"

"Yes, in Paris."

"May I ask your age?"

He squirmed a bit, knotting the tip of his gold silk scarf around an index finger. He acknowledged, "I have forty-eight years."

Glee looked up from her pad, slid her reading glasses down her nose, and stared over them at him. "My God, Bruno, you could pass for *thirty*-eight. This'll be *our* little secret." She winked at him confidentially—what a pro.

In response to her flattery, the man positively beamed. "You are too kind."

"Not at all." Without missing a beat, she asked, "Married?"

Bruno cleared his throat. "Divorced." Speaking slowly, he added, "My work, said my wife, has consumed all my love. We were together twenty years, but she wanted a new life. I could not refuse her, no? We have no children." He fell silent.

"I understand," Glee told him, not recording these particulars. Changing her line of questioning, she asked, "Would I be correct, Bruno, in telling my readers that you're the world's most renowned craftsman of miniature period furniture?"

"But of course." His attitude was not smug; he was being flatly objective. Then he raised a finger. "To be accurate, *chère* Glee, you might refer to me as a renowned 'artisan.' That is the term often applied to those of us who craft the miniature furniture of highest quality."

"Wonderful. Thank you," she said, making note of the distinction. "And the reason you're here for the convention of the Midwest Miniatures Society—is it in order to exhibit your pieces or to sell them?"

"Both. I shall conduct workshops as well. There are many who are eager to learn my methods, my 'tricks that click,' as you say." He chortled.

Glee leaned forward in thought, fingers to chin. "I have no idea, Bruno, and I'm curious: What is the price range of your furniture?"

"Ah"—he tossed his hands in the air—"that depends. It depends upon whether the piece is a simple side chair or an intricate cylinder-top desk, either of which would fit into the palm of your hand."

I asked, "What's a cylinder-top desk?"

Glee turned and explained to me, "It's a type of rolltop desk. The sliding hardwood cover is a solid cylinder instead of slatted."

Bruno continued, "The price further depends upon who is selling it, whether it is I . . . or . . . or Cantrell!" His eyes bugged and he became suddenly animated as he invoked the name of the king of miniatures.

"For instance," Glee persisted, "what is the price of one of your marvelous cylinder-top desks in the Louis Quinze style?"

Bruno fidgeted, converting francs on his fingers. "I would charge some six thousand dollars. His majesty Cantrell, however, would sell it for twelve, perhaps as high as fifteen."

"*Thousand?*" asked Glee, dropping her pen.

"*Dollars?*" I blurted.

"It is the truth," he told us calmly, sitting back in his chair, resting his case.

"I had no idea . . . ," Glee muttered as she retrieved her pen and scratched the numbers on her pad.

I joked, "You could buy a damned nice full-size desk for much less."

"Yes," he conceded, "but it would not be one of *my* desks." Harrumph.

Glee asked him, "Are these markups—a hundred percent or more—typical of Carrol Cantrell's profits?"

"Always." He sniffed.

I was tempted to comment, Good for King Carrol—whatever the market will bear. But I kept these thoughts to myself.

Bruno continued, "Cantrell, who cannot himself construct even the most simple miniature . . . *box*, is but a merchant, a 'middleman.' His arrogance is matched only by his lack of talent—unless, of course, one considers it a talent to merely sell the work of others. He has profited more from my labors than I myself have. His profits are obscene!"

I wondered wryly whether obscene profits fell under the purview of Dumont County's obscenity ordinance. Our hot-dog DA could make headlines by raiding the miniatures convention and hauling a group of shackled artisans into court for trafficking in obscenely priced toy desks. As I struggled to compose a clever caption to accompany the page-one photo developing in my mind's eye, Bruno verbalized his own concluding thoughts:

"Cantrell is not the *king* of miniatures, no! He is in fact the reigning *parasite* of our precious little world. The time has arrived to *expose* him"—he smashed his clenched fist once, thunderously upon the table—"to *topple* him!"

Glee and I glanced at each other, restraining our reaction to this outburst. With perfect composure, she studied her notes while asking, "In what sense, Bruno, do you wish to 'topple' your rival?"

"In the professional sense, of course." He smiled, instantly more calm, realizing that he had overplayed his position. "I do intend to vanquish Cantrell—in the marketplace." His smile turned devious. He rumbled, "And I have a plan."

Glee mirrored his smug grin. With lowered voice, she asked, "Care to share your plan?" The twitch of her pen betrayed that she now sniffed a real story. She leaned toward him, curling her red lips into a pretty-please pout.

He leaned back into his chair, now fully at ease, aware that he had tantalized her. Pausing for effect, he fluffed the knot of his silk scarf. "I would not have come to see you, *chère* Glee, had it not been my intent to speak openly. I thought you might appreciate—how do you call it?—a scoop."

"Why me?" she asked through a purr. The sound of her voice was underlaid by the scratch of her pen. "The trade press will be arriving in Dumont any day. I'm sure the *Nutshell Digest* would be eager to print your exclusive."

"I'm sure." He smiled. "But I prefer to speak to you." His tone insinuated an interest in Glee outside the realm of journalism.

"I'm all ears, Bruno." Her sensual tone echoed his; if she was faking it, Oscars have been given for shoddier performances. I suddenly felt like a voyeur and was tempted to leave the room. I stayed though—we were sitting in my own office. The rasp of her pen stopped as she waited.

Bruno cleared his throat. "I am prepared to announce the imminent opening of my own American workshop, showroom, and museum, the Petite Galerie Hérisson, which will eclipse the Hall of Miniatures—King Cantrell's monopolistic enterprise—in the grandeur of its scale and the scope of its offerings."

Glee got busy with her notes. "Where will this be located?" she asked, though we could both guess the answer.

"Los Angeles, naturally—not a block away from Cantrell. Negotiations on the property are all but finished. Installation will begin when the papers are signed."

Glee's tone was all business now. "You mentioned the 'scope of offerings' of your showroom. Can you be more specific?"

"Galerie Hérisson will be, most certainly, the exclusive purveyor of my own work to the American market—Cantrell will not reap another sou from the sweat of my labors. In the eyes of many, that alone would be enough to secure the superior reputation of my showroom. But there is more, far more. I have already secured agreements from many of the world's most noted artisans to represent them through my Petite Galerie. Cantrell will lose his most prestigious suppliers."

Glee and I looked at each other again, each with arched brows, acknowledging the volatile situation that had landed in Dumont. As Glee seemed at a temporary loss for words, I asked the next logical question: "Does Carrol Cantrell know of your plans yet?"

Offhandedly Bruno told us, "I intended to discuss my plans with him during our drive from the airport yesterday, but his majesty was more interested in a running critique of my road manners." He smiled as a thought occurred to him. "Perhaps it may not be necessary for me to broach this—perhaps he will read of it in your journal."

"It would really be better if he heard it from you," Glee suggested. "Telling him directly would be the polite thing to do."

"Ah, yes." He mulled the situation. "*Politesse*."

At that moment, the discussion was interrupted by a rap on the glass wall to the newsroom. Standing at attention outside the closed door was my managing editor, Lucille Haring—there could be no mistaking that bright shock of short-cropped red hair, which stood in such stark contrast to her drab-colored outfit, one of several mannish suits she always wore. I waved her in.

As she entered, Bruno stood, waiting to be introduced. I stood to take charge of the formalities. I did a respectable job of the Frenchman's name this time, briefly reviewing his background. Then I said, "Bruno, this is Lucille Haring, the *Register*'s managing editor." He seemed unsure of this title, so I explained, "Lucy is my second-in-command," which he absorbed with a flash of understanding.

I was the only person alive who called her Lucy to her face, and she didn't seem to mind. Nonetheless, everyone else addressed her as Lucille or Miss Haring, with the exception of a few older newsroom veterans who simply called her Haring. The reason for these name games, for my staff's reticence to get chummy with Lucy, was that she was easily the stiffest woman ever to spike a story.

"*Enchanté*," said Bruno with a bow of his head. I could tell by his expression that he was trying to size her up, wondering her age, perhaps. She wore no makeup, complicating the puzzle. As her employer, I'd seen her files, and I could recall that she was thirty-something, but to be more specific would be guesswork.

"My pleasure," Lucy responded without inflection, extending her hand and pumping his once, briskly. She may have snapped her heels.

Bruno seemed stunned by her military manner, but I had come to view it as unremarkable. I'd first met the woman some fifteen months earlier, while working on the biggest story of my career at the *Chicago Journal*. True to her bearing, she did in fact have connections to the Pentagon, and she was assigned by an army crony of the paper's esteemed publisher to direct a massive computer upgrade at JournalCorp. She turned out to be a key ally of mine in breaking my story that summer, demonstrating impeccable research skills and an innate nose for news. When I moved up to Dumont as publisher of the *Register,* she surprised me by applying for the editor's position. After some initial hesitation (I didn't like raiding the *Journal*'s staff, and her lack of "people skills" was disquieting at best), circumstances convinced me that she was in fact the right person for the job. I have never once regretted that decision.

"Sorry to interrupt," she told the group. "Mark, something's up. Thought you'd want to know." She stopped, glancing about the room with jerky little bird-twists of her head, as if she wanted to be alone with me.

Bruno decoded this signal with ease, offering, "I must be on my way, my friends. Besides, I have finished—I have told you of my plans."

Glee rose from her chair, flipping her notebook closed, her interview abruptly ended. She asked Bruno, "Can I reach you at your motel if I need a few more quotes for my story?"

"But of course, *chère* Glee." He edged toward the doorway, nodding a farewell to each of us. Then he stopped, remembering. "This weekend, however, I shall drive to Milwaukee—with regard to the matter we discussed. But you can reach me on Monday." And he left the office to retrace his path through the newsroom.

Crossing to the doorway, Glee called after him, "Travel safe, Bruno. Good luck." She waved.

I muttered, "He'll need all the luck he can get." Judging from the driving technique I'd witnessed the previous morning when he'd roared up to Grace Lord's house, I wouldn't want to share the same road with him.

Glee commented to Lucy and me, "He's quite a character."

I laughed at the understatement.

Lucy wondered aloud, "But is he 'news'?"

"Absolutely," said Glee with mock gravity. "He and Carrol Cantrell are the two biggest figures in the small world of miniatures, at least according to the experts at *Nutshell Digest*."

Lucy looked at Glee as if she were joking.

From the papers that Glee carried with her notes, she pulled a copy of the magazine in question, displaying its cover. The headline under the *Nutshell Digest* masthead read, DUMONT PREVIEW: MIDWEST MINIATURES SOCIETY TO CONVENE.

The trace of a grin twisted Lucy's mouth. She cracked, "It's aptly named." The comment was dry, but from Lucy it was the equivalent of a knee-slapper.

Watching this exchange, I couldn't help but notice how strikingly different these women were from each other. Glee Savage: fifty-two, still man-hungry, flashy dresser, glib talker, features editor (soft news). Lucille Haring: some twenty years younger, no interest in men (lesbian, in fact, but no active love life to my knowledge), not much of a dresser, not much of a talker, managing editor (hard news, hard as nails). In so many ways, they were polar opposites, and yet, their working relationship was comfortable and cordial, each respecting the other's talents, each admiring the other's success in a profession once dominated by men.

Continuing the discussion of *Nutshell Digest*, Glee nudged her glasses into reading position and flipped to a magazine page she had dog-eared, telling us, "The lead story details a history of bad blood between Carrol and Bruno. Apparently they've managed to keep out of each other's way for years, even though their success has been mutually dependent. The story closes by posing an unanswered question: 'Come September, when these feuding titans cross paths, will there be fireworks in Dumont?' "

"Tempest in a teapot," said Lucy, dismissing the petty dispute. She turned to me. "There's a *real* controversy brewing with the County Plan Commission, and it may well lead to fireworks."

That caught my attention. I had an inkling I was about to hear about Dr. Benjamin Tenelli for the second time that morning—not two hours earlier, at breakfast, Sheriff Pierce had told me about the retired obstetrician turned civic crusader. I asked my editor, "Their porn report?"

"Just issued. The Commission's report, authored by a Dr. Tenelli, concludes that the adult bookstores on the edge of town impede commercial development along the highway. What's more"—she snorted—"the porn shops are thought to 'scare away tourists.' "

Glee cracked, "Silly me—I always thought it was the brutal winters."

I added, "Not to mention Dumont's lack of casinos and discount malls."

Lucy said, "The report makes no specific recommendation regarding enforcement of the obscenity ordinance, but the implication is clear: Dumont County would be well served by a crackdown on smut."

I thought for a moment. "Is tomorrow's editorial page locked up yet?"

Lucy reminded me, "Not if you say it's not."

I paused again. "Ladies, if you'll excuse me, I've got some writing to do."

As they left my outer office, I retreated to my desk.

PART TWO

To Serve and Protect

OUR ENDORSEMENT

The Register backs Douglas Pierce for sheriff of Dumont County

---

by MARK MANNING
Publisher, Dumont Daily Register

Sept. 16, DUMONT WI—Sheriff Douglas Pierce, Dumont County's chief law-enforcement officer, has demonstrated during his first term of service that he is a dedicated, able, and effective public servant. By any objective standard of judging his performance as sheriff, he deserves to be returned to that office.

Mr. Pierce (45) points out that during his tenure, crime rates have fallen some 14 percent in our community. Department expenses have remained consistently within budget, and he has presented a responsible plan for the long-overdue modernization of the county's jail facilities. He has proven himself a skilled administrator—as well as a good cop.

Daniel Kerr (35), Mr. Pierce's opponent in this election, is a deputy lieutenant within the sheriff's department, having risen through the ranks as a detective in the footsteps of his mentor, Mr. Pierce. Interviewing Lieutenant Kerr at the *Register*'s editorial offices, we found him to be affable, intelligent, and committed to public service. If given the opportunity, he could doubtless dispatch effectively the duties of the office he seeks, and we applaud his eagerness to serve the community in this broader capacity.

We disagree, however, with Mr. Kerr's position that the sheriff's department should play a more aggressive role in enforcement of the county's obscenity ordinance, a wrongheaded bit of lawmaking that runs contrary to every journalistic principle as well as to the First Amendment.

We fear that Mr. Kerr's position, coupled with the curious findings of the County Plan Commission (reported elsewhere on these pages), neither serves nor protects the liberties of Dumont's citizenry. In our view, this issue alone disqualifies Mr. Kerr as a tenable candidate.

On November 7, Dumont's voters will be best served by returning Sheriff Douglas Pierce to office. We offer him our enthusiastic endorsement. ❑

Saturday, September 16

Naming names is part of my business. During my career as a reporter, I quickly learned that the name in the first sentence was the most crucial detail of the story: Who did it? As publisher of my own paper, I direct my staff in the reporting of news, but my own writing is generally limited to the occasional editorial. When a column appears under my byline in Dumont, readers know that my words are not restricted to the objective transmission of facts. Rather, I now tread boldly into the realm of opinion—and I'm still naming names.

As a publisher, I view election endorsements as one of my most serious responsibilities. They are also among my greatest risks. Even in a smallish town like Dumont, where the stakes aren't seemingly all that high, the election of public officials provides the thrust and rhythm of grassroots democracy; for most people, participation in government begins and ends in the voting booth. And in local elections, voters are far more likely to feel some connection, whether real or imagined, to the names on the ballot. Chances are, when I urge my readers to elect so-and-so, half of them will be miffed.

"Why so early?" asked Neil at breakfast that Saturday. He set the morning paper on the kitchen table, folding the editorial page to face out. "I support Doug too, but the election is nearly two months away. Tactically"—he tapped my endorsement with his finger—"wouldn't this have more impact in November?"

He'd raised a good point. Standing at the counter, waiting for the toaster to pop, I explained, "The report from the County Plan Commission needed a quick rebuttal, so I decided to rush ahead with Doug's endorsement, since the election could now be riding on the porn issue. Doug *deserves* to be reelected, and everyone knows it—why let the public be diverted by this censorship campaign?"

Neil raised a brow. "Censorship?"

The toast popped. "In the final analysis, that's what this porn battle really is. Regardless of whatever lofty motive is invoked to justify it—whether it's public decency or political correctness or economic expediency—it's still a case of using governmental force to restrict adult access to materials deemed offensive. In my book, that's censorship." I was buttering toast so vigorously, it broke, leaving my palm covered with greasy crumbs. Though agitated by the topic and by the minor mess, I couldn't help laughing.

"Let me do that," Neil volunteered, rising from the table, crossing to the counter, taking the knife from my clean hand. He set to work buttering the toast, stacking the slices with architectural precision on a bread plate. Since neither of us was rushing to work that morning, we hadn't dressed yet. Standing there at the counter, we both wore bathrobes, flannel for fall. I was barefoot, but Neil wore bulky gray boot socks—he'd had the foresight to realize the tile floor would be cold.

"You're right, of course," he told me, still buttering (there was a lot of toast, enough for Thad and Sheriff Pierce, should they join us). "Any attempt to define 'acceptable' reading—or viewing—is censorship, pure and simple."

Washing my hands under the faucet, wiping them with a towel, I razzed him, "Don't take it *too* personally."

He paused. "And what is *that* supposed to mean?"

"It means," I reminded him, "that you've always had a taste for smut."

"I resent that." His indignation wasn't genuine. "I've always had a *rarefied* taste for smut." Though his words sounded oxymoronic, they were a precise statement of fact. Long before I met Neil, he began amassing a sizable collection of videos—specifically, gay porn videos. Curiously, though, his interest in this material had always been more academic than prurient, and his favorite tapes could be described as cerebral, as opposed to down and dirty. His collection was stored back at the loft in Chicago; we both agreed that we'd be playing with fire if any of these videos were kept in Dumont, where an inquisitive sixteen-year-old might get ahold of them.

Returning to the topic of the election, I told Neil, "I just hope that the committee's report doesn't stir up enough public sentiment to hurt Doug's chances. This Tenelli character apparently has plenty of pull." The coffeemaker had finished brewing, and I carried the pot to the table.

Neil followed with his artful arrangement of toast, perfectly buttered to a golden sheen. "I doubt that Doug has anything to worry about—the *Register*'s endorsement ought to lock it up for him."

"Don't be so sure." I sat. "Endorsements can backfire, especially in small towns, where everyone seems only too eager to trash the 'local rag.' "

Neil sat next to me. "Are you being cynical?" He smiled. "Or just insecure?"

"A bit of both," I admitted, returning his smile, telling myself to relax. It was Saturday, after all, and far too early in the day to get worked up over "issues." Another cool autumn morning, it was a perfect opportunity to enjoy each other's company. We'd had precious few of these quiet times during the past year.

So I paused, rested my hand on Neil's, and stated the obvious: "I'm really glad you're here—I mean working in Dumont on the Quatro project. It feels like we're living together again."

"We *are*—at least for a few months. Then it's back to the old 'arrangement.' " He was referring to the routine of alternating weekends between Dumont and Chicago, requiring long hours on the road. This future separation was not a happy thought, so Neil brought his discourse back to the present. "I really need to set up a workroom here. I've been spending my weekdays working out of a spare office at Quatro, which is fine, but I feel like a squatter. I need a 'base' outside the plant."

"Take one of the spare bedrooms," I suggested. There was plenty of extra room in the house. "Or rent an office somewhere." There were plenty of vacant storefronts downtown; retailing in Dumont, as everywhere, had followed the population growth to the farther reaches of town.

"An office?" He seemed surprised that I suggested it, and I could tell that it had sparked some interest. Then he frowned, dismissing the idea. "Too permanent. I just need some space for a desk, a drafting table, and my computer."

I shrugged. "I'm sure you could find a short-term lease somewhere." I was scheming, of course. If we were to set him up in an office, he might begin to entertain the notion of moving his practice to Dumont. He could leave the Chicago firm and set out on his own here. But that would mean leaving the recognition and satisfying pace of his big-city career, which he would be reluctant to consider. What's more, building his practice here would be slow going at first. Still, there was no risk—I could easily support him and provide the capital for his venture. I dared not breathe any of this, however. My motives were unabashedly selfish, and I knew he would find any offers of financial assistance demeaning. From the start, we had lived our relationship as equal partners. Though my own fortunes had outpaced his, though eight years his senior, I could never assume the position of boss and provider. And I would never want to.

"Maybe one of the bedrooms would work," he thought aloud, adding, "though it doesn't seem very professional."

"No need to fret over it now," I told him, pouring coffee for both of us. "Let's just ease into the weekend and enjoy it."

He smirked. "Easy for you to say. I need to gird for battle at the supermarket. We're out of peanut butter, remember."

"Thad goes through that stuff awfully fast," I remarked innocently.

Neil eyed me askance. "You've been putting away quite a bit of it yourself."

I couldn't argue the point, as peanut butter had been a weakness since childhood. Shifting the topic, I joked, "Maybe Miriam Westerman was right—we're *terrible* parents, making the kid fend for himself at breakfast. We ought to be whipping up eggs and things."

Neil laughed. "He thinks they're gross—thank God."

In fact, in our early days under the same roof with Thad, we'd been through all this, attempting to "cook" breakfast for him, but he just wasn't interested, preferring whatever milk or juice, toast or cereal, was handy. During a weekend visit last winter, Neil had surveyed the assortment of boxes and bottles that provided our morning meal, quipping that we served the finest continental breakfast in town. Thad thought that was cool, and months later I happened upon a conversation he was having with a friend one day in our kitchen after school. The other kid was bragging about his mother's cooking, claiming that her eggs Benedict were as good as Egg McMuffins. Without blinking, Thad told him, "We much prefer a continental breakfast."

Neil looked over his shoulder at the wall clock—it was well after eight. "Speaking of the tyke, no signs of life yet?"

"He's at that age—he'll sleep till noon if you let him."

"So let him." Neil wiped butter from his lips with his napkin.

I poured more coffee for him. "Did Thad say anything about the school play?"

Neil shook his head before sipping from the mug. "We never really talked last night. You were late at the paper, he was on his way out to meet friends, and dinner was catch-as-catch-can. I assume he spoke to his teacher—no details yet." Then Neil slid his chair a few inches from the table, leaning back. He pushed the still-heaping plate of toast to the far side of the table. "It doesn't surprise me that Thad's sleeping in, but I was sure we'd see Doug this morning, especially on the heels of your endorsement."

"Guess he hasn't seen it yet." But Neil was right—of *course* I'd expected Pierce to bound up the porch stairs early that morning to thank me. He'd had no clue that the editorial would appear so soon, and I knew from our many past breakfasts that it was his habit to check the paper first thing upon rising. So where *was* he?

Neil's face brightened with a thought. He rose from his chair and stepped behind me, taking hold of my shoulders to massage my neck with his thumbs. "As long as it's 'just us,' why don't we go for a run? It's perfect weather, and we haven't been out for a while."

"Great idea," I told him, twisting my head to look up at him. We shared a smile acknowledging the erotic history that running had played in our relationship. Some three years earlier, on a Christmas morning in Phoenix, Neil and I had run together along a mountain road just prior to first making love. Ever since, our runs had taken on the magic of a private ritual that frequently served as a prelude to sex—all in the guise of aerobics. Ah, the joys of healthy living.

Sitting now with Neil standing at my side, I reached inside his robe and stroked his leg. Feeling the taut muscles of his calf, I worked my way up to his thigh. I don't know whether Neil was responding to my touch or to the stimulus of some mutual memory, but he began to breathe heavily as the first stages of an erection plumped the flannel of his robe near my shoulder. I leaned my head to feel his heat against my ear. Then he leaned over my face, upside down, to kiss me deeply. With my free hand, I uncinched my robe to tend to my own erection. Through the slits of my eyes I saw the unshaven stubble on his throat; in my mind's eye I saw the indelible vision of sweat darkening the crack of his faded gray cotton running shorts as he led me up that mountain. I heard the treaded soles of our shoes slapping the earth in unison, pounding the pavement.

Pounding the door. "Any coffee left?" The spring creaked as the screen opened.

Good God. Douglas Pierce—sheriff of all the land—was walking into the kitchen. Had he been half a minute later, he'd likely have witnessed two grown men in the throes of something torrid (which he might have enjoyed). As it was, Neil and I barely had time to disentangle ourselves, clumsily concealing our arousal in the folds of our bathrobes.

"Hey, guys. Beautiful day," said Pierce as he approached the table with jaunty steps, delivering a bag of muffins, apparently fetched on his way to the house. If Neil and I projected the guilty look of being caught in the act, Pierce didn't notice, oblivious to everything but the pleasant autumn weather. His cheery manner—his "glow," for lack of a better word—was the result, I assumed, of my unexpected endorsement in that morning's paper.

We greeted him, grinning, amused by his bright attitude, enjoying his company in spite of the untimely arrival. Neil got an extra mug from a cupboard, then joined Pierce and me at the table, pouring coffee for all of us. The muffins were fresh and smelled wonderful, with gobs of wet blueberries erupting from the dough, so Neil and I each took one—toast be damned.

Rearranging the table to accommodate our guest, Neil made sure everything was within easy reach of Pierce, including the folded newspaper, which he placed squarely above the sheriff's plate. We expected him to comment on the endorsement displayed there, but he seemed not to notice it, and I was certain he was being coy.

Beaming, I finally asked, "*Well . . . ?*"

He looked at me, then at Neil, then back to me, asking, "Well, what?" His blank expression told me that he was not being coy—he was clueless.

"*Doug,*" I said, tapping the editorial in front of him, "didn't you see my column?"

"No"—he laughed—"I didn't"—he stopped short, reading the headline. Picking up the paper, he broke into a broad smile as he flumped back into his chair to peruse my endorsement of him.

Watching as he read, I wondered how he could possibly have missed the editorial page earlier that morning—public officials invariably flip to it first, breath bated, wondering if anything has been said about them. Clearly, Pierce had not yet seen the paper that day. Then I noticed his clothes. Though it was Saturday, he wore a sport coat, dress slacks, and button-down shirt, as he would for the office, but without a tie. Though the collar of his shirt was open, little wrinkles radiating from the top button signaled that it had been worn before, with a tie, presumably yesterday. Focusing on his collar, I also saw that he was overdue, once again, for his daily shave. His chipper mood, his day-old clothes, his unread endorsement—it all added up. I was afraid to guess where he'd been overnight, but it was obvious that he hadn't woken up at home that morning.

"Mark," he said, putting down the paper, "how can I thank you?"

"By beating Deputy Dan and getting reelected." I raised my coffee and clinked it to his, Neil joining the skoal—a silly gesture, perhaps, but it seemed appropriate.

Pierce's expression grew pensive. "I assume this endorsement was prompted by the report of the County Plan Commission?"

I nodded. "That's why I ran it when I did, but you needn't doubt for a minute that the *Register* would back you, whatever the timing."

Neil was crumbling his muffin on a plate, picking out berries, popping them into his mouth; his fingertips were stained inky blue. He asked Pierce, "Do you suppose this Dr. Tenelli has a political agenda at work? I know you said he's a revered old guy who's dedicated his retirement to public service, but isn't it a little fishy to call for a crackdown on porn in the name of 'tourism'?" Neil had read details of the Commission's report in the morning paper, and we'd both had a laugh over it.

"A political agenda . . ." Pierce mulled Neil's notion. "I can't imagine what it would be. To the best of my knowledge, Dr. Tenelli has no connection to my opponent or to anyone in Dan Kerr's family. And I'm sure he has no taste for Miriam Westerman's campaign on moralistic grounds. Tenelli is a highly principled, ethical man—not a book burner."

"Hm." I traced a finger around the rim of my cup. "Maybe it's time we met."

"Maybe it is," Pierce agreed. "I think you'll like him, in spite of this obscenity business. So if you've got a slow day sometime next week, give me a call, and I'll take you over to his place and introduce you."

"Thanks. He sounds like an interesting character."

Neil interjected, "The interesting character *I'd* like to meet is the Frenchman, Bruno Hérisson." To Pierce, he explained, "Mark said he visited the *Register* yesterday. Trouble's brewing in the refined little world of miniatures."

I was glad Neil had steered the conversation in this direction, as it might lead Pierce to drop some clue regarding his involvement, if any, with Carrol Cantrell.

Pierce seemed confused by Neil's comment, asking, "Trouble's brewing? What do you mean?"

Neil explained, "Bruno claims to have signed agreements with an elite group of artisans to become their exclusive distributor in America."

I added, "Glee Savage sniffed a juicy story there, and I think she's right. We'll try to see Cantrell this weekend and get his side of it."

"But Carrol said"—Pierce stopped himself, rewording—"Cantrell said that he alone acts as distributor to all the big-name artisans, including Bruno."

Uh-huh. I asked, "When was that, Doug?"

"Just last"—again Pierce stopped to reword—"the other day, I guess. Sure, it was Thursday, Thursday morning right after he arrived. He mentioned it to me on the stairs while we were all helping him move into the coach house."

I had been there, of course, and recalled no such conversation. They had discussed this some other time, on their own.

So. I knew. I was sure: Dumont's chief law-enforcement officer, Sheriff Douglas Pierce, whom I had just publicly endorsed for reelection, had been buggering the king of miniatures.

Or vice versa.

Either way, the mind reeled.

Driving away from the house later than morning, I planned to spend an hour or two at the *Register* checking the wire services, meeting with Lucille Haring about the makeup of Sunday's page one, and generally catching up at my desk. Turning off Prairie Street and heading toward First Avenue along Park Street, I passed the park itself and a succession of side streets—Durkee, La Salle, Trevor. Not quite conscious of my surroundings, I was immersed in thoughts about the obscenity issue. Was I blowing it out of proportion? Was my obsession with the First Amendment merely academic, out of touch with the real-world concerns of a great many citizens? Should I keep the paper out of the debate, merely reporting the issues as argued by others, or should I commit the *Register* to an aggressive editorial stance in defense of civil liberties?

These thoughts were broken as I approached the intersection of Tyner Avenue, the street where Grace Lord's miniatures shop was located. Slowing the car, I glanced down the street and noticed activity there, with cars parked in both directions. My reporter's instincts kicked in, and I turned from my intended route to check out the action.

The congestion (if that term can apply to traffic anywhere in Dumont) was thickest in front of Grace's shop, The Nook. The miniatures show would open a week from that morning, but a mob of exhibitors had already arrived to set up for the meeting and to claim prime spaces for their booths. Cars and vans jockeyed to park near a service drive; I spotted license plates from Illinois, Minnesota, and Iowa, as well as Wisconsin. The people themselves—most middle-aged, most wearing windbreakers—ant-tracked their wares from the vehicles to the building.

The Nook, which looked something like a dollhouse in both its cutesy decorating and its diminutive scale, was far too small to accommodate this invasion, and the transformation of the adjacent space of the long-vacant Rexall store was by now in full swing. A crew of volunteers was unsoaping the plate-glass windows, revealing a buzz of activity within. Outside, more workers attempted to hang a banner across the space once occupied by the Rexall sign, but they were having a difficult time of it, thwarted by a brisk autumn breeze. Though this operation had a farcical quality, I quelled the urge to laugh, fearing that someone might fall from a ladder.

Cruising past this commotion, I assumed that Grace Lord was there in the thick of it, but I couldn't spot her low-set figure in the crowd. It would have been easy to pick out Carrol Cantrell's lanky frame, but I didn't see him either. With my curiosity satisfied, I decided there was no need to stop, so I drove a bit farther toward the Lord house, intending to turn around in the driveway and head back to the *Register*.

Approaching the drive, I noticed another car parking there at the curb, well removed from the crush near the shop. It was one of those drab sedans assigned to city and county officials, conspicuous in its anonymity, like an unmarked squad car—yes, it was tagged with "Official" plates. I thought at first it might be Doug Pierce, but his sedan was a lighter shade of beige. A man was driving, and he had a passenger, but I couldn't discern their features through the sun's glare on the windshield. So I pulled over to the opposite curb, cut my engine, and busied myself with a few notes, waiting to see who'd emerge from the other car.

I recognized the passenger as soon as she stepped out onto the parkway. A gust of wind caught her cape and furled it over her head, making a further mess of her ratted gray hair—she looked like a wayward witch making a clumsy landing from Oz. It was none other than Miriam Westerman, founder and leader of Fem-Snach. Attempting to unruffle the cape, she clattered a giant primitive necklace that weighed heavily upon her flat bodice.

Then the other door opened and the driver stepped onto the street. The sun gleamed blue on his jet-black hair, which was surely dyed, worn in an outdated pompadour. When the pesky breeze got hold of it, he looked like a poodle in a suit. This was Harley Kaiser, Dumont County's distinguished district attorney. While closing the car door, he tried to finger-comb his hair, but without success—now he looked like a poodle with a Mohawk.

Admittedly, my vision of these two characters was tainted by prejudice.

Miriam was the woman who had tried to steal custody of Thad from me. She was the woman who had instigated a hate-mail campaign against me when I first moved to Dumont, branding my homosexuality an "abomination against Mother Nature"—never mind her own past flirtations with lesbianism, which was just dandy in her book, since it didn't involve men. She was the woman I had bodily thrown from my home one evening when she invaded a family gathering and spat epithets at me, including the rather clever "penis cultist." And she was the woman who sought to violate the civil liberties of an entire community because pornography, in her view, was tantamount to "violence against women." Miriam Westerman openly hated me. In the face of such irrational animosity, I could only return the sentiment.

Kaiser was a different matter. As an elected official, he was instinctively sensitive to public opinion, accountable to every voter, or at least to fifty-one percent of them. Further, he was smart enough to recognize that he stood nothing to gain by antagonizing the publisher of the local paper. So he at least made an attempt to behave cordially to me, in spite of our polar disagreement regarding the enforcement of obscenity standards. As far as he was concerned, I had no grasp of political reality. As far as I was concerned, he'd landed on the wrong side of the issue, period, and I marveled at his lack of principle in selling out the First Amendment for the sake of some presumed political advantage. My friend Roxanne Exner had hit the nail on the head in her succinct appraisal of the district attorney: Harley Kaiser was a hot dog.

I had previously called Kaiser and Miriam "strange bedfellows" in their alliance to rid Dumont of porn. Now, watching them from my car, I found their pairing all the more unlikely. What were they up to? Why here? Why now?

They were doubtless asking themselves the same questions about me. Standing at the curb, they spoke over their shoulders to each other, glancing at my car, which anyone in town would recognize. So I let them continue wondering for a few moments, hoping that my presence would unsettle them. Behind tinted windows, I wrote a few last notes, then capped my pen, returning it with the pad to my jacket.

Opening the door, I got out of the car, donning a pair of sunglasses (the autumnal slant of midmorning light was not especially bothersome—in fact, I enjoyed it—but I figured the dark glasses might make me a tad more menacing). Pretending to notice them just then, I called to the opposite curb, "Miriam, Harley—what a pleasant surprise." It was a good act, but in light of our past run-ins, they could guess I was lying.

Kaiser crossed to meet me in the middle of the street, extending his hand to shake mine. "Morning, Mark. Didn't know you harbored an interest in dollhouses." The remark could have been intended to question my masculinity, but his tone seemed innocuous enough—he was just inept at small talk. If his words carried a hidden message, he was really trying to ask, What are *you* doing here?

Strolling with him back to the curb, I bulled, "Wherever there's news, there am I."

Miriam had made no move to acknowledge me, so arriving where she stood on the parkway, I dispensed with further pleasantries and asked her bluntly, "What are *you* doing here?"

"One might ask *you* the same," she snapped back with a defiant stomp of one foot, but the gesture lost its punch—her clog merely mashed the turf.

"Actually," said Kaiser, attempting to keep things civil, "we've come to see Carrol Cantrell. He's a distinguished visitor to the city, and we both wanted to wish him welcome." He smiled, as if that explained everything, wrapping it up.

"What a coincidence," I fibbed. "I was just on my way to see him myself. We're working up a feature." It would be Glee's story, of course, but for the moment, there was no harm in letting Kaiser think I was there on assignment. I found it unlikely that both he and Miriam were inclined to roll out the welcome mat for the king of miniatures as a simple matter of civic courtesy. Still, I had no theory that would better explain their visit. If I stuck with them, their motive might become plain to me. Brightly I suggested, "Let's all pop in on him."

Miriam and Kaiser exchanged an uncertain glance; in my presence they did not feel free to discuss my proposed intrusion. Miriam looked vexed, Kaiser wary. He hawed before relenting, "Sure, why not? Do you think he's at the shop?"

"Actually, no." I waved my arm up the street—"I drove from that direction and got a pretty good look at the mob. Carrol Cantrell is at least six foot four, so I'd have noticed if he were there. I think our best bet is the coach house."

Kaiser and Miriam were aware of Carrol's lodging arrangements, but neither of them knew the lay of Grace Lord's property, so my presence proved helpful in that I could guide them. The three of us walked in silence as I led them up the driveway beside the house, our feet crunching the gravel. Watching the DA and the feminist as they trudged toward the coach house for purposes not known to me, I found it difficult to imagine that they had grown up with Doug Pierce—their lives had taken such radically different directions.

Out on the street, with all the activity surrounding setup of the convention, there'd been a sense of merry confusion. But here, in the shadow of the house, all was still—save for us, save for the rustle of a bird somewhere in the soaring limbs of old trees. The bright day had taken on an eerie quality, and I instinctively removed my dark glasses, pocketing them. Our lack of conversation, prompted by nothing more sinister than distaste for each other, now seemed to radiate an active malice borne of tight-lipped silence.

I broke this lull by asking Miriam, "Did you get your school up and running?"

Without breaking stride, she turned to tell me, "You know very well that I did. Your own paper reported it—barely. It *is* news, you know. Wisconsin's—probably the nation's—first holistic, paganic New Age day school. Ariel would benefit from our curriculum and from our all-organic diet."

This last comment was made purely to nettle me. Ariel was the name Miriam and her Fem-Snachers had given to Thad, claiming him as a child of the Society. I reminded her, "The boy's mother named him Thad."

She was revving up for a diatribe when Kaiser shushed her, saying, "Not now, Miriam. We have other fish to fry."

So then—they were indeed paying this visit for some planned purpose. Trying to fathom what fish they meant to fry, I let our conversation lapse again.

Reaching the two-story garage at the end of the driveway, I led them around to the side of the building, where the stairs rose to the covered porch of the coach house. Climbing the first few of the green-painted treads, I looked out upon the vast, shade-dappled lawn. In a flash, I saw the same serene scene that had been captured in the framed photo of Grace's nephew, Ward Lord, whipping a Frisbee to his dog. The memory (which was not a direct recollection, but merely a visual impression of a years-old occurrence, preserved in a snapshot) gave me a perturbing sense of déjà vu, raising a mind-loop question: Did the scene there before me truly resemble the scene I recalled, or was my memory being rewritten by what I now saw? It was impossible to draw the distinction—even the trees looked the same to me, which I knew, intellectually if not in my gut, to be impossible. Continuing up the stairs, I searched for some small detail, any overlooked clue, that would prove a discrepancy between past and present. And I saw it. While making a turn at the landing, I noticed, tucked under a tree near the far end of the lawn, a garden ornament, a small stone obelisk that I had not seen before, either in the photo or in life. Though I should have been relieved by this discovery—it ratified my grip on reality—the effect of the obelisk was anything but heartening. No, the limestone monolith looked for all the world like a grave marker. This, combined with the uneasy stillness (even that morning's gusty wind had now died, as if holding its breath), created a mood of intense foreboding, and I suddenly dreaded what I might find at the top of the stairs.

Carrol Cantrell's scream shattered the silence, nipping my thoughts, confirming my fears—or so I assumed. Miriam, Kaiser, and I froze, unsure, in that first instant, how to react. During this moment of suspended animation, Miriam lost her footing. One of her lumpish clogs slipped from the tread where she stood, knocking a potted geranium over the edge. Just as it hit ground, the crash was drowned out by another shriek from Carrol's quarters.

Through the screen door, we realized, he was talking on the phone, now howling breathlessly—the waning aftermath of his explosive look-at-me laughter. I chided myself for indulging in morbid premonitions, inspired by a harmless garden accessory, and reminded myself that the success of my career stemmed in part from a ruthless objectivity that allowed no faith in superstition. Glad to be in touch again with the here and now, I focused my attention on Carrol's phone call. "Gawd, she's a *fright!*" he dished with abandon between gulps of air. "A total, fucking *ditz!*" Then he yelped with delight at whatever was said on the phone.

Miriam and Kaiser exchanged a disgusted look, rolling their eyes in disapproval. In truth, I didn't much approve of Carrol's performance either. His words, though, were not meant for our ears. He had no idea an audience was now on his porch, and if we were to let him continue unaware, we'd be guilty of eavesdropping, one-upping his bad manners.

So I approached the door, preparing to rap on it. Just prior to my knock, we heard one last comment, delivered in a far more sober tone: "What about the Miller standard?"

Caught unprepared for this question and confused by its meaning, I paused before knocking, mulling Carrol's words. Was he talking about . . . beer? Surely not. Was he referring to the work of some noted miniatures artisan named Miller? Possibly. Glancing back toward Miriam and Kaiser, I noted that Miriam seemed oblivious to Carrol's question. She was squatting to adjust her clog, which was quite a sight—she looked as if she were being eaten by her cape. Kaiser, on the other hand, seemed focused and intent, as if he understood Carrol's reference to the "Miller standard." Was it a legal term? I just didn't know.

So I knocked, calling inside, "Carrol? Anybody home?" There was no point in *telling* him we'd been hanging on his every word.

He approached the door from the shadows behind the screen, wearing a long silk bathrobe, carrying a cell phone. "Company's here," he said into it. "Gotta go, love. Later." And he snapped it shut.

"Sorry to interrupt," I told him lamely through the screen.

Recognizing me, he swung the door wide. "Mark, hon!" Then, squinting into the sunlight, he saw the others. "Oh?" His hair was a mess, and he hadn't shaven yet. It was late morning—I figured his daily rhythms were still on California time.

"I was in the neighborhood," I explained, "so I thought I'd drop by, and—of all people—I ran into a couple of friends who'd had the same idea." There was a moment's pause. It was clear he did not appreciate the disturbance, so I forged ahead with introductions, telling him, "First, this is Miriam Westerman, founder of a local feminist organization that has just opened a New Age day school."

Pocketing his phone, he cinched his robe tighter and reached to shake her hand from where he stood in the doorway. After an exchange of strained pleasantries, he asked, "Are you . . . a collector?"

She looked at him blankly. "Collector of what?"

As if addressing an idiot (I was enjoying this), he said, "Miniatures, of course."

She laughed awkwardly. "Oh—no—not really." And she said nothing more, offering no explanation for her presence.

Understandably, Carrol now seemed more baffled than annoyed. Assuming he would be equally confused by the appearance of his other visitor, I told Carrol, "And this is Harley Kaiser, district attorney for Dumont County."

"Really?" Contrary to what I expected, Carrol's tone carried no ring of surprise, but rather a note of recognition, as if he'd somehow been expecting Kaiser to appear at his door. It was apparent that the two had never met, but Carrol seemed fully aware of who Kaiser was. Shaking hands, he peered intently at Kaiser, as if attaching a face to a name. If my theory was correct that Sheriff Pierce and Carrol had been sleeping together, had Pierce told Carrol about the DA? Such a conversation didn't strike me as probable pillow talk.

In a tone that was instantly more gracious, Carrol continued, "How rude of me—leaving you all standing outdoors. Do come in." He stepped aside, admitting us. "But I warn you: the place is a fright. I haven't quite gotten settled yet." That was an understatement.

The space itself was charming. Grace Lord's coach house was essentially one big room under the barn-roof gables. Dormer windows fetched treetop views from both sides, framed by those lacy tiebacks I'd seen from the ground. At one end was a bathroom with a small closet and galley kitchen nearby, but most of the quarters was open space that served as living room, dining room, and bedroom. The furnishings all had a tasteful "country" feel, upholstered in cheery chintzes and crisp ginghams. The wide, painted floorboards creaked underfoot, muffled by a scattering of colorful rag rugs. The overall effect of the room was comfortable and tidy.

While the room's new tenant may have been comfortable there, he was anything but tidy. For starters, the contents of his luggage could not begin to fit inside the tiny closet, so clothes were hung wherever he could hook their hangers—from rafters, curtain rods, and doorknobs. The luggage itself gaped open from the seats of chairs, containing a variety of items still unpacked—shoes, stacks of magazines, little corrugated boxes, a hair dryer, and a prodigious array of toiletries and cosmetics.

This sense of disarray went beyond the obvious problem that Carrol had brought too much stuff. He'd had two days to get settled, and instead of making the best of a cramped situation, he'd created a shambles. Knotted bedclothes spilled from the king-size mattress to the floor. Damp towels hung from chair backs or lay wadded where they'd fallen. Magazines and file folders overflowed a diminutive writing desk. The dining table had been forced into duty as additional work space, where Carrol's laptop was open and running, a document displayed upon its glowing screen. Surrounding the computer, amid fanned-out piles of paperwork, were some of the little corrugated boxes, opened, containing pieces of miniature furniture—gorgeous tiny desks and curios and upholstered chairs, all incredibly detailed. Were these in fact examples of Bruno Hérisson's artistry?

Also near the computer were some of the magazines Carrol had unpacked, and I now noticed that the common theme of these publications was not dollhouses, but beefcake. Unfolded centerspreads displayed horny muscle-guys getting it on together. The unexpected sight of their oiled bodies sucked me, momentarily, into their frozen, glossy, four-color frenzy.

I was not the only one to notice the orgy on the table. Kaiser and Miriam, engaged in some pointless chatter with Carrol, had moved into the room and now stood within a foot of the table, both of them staring down at it, preoccupied by what they saw there. I got the impression that Kaiser had never before seen such explicit depictions of male couplings—his wide-eyed reaction seemed more amazed than aghast. Miriam, however, wrinkled her face in open disgust, which rather surprised me—her objection to pornography, after all, was that it constitutes "violence against women," and believe me, there were no women being violated on the dining-room table that morning.

I was also surprised by Carrol's nonchalance. There he was, blithely grousing about the "wretched wet weather" he'd left in California, seemingly oblivious to the fact that these two strangers were gawking at material that most people would hide somewhere. He made no move to tuck away the magazines or to steer his visitors from the table. Instead, he gabbed on while leaning to peck at his computer, shutting it down. With a bleep, the screen went dark.

He was something of an enigma, Carrol Cantrell. Not only was the king of miniatures a key figure in a bizarre little world that struck me as somewhat obsessive—possibly neurotic—but he also embodied a variety of contradictory traits. Consider: On the day he arrived, he was impeccably dressed and fastidiously groomed, so appearances obviously *mattered* to him. But now he looked like hell, his room was a wreck, and he had no qualms about baring this unvarnished glimpse of his morning to three unexpected visitors. Did he think us all rubes in Wisconsin, with opinions that weren't worth fretting over? Or was he jaded by his own celebrity status, no longer caring how he was seen or thought of, confident that his reign could withstand all? Or (and this was my best theory) was he simply sated by two nights in the sack with Doug Pierce? That could well explain Carrol's carefree attitude, his afterglow, his ready dismissal of protocol.

Once my thoughts had turned in this direction, I could not easily shake them. While drifting in and out of a conversation that eluded me (Kaiser made some disparaging remark about the American Civil Liberties Union, but it seemed gratuitous, lacking context), I scoured the room for any evidence that Pierce had been spending his nights there. My gaze began at the bed, naturally—as if the sheriff would have been absentminded enough to leave his holster hanging on the headboard. Finding neither gun, badge, nor handcuffs, my probing eye left the bed, circling the room.

I knew very well that this was none of my business. My curiosity was motivated by little more than—what, idle nosiness? Or was it something more akin to jealousy? Don't go there, I warned myself. What could I possibly regard as the object of jealousy? A quick fling? I was committed to a loving relationship, and I'd learned through experience that there are ways in which it must not be tested. Besides, I had no interest whatever in bedding Carrol Cantrell. But what about Doug Pierce? Though Doug and I . . .

This examination of conscience was interrupted when my eye tripped on something as it passed across the top of a dresser. More accurately, my eye tripped on "nothing," a space on the wall where something seemed to be missing. The top of the dresser held an unremarkable assortment of whatnot—little crystal figures, framed snapshots and other Lord-family memorabilia, an arrangement of dried strawflowers, a dish for change, a pair of brass candleholders with milk-glass chimneys. The candleholders were placed symmetrically at either end of the dresser, and between them on the wall hung nothing. It looked as if a mirror belonged there. And sure enough, there was a hook in the wall. Then I remembered the enlarged photo of Grace's nephew Ward, which I had helped remove from these quarters—surely that was what had hung above the dresser. Though I had solved this little mystery, the bare spot on the wall was oddly troublesome. Was I doting again on the image of the boy? Or was I simply reacting to the questionable aesthetics of the bare wall?

Completing my inspection of the room, my eyes came to rest again where they had started, on the bed. Just as I concluded that my search had been fruitless, just as I reminded myself to focus on Carrol's conversation with Kaiser and Miriam, I noticed something protruding from under a pillow that had been flung onto a nightstand. If I wasn't mistaken, it was a crimped tube of K-Y, a medical lubricant favored by many as sex grease. Though this discovery in no way provided hard evidence of the liaison I suspected, it certainly fueled that suspicion, and I found myself agitated by the image it conjured. Drop this, I told myself. This doesn't concern you. Doug's an adult. He's forty-five. He's alone. Maybe he *needed* this.

"As a matter of fact," said Carrol, "it is." He wagged his nickel Medic Alert bracelet, the only jewelry he wore that morning, explaining to Kaiser and Miriam, "I'm allergic to nuts, that's all. Severely allergic, in fact, but otherwise, I'm healthy as an ox." He dramatically pounded his chest as a demonstration of his manly vigor, but it would have been more effective in any costume other than his sweeping silk robe.

We all had a chuckle at his mock bravado, and in fact he chorused in with his powerful, practiced laugh. Then silence filled the room.

He asked, "Is there anything else? I really ought to put myself together."

"No . . ." Harley Kaiser hesitated. "We need to be going, actually. Miriam and I just wanted to welcome you to Dumont. Hope you'll enjoy your stay."

Miriam echoed, "Welcome to Dumont, Mr. Cantrell." Her inflection was flat and insincere, but that came as no surprise—she only showed signs of life when she had something to bleat about.

Moving with them to the door, I turned to wish Carrol a good day, shaking his hand. As I did this, he pulled me gently toward him, asking, "Stay a minute?"

So I remained while Kaiser and Miriam stepped through the door, clomped across the porch, and started down the stairs.

Carrol edged toward a window to watch their progress, and when he was confident that they were well out of earshot, he turned to me, gushing, "I'm *sorry,* Mark. I'm *mortified* that you caught me like this." His hands fluttered to rake his hair as he dashed across the room to close the magazines on the table, jogging them into several neat piles.

I laughed, relieved to note that his previous behavior wasn't really "him." But I was still confused. "Why the act for Kaiser and Miriam?"

Stepping to the bed, he whipped the sheets from the floor and tried, without much success, to make things more presentable. "I just didn't like those two," he explained. "Maybe it's instinct. I wanted them to leave, and frankly, I don't give a shit what they think of me." Surveying the rumpled bedding, he growled with frustration. Then a thought lightened his tone. "Thank God—Grace said she'd pop up this afternoon and help me put things in order. She's a dear."

"She really is," I agreed. "But what did they *want?*"

"You tell *me*." Carrol flung his long arms in exasperation. "Did you catch that crack about the ACLU?"

"As a matter of fact, I did. Kaiser's got pornography on the brain lately, putting him at odds with most civil libertarians. Your . . . uh, reading material must have set him off." I filled Carrol in on the background of Miriam's feminist antiporn campaign, the county ordinance, and the DA's imminent must-win obscenity case.

Carrol reacted, "Now *why* doesn't any of this surprise me?"

Indeed. I was tempted to ask if Doug Pierce had told him about it, but he'd surely suspect my ulterior, voyeuristic motive for asking, so I let the comment pass.

Frenetically working his way around the bed, smoothing a quilted comforter over the sheets, he arrived at the nightstand and fluffed the errant pillow back into position on the bed, fully revealing the still-gooey tube of K-Y. He tisked apologetically while opening the drawer of the night table, dropping in the lube, and sliding it shut. On top of the night table, along with a disheveled pile of papers, I now noticed Carrol's fat fountain pen, the ugly one I'd seen in his pocket on Thursday morning.

Gathering up the papers and scurrying to the writing desk, he piled them atop the rest of the clutter while asking, "And what brought *you* to see me this morning?" There was a lilt to his question that begged a salacious answer.

"Actually," I confessed, "I wondered what Kaiser and Miriam were up to, so I tagged along, telling them I was working up another story about you. Truth is, Glee Savage would like to interview you again—we had a visit from your old friend Bruno yesterday, and—well, I'm getting ahead of myself. Could Glee and I spend a bit of time with you, possibly tomorrow morning?"

"Sure, Mark, happy to oblige—the more press the better. I'd planned to look in on the hubbub at Grace's shop, so let's meet there."

"Great." I took out my pen and pad, suggesting, "Nine or ten o'clock?"

He beaded me with a get-real stare. Grinning, he reminded me, "Tonight is Saturday, Mark. Let's make it eleven tomorrow."

"Done," I said, making note of it.

"And now," he said, playfully shooing me toward the door, "I really must do something about *this*"—he whisked a hand from head to toe, implying that he needed a complete makeover, which in fact he did.

"Thanks, Carrol." I opened the screen door to let myself out. "See you tomorrow at The Nook."

"Tomorrow," he echoed, waltzing off to the bath, stooping en route to retrieve a towel from the floor. Then he swung the bathroom door shut behind him.

Stepping out to the porch, I laughed quietly at the scene that had just transpired, then paused. Something was troubling me. Something seemed amiss, but what? So I poked my head back into the room, hoping the sight would nudge my thinking. And I saw it—Carrol's fat pen.

During his brief, obsessive burst of housekeeping, he'd moved a pile of papers from the bed to the desk, but left his ugly pen on the nightstand.

Logically, didn't the pen belong with the papers on the desk?

Or was it now I who was being obsessive?

Closing the door and crossing the porch, I started down the stairs. A frown pinched my mouth. The riddle of the pen was nothing, surely. A larger riddle still perplexed me. An unanswered question still loomed over the cool morning.

What the hell were Harley Kaiser and Miriam Westerman up to?

Sunday, September 17

Sunday morning, I left the house on Prairie Street and drove along the park, headed toward downtown. Crossing the succession of side streets, including Grace Lord's, I continued past Vincennes and Wisconsin, slowing the car as I approached the intersection of Third Avenue, where Glee Savage lived in a solid, old red-brick apartment building at the edge of Dumont's business district. She was standing at the corner, dressed in her stylish best, replete with hat, gloves, and one of her oversize purses. One might have assumed she was dolled up for church, but she wasn't, of course—she was waiting for me.

I circled under her building's portico, lowering the passenger window to blow her a wolf whistle. She strode toward the car, heels pecking the sidewalk, looking absolutely vibrant—nothing pleased her more than a juicy assignment, and she was raring to probe the feud that was set to blow up between Carrol Cantrell and Bruno Hérisson. I unbuckled my seat belt, intending to help her into the car, but she was too quick, hopping in next to me before I got my door open.

"This ought to be good," she told me, checking her purse for her notebook. Satisfied that she was fully equipped, she closed the bag with a decisive snap.

I agreed, "There's a story here, all right, but there may be more to it than petty rivalry within the mini world. My impromptu visit with Carrol yesterday raised more questions than it answered. You should do the talking today, but I may make a few notes of my own."

I had already discussed this with Glee by phone on Saturday afternoon, but I continued to review our plans as I drove back up Park Street, crossing Wisconsin and Vincennes.

"Hey, boss," Glee interrupted me, with a facetious grin, "don't miss our turn."

I had nearly blown through the intersection on Thursday morning, but by now I was well trained in finding Grace Lord's shop, executing a smooth, flawless turn. A few blocks ahead lay The Nook and the adjacent former drugstore. The scene was much as it had been the day before, with cars and vans parked on either side of the street, people in windbreakers milling near the buildings. I drove past the shops, parking beyond them, near the house. Checking my watch, I told Glee, "It's not quite eleven, and I got the impression Carrol wouldn't be early."

"Let's go in anyway," she suggested. "Maybe we can get a feel for the exhibits."

So we got out of the car. Standing on the street, I opened the back door and retrieved the blazer I'd laid on the seat, checking its pockets for my notebook and pen. Locking the car, I was glad to have the jacket—the cool morning had clouded over and turned cold.

Shrugging into my coat, I fastened a single button while stepping to the curb to escort Glee to the sidewalk. I reminded her, "You're the boss today. Do you intend to reveal to Carrol that Bruno plans to open a competing gallery in Los Angeles?"

She thought for a moment, walking next to me as we ambled toward The Nook. "That depends. Mainly, I just want to get the background of their rivalry from *his* point of view. There are two sides to every dispute. But if the interview shifts in the right direction—who knows?—I just may break the news to Carrol. After all, Bruno all but invited me to do the dirty work for him."

Reaching the front door of the shop, we sidled in through the crowd, arriving in a cramped showroom where glass cases lined the walls from floor to ceiling, displaying all manner of dollhouse paraphernalia. It would have been interesting to browse a bit, but the space was simply too jammed. Surveying the tops of heads, I could tell at once that Carrol had not yet arrived—there was no one that tall. So I asked a woman with a clipboard, "Is Grace Lord around?"

"I saw her in the hall." She pointed to a doorway at the back of the shop.

Edging through the crush of bodies, Glee and I arrived at the doorway and discovered that it connected to the Rexall store, which the woman had called the "hall." The description was apt, at least in comparison to the claustrophobic confines of The Nook—the interior of the drugstore, long denuded of its shelving, showcases, and other fixtures, seemed cavernous. Though a good number of people were busy transforming the vacant store into the temporary headquarters of the Midwest Miniatures Society, the room did not feel overcrowded, and the buzz of activity was restrained and focused. The yawning space was brightly lit by the windows on the front wall and by banks of fluorescent tubes that hummed overhead. The floor had been taped off into rows that were subdivided into exhibit spaces, labeled by number.

Most of the area was occupied by vendors, setting up their wares on folding tables, many with backdrop signage extolling some special expertise: LILLIPUT LAMP SHOP; TEENY TINY TRIM FACTORY; BITSY BOOKS & BAUBLES. A smaller area at one end of the space would be devoted to workshops, where would-be artisans could learn some hands-on tips from the pros: CURTAIN FOLDING; CARPENTRY TECHNIQUES; FAUX FINISHES. At the opposite end of the hall was the competition area, where several entrants already fussed with their roomboxes, unpacking the delicate furnishings, touching up details with slim sable brushes, checking thread-size electrical connections for pea-size lights. Mingling among these contestants was Grace Lord, hostess of the entire proceedings. Her short stature and sprightly manner seemed perfectly at home in the little world that surrounded her.

Glee had donned her reading glasses, perching them low on her nose to scrutinize a display of intricate floral arrangements, none of them more than an inch high. She gasped at the meticulous workmanship, noting the exhibit number.

I tapped her shoulder, directing her gaze toward the competition area. "There's Grace. She's had Carrol in her coach house for three days now—maybe she can share a few reactions before he arrives." Glancing at my watch, I noted that it was just past eleven. I'd been correct in my hunch that Carrol wouldn't be prompt.

Glee peered over her glasses at Grace. Slyly she agreed, "Let's talk to her."

Moving through the aisle together, stepping over boxes and packing material, we approached Grace, who was now busily at work on something, from behind. "Morning, Grace," I called to her. "Got a moment to meet the press?"

She turned to us with a wide grin. "Of course, Mark. Good morning, Glee. Welcome, both of you." And she strode toward us to shake our hands. With that endearing self-disparaging laugh, she told us, "You've managed to catch me at my worst again, looking like hell." She wore jeans, a shirt, and comfortable old shoes, dressed for work—she looked just fine.

Glee assured her, "It's Sunday and you're busy—no need to put on airs for us," which was an odd comment coming from my features editor, who looked as if she'd stepped straight off the fashion page.

Dropping the topic of clothes, Grace told us, a touch of excitement coloring her words, "I'm glad you popped in. It's not quite finished, but if you'd care to see it, I'd be happy to give you a sneak peek." She winked.

Since my thoughts had been occupied by Carrol Cantrell, I wasn't quite prepared for this offer. In fact, I couldn't imagine what she was referring to.

Reading my confused expression, she explained, "My *roombox.* Lord's Rexall."

"Oh, of course." I smiled, truly eager to see it.

Glee echoed my sentiments, "We'd be honored, Grace. I wish we'd brought a photographer."

"This is just a preview," she reminded us. "No pictures yet, please." Then she waved an arm in the direction of a row of roomboxes, all arranged at eye height. Some were covered, some were being worked on, some lit, others dark—all in various stages of completion. She directed us to one of the larger shadow boxes, partially obscured with a cloth. Unveiling it, she intoned a simple fanfare: "*Tuh-daaah!*"

Glee and I stepped forward to peer into the miniature drugstore, gratifying Grace with an initial reaction of oohs and aahs. It was eerie to note that we actually stood in the same space that was being depicted. Though the passing of years and the abandonment of the business had greatly changed the appearance of the interior, the two structures were clearly identical, except, of course, for their scale. The proportions of the space, the placement and detail of architectural features such as doors, windows, and remaining cabinetry—all was exacting.

But Grace's project went well beyond the slavish reproduction of an empty room. To the contrary, she had created a tiny space chockfull with the products and fixtures and icons of midwest America in an earlier generation. Though inanimate, the scene bristled with life. The soda fountain stood ready to serve an onslaught of kids, yet to arrive from school. The prescription counter was stocked with its cryptic inventory, its pharmacist having stepped away for a moment, perhaps to place a four-digit phone call to some local doctor—just double-checking. The aisles of the store brimmed with an assortment of tonics and salves, brushes and hairpins, seltzers and bromides, douches and laxatives, candies and One A Days, greeting cards and pocket novels. No condoms though—you had to ask.

Glee and I fired a series of bemused questions, amazed that Grace had been able to accomplish this theatrical deception so convincingly in her first roombox. With cheer and supreme patience, she answered all our queries, telling us about the hundreds of hours she'd spent at her worktable piecing together this testament to the Lord family's past, checking each step against store records, old photos, and the scrutiny of her own memory. She proudly pointed out the miniature portraits of her father and grandfather hanging behind the cash register. "I once planned to add my own mug to that lineup," she told us with a pensive sigh, "but it wasn't meant to be."

The nostalgic moment passed, and I still had plenty of questions left regarding technique. "What about all this . . . *stuff?* I mean, how did you get the little printed labels for everything? Did you actually *make* all of it?"

"Heavens *no,*" she gasped. "There are various sources for furnishing just about any miniatures project you could dream up. I built the room itself, but the inventory of commercial products was bought wherever I could find it—that's quite a specialty, as you can imagine."

Glee asked, "How did you track it all down?"

"Through various magazines and catalogs. There's a lot out there, especially at some of the regional shows. But the real godsend has been the Internet. Just hop on the Net, and you can find nearly anything, regardless of how specialized."

I had to remind myself that Grace was sixty-four. Many people of that age have never gotten friendly with computers, some out of fear, others for lack of opportunity. I admired Grace for making the leap—it fit her rambunctious personality, and I liked her all the more for it.

We continued to gab about Grace's drugstore project, Glee taking copious notes. I could tell that she'd decided to spin a full-blown feature out of this, and I was eager to see what she'd do with it. When at last we'd exhausted the topic, Grace offered, "Can I give you a guided tour of some of the other entries?"

"By all means," Glee answered, enthused.

Tapping my watch, I laughed while reminding her, "We were *supposed* to see Carrol Cantrell. But it's nearly eleven-thirty—he's late."

"My God," said Glee, hand to her mouth, "I'd forgotten."

"I noticed," I told her wryly. Turning to Grace, I said, "Your distinguished visitor planned to meet us here at eleven. Was he up and about this morning?"

"Not that I noticed. But that's not unusual. He's not the 'early to bed, early to rise' type." She chuckled at the understatement.

I related a bit of my previous morning's visit, how I'd found both him and his quarters in need of a serious makeover.

Grace rolled her eyes. "I have no idea what sort of shape *he's* in right now, but his room ought to be more presentable—I helped him tidy up yesterday."

"He mentioned that you'd offered to help. That was most kind of you." I hoped to God that Carrol had had sense enough to put away his porn collection. It was a perverse stroke of luck that he had managed to shock Kaiser and Miriam with it, but Grace Lord deserved more considerate treatment.

She suggested, "Shall we walk over and see if he's in?"

"Yes, let's."

So we filed back through the exhibit hall, headed for the connecting doorway to The Nook. But Grace made a sharp turn toward the rear of the building, telling us, "The shop's too crowded. Let's sneak out the back." And she opened an obscure door that led directly to the yard behind the shops and the house.

We emerged onto a brick walkway that I'd noticed Thursday morning, one of several that crisscrossed the backyard. During the past half hour, the weather had grown cloudier still, colder too. The wind had picked up, and robins sang for rain. Following Grace along the path toward the house, Glee struggled to control her big flat purse. I would have found this funny had I not been fighting the gusts myself, hunkering into my jacket, warming my hands in my pockets.

Arriving at the porch of the house, Grace turned onto the path that led back to the garage. Glee and I followed, and within moments we were climbing the open stairway to the coach house. Under a threatening sky, the white building had paled to gray, the green banister looked almost black, and the potted geraniums flanking each step took on a hue of deep, velvety burgundy.

Halfway up, at the turn of the landing, Grace stopped. "Well, I'll be," she said, plucking from the banister a silk scarf snagged there on a splinter. Glee and I backed up behind her on the landing as she held up the scarf, examining it as it snapped in the wind. Lushly patterned in gold with a small repetitive design, its center area was badly wrinkled, as if it had been knotted. Glee and I glanced at each other, silently sharing our assessment—it looked for all the world like Bruno's cravat.

But Grace thought otherwise. With a laugh, she wadded the scarf into a pocket, telling us, "Carrol certainly needs a lot of picking up after. Looks like he stumbled in late last night."

I asked, "That's *his* scarf?"

"I assume so. I cleaned his room yesterday, and he's quite the clotheshorse. He has lots of silk scarves."

She should know, I told myself. But even so, the scarf in her pocket looked exactly like the one I'd seen twice around Bruno's neck. Had he been here?

As I spun these thoughts, my gaze left my companions huddled there on the landing and drifted out to the expansive lawn, where the wind rushed in waves across the thick grass. The ripples led my eye to the far end of the lawn, to a tree that drooped protectively over a small stone obelisk. Once again, the pointed obelisk snagged my thoughts as securely as the splintered banister had snagged that silk scarf.

"It's *cold* out here," said Glee, urging me to get moving.

Grace added, under her breath, "Let's go see if his majesty is receiving."

I laughed at her comment, hoping to lighten my mood, but I couldn't shake the morbid thoughts inspired by the sight of that unassuming garden ornament—it looked like a tombstone. It was time, I decided, to lay the issue to rest (even my thoughts were cluttered with funereal euphemisms). No longer laughing, but still forcing a smile, I said, "Just a second, Grace. That obelisk over there." I pointed to it. "I first noticed it yesterday, and I got the crazy feeling that—"

"That's Rascal's grave," she interrupted matter-of-factly.

Huh? Who? My mind spun with the realization that although my premonition may have been irrational, it was nonetheless well-founded.

"The dog," she explained.

Of course. I remembered aloud, "The collie in the photo with your nephew."

She nodded. "The very same. He meant a lot to all of us. When he passed on, we didn't have the heart to just . . . to just *throw him away*." She smiled sheepishly, as if we might fault the sentiments that inspired so lavish a tribute to a lost pet.

I rested a hand on her shoulder, a gesture intended both to assure her that I understood and to offer much belated condolences on the loss of the dog. "I'm sorry," I told her. "I shouldn't have pried."

"Oh, posh." She smiled. "No harm in sharing another tidbit of Lord family history—though I wouldn't be surprised if you suspected we're all nuts." Her smile widened as she laughed.

"Hardly," I said.

Glee butted in, "It *is* getting cold out here—and we're on assignment." Both hands were now busy, battening down her hat as well as her purse.

"Okay," I conceded. "Onward."

Climbing the remaining stairs, I tried to focus on our imminent meeting with Carrol Cantrell, but the subject of Grace's nephew had been raised, and once again, I couldn't get the kid out of my mind. Ward Lord—I now knew the fate of his dog, but what of the golden child himself? My only glimpse of him had been snapped untold years ago as he leapt into manhood, flexing his whole body while launching a Frisbee that was captured on film as a gray blur in the sky. Where was he now? Was there a tactful way to find out? More important, why did I care? Did I want to call him, meet him? *Then* what?

"My God!" hollered Glee from the top of the stairs as the wind caught her hat.

"I've got it," Grace told her, grabbing the hat from midair—conjuring a brief, bizarre image that morphed her into her nephew with the Frisbee.

Clearly, it was time to get indoors. I stepped ahead of them, crossing the porch to the door. I could see through the screen door that the inner door was open, so it was a safe bet that Carrol was indeed within. But why would the door be open? The weather that morning was far from pleasant. I rapped, calling, "Carrol?"

"Oh *no!*" cried Glee. This time it was her purse, snatched from her hand by a powerful gust that sent it sliding across the porch—sideswiping some half dozen geraniums, which tumbled over the edge. As the pots crashed in succession on the ground below, Glee scrambled to retrieve her purse.

I cracked the screen door open, telling Carrol with an uncertain laugh, "We'd really *like* to come in." But there was no answer.

So I opened the door wider and looked inside. Gasping at the sight of someone sprawled across the bed, I turned to tell Glee and Grace, "Wait here."

Entering the room, I rushed to the bed—it was Carrol. Dressed as on the day before in his long bathrobe, he had collapsed near the corner of the bed, as if he'd stumbled there and fallen. The robe was askew, exposing much of his body. His skin had the bluish tinge of suffocation, and his neck was ringed with purple abrasions, suggesting strangulation.

"What's wrong, Mark?" the ladies called from the porch. "What happened?"

"Stay there," I warned, hoping to spare them the sight of the apparent murder while trying to analyze what I could of the scene. Although Carrol had obviously met a violent end, there were no signs of struggle, and there was no suggestion of forced entry. The room itself, compared to the previous morning, was immaculate and tidy—no burglary or ransacking. The bed, though slept in, was generally neat, and there was no clutter on the nightstand—no papers, no K-Y, no big ugly pen. His laptop, with its screen folded shut, was still on the dining table. A few orderly piles of paperwork were stacked nearby—no porn magazines. Also on the table was a partially eaten cake, not pretty enough to be store-bought.

By now, of course, Glee and Grace had braved their way into the room. Both proved themselves tougher than I'd have guessed, forgoing the indulgence of shrieks or sobs or hightailing out the door and down the stairs.

Glee stepped boldly forward, surveying the corpse in silence. Carrol's genitals were exposed, and Glee's eyes popped—after all, the guy was six foot four. Shame on you, Glee.

More timidly, Grace approached the body on the bed. "Is he . . . ?"

"Yes," I answered. Given the circumstances, I could not resist adding a wry proclamation:

"The king is dead."

PART THREE

Fingers of Suspicion

CARROL CANTRELL SLAIN

'King of miniatures' found strangled at Lord residence

by CHARLES OAKLAND
Staff Reporter, Dumont Daily Register

Sept. 18, DUMONT WI—Carrol Cantrell, widely recognized as the world's reigning "king of miniatures," was found dead Sunday morning in his guest quarters behind the Grace Lord residence on Dumont's quiet north side. Victim of an apparent strangulation, Cantrell (50) had arrived in town from Los Angeles on Thursday, planning to serve as celebrity judge of a roombox competition to be held in conjunction with a convention of the Midwest Miniatures Society.

Sheriff Douglas Pierce was first to arrive on the murder scene after the body was discovered by two *Register* staffers, escorted there by Grace Lord. Pierce estimates that the death occurred sometime between dawn and 10 A.M. yesterday. He added, "A complete postmortem will be performed, allowing us to pinpoint the exact time and cause of death."

Pierce has pledged the total resources of his department toward solving the crime. "Murder is murder," he stated, "but this instance is particularly heinous in that it victimized a distinguished visitor to our city. Justice will be served."

As of late Sunday, detectives assigned to the case had interviewed dozens of locals who had interacted with Cantrell since his arrival. A list of possible suspects was being compiled, but no arrest had yet been made.

Knowledge of Cantrell's past is currently sketchy. Though outwardly flamboyant, he held his business matters private, and little is known of his finances, except that he appeared highly successful. It is hoped that a probate investigation will clarify whether a motive for murder may reach beyond Dumont.

Grace Lord, who invited Cantrell to Dumont and hosted his brief stay here, mourned the loss of a figure known simply as Carrol to miniatures enthusiasts everywhere. She told a reporter at the scene, "Our little world will never be the same." ❑

Monday, September 18

Dreams have always perplexed me. I've taken pride in building my career on the methodical gathering and rational scrutiny of facts, and I confess to a degree of smugness in judging myself intellectually superior to those who are less objective. Superstition, mysticism, dogma, and the occult are all products of a rankly subjective realm, and I have little respect for the opinions of those who place faith in such illusory nonsense.

Yet, we all dream. Over the ages, attempting to explain our dreams, we have imbued this phenomenon with all manner of ominous powers. From the totems and fetishes of the ancients, to the religious ecstasy of the Middle Ages, to the labyrinth of psychoanalysis, we have struggled to make sense of the images spun by our sleeping minds. Most of us have come to understand that these nocturnal fantasies are not supernatural visitations from the beyond; rather, they are generated from deep within. While this knowledge has helped to unscramble the neurological mechanism of our dreams, it has done little to render them less freaky.

Especially unsettling are those long, rambling dreams that often occupy our last hours of slumber before daybreak. These are the dreams that seem so confoundingly real, that speak to us with the narrative precision of a film loop fluttering behind our closed eyes. These are the dreams that stick.

Early the next morning after Carrol Cantrell's murder, I had such a dream.

I am behind Grace Lord's house, looking into the vast backyard with its carpet of lawn and canopy of trees. Music thumps from somewhere—a low-fi disco tune that sounds dated and seedy. The synthetic music doesn't match the natural simplicity of the scene. I turn my head to search for the source of the sound, but my field of vision is limited to the horizontal rectangle in front of me—I am unable to look up into the sky or beyond the sides of the scene.

A dog barks. It's a canned sort of bark, synchronized to the disco beat. The dog, a big friendly collie, a dead ringer for Lassie, bounds into view from the right side of the scene. It stops, looking back, wanting someone to follow. Then its head snaps skyward, following a Frisbee that arcs past. The dog leaps after it, barking to the beat. Just as the dog exits to the left, a young man (perhaps twenty, a grown boy, really) enters from the right.

It is Ward Lord. Dressed for summer in cutoffs and T-shirt, he flashes a perfect smile, flexes a perfect body. He gleams in the bright daylight, sweating from his romp with the dog. But he doesn't follow the dog—their game is finished. Instead, he turns from the scene and fixes me in his stare, grinning seductively, beckoning me.

I have watched all this from some distance and would gladly step forward to meet young Mr. Picture Perfect, but I am powerless to move, unable to walk. Then, responding to *his* will, not mine, I begin drifting toward him, gliding as if propelled along a frictionless track, arriving at some middle distance where his body fills my field of vision.

The music has grown louder, and Ward has caught the rhythm, moving to its pulse. His gyrations aren't exactly a dance—not one that you could name—but more of a visceral interplay between his body and the beat. His feet barely move from the patch of grass where he stands, but his legs sway to the sound. His torso jerks. His hands explore the fine nap of hair on his thighs. Then his fingers reach up the frayed legs of his cutoffs, feeling his crotch. And all this time, he's watching me.

Transfixed by this erotic spectacle, I respond with my own arousal. I want to zip open my pants and take hold of myself, stroke myself, but again I am powerless to move. I cannot even glance at myself to see if I am clothed or naked. I can see only Ward Lord—framed in the hard-edged rectangle of my vision.

He's clearly enjoying himself, judging from the lump in his shorts. Curiously, though, the purpose of this performance seems to be *my* satisfaction, not his. With a wink, he bids me to move closer as he peels the damp T-shirt from his chest and lifts it past his face. Tossing it aside, he shakes his head and swipes a hand through his mussed hair. With his other hand, he unbuttons the waistband of his cutoffs, letting them drop.

Zooming toward him (there is no sense of my own movement, but simply a larger, closer image of him within my view), I absorb every detail of his groin, the bluish ridge of every vein that feeds his penis, the sandy crater of every follicle that peppers his testicles. With my face between his legs, I feel the heat that radiates from him as he writhes to the rhythm of some disco diva. I feel his heat, but I do not feel *him*. Though close enough to lick him, to aid him in his mounting quest for orgasm, I cannot touch him. He is right there in front of me, and yet he is not.

It's a dream, I remind myself. Just enjoy it.

So I submit to the fantasy being played out around me. I indulge in the sensory treats that are offered, taking in stride the restrictions of my surreal presence, my disembodied participation. Though I cannot see Ward's hands, I can now feel them between my legs—surely it is he who rolls my balls through his fingers while stretching my cock stiff.

And so it continues, this sensual joyride. I am suspended—neither in space nor in time—adrift upon waves of pure but incomplete ecstasy, rising and falling to the cadence of Ward's carnal ministrations, both of us lost in some pumped-up, never-ending disco beat. Over and over, measure after measure, the music goes on. Seconds, minutes, hours (who knows?) pass in a long instant of sightless lust.

"Ward," I warn, "stop."

But of course he does not. Flashing that perfect smile, he grooves onward, slipping a finger inside me.

And I'm slipping off to some other zone, rushing toward a climax that I couldn't forestall even if I wanted to.

Ejaculating, I awake.

That morning in the kitchen—it was a Monday—the pace was brisk on Prairie Street, with our household preparing to begin the week. Neil and Thad stood at the counter, talking about something while opening the assortment of bags, boxes, and bottles that would dispense our "continental breakfast." I was already at the table with my coffee, looking over the morning paper. The big news was of course the story of Carrol's murder, which even upstaged the rehash of yesterday's Packers game, at least in the *Dumont Daily Register*.

My mind wasn't on the murder, though. I was still mulling the dream that had launched my morning with such a disconcerting, if pleasurable, bang. Am I, I wondered, so sexually needy that I can find fulfillment only in fantasy? Wet dreams are more properly the amusement of Thad's generation, at sixteen, not mine, at forty-two. After all, I have Neil, an experienced and eager partner who seems no less attracted to me than when we met three years ago. Granted, the frequency of our intimacy has waned of late. Living apart has put a predictable strain on our relationship, and even now that Neil has been spending more time in Dumont, our sex life has been inhibited by family life with Thad. Is this whole setup a mistake? Should I simply have stayed in Chicago at the *Journal*?

Even more rattling was the cast of my dream. Star billing went to Ward Lord, with his dog featured in a walk-on and me as an anonymous, lucky extra. My subconscious was lusting after Grace Lord's *nephew*, for God's sake—a "kid" just a few years older than Thad. I wondered, Was Miriam Westerman correct after all? Am I totally unfit for fatherhood? I ought to be ashamed of myself.

I *was* ashamed. When I woke from the dream, sticky with my involuntary orgasm, I felt as embarrassed as a child who'd wet the bed. Neil lay next to me, waking, it seemed, at the same moment. Had I perhaps thrashed or moaned at the climax of my dream, rousing him? It was still early, but the sun had risen and we both anticipated a busy day, so we kissed, deciding it was time to get up. I lingered, waiting for Neil to pad off to the bathroom, then scrambled to my feet and stripped the bed, wadding the soiled sheets. When Neil returned, he stopped at the sight of my feverish housekeeping. I explained, "Monday. Wash day."

"Who's Charles Oakland?" asked Neil as he sat next to me in the kitchen, snapping my attention back to the moment. He tapped the front page of the *Register*, which displayed the murder story under Charles Oakland's byline.

"Staff reporter," I answered with a shrug. "General assignment."

"Never heard of him." Neil slurped some coffee, warming his hands with the mug. Sunday's change of weather had brought a cold rain overnight, and the morning felt damp and chilly. "How was he lucky enough to land such an important story?"

Again I shrugged. "He happened to be covering the Sunday shift in the newsroom." I turned the page, landing Charles Oakland's story facedown on the table. I glanced over the contents of pages two and three.

Thad sidled up behind me. I knew from the heady aroma that followed him that he carried peanut-buttered toast—our pantry had been replenished. He asked, "So this guy got killed, and you like . . . *saw* him?" From his tone, I expected him to add, Too cool!

"Yes," I answered dryly, "Mr. Cantrell died yesterday, and by sheer coincidence, I discovered the body."

"How cool is *that?*" (Okay, I was close.) Setting his milk and the plate of toast on the table, Thad sat next to me, across from Neil.

Leaning toward him, I looked him in the eye and tried to explain, soothingly, "No, Thad, there was nothing cool about it. The murder was a tragedy both for Mr. Cantrell and for the city. Sheriff Pierce is under lots of pressure, and Miss Lord is utterly devastated." I was tempted to remind him of how he had felt last winter when his mother died too young, but in truth, I felt he had never properly grieved that loss, and I suspected he was still suppressing those feelings with an adolescent veneer of fascination with the morbid.

He nodded, grudgingly conceding my point that murder's not cool. Then a thought brightened his eyes. "So he was like . . . *strangled?*"

Lord. There was nothing to be gained by lecturing him on the appropriate tone of this discussion, so I simply answered, "It appears so, yes."

Neil jumped to my rescue, pouring more coffee while changing the topic. "On Friday, Thad talked to Mrs. Osborne, his English teacher, about the school play. She's directing it, and she encouraged him to audition."

"Oh yeah?" With the events of the weekend, I'd forgotten about Thad's budding interest in theater. He needed *something* to get enthused about, and drama was vastly preferable to homicide. I asked him brightly, "What's the play?"

"*Arsenic and Old Lace*." He actually licked his lips while leaning to explain, "It's about two old ladies who poison a bunch of men and bury them in their basement!" He'd risen a couple of inches from his seat.

I laughed, telling him, "I *know* what it's about, Thad." Hell, in my day there wasn't a school in forty-eight states that hadn't produced it, and the movie version with Cary Grant had been on television countless times. But to Thad and his contemporaries, this theatrical chestnut was brand-new, and I understood his delight in discovering its ghoulish humor. Recalling that the play is often produced in the fall, I asked, "When does it open—Halloween?"

Thad's eyes bugged, as if I'd performed a psychic feat. "Mrs. Osborne said she *wanted* the play to open on Halloween, but she'll need a couple more weeks."

Neil told him, "I was *in* that play, Thad."

"You *were?*" we both asked him.

"Wasn't everyone?" Neil began peeling an orange.

"No," I assured him. "Who'd you play?"

"Just a small part, one of the cops. But the role I came to love was the aunts' goofy nephew who thinks he's Teddy Roosevelt." Neil broke the orange into sections, sharing one with each of us. He asked Thad, "Is there any role you're particularly interested in?"

"I've never seen the play," he reminded us, "but Mrs. Osborne said I could borrow a script today. I'll start reading during study period this morning."

"Good idea," I told him. "Be prepared."

"Well"—he squirmed—"I can try to get the script read, but I don't know how to prepare for the tryouts. I've never done it before. It makes me sort of nervous."

Neil smiled. "That's perfectly natural. Just do your best. Most of the others won't know what they're doing either. Listen to the director—that's why she's there."

Thad nodded, weighing all this, taking courage. "All right," he told us. "If I like what I read, I'll go for it." He stood. "Nothing to lose, right?"

"Right," we both answered.

"Then I'd better get going." He wiped his mouth, picked up his dishes, and carried them to the sink, telling us, "Mrs. Osborne is usually in her office early. If I catch her, I can get the script." He grabbed his books from the counter.

Neil and I rose and sandwiched him in a hug. "Have a great day at school," I told him, "and good luck with the audition."

Neil reminded me, "Don't wish an actor good luck—it's a jinx." He told Thad, "Break a leg, kid."

I rolled my eyes in response to this superstitious ritual, but I let it pass, smiling, without comment. Thad, though baffled by it, chalked it off as the first of many lessons he was willing to learn as a novice seeking entry into the world of theater. Returning our hug, he thanked us for our wishes and headed for the door.

"Take a jacket," Neil told him. "It's wet."

Leaning into the back hall, Thad grabbed a zippered sweatshirt from a coat hook before leaving the house with an upbeat "Later, guys."

Neil and I shared a soft laugh. I asked, "Think he stands a chance? It's great to see him revved up about this, but it could backfire. He might be setting himself up for a bitter disappointment."

"That's just a chance he'll have to take," Neil answered with the voice of common sense. Stepping to the counter, he tidied some breakfast debris while reminding me, "His teacher encouraged him to audition—that bodes well."

"True," I admitted. Returning to the table to finish my coffee, I sat and turned the newspaper back to page one, which silently trumpeted news of the local murder. Gesturing toward the story, I thought aloud, "I wish Thad weren't quite so intrigued by the gruesome details."

Neil sat next to me, having poured himself a bowl of cereal. "He's at that age—kids, growing up, seem fascinated by death. Thinking they're immortal, they defy death with that adolescent brand of gory humor. I wouldn't worry about it." Again the voice of common sense.

I nodded. Silently, I sipped my coffee. Finding it tepid, I warmed it with more from the pot.

Neil looked up from the cereal he was eating. "You're rather pensive this morning. It seems Carrol's murder has really thrown you."

I could have dismissed my mood by simply concurring that I'd found the murder unexpectedly disturbing. "Actually," I explained, "there's something else on my mind." I paused—did I really want to get into this with Neil? "I had a strange dream last night."

He put down his spoon. He grinned. "A hot one?"

I'd made him privy to some previous reveries. Returning his grin, I admitted, "It was a scorcher."

Common sense again: "Then enjoy it. Why the angst?"

I leaned over my cup to tell him, "Because the young object of my middle-age lust was none other than Grace Lord's *nephew*."

Neil's grin sagged. With a look of blank astonishment, he said, "I wasn't even aware that Grace Lord *has* a nephew. How'd you meet him? And, uh—just how young *is* he?"

"Relax." I felt my mood lightening even as we spoke. Voicing my concerns had put them instantly into perspective, and I now found the dream considerably less vexing. I explained to Neil, "I didn't meet him—I only saw his picture, once, while helping Grace move some things out of the coach house. And don't worry—he's not twelve, more like twenty, at least when the picture was taken, which must have been years ago. He's Grace's brother's son. His name—get this—is Ward Lord."

Neil twitched a brow. "Yow. Sounds hunky." With a laugh, he added, "Sounds like a porn star."

I laughed with him. "Believe me, he *looks* like one! And in fact, my dream had the feel of a porn video, as if I were a detached spectator, watching him perform on a screen. There was even a cheesy sound track of background disco music."

With a heartier laugh, Neil remembered, "Those were the days. Production values have come a long way since then, but some of those early videos, crude as they were, remain some of the best. The video medium was still new, still defining itself. That early work was seminal—no pun intended."

Amused by the near academic slant of Neil's interest in porn, I reminded him, "This stuff isn't *art*—we're talking about jackoff tapes."

"Even trash," he lectured drolly, "can rise to greatness in its execution."

Though I found this assertion dubious, I conceded, "Ward Lord certainly 'rose to greatness' in my dream." I leaned back with my coffee, sipping. Neil resumed eating his cereal.

The more I thought about it, the more obvious it became why I had spun my dream with Ward as a porn star. Undoubtedly, my nighttime subconscious was still dealing with pornography because, for several days, my waking mind had been wrestling with matters related to smut. The obscenity ordinance, the looming trial, the report of the County Plan Commission, my editorial endorsement of Doug Pierce—all these concerns rose from the issue of pornography. Also, while visiting Carrol Cantrell at the coach house on Saturday, I had absorbed an eyeful of hard-core erotic images from the open magazines scattered on his worktable. No *wonder* these snippets of my waking life had taken the form they did in my dream.

Neil got up from the table with his bowl and rinsed it in the sink. Loading the dishwasher, he said wistfully, "My interest in collecting gay videos goes back fifteen years or so, to my college days. Can you guess who got me started?"

From the tone of the question, and from my limited knowledge of his college circle, I had an inkling where he was headed.

He answered his own question, "Roxanne. She's a couple of years older than I—and had no qualms about procuring my first tape for me on the day she turned twenty-one." He chortled at the recollection.

I laughed with him—this revelation came as little surprise. Roxanne Exner, the spunky Chicago lawyer who had introduced Neil and me, had first befriended Neil during college, and I could well imagine that she'd taken perverse pleasure in purveying to him the forbidden fruit of pornography. I would later come to know her as a news source while working on several high-profile stories at the *Journal*.

Younger than I but older than Neil, Roxanne had set her sights, romantically, on both of us. As for Neil, she was simply barking up the wrong tree. As for me, though, before committing myself to a new way of life with Neil, I did in fact indulge in a brief fling with her. The experiment was destined to disappoint both of us, and she seethed with resentment at the irony of having played matchmaker to the two men she wanted most. But in time, Roxanne's affection for both of us won out, and we came to think of her as our best friend—a relationship we managed to maintain in spite of my move to Dumont.

Having learned a hard lesson, Roxanne kicked the habit of falling for gay men and was now in a serious relationship with Carl Creighton, twelve years her senior, a deputy attorney general for the state of Illinois. Neither Neil nor I had seen much of Carl lately, but we still saw Roxanne with surprising regularity, considering the distance. Due to my board work at Quatro Press and Neil's involvement with the plant expansion, there were ample excuses to call in big-gun Chicago legal talent to handle the thicket of issues routinely faced by Quatro or by any thriving industry. And the person we called, of course, was Roxanne.

"Is she coming up this week?" I asked Neil.

He turned to me. "Today," he informed me, as though I should have known.

"Really?" I couldn't recall any board matters pending that required her attention, so I assumed that Neil had summoned her for matters pertaining to construction—environmental impact or some other hoo-ha. I asked, "What about dinner? Is she spending the night?" Details, details . . .

"It's just a day trip this time," he told me, rinsing his hands, closing some cupboards. "But if she arrives in town early enough, she'll see you for lunch—remember?"

The plan had a familiar ring to it. "Can't you join us?"

He crossed to where I sat, standing behind me, hands on my shoulders. "Not today, I'm afraid. Too much going on at the plant—meetings all morning."

I reached up to take hold of his fingers. "Things are bound to be busy at the *Register* too—the murder, the obscenity trial." I sighed.

Neil pulled back, planting hands on hips. "I thought you *relished* this stuff."

I couldn't help laughing, embarrassed to admit, "I do. But now and then—"

A knock at the back door interrupted us. Through the window, we could see that it was Doug Pierce. I expected him to holler, Any coffee left? I expected him simply to walk in. But he stood quietly outdoors in the drizzle, like any stranger waiting to be admitted.

"Come on in, Doug," we called to him. "It's not locked."

Pierce opened the door and stepped inside. "Nasty weather," he said, thumping the door closed. He wore one of those Australian-looking rubberized raincoats with big flaps and heaps of hardware. He shrugged out of it and hung it in the hall—on the hook that had been vacated by Thad's sweatshirt.

"Have some coffee, Doug," Neil told him, grabbing an extra mug from the counter and pouring from the pot on the table.

"Thanks." Pierce crossed the room and sat next to me. His mood and bearing were altogether different from the chipper afterglow that had marked his recent visits, when he'd arrived unshaven in day-old clothes. By contrast, this morning he was freshly dressed and groomed—he'd obviously spent the night in his own bed. There was no bounce to his step, no lighthearted banter—he'd slept alone.

I told him, "Looks like we've all got a tough week ahead." In truth, I was looking forward to a brisk Monday of meaty news at the paper, but he seemed in need of commiseration.

"Christ, what a mess," he muttered between slurps of coffee. "Dumont's celebrity visitor has been dead for twenty-four hours, and there isn't an arrest warrant in sight." He did not need to mention that his reelection might now very well rest on a speedy resolution of the crime. Nor did he mention that he'd been sleeping with the victim—a minor but tawdry detail that, if true and if made public, would be a political windfall for his opponent.

Neil joined us, sitting at the table. "You'll have an arrest as soon as Bruno returns to town, won't you? I mean, isn't it obvious?"

Good question. I waited with Neil for Pierce's answer.

He told us, "Bruno arrived back in Dumont late last night from Milwaukee, which was the plan he'd announced to several people. On the surface, he appears to have a clean alibi—he was out of town at the time of the murder. What's more, he's a French national, so even though I still consider him our prime suspect, we need to treat the situation with kid gloves. There's no point in setting off an international incident unless we have the case against him absolutely nailed."

I asked, "Have you talked to him yet?"

"Briefly, when he got in last night after midnight. We'd been waiting for him, and I helped carry his bags from the car to his motel room. I immediately informed him of the murder, but it came as no surprise—it was all over the news yesterday, and he claimed to have heard the story in Milwaukee. He was clearly tired, and so was I. I figured that since he returned to Dumont on his own, he wasn't likely to bolt, so we agreed to meet again this morning. For whatever it's worth, he didn't *act* suspicious—just his usual weird self."

Attempting to lay out the case against Bruno, I thought aloud, "There are three classic criteria that point to a suspect: motive, means, and opportunity. First, we know that Bruno was amply motivated to want Carrol dead. Their professional rivalry was legendary, and Bruno said in my presence at the *Register* on Friday that he considered Carrol a 'parasite,' that he intended to 'topple' him. Though he claimed to be speaking figuratively, the fact remains that both Bruno and Carrol are big men, and it would take someone of Bruno's heft to physically subdue Carrol, which brings us to classic criterion number two: means. Carrol was apparently strangled, and Bruno would have the strength to do it."

"*And*," Neil contributed, leaning into the conversation, "Bruno also had the silk scarf, the likely weapon. You'd both seen him wearing a patterned gold cravat that looked exactly like the wrinkled one found snagged on the banister of the coach-house stairs yesterday morning, moments before the body was discovered."

"*But*," said Pierce, also leaning forward (our three faces were now mere inches apart), "classic criterion number three doesn't seem to wash. Where and when was Bruno's *opportunity* to commit the murder if he was out of town all weekend?"

"So it all hinges on that 'if,' " I summarized. "Was Bruno in fact in Milwaukee as he claimed?"

"That's what we need to find out." Pierce leaned back in his chair to explain, "If there are any holes in his alibi, this'll be the easiest homicide of my career. If his story's tight, though, we're back to square one."

I asked, "When do you plan to see him?"

Pierce glanced at his watch. "I'm due now. We agreed to meet at The Nook early—he has some business appointments there as well." Pierce took a last drink of coffee, then set aside the mug. His face wrinkled with a new thought. "I won't be treating this as an official interrogation, so if you'd care to come along, Mark, I'd be grateful for your reactions—so long as the meeting stays off-the-record."

Big smile. "I thought you'd never ask." I stood, raring to go.

Neil and Pierce rose also. Neil mused, "It's a question of opportunity. If it turns out that Bruno wasn't here to strangle Carrol, who else had access to the victim?"

"I've been over that again and again," said Pierce, rubbing his neck, perplexed. "Lots of people had access to the coach house—there's little or no security—and Cantrell had a steady stream of visitors since the morning he arrived."

I offered, "I myself have been there several times; I accompanied Harley Kaiser and Miriam Westerman in one instance, Glee Savage another time. Grace Lord had total access, of course. And those are just the people I *know* to have been there." I might have added Pierce's name to the list, but refrained, hoping he might volunteer it. But he did not. So I continued, "The question we need to answer is: Who was there on Sunday morning?"

"Grace Lord," Neil suggested with a snicker, clearing the table. Carrying coffee and cups to the counter, he turned to elaborate, "She was there *every* morning—the place belongs to her. If it's a question of opportunity, Grace is your gal."

Though Neil's hypothesis was not meant to be taken seriously, Pierce felt compelled to weigh it objectively, looking beyond the gut response that Grace was far too kindly a soul to be involved in such heinous devilry. "She may have had ample opportunity," he reminded Neil, "but she had no motive. After all, her prestige with the Midwest Miniatures Society hinged on her ability to deliver Cantrell to their convention *alive*. Understandably, she's been really shaken by this—her big coup has turned into an unmitigated disaster."

"What's more," I reminded both of them, "whoever killed Carrol needed sufficient physical stature to subdue and strangle him. Grace's five-foot frame is no match for Carrol's, at six-four."

"Fine," Neil conceded with a laugh, "no need to give Grace the rubber-hose treatment. Just keeping you guys on your toes."

Pierce turned to me. "We'd *better* be on our toes—with Bruno. He's a foreign national, which not only complicates our usual procedures, but also presents us with a bit of a language barrier. Still, he's our only promising suspect."

I moved toward the door. "Let's get going then." I pulled my own raincoat from the back hall—a classic tan Burberry, not nearly so trendy as Pierce's olive-colored duster, which I handed to him. I told Neil, "Leave that stuff in the sink; I'll take care of it later. You've got a busy morning at Quatro."

"I can't leave yet." He paused before explaining, "It's not just the dishes. It's wash day, remember? And I can't put it off—you stripped the bed already."

"Sorry," I told him, suddenly sheepish.

"No problem." His amiable tone made it clear that he wasn't complaining. "But I *need* to do laundry."

What we *needed* was a housekeeper.

Since Pierce and I would be going to our respective offices downtown after meeting Bruno Hérisson, we drove both of our cars to The Nook. Following Pierce as he turned off Park Street, I noticed that the activity down the block in front of the miniatures store had a quieter, more somber pace than the hubbub I'd witnessed over the weekend—fewer vans, less milling of people. Had the news of Carrol Cantrell's murder sent the mini masses into mourning? Or perhaps the rush was destined to subside on Monday, when weekend dilettanti would trudge back to their day jobs. Or maybe it was just the rain—we had all gotten off to a slow start on that cold, damp morning.

Parking at the curb, Pierce and I got out of our cars, clapping their doors closed in unison. We stepped onto the sidewalk, glancing about for Bruno's rented compact. "He seems to be running late," said Pierce, a wrinkle of concern creasing his brow.

"Let's get indoors." As I led the way to The Nook's entrance, our leather soles softly slogged the wet concrete, leaving a trail of spots that glowed silver for a moment, then vanished beneath a fresh layer of gray drizzle. Opening the door for Pierce, I let him pass in front of me.

Inside, fluorescent lights burned coldly, magnifying rather than dispelling the Monday gloom. I felt like a kid arriving at school after a perfect fall weekend that had brought a change of weather for the worse. The place even smelled like a long-ago school in autumn—damp clothes, dry old wood, fresh paint—a whiff of Ditto fluid would have made the illusion complete. The sounds, however, were not those of a school—adult voices engaged in subdued chatter, the thud and slide of cartons and furniture, a crackling radio tuned to some nostalgia station, played low.

Pierce had not been inside the store before. He stood there with me in the front hall, peering into the showroom, not sure what to make of this odd little world. Unbuttoning his long coat, he looked about for somewhere to hang it—a good idea. I removed my Burberry as well, checking first to confirm that my pen and notebook were in my jacket, then we draped our raincoats together on the back of a wooden chair that had been shoved into a corner, out of the way.

As we entered the showroom, some of the people there glanced at us, but no one recognized us—they were out-of-towners. I spotted the clipboard woman whom I'd seen the day before, so I asked, "Has Mr. Hérisson arrived yet?" My pronunciation of his name had improved some.

"Haven't seen him." Her terse style had not improved. "Ask Grace."

Reluctant to engage her in more of this sparkling repartee, I nodded my thanks and led Pierce to the back of the room, where I now knew a doorway would connect to the defunct Rexall store, converted that week into a makeshift exhibit hall.

Entering the hall, I noted that the convention setup was at a standstill, having progressed little since the previous morning. News of Carrol Cantrell's murder had completely bollixed Sunday's work crew, and the few who remained on hand today were still preoccupied by the tragedy, gossiping in clumps, aghast at the brutal demise of the king of miniatures.

I saw Grace Lord where I had found her yesterday, at the far end of the hall, in the competition area among the roomboxes. Directing Pierce's glance toward her, I led him through the main aisle and approached Grace quietly, not wishing to interrupt a discussion she was having with several exhibitors.

"I just don't know," she told the others with a sigh. "If we drape the entrance in black, it'd be a fitting tribute, to be sure, but at the same time, it might keep the public away—what a downer." She wasn't being disrespectful, just pragmatic, and I admired her attempt to remain objective in such an emotional situation.

Then she noticed Pierce and me. "Oh. Good morning, Mark. Morning, Sheriff." The others backed out of the conversation as Grace continued, "I had a hunch I'd be seeing you fellas today. And wouldn't you know it—me looking like hell again." She laughed halfheartedly.

It seemed she was always apologizing for her appearance, which was never warranted—till now. That morning, in fact, she looked pretty bad. "Under the circumstances," I fudged, "you're looking very well today."

She rolled her eyes—she knew better. "We're doing the best we can. I met with the rest of the organizers late into the night and again this morning. We decided to push ahead—'the show must go on.' But it's hard to muster any energy now, let alone enthusiasm. Carrol was our top attraction, the biggest name in miniatures, and now he's gone. He *died* here. Murdered. Oh, Lord . . . ," she trailed off, lost in thought.

Pierce offered words of sympathy and assurance, explaining that the murder was his department's top priority, that he hoped to resolve it quickly, hoped to dispel any clouds of uncertainty that might hang over the convention's opening, now only five days away. "In fact," he concluded, "we may wrap this up as soon as this morning. Bruno Hérisson agreed to meet me here, but he's late."

Grace had heard Pierce without really listening—his speech was predictable—until his reference to Bruno and the unspoken implication that the Frenchman was thought guilty. Her eyes widened with astonishment and a tinge of fear. "No," she told Pierce, touching his arm with her fingertips, "you can't possibly think that Bruno killed Carrol. That would be just *too* terrible. He's the *second* biggest name in miniatures. If he as well as Carrol met his downfall here in Dumont, I'd never be able to forgive myself—and no one else would either."

Her fretting over these names and their ranks reminded me of the name games that had played through my mind since the previous Thursday, when I'd met Carrol. The irony of Grace's statement, when she called Bruno "the second biggest name in miniatures," was that she had not yet assimilated the new pecking order of her little world. With Carrol's death, Bruno had moved up a notch.

Pierce explained to Grace, "I haven't drawn any conclusions about Bruno, not yet. That's why I need to talk to him. But you must admit, he had the most to gain from Carrol's death, also the biggest ax to grind—at least as far as we know."

I added, "And remember the silk scarf we found on the banister, Grace? It may very well have been used to strangle Carrol, snagged from the killer's pocket as he fled the scene. The point is, we've all seen Bruno wearing just such a scarf."

"But I *told* you," Grace insisted, "that scarf was probably Carrol's. When I cleaned his room, I saw that he had many silk scarves."

"She's right," conceded Pierce, whose investigators had already inventoried the contents of the coach house.

"There now," said Grace, satisfied that an important point had been made. "I'm sure if you just *talk* to Bruno, he'll explain everything to your satisfaction."

"We're eager to hear him out." Pierce tapped his watch. "But where is he?"

Right on cue, amid a flurry of activity from the doorway to The Nook, Bruno entered the hall, surrounded by exhibitors who followed him from the showroom. To characterize his entrance as triumphal would sell it short. He had newly assumed the mantle of the reigning sovereign of miniatures, and his subjects fawned about him to troth their allegiance—one woman skittered forward to introduce herself, and she actually made a clumsy attempt at a curtsy. Bruno sopped up the attention and flattery of his minions, strolling forward among them at a regal pace. His refined manner and delicate movements seemed impossible from a man of such burly bearing and sheer heft. With one arm he clutched a dog-eared notebook; in the other hand he carried a gnawed pencil, punctuating the air as he spoke. The way he handled these pedestrian articles, you'd have thought they were an orb and scepter. Yes, King Bruno had arrived.

Spotting us at the far end of the hall, he shrugged a gesture of apology for his tardiness, unable (or unwilling) to extricate himself from the little throng of admirers. "*Oh la la*," he singsonged to them, "I am late, my friends. Truly, I must take my leave," at last shooing the crowd aside and crossing the room to meet us.

"Morning, Majesty," I told him wryly, extending my hand.

"Yes, Mark? Good morning?" he said, pretending to be confused by my greeting. He shook my hand, then Pierce's, telling him, "Do forgive my late arrival. I hope you did not begin to suspect that I had"—he paused, searching for the phrase—"skipped town." He chortled.

Grace cast both Pierce and me a visual jab, shaming us for the suspicion that Bruno had so colloquially nailed.

Getting into his cop mode, Pierce replied flatly, "We've got a murder on our hands, Bruno. It's our job to be suspicious." His serious tone effectively quelled any instincts to keep our conversation lighthearted.

Grace seemed irked by this, as if Bruno—a foreign visitor, her guest—were being treated rudely. She told Pierce, "I can tell that you gentlemen would prefer to be alone. Would you like to use the old office?"

"Thank you, Grace. That might be best."

Wordlessly, Grace led us to a back corner of the exhibit space, where a door opened into the bygone drugstore's office. A small, windowless room, it was clean but barren, containing only a card table and a few folding chairs, probably used as a lunchroom by the exhibitors. The lighting was too bright, the walls too white. Had the furniture been heavier, the setting could have passed for a police interrogation room in some forties-vintage gangster B movie. This imagery did not escape Bruno (had he seen a lot of old American films?), for his features dropped and he hesitated in the doorway before gingerly proceeding in, approaching one of the chairs as if on tiptoe. Grace excused herself, closing the door behind her with a hearty thud (I don't think she meant to slam it—perhaps the jamb had warped), which made both Bruno and me jump. But Pierce was cool, suggesting, "Let's all sit down."

Without carpet or drapes or upholstery to soften the room's harsh acoustics, our metal chairs squeaked and scraped grimly as we settled around the table. It was a challenge for Bruno to perch his corpulence on the banged-up chair's perforated seat. He squirmed to cross his legs, attempting an air of nonchalance, but the darting of his eyes revealed apprehension as well as physical discomfort.

Pierce flipped open a folder and clicked his ballpoint. I readied both my steno pad and my Montblanc, but did not uncap the pen, recalling Pierce's admonition that this meeting was off-the-record. Bruno, mimicking our actions but unsure of his purpose, riffled through the pages of his shabby notebook, marking one of them with his chewed pencil.

Pierce calmly reviewed his notes, saying nothing as he read. I waited, as this was Pierce's meeting—anything I might say would arise from my reporter's instincts and could possibly run contrary to police procedure. But Bruno fidgeted, finding the lull unbearable. He broke the silence, asking, "Am I to be arrested? Shall I procure the services of an advocate, or perhaps phone the consul general? He is—where, Chicago?"

He had punched precisely the hot button Pierce hoped to avoid—the prospect of a diplomatic incident. "Of course not." Pierce gave Bruno a comforting smile, then hesitated, explaining, "Of course I presume your innocence in the matter of Carrol Cantrell's murder, and we do not arrest the innocent. But because your rivalry with the victim was well known, it is my duty to question you about the *possibility* of your involvement with the crime. If you have any misgivings about how to answer these questions, or about the future consequences of your answers, then you would be well advised to have a lawyer present, which is your right." Pierce skirted the issue of the consulate entirely, concluding, "Would you care to postpone this interview until you've secured representation by an attorney?"

Under the circumstances, *I* certainly would have. But Bruno surprised both of us. His manner turned suddenly calm as he answered, "That will not be necessary, as I have nothing to hide. Let us proceed."

Pierce and I glanced at each other as he made note of Bruno's decision. Was Bruno, our prime suspect, in fact innocent—and sufficiently confident to risk self-representation? Or was he bluffing, suspecting that his foreign citizenship would keep Pierce's investigation at arm's length, at least long enough for Bruno to weigh his next move, which could take him out of the country? Tough call.

Pierce began, "I'm sure, Mr. Hérisson, that you share the sadness felt by everyone else in Dumont regarding Mr. Cantrell's tragic and untimely death."

Bruno eyed him skeptically. "You have made this observation as a statement, Sheriff Pierce, but I sense that you have posed it as a question. Is it your intent to ask me how I 'feel' about the murder?"

"Actually," Pierce admitted, "yes."

Bruno responded with one of those characteristically French isn't-it-obvious shrugs. "Murder is wrong, and one must mourn the victim. Cantrell and I were not good friends, as you know. I cannot even say that I liked the man—but he did not deserve the garrote."

"I understand that you've developed plans to open"—Pierce checked his notes—"a Los Angeles miniatures museum and showroom that would go into direct competition with Cantrell's establishment, the Hall of Miniatures."

"Competition is the American way, no?"

"Yes," said Pierce, allowing himself a laugh, as did I, "but some people might get the idea that Cantrell's death works to your professional advantage."

Again that shrug. "Indeed it does. I do not deny it—Cantrell's misfortune comes as a great blessing to me. Does that aspect of this tragedy please me? But of course!" He leaned back to assume a self-satisfied pose, but the rickety chair would not cooperate, and Bruno almost lost his balance. Heaving himself forward again, he barely managed to avoid toppling. The image of the chair's near collapse, which would have landed Bruno on his ass, legs wagging, lent a note of absurd humor to the dry dialogue, and I suppressed a nascent laugh.

With laudable discretion, Pierce pretended not to notice Bruno's mismove, focusing instead on his words. "What we've established, then, Mr. Hérisson, is this: You and Mr. Cantrell were professional rivals, and his demise has proved advantageous to you. Some might conclude that you had sufficient *motive* for murder. Further, Mr. Cantrell was probably strangled to death, possibly with a silk scarf that was found at the crime scene. He was a tall and able-bodied man, and it would take someone of your size, Mr. Hérisson, to subdue him. What's more, you have often been seen wearing a scarf much like the one found on the premises. In other words, some might conclude that you had sufficient *means* for murder . . ."

I realized, as Pierce spoke of the scarf, that Bruno was not wearing the patterned gold cravat today; it was the first time I'd seen him with a bare neck. Surely this detail was as evident to Pierce as it was to me, for he casually made note of something while speaking. I expected Bruno to react nervously to Pierce's mention of the scarf—perhaps he would fuss with his shirt collar or rub his chin in an attempt to conceal his neck—but he made no move at all, letting the comment pass. Indeed, there was almost a smugness to his expression, as if he knew exactly where Pierce's discourse was leading.

Pierce continued, "You may have had a motive to want Cantrell dead, and you may have had the means to kill him, but—"

"But," Bruno interrupted, concluding the thought, "I could not have committed the crime if I was not here to do it." He crossed his arms.

"Correct, of course. So it's vitally important that we establish—I'm not sure if you know the word—a firm *alibi*."

Bruno nodded. "Yes, it is the same in French, *alibi*," he repeated the word, but pronounced it with a soft *a* and with *e* sounds instead of *i*'s.

Pierce again referred to his notes. "You told several people last week that you planned to visit Milwaukee over the weekend, leaving Dumont by car early Saturday and returning late Sunday."

"Precisely," said Bruno, flipping both hands in the air, as if that settled the matter. "Cantrell was murdered, I understand, early yesterday morning, and you witnessed my return to Dumont late last night."

"But can you *prove* you were not in Dumont at the time of the murder?"

Bruno puffed himself up. "Do you call me a liar?"

"Certainly not. But *someone* will eventually be charged with this murder. Though it is not incumbent upon you to prove innocence—it's the responsibility of the state to prove guilt—a case could never be brought against you or anyone else who could demonstrate up front that he'd had no *opportunity* to commit the crime."

"I see," Bruno said in a conciliatory tone that served as apology for his brief show of indignation. With eyes cast toward the ceiling, he whirled a hand, recalling, "I left Dumont early Saturday, perhaps eight o'clock, arriving in Milwaukee well before noon. I could not yet check into my hotel there, the Pfister, because the room was not yet ready. So I spent some time downtown, took lunch, and returned to the hotel after one. It was then that I registered, as I am sure the hotel records will verify. That afternoon, I napped in my room and also phoned friends whom I planned to see that evening—that was the purpose of my visit. Several well-known miniatures artisans had arrived in Milwaukee and were staying in the city prior to the convention's opening in Dumont. I wanted to meet with them in order to present my proposal regarding exclusive representation in this country by the Petite Galerie Hérisson. We met that night for dinner, and any of these colleagues will be able to verify that I was there, in Milwaukee, as I have claimed. My mission was a complete success, and I returned with signed contracts granting me exclusivity."

Pierce was recording details of this story in his notebook. He looked up to ask Bruno, "And Sunday morning?"

"What about it?"

With a tinge of exasperation, Pierce explained, "We can vouch for your whereabouts on Saturday afternoon and evening, but the period we need to nail down is Sunday morning, the time of the murder."

"I was *asleep*," Bruno told him, as if the answer should be self-evident. "I arose late, then left the hotel just before noon."

"Can you remember who you spoke to at the desk when you checked out?"

Now it was Bruno who sounded exasperated. "I spoke to no one. One may simply sign a card and leave it in the room with the key."

"Did you order room service that morning—or speak to a maid in the hall?"

"No, I simply left. Had I known that this action would be deemed culpable, I would have arranged to have witnesses." He sniffed.

Pierce reminded him, "You left the hotel around noon, but you didn't arrive back in Dumont until after midnight. That's twelve hours, and the drive takes about three. What did you do with the rest of the day?"

"I enjoyed the city—there was a festival at the shore of the lake. I saw thousands of people, and they saw me, but there was no one I knew, no one who could swear I was there."

"You must have parked your car somewhere. Do you have a stub from the lot?"

Bruno thought. "I am not certain. I can check my things."

"Good," said Pierce, underscoring a word on his pad, "try to find it—or *anything* that places you in downtown Milwaukee during the day yesterday."

Bruno nodded, making a note of his own.

There was a moment's silence before Pierce continued, "It would be useful, Mr. Hérisson, if you could recall anything distinctive or peculiar about your trip, anything that we could independently verify that would help prove where you were over the weekend. Does any incident spring to mind?"

"No . . ." He shook his head gently, his brow furrowed in thought. Then he froze momentarily as something occurred to him. He looked Pierce in the eye, telling him tentatively, "There was . . . the dog."

Pierce looked at me, then back at Bruno. "Yes? What dog?"

"A large dog, a brown dog, the breed sometimes used by police."

I suggested, "A German shepherd?"

"Yes, Mark," said Bruno, "exactly. Shortly after I left town on Saturday, I drove onto the highway, going south. It was still quite early, and I was not quite awake, and my thoughts were perhaps not so much on the road as on my mission. I had driven no more than a mile from the edge of town, when a dog, a German shepherd, appeared on the roadway, perhaps chasing a small animal—a rabbit? Seeing the dog just in time, I turned the car and managed not to hit it. But behind me there was another car, an odd car like a Jeep, that had not seen the dog because I was in front."

Bruno paused, mopping his brow, agitated by the recollection. "Watching through my mirror, I then saw the Jeep hit the dog, which was pushed into the air before falling by the roadside. It disappeared into the, uh . . . trench, the ditch."

Neither Pierce nor I said a word, silenced by Bruno's upsetting story. With sticky mouth, he continued, "I thought to turn back, but I noticed that the Jeep had already stopped, and I was certain that the poor dog was beyond helping. So I drove on, trying to shake the unfortunate incident from my mind. When I drove home last night, I slowed my car there, wondering what I might see, but of course it was too dark."

Pierce asked, "Can you be more specific as to where this happened?"

Bruno nodded without hesitation—the scene was apparently still vivid to him. "At the edge of town, there are a few shops on the highway. Further south, on the right, there is a farm—there are many after that, but this is the first one. In a field, beyond the barn, there is a *moulin à vent*"—he whirled a hand in the air, searching for the word—"a windmill. At the point where the road comes closest to the mill, that is where the poor dog flew into the ditch."

The story, while touchingly told, did nothing to confirm that Bruno had not killed Carrol, but it revealed a quiet facet of the man that neither Pierce nor I had yet seen.

"Thank you, Mr. Hérisson," Pierce told him. "If you need to be going, feel free. And do see if you can locate a parking stub for me." Pierce smiled, rose, and shook Bruno's hand.

Rising, Bruno told him, "Thank you, Sheriff Pierce. I shall search for this evidence." Bruno turned to me. "Good day, Mark."

I rose to shake his hand, and without further discussion, he left the room.

Pierce glanced over his notes in silence for a moment.

Closing his file, he told me, "Let's find that dog."

Since the incident had occurred on the outskirts of Dumont, nowhere near our downtown offices, we decided to ride together in my car, which was bigger and more comfortable than Pierce's. From Bruno's description of the area, Pierce knew exactly where to look.

Still something of a newcomer to Dumont, I needed directions. "South on the highway, right?"

Pierce nodded at the turn. "Just as if you were hopping on the interstate toward Chicago." I'd done *that* often enough.

We weren't going far, but the trip gave us a few minutes to recap the meeting with Bruno. "Do you still consider him a suspect?" I asked.

"You bet." Pierce turned in his seat to face me as I drove. "Bruno's trip to Milwaukee sounds almost as if it was *invented* to give him an alibi. The problem with his story, of course, is that he can't account for the critical hours when Cantrell was killed. Since there's no clear record of when he checked out of the Pfister, he could have left Milwaukee at, say, six yesterday morning, arriving back in Dumont by nine. That would put him at the crime scene at the time of the murder. Then he could have simply left town again, hanging out somewhere—even Milwaukee—till his return at midnight."

My eyes were on the road, but my mind was absorbed by the possibilities raised by Pierce. I added a theory of my own: "Even if Bruno is able to produce some evidence that he was in Milwaukee when Cantrell died, he could have arranged for some third party to do the dirty work during his planned, well-announced absence."

"That would fit," agreed Pierce, turning his own gaze back to the road. Thinking aloud, he added, "Since Bruno is such a conspicuous figure, he'd have a tough time sneaking into and out of town unnoticed, especially on a morning when everyone presumed he was in Milwaukee. If in fact Bruno was savvy enough—or sinister enough, or stupid enough—to put a hit on Cantrell, it should be easy to trace the arrangements. After all, this guy's milieu is dollhouses, not organized crime."

We shared a laugh at the image conjured by Pierce's words: Bruno squeezing into a phone booth with a satchel of loot, placing a clandestine call, lamely disguising his voice but not his accent as he whispers through a silk scarf wrapped over the receiver. It was absurd. And yet, it was a workable theory.

Something had been troubling me. "I'm curious—what are we doing out here? The Pfister's records can easily verify whether Bruno was in Milwaukee on Saturday, as claimed. But his story about the dog being hit that morning, whether true or false, does nothing to prove that he was in Milwaukee on *Sunday* morning. So why check out the dog story?"

"Because," Pierce stated simply, "if there's no dead dog, Bruno lied to us."

"Aha."

We had passed the city limits and traveled into the sparser environs of Dumont County, along the highway that led to the interstate, an area ripe for development. Under consideration for annexation to the city, this stretch of land was the subject of the study just completed by the County Plan Commission. Not far ahead, scattered on either side of the road, were the "few shops" that had been noted by Bruno. These were in fact the adult bookstores (i.e., porn shops) that so nettled certain factions within the community—including fundamentalists of every stripe, feminists like Miriam Westerman, and politicians like Harley Kaiser.

Even on an overcast Monday morning, the porn shops were open, mongering their selection of videos, magazines, peep shows, and novelties to motorists who had hopped off the interstate, few from the town itself. The stores themselves were windowless, spartan structures converted from a mechanic's garage, a long-defunct roadhouse, a barn or two. Helium balloons and wheeled marquees lured drivers from the highway with promises of SEX TOYS FOR HIM AND HER! and TWENTY-FOUR-HOUR VIDEO ARCADE! and EXOTIC LINGERIE FANTASIES! The largest of these emporiums, Star-Spangled Video, one of the defendants named in the impending obscenity trial, was located in a barn painted pink. A banner across its entire width hyped the latest in sizzling CD-ROMs. I wondered aloud, "When did smut go high-tech?"

Pierce chortled. "When computers came home from the office."

The gravel parking lot in front of Star-Spangled Video was filled with big amorphous puddles from the overnight rain, reflecting the gray sky. Trucks and vans outnumbered the cars there, most with out-of-state plates. Whatever the drivers were doing inside the pink barn, it struck me as an odd amusement to occupy a dreary morning. But then, to each his own.

Nearing the parking lot, I slowed the car, telling Pierce, "I wonder who they are. Mostly men, I presume. Some gay. They don't seem to mind being seen here—their cars are in full view of the road."

"Most of them," Pierce reminded me, "are from out of town. They wouldn't know a soul here."

As he said this, a trucker revved his engine and backed his rig away from the building. I stopped at the roadside, watching him shift into low gear while pulling out of the lot. As the truck passed in front of us, I noticed the profile of another car parked near the pink barn. It had been there all along with the others, but obscured by the truck's trailer. It caught my eye now because it was nearly identical to my own, a Bavarian V-8, looking brand-new—there were still tape marks on the window where the price sticker had been removed. The sedan was a deep emerald green; my own, black.

It caught Pierce's attention too. He quipped, "Don't get nervous, Mark. I'll bet it's out-of-state. You still take top honors for the slickest wheels in Dumont." He stroked my dashboard as if patting the flank of a thoroughbred.

I asked through a laugh, "Was I that obvious?"

"You were bug-eyed."

Driving onto the road again and cruising past the parking lot, I glanced over for another look at the green car and, seeing it from the rear, noticed that Pierce's bet was wrong—it was tagged with Wisconsin plates. Though tempted to point this out to him, I let it pass, as it would only reinforce the impression that I was overly fond of my own car and its exclusivity. Pierce was embroiled, after all, in a murder investigation, and my flustering about some stranger's car invading my turf amounted to nothing more than petty one-upsmanship. Chiding myself for wasting mental energy on such a niggling nonissue, I drove away in silence.

As the porn shops grew smaller in my mirror, expansive farmland dominated the view ahead, stretching to the horizon, where the delicate ribbon of the four-lane interstate met the two-lane blacktop on which we traveled. Pierce said, "Bruno told us the dog was hit near the first farm on the right. It's just ahead, the Norris place."

Set well back from the fields, on a side road, was the house. Behind it was the barn and a scattering of smaller buildings. And there, in the midst of a soy field along the road where we drove, was a rusty old windmill, missing a blade or two. Though it hadn't pumped water in decades, the Norrises apparently felt that it made a quaint landmark—either that, or they figured that someday a good storm would knock it over, saving them the bother of dismantling it.

I pulled off the road where it passed nearest the windmill, along the ditch where Bruno said the dog had been thrown. Without speaking, Pierce and I both got out of the car. The rain had stopped, but a damp wind still blew, and we both reflexively huddled into our trench coats, raising their collars. I walked a few yards ahead, scanning the ditch; Pierce moved in the opposite direction.

"There it is," he said flatly, and I joined him, peering down the steep embankment of weeds along the roadside.

The dog (I *thought* it was a dog, but only because a dog was the object of our search—it certainly didn't *look* like a dog, or any other animal, for that matter) was curled in the water that trickled along the bottom of the ditch. The overnight rain and two days of death and insects had transformed the stricken creature into a black, bloated ball of a thing that looked like a wad of tar. I was perfectly satisfied that Bruno had been truthful, that he'd witnessed the poor dog's misfortune, and I was ready to leave. To my dismay, though, Pierce began sidestepping his way down the embankment, preparing to get a closer look. With difficulty, he barely maintained his balance, as his office shoes were not designed to grip the grassy, wet incline. Stumbling to the bottom, he straddled the stream of rainwater and waddled to the dog. Crouching clumsily in his greatcoat, he lifted the dog's head. As he did this, I suddenly saw the dog's form emerge from the carcass I had thought shapeless. I also saw that the dog wore a chain around its neck.

"It's Rambo," said Pierce, "the Norrises' shepherd." Standing, he pulled out a handkerchief and wiped his hands. To my great relief, he started climbing up to the road—I'd feared he might want to move the dead animal. Needless to say, I didn't want it in my car, not even in the trunk, not even if covered with a makeshift shroud, which we didn't have. As if reading my mind, Pierce explained, "The county road crew will dispose of it eventually, but I'd better tell the Norrises—I'm sure they're worried. The kids'll be sick about this."

I was a bit queasy myself. I could well imagine the kids' mounting dread—they'd doubtless been out here searching for Rambo, and they'd probably glanced right over the bloated corpse, not recognizing it, concluding that their dog had run away from home, had left them. Extending my arm, gripping Pierce's hand to help hoist him onto the road's shoulder, I felt a visceral surge of melancholy, a reaction I had not expected. After all, we'd driven out here for the specific purpose of finding a dead dog, and we found it—mission accomplished. It wasn't *my* dog. I'd never known the dog in life, I'd never met its owners, and I'd never much cared for German shepherds anyway, thinking them mean. And yet, here lay Rambo, a farm dog, a family pet, stricken in his feral prime (was I romanticizing this?) by a car, a machine, the handiwork of man. Yes, I was romanticizing poor Rambo's demise.

Pierce stomped his feet, trying to clean his shoes on the bumpy surface of the wet asphalt. His eyes were still aimed into the ditch, and he seemed lost in thought, as I was. He asked, "Did you ever have a dog, Mark?"

I shook my head. "No. Cats. How about you?"

"Oh sure, I had a dog. Well, my *folks* had one, a cocker spaniel—a popular breed when I was growing up. They named him Checkers. Original, huh?"

I shared his soft laughter. I wasn't old enough to remember Nixon's television speech in the early fifties, but my mother had found it a source of endless amusement for years to come. I finally saw clips of the "Checkers speech" during the final days of the

Watergate scandal, when the networks scrambled to patch together swan-song videos documenting the background of the nation's first failed presidency.

"Later," said Pierce, "after Checkers died, while I was in high school, I got a dog of my own. Just a mutt from the pound, but he was sure great." Pleasant memories showed on Pierce's face, taking the form of a boyish grin.

"What was his name?"

"I called him Squire—it sounded sort of lordly, like Prince or Duke, but *those* names were so common, and I wanted something special." With his hands, he framed the name in the air, as if reading it in lights. "Squire."

As he spoke of his younger years in Dumont, a thought occurred to me: Had Doug Pierce and Ward Lord grown up together? I had no idea how old Grace Lord's nephew would now be, but there was a chance that he and Pierce were contemporaries. Maybe they'd tossed Frisbees to their dogs together. I was tempted to ask about this, but the question would surely have struck Pierce as a non sequitur. Further, he would wonder what interest I had in Ward, which I was at a loss to explain. So I simply asked, "How long did you have Squire?"

He sighed. "Only a couple of years. My parents sort of 'inherited' him when I went away to college, and by the time I'd finished police training, they'd all gotten used to each other—in fact, they'd grown old together. So when I moved back to town and got a place of my own, Squire stayed home with Mom and Dad. He lived another four or five years, and when he died, it was rough on all of us. Afterwards, none of us breathed a word about getting another pet."

There wasn't much traffic that morning, and only a few cars drove past us from either direction as we spoke, some slowing as they approached, motivated by either caution or curiosity. But there was nothing to see—two men in trench coats talking on the roadside.

I asked Pierce, "How did you, uh . . . dispose of Squire?"

Frankly, this conversation had gotten weird, but Pierce wasn't troubled by it. He answered, "Buried him in the backyard, no big deal." Then he turned the tables. "Tell me about your cats."

I really hadn't thought about them in years, but my childhood pets still lived just beneath the threshold of memory, spurring recollections that may have been only imagined: awakening to the soft nuzzling of my ear, or recoiling from the snap of static electricity that arced from a wet nose-kiss on a dry winter night, or picking stray strands of fur from my lips after napping together one afternoon. Though these impressions were vivid, they were not, I knew, the sort of boy-and-his-dog anecdotes that Pierce could relate to. A dog's master often regards the animal as his best friend, a loyal guard and servant. Not so with cats, of course—the term *master* doesn't even apply. No, cats are simply a presence in their owners' lives—a magnificent, sculptural, regal, sometimes haughty presence that deigns to share a home and be kept. Dog people just don't get it.

So I told Pierce, "My dad died when I was three, and Mom worked. With me in school, there was no one around the house during the day, so having a dog just wouldn't have been practical." In truth, neither Mom nor I had ever felt inclined to get a dog, but for Pierce's sake, I decided to give him the impression that we'd settled for "second best." It was simpler.

I continued, "Since cats are relatively easy to care for, that's what we got. The first was a stray that showed up while I was in grade school—I was seven or eight. We took him in, and I named him Charlie. God knows why—it just seemed to fit."

"Charlie the cat." Pierce laughed. "That was in Illinois, right?"

"Yes." I reminded him, "Mom, who was a Quatrain, moved from Dumont to Illinois about the time she married Dad. They settled in the suburbs north of Chicago, and I grew up in a gray house with white trim on a quiet street named Oakland Avenue. Those were peaceful times, and it was a peaceful place, not unlike Dumont."

"What happened to him?" Pierce clarified, "I mean Charlie."

Moving toward the car—there was no reason to remain standing there on the roadside—I told him, "Charlie was always getting battered up in cat fights, then he'd stay in the house for a while, licking his wounds, literally. But one night, something got the best of him, probably a dog." Saying this, I realized that I'd doubtless hit upon the reason I'd never found dogs alluring, but I also realized that it was a comment Pierce might not appreciate, so I quickly added, "Or it may have been a big raccoon. In any event, I found Charlie in the yard one morning, and it was awful. Mom stayed home from work to help me bury him."

"That's rough," said Pierce, extending his sympathies thirty-some years after the central tragedy of my youth.

I nodded. We were by now both buckled into the car, so I turned the key in the ignition. "It's funny, Doug. When Dad died, I was too young to understand what was happening, and his funeral, from my child's perspective, was 'sanitized' and essentially meaningless. But a few years later, when that cat died and I dug a hole and buried him—boy—*then* I understood the meaning of life and death."

As we pulled onto the road, Pierce asked, "You got another cat?"

"A while later, yes. A big orange tabby. I named him Willy. Again, no reason, no namesake. He lived with us for years. Funny, though"—a disturbing thought occurred to me as I brought the car up to highway speed—"I can't quite remember what happened to him. He almost always went outdoors overnight. I guess he just didn't come home one morning."

"That's a terrible feeling—not knowing," Pierce commiserated.

In his line of work, Pierce often consoled distressed families in the midst of calamities far more weighty than lost pets. It was kind of him to judge my uncertain recollections worthy of his sympathies. It was the same kindness that had prompted his concern for the feelings of the Norris children, who still wondered what had become of their German shepherd. As we approached the crossroad leading to the farmhouse, I asked, "Did you want to stop to tell the Norrises about Rambo?"

"I need to check in at the department. I'll call them from there."

So I passed through the intersection, heading back toward town, and our conversation lapsed. I still entertained thoughts of Charlie and Willy, and chances are, Pierce continued to ponder Checkers and Squire.

These musings of more innocent times were interrupted when we passed the porn shops, specifically the blushing-pink barn that housed Star-Spangled Video. What drew my attention was not the building itself, not its lurid signage, but rather an empty space in the parking lot—the fuzzy edge of a dry rectangle was still visible on the wet gravel. The Bavarian V-8, my car's green twin, was gone.

It had not passed us while we searched the ditch (I'd surely have noticed it), which meant that it had not headed out of town, toward the interstate. Instead, it must have driven into Dumont. I'd never seen another car like mine in the area. Whose was it?

"I just had a thought," said Pierce.

"Me too." I assumed that he had also noticed the missing green car.

But he continued, "Bruno's story. Obviously, he saw the dog get hit, but I wonder if he really saw a Jeep do it through his rearview mirror. Somehow, that part of the story had the ring of fabrication. Maybe he hit the dog himself." Pierce pondered this a moment before allowing, "But then, Bruno may be an excellent driver. I've never seen him behind the wheel."

"I have," I assured Pierce.

Then I added, "Poor Rambo."

Late that morning, in the conference area of my outer office at the *Register,* I sat with the paper's managing editor, Lucille Haring, and features editor, Glee Savage, planning our coverage of Carrol Cantrell's murder investigation. Glee would not normally be involved with such a story, but she had, after all, first covered Carrol's visit to Dumont, so she was now our staff authority on the victim. What's more, it was impossible to separate the murder story from that of the soon-to-open miniatures convention, which fell squarely within Glee's domain. All three of us took the attitude that traditional roles didn't matter as much as our ability to report news, so we didn't bother fretting over job descriptions. We were a team.

"I thought I'd develop a sidebar," said Glee, adjusting her half-frame glasses while skimming her notes, "profiling some of the other artisans who'll exhibit at the convention. These are the gentlemen visited by Bruno in Milwaukee over the weekend. I ought to be able to reach most of them by phone before they arrive—maybe they can shed more light on the rivalry."

"That sounds good," said Lucy, scratching out an item on her list. Shifting toward me in her chair, she crossed the legs of her twill pantsuit and asked, "Can I assume we'll keep the story on page one till there's an arrest?"

"For now, sure. If Bruno can't come up with any proof that he *was* in Milwaukee at the time of the murder Sunday morning—or if Pierce comes up with evidence that he *wasn't*—we should see an arrest fairly soon. Otherwise, there's no way of telling how long this could drag on."

Listening to this, Glee had been sucking the tip of her pen, troubled. She asked both Lucy and me, "Is Bruno the *only* active suspect? He's kind of a flake, and we've seen him vent a vindictive streak, but my gut tells me he didn't do it."

Lucy answered, "We're following Cantrell's probate proceedings in California to see if they reveal any interests that could have motivated murder. And here in Dumont, we're still waiting for the coroner's report, which ought to be cut-and-dried. Barring any surprises on those two fronts, everything points to Bruno."

"*Unless*," I reminded her, "his alibi checks out."

"Duly noted," Lucy assured me.

"What's troublesome about this case . . . ," I began to tell both of them, but I was distracted by a figure crossing the newsroom toward the glass wall of my office.

Following my glance, Glee told me, "You seem to have a visitor, Mark. Miss Exner, I believe."

"Oh?" said Lucy, sounding uncharacteristically chipper. Sitting with her back to the newsroom, she spun her short shock of red hair, looking over her shoulder to confirm the arrival of my Chicago lawyer friend, Roxanne Exner. Both Glee and Lucy knew Roxanne from her frequent visits to Dumont during the past year, but Lucy had first met Roxanne earlier, in Chicago, while Lucy and I were still at the *Journal*. Lucy had snapped to attention at the mention of Roxanne's name because she still carried something of a torch for the woman. On the summer night when they had first crossed paths at a cocktail party hosted by Neil and me at our loft in the city, Roxanne had just cropped her hair into a mannish bob that left Lucy breathless. What Lucy didn't know, though, was that Roxanne had done this only as a temporary concession to Carl Creighton, her lover, who had acquired a new convertible. The misunderstanding was quickly corrected, but not until after Lucy had made a move on Roxanne. Though unsettled by the experience, Roxanne—always self-assured—had dismissed the incident as the unfortunate aftermath of a bad haircut, deciding on the spot to grow back her tresses. Less confident women might thereafter have eschewed Lucy, but not Roxanne. She seemed to take perverse pride in the knowledge that she was attractive to women as well as to men. All this only served to convince Lucy that there was still hope.

Roxanne rapped on the glass wall, and I waved her in. Opening the door, she apologized, "Didn't mean to interrupt. This looks important."

Rising, I checked my watch. "God, it's past noon. We ran late." Stepping to her, I offered a kiss. Her lips met mine, but not fully; the side of my mouth touched the opposite side of hers. I told her, "You're looking great, as usual, even after a four-hour drive."

Roxanne had always struck me as the most stylish woman I knew—not stylish in the hyperconscious "fashion" sense epitomized by Glee Savage, but stylish in the "personal" sense—she always seemed to know precisely what to wear, always understated, always quietly glamorous. That day in my office, she wore a handsome gray flannel business suit (Donna Karan, if my eye can be trusted) with a tight skirt that dropped to midcalf, slit up past the knee. For color, she wore knotted around her neck a gold-hued silk scarf that bore an uncanny resemblance to Bruno's cravat. I couldn't imagine how she'd managed to arrive looking so fresh and unrumpled, ready to do her law thing.

In response to my flattery, she rolled her eyes as if she didn't believe me. That too had always struck me about Roxanne: even at thirty-seven, approaching the maturity of middle age, she didn't quite understand that her beauty was more than physical. She was smart, pleasantly aggressive, and at times truly loving. But she also honed a cynical edge that both marked her humor and marred her ability to "connect." Not that she lacked confidence (just watch her in a courtroom); she'd simply never been adept at accepting compliments.

There was no need for introductions, as everyone in the room was already well acquainted, so our opening lines of small talk focused on the weather, the long drive, the quickening pace of life as the transition from summer to autumn unfolded that week. But Roxanne soon brought the conversation down to business—not her legal dealings with Quatro Press, but the murder story that was the topic of the meeting she had interrupted. "*Well* now," she said, "it seems that sleepy little Dumont is in the news again. I hate to point this out, Mark, but the crime rate has taken a decided turn for the worse since your arrival here."

Though her comment had a morbid ring, it was nonetheless funny, eliciting a good laugh from Glee, Lucy, and me. I asked Roxanne, "You've heard all about it?"

She sat, lolling. "It wasn't exactly front-page news in Chicago, but the strangulation of the 'king of miniatures' made an irresistible headline—as I'm sure *you* can appreciate." She smirked.

I sat, joining the rest of them around the low table. "Doug Pierce really has his hands full with this. Murder is serious enough in its own right, but the timing makes this case doubly urgent—he's up for reelection."

"Doug can handle it," Roxanne said flatly. She'd come to know Pierce shortly after my move to Dumont, when he'd befriended me during an ugly incident that sullied my arrival. "He's an able sheriff and a good detective—at least in my book." And that said a lot. If Roxanne had harbored any doubts about the man, she'd not have hesitated to voice them. Pressing on, she asked succinctly, "Any suspects?"

"Just one—"

"Mark," Glee interrupted me, "this is basically where Lucille and I left off. If you don't mind, I'd like to get hopping on that sidebar." She gathered her notes.

"Oh. Sure. Fine, gals. Roxanne has an appointment after lunch, so we should be on our way. I'll fill her in at the Grill."

Glee was already on her feet, chomping to get to her desk. She extended her hand to Roxanne, exchanged a lady-shake, and excused herself from the room.

Lucy took a little longer leaving. She knew that Glee was right—there was plenty of work to be done—but even so, now that Roxanne had arrived, she'd have liked to hang around. I briefly considered inviting Lucy to lunch with us, but she did have a deadline, and besides, Roxanne and I would enjoy being alone. So I waited while Lucy rose, checking her clipboard once more. She told me, "I'll get writers assigned to these other two stories—we need someone at the sheriff's department, and another at the morgue."

"Great. Let's put our heads together later this afternoon."

"Miss Exner," Lucy said, "nice to see you again." She was obviously flummoxed, addressing Roxanne by her last name.

"My pleasure, Miss Haring." Roxanne offered a smile with a farewell nod.

Lucy literally backed out of my office, as if to prolong sharing Roxanne's space before disappearing into the newsroom. I had rarely, if ever, witnessed scatterbrained behavior from her—she was normally, in fact unerringly, a model of military precision. So I told Roxanne, who was accustomed to giving gibes, not receiving them, "I think she likes you."

"I *know* she likes me." Coyly she added, "But she's not my type."

"Hungry?"

"Starved—I got an early start this morning."

So we got up to leave the office. I noticed that Roxanne hadn't carried an umbrella; assuming the weather was now dry, I didn't bother to grab my coat. We zigzagged through the newsroom together and descended the front stairs, arriving in the *Register*'s lobby. I told Connie, our receptionist, who resembled a bank teller perched behind a window there, "We're on our way to the First Avenue Grill. I'll be back in an hour or so."

"Enjoy your lunch, Mr. Manning."

Out on First Avenue, people and cars rushed to lunch or errands, lending Dumont's main drag a hint of urban buzz. It was a far cry from Michigan Avenue, the swank Chicago boulevard that I had walked every day when I worked at the *Journal*, but this quieter streetscape had its own allure—no belching buses, no drug-crazed cabbies, no wailing sirens.

The sky was doing its noontide best to brighten, but a thick layer of clouds reduced the sun to a white glow in the damp, gray air. That morning's drizzle had spent itself—the trees and awnings had stopped dripping—so we strolled the block or so toward the restaurant, talking, poking along while others hustled past.

Roxanne revived the topic of the murder, asking, "You said there's a suspect?"

"Right—Bruno. He's all we've got right now."

She broke stride briefly. "Bruno?" she asked, finding the name unusual.

"He's French, a rival of the victim's, a big name in miniatures, and quite a character. Our best theory is that Bruno strangled Carrol with his own silk scarf."

Roxanne looked confused. "*Whose* silk scarf—Bruno's or Carrol's?"

"Bruno's. He wore it all the time, up till the murder. In fact, it looked a lot like yours." I fingered the gold-toned scarf that hung over her shoulder.

She stopped there on the sidewalk and unfurled the long end of her scarf, displaying it for me. "I find that unlikely. This is Hermès. It's for women."

"He *is* French," I glibly reminded her. But even as I spoke, I noticed that her scarf, held open for me, was patterned with an irregular design of big horse bridles, saddle buckles, and other equestrian motifs, all in a jumbled palette of yellows, browns, and golds. From a distance, wrinkled, it had looked just like Bruno's cravat. Up close, though, it bore no resemblance to the scarf found snagged on the banister—that scarf was patterned with a smaller, repeating design, like wallpaper.

"You're right," I conceded, smoothing the Hermès scarf over her shoulder again, "this isn't the same as Bruno's." Draping my arm (as well as the scarf) across her shoulder, I guided her onward.

Continuing our walk, she slid her arm around my waist; any passerby would have assumed we were romantically involved. There was a time, of course, when we *were* so involved, but our lives had changed profoundly since then, and we now contented ourselves to share a loving friendship that had survived even intimacy.

"Bruno . . . ," she thought aloud. "Can't say I've heard of him, but then, I'd never heard of Carrol Cantrell either."

I explained, "Bruno is his first name. I usually mangle the rest of it—Hérisson."

"Harrison?" she asked. (I had mangled it again.) "Sounds English, not French."

I gave it another try: "Hérisson." Then, just to make sure, I spelled it for her.

"Ah," she said, affecting a comic, throaty accent, "but of course—Hérisson," pronouncing it masterfully. Her features paused in thought for a moment, then she laughed, dropping her hand from my waist.

I turned to her. "What's so funny?"

"Hérisson," she repeated the name. "If my college French serves me correctly—I'd need to check the Larousse, but I'm almost certain—*hérisson* means 'hedgehog.' " She laughed again.

I joined in laughter at the image she'd conjured—a roly-poly Bruno in cravat and beret, covered head to toe with quills. I asked her rhetorically, "How do people come *up* with this stuff?"

She waved an arm in a theatrical flourish, posing a rhetorical question of her own, courtesy of Shakespeare: " 'What's in a name?' "

Mirroring her flourish, I declaimed, " 'That which we call a rose by any other name would smell as sweet.' "

A few people actually stopped to watch us, one lady breaking into applause. To my way of thinking, our brief performance wasn't all that good, but so as not to disappoint our little audience, we offered a series of elaborate bows to our onlookers and to each other. Our parody of star-crossed tragedy soon degenerated into a genre more akin to slapstick, and we moved on.

Nearing the end of the block, we paused at the intersection, waiting for traffic. The corner storefront, I noticed, was vacant—one of several along the way—and I couldn't help musing that this one would make an attractive office for Neil. I didn't know what the store had been, as it was empty when I'd arrived in Dumont and its signage was removed. But the facade was tastefully subdued, and it didn't take a lot of creative vision to see that it could easily be adapted to the needs of an architect who would, perhaps eventually, retain a small staff.

In my mind's eye, a sign already hung from the eaves near the door: NEIL M. WAITE, AIA.

"Hey, Mark," said Roxanne with a nudge, "it doesn't get any greener." She was referring to the traffic light, which had turned. I hadn't been paying attention, and other pedestrians now streamed around us, casting annoyed glances.

So I shrugged an apology, locked my arm through hers, and proceeded into the crosswalk. Our destination, First Avenue Grill, was still a half block ahead, and my mind was still occupied by the possibility, however remote, that Neil could be persuaded to move his practice from Chicago. The WALK light changed, flashing amber, as we stepped onto the opposite curb. On the corner was a tavern; in its windows were neon signs extolling various brews, flashing out of sync with the traffic light. This visual noise would not normally make a dent in my thoughts, but one of the signs flickered nervously, tugging for my attention: MILLER BEER.

I snapped my fingers. "Miller," I said, waltzing Roxanne under the awning to the window where the feeblish neon blinked and quavered.

She shook her head, tisking. "It didn't take long for Wisconsin to cast its spell. You used to be a vodka man. What's next—bratwurst?"

"No, listen, I forgot about this. A couple of days ago, I overheard part of a phone conversation—and a reference to the 'Miller standard.' I didn't know what was meant by this, but I was left with the impression that it might be a legal term. Have you ever heard of the 'Miller standard'?"

"Of course." She paused as if I were an idiot.

"I'm not a lawyer," I reminded her. "So—what is it?"

Clearing her throat, she lectured, "The Miller standard was established by a 1973 Supreme Court ruling in the case of *Miller v. California*. It partly defined obscenity as material that appeals to a prurient interest in sex. The Miller standard has not been significantly reduced over the years, and to this day, it remains the darling of book burners, the bane of free-speech advocates."

Enlightened by this bit of information and stunned by its implications, I asked, "Would the Miller standard have any bearing on the obscenity trial that's looming in Dumont County?"

"You betcha." Then a puzzled look crossed Roxanne's face. "Who was talking about this?"

"Carrol Cantrell, king of miniatures."

"*Slain* king of miniatures," she corrected me.

Arriving at the Grill, we found the place crowded—in fact, full. Generally regarded as Dumont's best restaurant, it attracted a loyal clientele of business people at lunch, including me. Shortly after I'd arrived at the *Register*, the Grill had extended to me a standing noon reservation at my favorite table, held for me until twelve-fifteen. Today, having lost track of time during my meeting at the office, I was late.

The hostess rushed to greet me at the door. "I'm so *sorry*, Mr. Manning. We assumed you weren't coming." It was twenty past the hour.

"That's okay," I assured her, "I should have phoned."

She glanced about, wringing her hands. "The kitchen's running slow today, so there won't be a table for at least twenty minutes." She repeated, "I'm so sorry."

As Roxanne had commitments, we couldn't afford to dawdle, but still, we'd save no time by walking back to my car and driving somewhere else. So I told the hostess, "We'll wait. Maybe we could look at menus and order before we sit down."

"Certainly, sir. May I bring you and the lady something from the bar?" There was no actual bar with stools, but they served liquor at the tables.

I asked Roxanne, "Would you like something?"

"Just mineral water, thanks."

The hostess nodded. "And you, sir—Lillet?"

I didn't realize till then that the soft-tasting, blond-colored aperitif had become my "usual" at lunch (I still saved the vodka ritual for evening). The week I moved to Dumont, I was surprised to discover that Lillet was available at this modest (by city standards) storefront restaurant. One evening, at table with Barret Logan, the *Register*'s founding publisher, I noticed that he ordered it. Assuming that it had been stocked at his request, I thought it fitting to continue the tradition—after all, I was assuming his position at the paper. More often than not, then, if I drank at lunch, I ordered Lillet. Curiously, though my tongue often tripped on French words, it had no problem whatever with *Lillet* (lee-*lay*).

Today, though, in deference to Roxanne, I thought it best to nix the booze. Roxanne had managed to kick a drinking problem three years earlier, around the time she introduced me to Neil. While the early phases of withdrawal were surely rough for her, she had since shown no difficulty with social situations involving liquor. Indeed, she routinely insisted, "Do enjoy yourself; don't mind me," finding it condescending if others abstained on her account.

Still, I didn't want to be the one to tempt her, and I certainly didn't *need* a drink. I told the hostess, "Mineral water sounds good—La Croix is fine." I smiled without enthusiasm.

"Mark!" a familiar voice interrupted these weighty deliberations. It was Sheriff Pierce, approaching us from a table, napkin in hand, as the hostess retreated into the crowded room.

"Hi, Doug," I told him. "You remember Roxanne Exner, from Chicago."

"How could I forget?" he queried graciously, shaking her hand. I noticed her eyes widen as he continued, "What brings you back to Dumont—Quatro business, or our latest manhunt?" His tone was light and amiable, surprisingly so, in light of the pressures of the murder investigation.

"The former," she answered, practically cooing, "which I assure you is considerably less interesting than the latter." Then she added with a chortle, "It seems you've got your hands full again, Doug." Her manner was more than friendly, almost flirtatious. In a sense, I didn't blame her—they were both attractive single professionals. Roxanne knew very well, though, that I had long harbored suspicions Pierce was gay. What I hadn't yet told her was that I was now convinced Pierce had been sleeping with Carrol Cantrell.

Determined to prevent Roxanne from getting any giddier, I made the insipid observation, "Quite a crowd today. Must be the weather."

Roxanne moaned, "Twenty minutes for a table . . ."

Pierce's head bobbed around the room, surveying the situation, then he turned back to ask, "Care to join us?"

That might work, I thought. "Who's with you?"

"Harley Kaiser." Pierce motioned to a table along the far wall, where the district attorney sat, finishing his salad. Another plate, presumably Pierce's, had been abandoned. There were two vacant spots at the table, chairs tucked beneath. Pierce explained under his breath, "Harley's not exactly my idea of a congenial lunch date, but this was *his* idea—said it was important. So far, though, nothing of substance, just routine shoptalk on the case. We're well along with our meal, but if you'd like to join us, there are two empty chairs."

Though the prospect of lunch with Pierce was enticing, I did *not* want to share a table with Kaiser. I assumed Roxanne would also be averse to Pierce's suggestion, as she'd had a previous, disagreeable encounter with the DA, judging him a "hot dog," a slur that got back to him.

"Maybe we *should*," said Roxanne, tapping her watch. "Thanks, Doug."

Thanks, indeed. The lady had spoken, so the three of us wended our way through the packed room, sidling between tables like a stunted conga line.

Kaiser rose when he saw Pierce returning to their table with Roxanne and me in tow. The look in his eye (a look of quizzical apprehension verging on panic) suggested that he'd had no idea Pierce would ask us to sit with them; it also suggested that he had no more taste for the idea than I did.

Seemingly oblivious to all this interplay, Pierce casually announced to his lunch companion that Roxanne was rushed and we'd be sharing their table.

"Very well," said Kaiser with a smile so twisted, it must have hurt.

Without further discussion—and pointedly, without the niceties of greetings or handshakes—we all sat down, arranging ourselves around the table. The hostess had eyed this maneuver from across the room, sending a waitress with our bottled water. A buxom, middle-aged woman in a crisp white uniform (she looked like a nurse), she produced, seemingly from nowhere, a complete set of tableware for Roxanne and me, whisking everything into position with a few adept snaps of her wrist. Tucked under her arm were two menus, which she handed to us. "Today's special is meat loaf—it's real good," she told us. "I'll check back." And she vanished.

Roxanne and Pierce suppressed a snicker. In defense of our earnest server, I told the others, "I've had their special meat loaf—many times—and it *is* real good."

Roxanne now broke into open laughter, clamping her hand on my arm, as if telling me to stop. Pierce also laughed, but tried to cover it with a cough, which only added to the noise. Kaiser watched us sternly, sitting ramrod stiff, telegraphing his disapproval of the merriment. His blue-black pompadour jittered atop his head, and he suddenly looked like a *pissed* poodle. This ludicrous image was more than I could stand. Staring at the DA's hair, I too broke into laughter. Good grief—Fifi Kaiser, poodle with an attitude.

Everyone at the table, including myself, seemed at a loss for words, as if afraid that whatever was said would take on comic overtones. In truth, our antic behavior had turned a tad juvenile, and it was time to shape up. Mercifully, our waitress returned at that moment to deliver Pierce's and Kaiser's main courses, removing their salad plates as she did so—an impressive feat of juggling that proved sufficiently distracting to curtail my laughing jag.

"Decided?" she asked Roxanne and me.

Though we hadn't even looked at our menus, we were pressed for time, so I ordered the meat loaf without even considering other choices. Roxanne queried the woman about fish; learning that the closest available species was shrimp, she ordered the ubiquitous chicken Caesar.

When the waitress had waddled off, I insisted that Pierce and Kaiser begin without us, which was of course the only sensible option under such awkward circumstances. With hesitation and apologies, they began to eat, which hampered their ability to converse. Roxanne and I were therefore left with nothing to eat and little to discuss. Speaking idly to each other, we attempted to include the other two in our patter, but their participation was limited to an occasional smile or nod while chewing.

Our small talk could be stretched only so far. The unspoken topic of Carrol Cantrell's murder hung over the table like a massive chandelier, supported by an impossibly weak thread, threatening to crash. What's more, only moments before our arrival at the Grill, I had learned from Roxanne that Carrol's overheard reference to the

Miller standard was in all likelihood related to the issue of obscenity—what was *that* all about? And here we sat with the district attorney—not only did he have a vested political interest in an impending obscenity case, but he'd also invited the sheriff to lunch to discuss something important. The DA wasn't talking, though, and my reporter's instincts had revved into high gear. That metaphorical chandelier now creaked and swayed overhead.

Avoiding the obvious issue of the murder, I said to Kaiser, "So then, Harley, do you think you've got a fighting chance to get an obscenity conviction this time?"

Slowly, he swallowed what was in his mouth and placed his fork on his plate. He knew only too well that I was philosophically opposed to his antismut campaign; he had read my editorial rejoicings when his previous efforts had failed. He probably assumed that I now raised the issue to taunt him, an assumption that, while correct, was incomplete, as my deeper motive related to the intriguing possibility of some connection between the obscenity issue and Carrol Cantrell.

In a flat, emotionless tone, he told me, "I have no comment on the impending trial, Mr. Manning." He often addressed me as "Mark," I noted, but not this time; today he saw me as the press, which is to say, the liberal press, the enemy. He continued, "The war against pornography will not ultimately be won in the courtroom, but in the hearts of the public." This struck me as an odd statement, coming from Kaiser. Though there were many things I didn't like about the man, I generally admired his sapless pragmatism; he rarely indulged in such flights of rhetorical blather. As if to explain this seeming inconsistency, he reminded me, "The County Plan Commission has issued its report, you know, and Dr. Benjamin Tenelli speaks with a highly persuasive voice in our community." He said no more, but continued to eye me, smiling wryly. His implication was clear: Dr. Tenelli had called, in effect, for a crackdown on porn, so public opinion was destined to heed that call. This meant that Kaiser was more apt to recruit a sympathetic jury in his case against the porn shops at the edge of town. It also meant that Sheriff Pierce was less apt to find a sympathetic electorate in his bid for reelection.

Roxanne seemed befuddled by this exchange, knowing nothing

of Dr. Tenelli. Pierce seemed wearied by it, preferring to focus, no doubt, on a murder investigation that needed quick and total attention. As for me, I was truly angered by Kaiser's smug attitude and prim self-righteousness. These were character traits I would find disagreeable in anyone. In a public servant, they were nauseating.

"Listen," I warned him, dropping any pretext of kissy-face, "if you're planning to wage a public-relations battle, you'd better be aware of what you're up against. The power of the press, especially in a small town, can be brutal, Harley."

"Is that a veiled threat, Mr. Manning?"

I laughed. "It's not the least bit 'veiled.' I'm telling you to watch your step."

He wadded his napkin and tossed it on the table. "If you think for one moment that you can flounce into town and—"

"I know a homophobic crack when I hear one, Harley, so again I warn you: Watch your step."

He seethed; I seethed back at him.

Roxanne watched eagerly, waiting for the next volley.

Pierce just sat back in his chair, shaking his head, having lost interest in his lunch. Assuming the role of mediator, he told us, "That's enough, guys. For the moment, I, for one, could care less about obscenity. What I *am* concerned about is the murder of Carrol Cantrell. I'm beginning to fear that this case isn't as open-and-shut as we'd hoped."

"Sorry, Doug," I told him, feeling duly chastised. I added, "Sorry, Harley. Roxanne and I didn't mean to horn in on your lunch meeting with Doug. I understand you've got important business to discuss." Naturally, I wanted to add, What's up? But it was none of my business, and I doubted that Kaiser was in the mood to gift me with a hot news tip.

Roxanne, who had remained atypically mute during all this, now ventured further than I dared, asking Kaiser point-blank, lawyer to lawyer, "Why would Cantrell have any knowledge of, or interest in, the Miller standard?" She sipped from her glass of mineral water, fingering the stem casually, as if she'd just asked nothing more consequential than the time of day.

Judging from Kaiser's reaction, though, the question came as something of a bombshell. His jaw drooped; his hand gripped the napkin crumpled on the table. It was clear enough that Roxanne had heard about the Miller reference from me, so Kaiser could guess that I had since learned from Roxanne the meaning of Carrol's words. Was there in fact some connection between Carrol's visit to Dumont and the obscenity case that Kaiser was preparing to bring to trial? It hardly seemed likely, but why else would Kaiser be so shaken by Roxanne's question?

"There's something I'd better explain," he said tenuously, voice lowered. "On Saturday morning, when Miriam Westerman and I visited the coach house and Mark guided us up the back stairs, I was astounded to overhear Cantrell mention the Miller standard as he talked on the phone. I was further astounded by the sheer quantity of obscene material that was openly displayed in his room. But you must understand this: I did not go there with any such expectations, and in fact, I was baffled by the point of our visit in the first place. It was Miriam's idea."

For his part, Pierce was confused both by the meaning of Roxanne's original question and by Kaiser's convoluted reply. He asked the DA, "What's this about, Harley—obscenity or murder?"

"*Murder!*" Kaiser assured him, assured all of us, beating both palms once, simultaneously, on the table. His abrupt response had sufficient intensity to quell conversation at several surrounding tables. Without wavering, his eyes held Pierce's for a long moment while the nearby babble rose again to its previous level. Then he leaned to tell Pierce, speaking loudly enough that his words were intended for Roxanne and me as well, "Damn it, Doug, something's happened—something on the case. I brought you here so that I could confide this development to you first."

"Great," said Pierce with an uncertain laugh. "What's the new wrinkle?"

"*Wrinkle?*" repeated Kaiser. "This is *serious*, Doug."

Pierce exchanged a glance with Roxanne and me before asking Kaiser, "Well?"

Kaiser hesitated. Then, to my surprise, he turned to address me. "Don't be offended, Mark, but this information simply isn't intended for your ears—not yet."

Though disappointed, I understood his position. Their investigation stood to gain nothing by involving the press at this stage. I offered, "No offense is taken, Harley. Roxanne and I would never have intruded, had we understood your need for privacy. Excuse us, please, and we'll wait at the door for another table." I started pushing my chair back.

Pierce made a silent be-seated gesture, urging us to stay.

Kaiser echoed the gesture, telling Roxanne and me, "No, Doug and I are finished anyway. We can talk in the car. Take the table and enjoy your lunch."

The waitress was waddling toward us with our food, so I offered no argument. "Thanks, Harley. We hate to inconvenience you."

He rose. "No trouble at all." His tone was oddly inflected, as if to tell me that I owed him one.

Pierce rose with him, telling all of us, "Sorry this turned so awkward."

Roxanne assured him, "You were only trying to be gracious." Then she barbed Kaiser, "Besides, I rather enjoyed the display of raw emotions—it rouses the appetite." The irony of her little joke was that she *had* enjoyed the tension.

Kaiser ignored her comment, moving off toward the door, followed by Pierce, while the waitress wordlessly delivered our lunch. As Kaiser stopped near the entrance to sign his check, Pierce turned back to us, miming a phone in his hand. The message was clear enough—he'd call me later with the poop.

When they'd left, I turned to Roxanne. "What was *that* all about?"

She forked a strip of chicken from her salad. "Good question." Pausing in thought, she tasted the charred bit of meat. "Not bad"—quite a compliment, considering the jaded standards of its source.

The Grill's special meat loaf was perfect for the cool, soggy day; the taste, texture, and warmth all said "comfort food." I savored it slowly, ate it deliberately, as if storing calories for the colder weather that would arrive unannounced some night during the approaching weeks. Silently, I laughed in appreciation of the rhythm of life—

summer was barely over, and there I was, packing away meat loaf like a squirrel hoarding nuts.

Roxanne and I enjoyed our meal together, alone. Back in Chicago, we would frequently phone each other at the last minute for an impromptu lunch date, meeting somewhere between our offices. Those days, however, were behind us. While she proved to be a frequent visitor to Dumont, she was often accompanied by Carl Creighton, her "love interest," and our meals together always included Neil. I loved Neil, and I had come to think of Carl as a friend, but my relationship with Roxanne predated those others by years, and at times I simply wanted to be alone with her. So our lunch that Monday in September was a rare opportunity, dampened only by the knowledge that she was soon due at a meeting on the far side of town. We attempted to be inconspicuous while checking our watches, but it was obvious that we both felt rushed.

Our conversation brought us up-to-date on each other's life, covering such topics as her law practice, Neil's architecture practice, Thad's interests at school—but we kept drifting back to the murder. She asked, "You'll let me know if you learn anything juicy from Sheriff Pierce?"

Laughing, I reminded her, "I'll tell the whole *town* if I learn something juicy."

"I'm sure. But I don't get to see the *Register* back in Chicago. And the news will be stale by next Monday."

"You're driving up again next week?"

Adopting a lawyerly tone, she explained, "Neil's Quatro project necessitates frequent face-to-face meetings." Wryly, she added, "Wait till you get the bills."

Just as wryly, I told her, "They won't make a blip in Quatro's budget."

"Glad to hear it."

"Hey." Thinking of something, I dabbed my mouth with my napkin. "Why don't you come up early—for the weekend. There's always plenty of room for guests on Prairie Street. And you won't face the drudgery of a Monday-morning drive."

Her features brightened as she flipped through a mental calendar. "Carl will be out of town next weekend. I'd love to come up."

"Consider it booked."

Finishing lunch, we walked back from the restaurant together, then each went our separate ways—Roxanne got into her car and drove off to her meeting with Neil at Quatro Press, and I zipped through the lobby of the *Register*. Prepared for a busy afternoon, I started up the stairs, taking them by twos, headed for the newsroom.

"Mr. Manning," Connie warbled through the hole in her glass cage, "yoo-hoo, Mr. Manning."

"Yes?" I asked, stopping to peer back down at her.

"Sheriff Pierce called with a message." She hesitated, presuming it improper to shout the message across the lobby.

I came down to her window. "What'd he say?"

She held a pink slip in her hand, but didn't need to read from it. With lowered voice, she told me, "He said it was very important." She lowered her voice even further. "He's over at Grace Lord's house and wants you to join him there." She added, mouthing the word without voicing it, *Alone*.

"Thanks, Connie." I checked for my keys—yes, I'd put them in one of my blazer pockets, along with my notepad and Montblanc, so I was ready for anything.

Or so I thought. I left the lobby by the rear door, which led to the reserved lot where my car was parked. Getting in, I started the engine and pulled onto First Avenue, collecting my thoughts.

I'd left the radio switched on that morning, and it now played a local talk show, *Denny Diggins' Dumont Digest*, hosted by a virulent announcer with an affected BBC accent—he came across as an amalgam of Rush Limbaugh and Alistair Cooke, if one can imagine such a fusion. Everyone knew the accent was fake because Denny was born and raised in Dumont. He claimed to have studied in England, but he never said when, and it was common knowledge that he'd gone to college in Madison.

Though I didn't think much of the program, I sometimes listened to it, as its guests occasionally provided fresh insights into current stories of importance to the community. In that sense, *Dumont*

Digest was the town's only news outlet other than the *Register*—a distinction that Denny never ceased touting to his listeners, missing no opportunity to publicly trash the paper—*my* paper. More often than not, I listened to him defensively. That afternoon, he was blathering about some inane crafts show being planned by the ladies' auxiliary of the local hospital—"an utterly *mah*-velous extravaganza," he called it—so I switched him off. After all, I had murder on my mind. (Carrol's, not Denny's, though the thought had merit.)

Turning off Park Street, headed toward The Nook and the Lord residence, I expected to see something of a commotion on the street. Pierce's message had implied a breakthrough in the investigation, so I would not have been surprised to find a convoy of police vehicles scattered about the property. Instead, there was just one car, Pierce's tan sedan—even the convention's setup crew had better things to do that afternoon.

Parking across the street from the house, I saw that Pierce was waiting for me in his car, parked at the opposite curb. Checking for pen and pad (an obsessive-compulsive habit, as I knew very well that I'd brought them), I got out of the car and met Pierce in the middle of the street.

"Let's talk," he said flatly, then led me to the sidewalk, ambling away from the house, toward the fringe of the quiet neighborhood, where vacant lots still had the look of virgin prairie.

He'd called this meeting, he'd wanted to talk, and he'd set the course of our stroll. But after a full minute, he'd said nothing. So I asked, "What is it, Doug?"

"Uh . . . ," he suggested, "let's sit down."

A creek ran through the vacant land there—no more than a crease in the terrain, but it flowed that afternoon with runoff from the recent rains. Near the sidewalk, in a cluster of small trees, a concrete embankment allowed the water to trickle under the street, and this structure offered a convenient, dry slab where we could park ourselves. Settling onto this makeshift bench, I found that it offered a pleasant, secluded setting, which I hoped would be conducive to the discussion that Pierce was hesitating to open. I prompted, "Yes?"

"Mark," he said, swallowing hard, "I'm gay."

Well, hallelujah—he'd finally said it. But why now? Somehow, I gathered from his tone that this coming out was not motivated by the joy of self-liberation. I wanted to give him a hug, and in fact, neurons fired from some remote recess of my brain instructing my muscles to begin moving in that direction. But as I leaned toward him, something felt wrong, and I aborted the hug by simply shifting my weight. I nodded pensively, telling him, "I'd always wondered, but I didn't want to ask. Thanks for taking me into your confidence."

He managed a smile—a smile of truth that at last acknowledged what had gone unspoken since we'd met—and in that instant, he was made . . . *beautiful.* An odd word, perhaps, to describe this ruggedly handsome man, this cop in designer clothing. But a barrier between us had just fallen; he now allowed me to see him openly. And I saw that he was beautiful.

"To be perfectly honest," he said, "I'm not sure I was ready."

"I doubt if anyone's ever 'ready' to say he's gay for the first time."

He shook his head with a soft laugh. "That's not what I mean, Mark. I've never had a problem with who or what I am, not really. From the day we met, it was clear that you understood me. I'd have said the words to you eventually, but I never felt rushed because it didn't seem necessary."

His logic made sense, but it led me to the inevitable question: "Then why say the words now?"

"To lay the groundwork for the rest."

Now I *was* lost. Where was this leading? Was I about to learn of some long-guarded fetish? Was this cop in designer clothing actually a cop in lady's underwear? Dismissing this image, I asked, "Lay the groundwork for what?"

After a long hesitation, replete with lip-pinching and neck-scratching, he told me simply, "Carrol Cantrell."

Ahaaa . . . Attempting not to seem surprised by this news (which, in fact, I wasn't), I explained, "I had a hunch you were having a little fling—to each his own, Doug. And if you prefer to keep your liaisons discreet, that's your prerogative. No one else needs to know."

He leaned toward me on the concrete slab. "But they do know."

Uh-oh. I'd nearly forgotten that the object of Pierce's tryst was also the subject of a murder investigation. The sticky nature of our conversation was quickly becoming clear to me. I asked, "Who else knows about this?"

Pierce paused—not so much with hesitation, it seemed, as for dramatic effect—before answering, "Harley Kaiser."

I puckered and whistled a sigh of commiseration, telling myself that this couldn't get much worse. "How'd he find out?"

"That's the best part." Pierce's voice now carried the slightest ring of sarcasm, suggesting that the situation could indeed get worse. "My relationship with Carrol was nothing more than a fling, as you've described it. We certainly didn't 'love' each other, but we, well . . . enjoyed what we did together, and after spending three nights with the man, I came to feel a measure of affection for him. You can well imagine my shock at learning he was killed yesterday, mere hours after I'd left him. I hate to sound melodramatic about this, but I've been driven to solve his murder not only because it's my job, but because I want to see his death avenged—I owe him that much."

He paused, and I could see that he was choked up over what had happened—a rare display of emotion. With his voice momentarily silent, the gurgle of the creek seemed magnified. A bird chirped somewhere, sounding faraway. I offered Pierce the consolation of a pat on the knee, and he nodded his thanks.

He continued, "Since the discovery of Carrol's body yesterday, I've been directing an ongoing investigation of the crime scene. I've relied heavily on the efforts of Dan Kerr, the department's top-ranking detective—other than myself."

Thinking aloud, I interjected, "Deputy Dan also happens to be the man who has aspirations for your job."

"True, but he's a professional, and the issue of the election, believe it or not, has never come between us on the job. He's a good detective. So I gave him, among other items taken from the crime scene, Carrol's laptop computer, hoping we could get into his files. We weren't sure what we were looking for, but it seemed reasonable to expect that we could learn something of Carrol's business dealings in Los Angeles, which could possibly shed some light on the murder."

"Did Deputy Dan find anything?"

"Yes, indeed. But it didn't relate to the victim's business ties in California. No, what Deputy Kerr found was the draft of an extortion note."

"A note *from* Cantrell? To whom?"

"To me." Pierce waited for the full impact of these words to register on my face before elaborating. "Kerr found a computer file of a document, supposedly written by Carrol, demanding hush money from me, or else he'd go public with information about our 'dalliance'—that was the word used. It went on to suggest that this would do irreparable harm to my bid for reelection."

"It just might," I thought aloud, spicing the comment with a dash of understatement, immediately wishing I'd kept the opinion to myself. "Do you have a copy of the note?"

My question was already answered, as Pierce was extracting something from the inside breast pocket of his jacket. He unfolded the single sheet of bond and handed it to me, explaining, "Carrol didn't print this; Kerr did, downtown. Carrol didn't even have a printer with him, which raises two questions to my advantage: If Carrol was going to blackmail me, why would he write an electronic note that he couldn't print and deliver to me? And if I never saw the note—the hard copy wasn't printed till after he died—what motive would I have to silence him?"

While Pierce spoke, I looked over the printout, finding the message to be exactly as he'd described it. The wording was terse and generic-sounding, using only the term *dalliance* to describe their sexual encounters, offering no details. The amount of money being demanded was not specified, nor was any deadline. The ostensible purpose of the note, extortion, was barely addressed; seemingly, its underlying purpose was simply to incriminate Pierce.

He continued, "Kerr found the message this morning, and because it implicated me, he took it directly to Kaiser—a tough call, but under the circumstances, I don't blame him. This, of course, is what Kaiser wanted to tell me about, and in retrospect, I have to thank him for his discretion at lunch. Obviously, this'll all come out—it's part of the investigation. But at least I've got a bit of time to work on a strategy to deal with it."

Handing the note back to him, I asked, "What's your plan?"

He shook his head. "It's hardly a 'plan,' more like 'damage control.' I'm still thinking it through."

"Talk it out. Maybe I can help."

"First of all, Mark, do you *believe* me? I'm telling you plainly: Yes, I'm gay. Yes, I had sex with Carrol—three nights running, in fact. But no, he never even hinted at the threat of blackmail. And no, I certainly didn't kill him."

My answer didn't require a moment's thought. "Of course I believe you."

He reacted with a decisive, satisfied nod—at least he had *that* resolved in his favor. "Now, then. If we assume that Carrol didn't write the note, we can only conclude that someone else did. But who? And why?"

Though his questions were posed rhetorically, I answered, "Offhand, I've no idea who could have done it, but the motive seems clear—to cast suspicion away from himself. Whoever planted the note is probably the killer."

"Right. That fits. Whoever strangled Carrol was there in the same room with the computer, so he had the *opportunity* to plant the note."

By that point, I was scribbling a few notes of my own, trying to make sense of this new puzzle. I mentioned to Pierce, "The stilted wording of the extortion note is unconvincing—it just doesn't sound as if it was written with knowledge of the situation's intimate details. *Dalliance*—what kind of word is *that?*"

Pierce wondered aloud, "Is it French?" His features brightened.

"Might be," I conceded, attuned to his reasoning. "But my point, Doug, is this: the person who wrote the note may have no direct knowledge that you actually slept with Carrol. I doubt that Carrol *bragged* about it to anyone local, and it's even more unlikely that you were watched by a Peeping Tom. Whoever wrote the note may simply have reasoned that casting suspicion on you, however farfetched, would throw a wrench into your investigation."

"That's putting it mildly." Pierce chuckled—his first show of humor since our conversation had turned heavy. With his tone considerably lightened, he said, "If the computer note can be proven a fake, and if its reference to our 'dalliance' was just a lucky guess, then I'm off the hook. There's nothing to implicate me in the murder, and there's nothing to 'out' me during the campaign."

Closing my notepad, I knew that Pierce was right, but I was troubled. I could well understand his eagerness to quash any implication that he'd stoop to murder, but I was disappointed by his apparently equal eagerness to slip back into the closet and tug the door shut behind him. Granted, there are more opportune times to bare the truth about one's sex life than during an election campaign, but I couldn't help feeling—

"Mark," Pierce interrupted my thoughts, having read my concerns from my silence, "you and I are both public figures, but we work in very different arenas. As a writer and now a publisher, you deal in the realm of words and ideas; ruthless honesty is your stock-in-trade. As sheriff, I'd better be honest, but I'm also a politician, and unfortunately, that's a realm in which the acceptable scope of honesty is very narrow indeed. At the moment, sexual orientation is not included in that scope, and frankly, it's nobody's business. Here's the bottom line: I'm convinced that Dumont County is better served by me as sheriff than it would be by Dan Kerr and the family-values crowd. And I'm far more likely to stay in office if the electorate isn't forced to wrestle with the issue of whether they can stomach the notion of a gay sheriff."

He was finished, and I could tell by his tone that he was annoyed. What I could not decipher, though, was the cause of his annoyance. Was it I, for having forced him to explain his view? Or was it the sad reality of his own pragmatism that nettled him?

"It's your decision, Doug," I told him quietly. "I'll support you either way."

He smiled and, almost imperceptibly, leaned toward me. I thought it was now he who was moving in for a hug, as I had been tempted to do earlier, but I'll never know because it didn't happen. Standing, he simply told me, "Thanks, Mark."

I stood with him, twisting a crick from my back—the concrete slab where we'd been sitting had also left my butt numb. "What's next?"

"As long as we're here"—he gestured back up the street—"I'd like to talk to Grace Lord again. Care to join me?"

"Try to stop me."

The afternoon sky darkened some as we walked the short distance from the vacant lot, and a light drizzle began falling again, adding a layer of translucent mist to the still, cool air. As neither of us had brought a raincoat, we quickened our pace to the house and up its driveway, taking cover under the roof of the back porch. Pierce knocked on the kitchen door. As we waited, I noticed that our sport coats had that faint, sweet smell of wet wool.

The storm door opened, and Grace Lord peered up at us through the screen. "Oh," she squeaked, "good afternoon, Sheriff. Afternoon, Mark. Please, come in." She swung the screen door wide for us.

"Thanks, Grace," said Pierce, "but our feet are wet—wouldn't want to track."

"My floor's due for a good mopping anyway."

But Pierce shook his head. "This'll only take a minute, Grace."

So she joined us on the porch, huddling into the copious folds of a comfortable old cardigan she wore. "What can I do for you boys?" Her friendly tone turned momentarily serious: "You haven't arrested the Frenchman, have you? My name really *will* be mud."

"No," Pierce assured her, "we're still checking his alibi."

She shook her head, tisking. "Bruno just *couldn't* have done it. I know that he and Carrol were big rivals and all, but I can't believe he'd stoop that low."

"*Somebody* sure did," I reminded her.

"You're right about *that*," she conceded. "I just hope you fellas can wrap this up quick. It'd be awful to have this still hangin' when the show opens at The Nook on Saturday."

"We're doing our best," said Pierce. "Do you have time for a few questions?"

"Anything to help, Sheriff. Shoot."

He shoved his hands into his pants pockets, thinking. "I'd like to ask about anyone you happened to see around the coach house over the weekend." He made no move to take notes, so neither did I, though the itch was hard to suppress.

Grace stepped to the edge of the porch and peered over the railing at the coach house, no more than ten yards away. The yellow police ribbons that now festooned the crime scene, combined with the lush red geraniums and bright green stairs, gave the place an oddly jolly look. Grace turned back to us with a quizzical expression. "We went over all that yesterday. Twice. There were lots of visitors to the coach house. I helped you make a list."

"I know," he said patiently, "but there's been a new development, and it's promising. Trouble is, of all the people on the list you gave us, there's no one who matches all the criteria we're looking for. Think hard, Grace. Is there anyone you might have overlooked?"

She glanced back at the coach house. When her gaze returned to us, she was biting her lip, wrinkling her brow—it was an almost comically cliché expression that said she was hiding something.

I asked, "Is there something you haven't told us?"

Pierce added, "It's important, Grace. If there was someone at the coach house, someone you haven't told us about—please, we need to know."

She wrung her hands, glancing from side to side at nothing in particular. Then, overcoming her reluctance, she told Pierce, "Well, *you* were there, Sheriff."

He froze. I said to Grace, "Sunday afternoon, during the investigation?"

Frustrated, not knowing how far she should take this, she waffled, "Well, *sure*. But, *no*. I *mean:* I saw the sheriff visit Carrol several times. He came at night, and I saw him leave early each morning."

Pierce managed to stay remarkably unruffled by this disclosure. Maintaining his professional tone, he asked, "Why didn't you mention this yesterday?"

Groping mutely for an explanation, at last she blurted, "Because I didn't think you'd *want* me to mention it. This probably won't set too well with certain people."

No, it certainly wouldn't. Pierce briefly pronged his fingers to his forehead, as if staving off a headache. He told her, "Thank you, Grace. I appreciate your concern for the delicacy of the situation, but we need to know everything. It's easier to solve a puzzle when you have all the pieces. We need everything out in the open."

It was a brave little speech—he'd handled himself better than I would have under the circumstances. His hopes of neatly dispatching the matter of the bogus extortion note had just vanished, as there was now an eyewitness (a highly credible one, at that) placing him at the crime scene on the morning of the murder, consistent with Deputy Dan's discovery of the computer file. Chances are, even as Pierce spoke, he saw his career in law enforcement swirling down an imaginary drain, replete with gurgles and a final belch from the plumbing.

After an awkward pause—even the birds stopped yattering—Grace asked, "Is there, uh, anything else?"

"No, Grace. Again, thanks for your time. Thanks for the information."

Nodding an uncertain farewell to both of us, she retreated into the kitchen and softly closed the door.

Pierce and I stepped to the edge of the porch and stood there side by side, hands on the railing, looking out at the coach house, not at each other. I asked, "Now what?"

He thought, but not very long, before answering, "Now that I've been so clearly implicated, I'll have to remove myself from this case. The irony is, you know who will now be driving the investigation."

I supplied the implied name: "Deputy Dan."

"He'll have a field day with this. It fits his agenda perfectly, and it may very well cinch his election." After a moment's pause, Pierce added, "Unless . . ."

I swung my head to face him. "Unless what?"

He faced me. "Unless we undertake our own investigation. Behind the scenes." He arched a brow.

I smiled. "How can I help?"

Tuesday, September 19

Lucille Haring said, "Let me get this straight, Sheriff. You had sex with the victim on the morning he was killed. Your name popped up on a computer file in which the victim demanded hush money from you, threatening a preelection scandal. Now you've withdrawn yourself from the investigation, handing it over to your political opponent." She looked up from her notes. "Did I miss anything?"

"That about sums it up," Pierce told my managing editor.

We were huddled around the table in my outer office at the *Register* on the morning after Pierce had recruited my help. Glee Savage was also present, eager to test her skills on some hard news—our local murder story, now spiced by blackmail and the whiff of political intrigue, was a far cry from the usual social reporting and personality features that occupied most of her time.

Lucy rose from the table and paced across the room in thought. Her steps had a deliberate, marchlike quality—an impression made all the more vivid by the military styling of the suits she frequently wore. She turned to tell all of us, but particularly me, "I'm just not sure what role the *Register* should play in all this. A police investigation is already under way."

I understood her concern, and indeed, I shared it. Our journalistic integrity was at stake, an issue I had tussled with overnight. Ultimately, though, I'd slept well, having concluded that the paper's involvement in this mess was justified.

I explained to Lucy, "There's more to this story now than the murder of Carrol Cantrell. If this were simply a matter of Lieutenant Kerr taking over the investigation from Sheriff Pierce, I'd agree—that's police business, and we shouldn't get involved. Consider, though, the intriguing circumstances that have prompted Doug to step into the background.

"First, he's been implicated in the murder itself, on the basis of an extortion note drafted on the victim's computer. The wording of the note, which you've all seen, is peculiar enough to suggest that it's bogus, leading us to conclude that it was written and planted by someone other than Cantrell, most likely the killer himself. That's more than just a new wrinkle in the investigation. That's *news*.

"Second—and this is what kept me awake last night, at least till I sorted it out—second is the question of what motivated the bogus note. The obvious reason for implicating Pierce is to cast suspicion away from the real killer. But there's another possibility, one that we've overlooked." I paused, letting them mull this.

Pierce, Lucy, and Glee glanced at each other, puzzled. Then Glee suddenly sat up rigid and alert, enlightened. She slipped her reading glasses off her nose, letting them drop to her chest on their gold chain. She told the others, "Election shenanigans!"

"Of course," I said. The others nodded, now seeing this secondary motive as clearly as Glee had. "Whoever framed Doug was not only trying to pin the crime on the wrong man; he was also well aware that he was jeopardizing Doug's chances for reelection. The note's reference to Doug and Carrol's sexual 'dalliance' has the smell of a classic smear campaign. Ironically, the writer may have had no direct knowledge of their fling."

"A lucky stab," Lucy commented, sitting with us again at the table.

"That depends on your perspective," Pierce dryly reminded her.

"In any event," I told everyone, "if election shenanigans have in any way tainted the murder investigation, it falls to the press—it falls to *us*—to expose them. That's why I feel the *Register* is more than justified in pursuing this." I paused, then added for Pierce's benefit, "I also feel obligated to help a friend to clear his good name." I didn't need to mention that I'd already endorsed that friend for reelection, so in a sense, my own reputation was at stake as well.

Glee drove our discussion forward (I was pleasantly surprised by her analytical approach to our discussion—had she been wasting her time in features all these years?), suggesting, "If the motive for framing Doug was election shenanigans, we need to ask ourselves, 'Who would have the most to gain by hurting Doug's chances?' Obviously, the opponent, Deputy Dan Kerr."

Lucy tapped her notes with her pencil. "And Deputy Dan is now in charge of the investigation—an investigation that has implicated Doug on the basis of a computer file found by none other than Deputy Dan himself. Pretty slick."

"Hold on," said Doug, leaning toward the rest of us, tightening our circle. "Dan Kerr may be my political opponent, but he's also a good detective and an honorable cop—I trained him myself. If you're suggesting that Kerr is behind all this, forget it."

Pointedly, Lucy asked him, "The laptop computer containing the extortion note—was it fingerprinted to determine if anyone had used it other than Cantrell?"

Pierce squirmed, settling back in his chair, admitting, "No. Kerr had no idea—"

"*Claimed* to have no idea," Lucy interjected.

Pierce rephrased, "Kerr claimed to have no idea that the computer might contain material not authored by Carrol, and in fact, the official stand of the investigation is that Carrol himself wrote the note. Anyway, Kerr didn't bother to dust the laptop before going to work on it. At this point, I'm sure the only prints we'd find all over it are his own."

Glee perched her glasses on her nose again and added a note to her pad, musing, "A handy oversight on the lieutenant's part."

"Here's a thought," said Lucy, running a hand through her mannish crop of red hair. "We've been assuming that whoever wrote the note is Cantrell's killer. But let's consider Kerr. Presumably, he had no motive whatever to want Cantrell dead. On the other hand, he has a strong motive to want the murder pinned on Doug. Maybe he was cunning enough to recognize a golden opportunity when he got hold of the laptop. It wouldn't take a genius to figure out that he suddenly had the means to divert the murder investigation and secure his own election."

Pierce seemed stunned by this observation, not only by Lucy's solid reasoning, but by the feasibility of foul play from his opponent, who happened to be his protégé. Pierce had already made it clear that he believed Kerr incapable of murder. Was he now willing to believe that Kerr was capable of this lesser crime? Lucy had raised an intriguing and compelling possibility.

"Uh, Doug?" There'd been something on my mind that needed to be dealt with, and now was as good a time as any. Everyone at the table could tell from my reticent tone that I was broaching something awkward.

Pierce cracked a smile, unable to fathom where I was headed. "Yes, Mark?"

"I believe you—we all believe you. There's no one in this room who thinks that you murdered Carrol Cantrell. We know, however, upon your own admission, that you did have sex with him, which is disturbingly consistent with the tenor of the blackmail note. What's more, Grace Lord has come forth as an eyewitness to your overnight visits with Carrol. My point is that you're now in a weak position to make a public denial of your relationship with Carrol, even if your sense of ethics would allow that. If you did make such a denial, and it were proven that you lied, you'd arouse serious suspicions that you just may be the murderer."

I paused a moment, making sure everyone had followed this logic. Perhaps the deeper-seated reason for my pause was that I had reached the stickiest aspect of what I had to say. So I rose, pacing a few steps from the table, not looking at Pierce as I asked him, "Will the autopsy reveal the presence of semen, other than his own, in Carrol's body?"

"No," said Pierce, surprisingly calm and objective. As I turned to listen, he explained, "We 'played safe.' Still, I'm well aware that if I deny our relationship, it'll trigger a scrupulous search for any physical evidence linking me to Carrol—a stray hair, a loose button, anything. It would be easy to prove I'd been in that bed. So there's no point in denying it. My best hope is to be forthright. Before this is all over, my private life will be very much a matter of public record."

We were all silent. I knew how painful this was for Pierce. Though I'd thought all along that he'd be better off "out," he didn't deserve the ignominy of being outed, especially under circumstances that accused him of murder.

Glee spoke first, and as she attempted to comfort him, I realized an embarrassing irony—she was the only straight person in the room. "Listen, Doug"—she leaned to tell him—"this town is full of your friends. You've never done anything to betray your office, and you've never given anyone cause to distrust you. When a man in his midforties is still a bachelor, assumptions are made about him. This news will barely raise an eyebrow, in spite of the headlines."

I jumped into the conversation, assuring him, "And there won't *be* any headlines. As the story breaks, of course we'll report it—we have to—but it won't be sensationalized, at least not in the *Register*."

He sighed. "I appreciate that—*believe* me."

I sat again, joining the others around the low table. "Okay, then. We've all got our work cut out for us. We've got news to report, but at the same time, we're investigating a murder and the possibility of election antics. Let's concentrate on the murder and assume, for now, that the bogus extortion note is the work of the killer. Let's review the possible suspects."

"There still aren't many," said Pierce with a toss of his hands. "By my count, we've got three: Bruno Hérisson, Deputy Dan Kerr, and . . . me."

"Now, Doug—"

"Stay objective," he reminded me. "I've been implicated. And you'll note that none of these three suspects are puny. Any one of us would have had sufficient physical stature to subdue and strangle Carrol."

"Fine," I said, adding Pierce's name to the lineup on my pad, "the sheriff himself has joined the ranks of the suspicious, but he's at the bottom of *my* list, so let's start at the top. Where are we with Bruno?"

Pierce told us, "His alibi checks out, as far as it goes. The Pfister confirmed that Bruno arrived late Saturday morning before his room was ready, then checked in after lunch. The computer log verifies this, and the desk clerk remembers him vividly. As for his departure on Sunday, the facts are consistent with Bruno's claim that he simply left before noon; housekeeping had his room turned by one o'clock. The sticking point, of course, is that there's no way to pinpoint how long before noon he left—was it mere minutes, as he claims, or possibly six hours? He still can't seem to establish proof of his whereabouts at the exact time of the murder; a simple parking stub would do the trick. Clearly, Bruno had the most obvious motive to want Carrol dead, so he's still first on my list."

I reminded him, "There's also the matter of *dalliance*."

Glee and Lucy exchanged a puzzled look.

I explained, "The extortion note uses the word *dalliance* to refer to Doug's fling with Carrol. Both Doug and I found the word not only vague, but downright peculiar—who would talk like that? Is the word perhaps French?"

Glee and Lucy both nodded that they now understood the implication, but then Glee shook her head uncertainly. "*Dalliance* may have the *look* of other French words, but I have a hunch it derives differently." She rose, asking me, "Okay if I check the unabridged in your office?"

"Please do." I chided myself for not having already done it.

She stepped from the conference room to my inner office, where *Webster's Third* lay open like a Bible on a stand behind my desk. With one hand, she riffled to the *d*'s; with the other, she adjusted her glasses. Leaning over the book, she read, telling us, "No. It derives from *dally*, which in turn comes from Middle English. It was Anglo-French five hundred years ago, but that's not exactly *au courant*." She laughed at her clever understatement.

Lucy called to her, "Check with the morgue. They have French dictionaries."

We waited while Glee used the phone on my desk to call the paper's reference room. After a short conversation, she joined us again at the table, reporting, "There's no *dalliance* in common usage in modern French."

Lucy said to me, "Nice try—it sounded promising. It would have been tidy if the extortion note had pointed directly to Bruno."

I scribbled over *dalliance* on my pad. "Okay," I conceded, "the note doesn't point to Bruno, but it doesn't exonerate him either. His English is fluent, if stilted—he may very well know the word."

Glee, thinking, tapped her pencil on her pad. "It *is* an odd word choice. Who'd say *dalliance*? It's so . . . affected."

Pierce reminded us wryly, "Carrol Cantrell was highly affected. Maybe he *did* write the note—and someone killed him before he had a chance to deliver it."

Lucy eyed him askance. With a tinge of sarcasm, she asked, "And just what is it, Douglas, that Carrol Cantrell might hope to wring out of you? He seemed like a big-bucks kind of guy, while you . . . well, your salary's a matter of public record. Not that you're 'hurting,' but—"

Pierce laughed, interrupting her, then finished her sentence. "But people in my line of work aren't in it for the money. I'm an unlikely target for extortion."

"Unless," Glee interjected, "Carrol was desperate. Maybe he was having financial difficulties. We still don't know much about his background."

Pierce opened a file he'd brought along. "This might help for starters," he said, extracting a sheet of paper that appeared to be a printout of raw data. "We got a record of his cell-phone activity since his arrival in Wisconsin. Mostly calls to California, probably business. Quite a few Chicago calls too. It proves *one* thing"—Pierce chortled while passing the page over the table to me. "He talked a lot."

I could tell at a glance that the rows of numbers would be meaningless to me, so I passed the printout to Lucy, asking, "Could you run a check on these?"

She nodded, placing the document atop her to-do pile. When it came to hard research skills, few could match Lucille Haring. This would be child's play at her computer terminal.

"Back to the extortion note," I said, returning to our original topic. "Moneywise, the murder-to-silence-blackmail scenario doesn't seem to fit our profile of Doug or the victim. So let's maintain our assumption that the note was faked and planted. What else does the word *dalliance* tell us?"

Lucy whirled a hand in the air, rattling off, "It's affected, it's stilted, it's poetic, it's old-fashioned, it's academic . . ." She ran out of adjectives.

"Which could be Bruno," Pierce summarized, "but it doesn't fit our other active suspect at all. Deputy Kerr is as corn-fed and plain-talking as they come."

Glee suggested, "He's also smart. The question is, is he clever enough, devious enough, to invent an extortion note that doesn't 'sound' like himself?"

"*No*," Pierce answered emphatically. "I've worked with Dan Kerr for years. Granted, I don't agree with his stand on the pornography issue, and I certainly don't appreciate his ambition to take my job, but I refuse to believe he's capable of criminal action. He's a cop to the core."

"But he also has a motive," I reminded Pierce. "The circumstances of his involvement in all this are highly suspicious—the note he found, *supposedly* found, on a computer that he didn't bother to check first for fingerprints—"

"Hey," said Lucy with a snap of her fingers. "Computers always notate their files with a date-and-time stamp. Do we know exactly when the extortion note was written? That should easily clarify whether Cantrell wrote it or not."

"Good point," said Pierce, jotting something. "I'll try to find out."

Something Pierce had said was triggering a new thought—then it came to me. "Pornography," I blurted.

The others looked at me.

I elaborated, "Doug just mentioned that he doesn't agree with Kerr's stand on the pornography issue. That's an issue that keeps popping up—not only in the context of the obscenity trial, but also in the context of this murder. Why?"

Lucy looked up from her notes. "You've lost me, Mark."

I related to everyone the details of my Saturday-morning visit to the coach house: the odd "welcoming committee" that consisted of antiporn crusaders Harley Kaiser and Miriam Westerman, the piles of porn strewn about Cantrell's quarters, and—that most intriguing of details—Cantrell's telephone reference to the Miller standard.

"I've since learned that the Miller standard is a set of legal guidelines used in judging obscenity—an odd thing indeed for the king of miniatures to be chatting about on the phone in his bathrobe on a Saturday morning—the morning before he's killed. Harley Kaiser overheard the telephone conversation as well. At the time, I didn't understand what Cantrell was talking about, but it was clear from his reaction that Harley did. Then yesterday, when Roxanne and I joined Doug and Harley at lunch, Roxanne raised the topic of the Miller standard. Harley got uncharacteristically sheepish, acknowledging that he'd heard Cantrell mention it, but insisting that it took him by surprise. Squirming, the DA went on to tell us that the visit was entirely Miriam's doing, that he'd had no idea what he was walking into."

The others looked at each other in silence for a moment. Glee asked, "What *was* he walking into?"

"*I don't know*. But it strikes me as unlikely that a pair of antismut zealots would just 'happen' to waltz in on a visitor's conversation regarding the legalistic definition of obscenity." I sat back, as if resting my case, but in truth, I was wondering, What next?

Glee answered my unspoken question. "We should talk to the defense team," she said, adjusting her reading glasses while scribbling a note.

Lucy's eyes widened with interest. "*Of course*," she said, adding something to her own notes, "let's check with the legal team handling defense of the porn shops in the obscenity case. It's a big-city firm somewhere—I'll find them. Maybe they can shed some light on the 'coincidences' of the Saturday visit."

"Sounds promising," Pierce conceded with a thoughtful nod.

It *was* a promising new turn, perhaps one too many, and I felt compelled to rein in the various possibilities we'd discussed that morning. "Okay, Lucy"—I was now writing notes of my own—"you need to do a bit of digging. Track down those numbers from Cantrell's cell phone, see what you can find out about his finances, and talk to the pornography defense team. Meanwhile," I told the others, "we were weighing the possibility that Deputy Kerr might have played a role in this—if not in the murder, then at least in planting the extortion note. Kerr ought to be the subject of a separate investigation."

"Have you forgotten?" asked Pierce. "Kerr's now in *charge* of the investigation."

"Not *our* investigation. We need to at least talk to him, question him."

"Good luck." Pierce closed his notes. "Kerr won't talk to you. Why would he?"

Stymied, we sat in silence for a moment.

"Hey." Glee again. "The endorsement. Tell him that 'circumstances' have caused the *Register* to reconsider its endorsement in the sheriff's race."

I told the others, "I'll bet he'd trot right in for an editorial-board interview."

Pierce said, "I'll bet he would too."

Lucy said, "I'll phone him right away."

We had our plan.

Neil was meeting me for lunch that day at the First Avenue Grill, and I invited Glee Savage to join us as well. When Glee and I arrived shortly after noon, I found the crowd considerably sparser than it had been on Monday. The hostess, looking less harried, greeted me at the door and showed us to my usual table, a prime spot between the fireplace and a corner window. The fireplace was dark and bare—though September had brought its cooler weather, it would be many weeks, I hoped, before winter would justify a fire.

Waiting for Neil, we ordered tea, hot for Glee, iced for me. I could predict with near certainty that Neil would want iced cappuccino (a recent kick of his), so I ordered this for him in advance, as it was apt to throw the kitchen into a panic.

Glee straightened her hat—it looked for all the world like a priest's biretta, except that it was made of a leopard-print damask that matched her flat two-foot-square purse. She said, "I can't thank you enough, Mark, for including me on this project. Your predecessor, Barret Logan, wouldn't let me anywhere near 'hard news.' I think he considered it unladylike."

"Barret and I are products of different generations," I reminded her.

"Thank God," she told me under her breath, in spite of the fact that her own age, fifty-two, nearly split the difference between Logan and me.

"Truth is, keeping you on this story was common sense. One way or another, this all seems tied to the miniatures world, and that's *your* area of expertise."

Glee had arranged with Grace Lord to do a follow-up story at

The Nook that afternoon, assessing the impact of Carrol Cantrell's death on the convention that would open on Saturday. When Glee invited me along for the interview, I gladly accepted, eager to get a firsthand impression of the situation. Now she told me, "Few publishers would take such an active interest in a story."

Pretending to weigh her comment gravely, I figured, "Maybe I should spend more time at my desk."

"Don't you dare!"

Laughing at this exchange, I noticed that Neil had arrived. Well acquainted with "my" table, he knew exactly where to find me and was already headed across the dining room in my direction. Glimpsing him now as if for the first time ever, I found him as attractive as on the evening three years prior when Roxanne had introduced us at a cocktail party she'd thrown in his honor.

Does anyone really understand physical attraction? Sure, Neil was and still is an undeniably handsome man; anyone would say so. But in our case, the instant vibes were much deeper. It wasn't just sex—I wasn't even out yet. Nor was it just our intellectual mating, which was immediate and complete and extraordinary. I've never put much credence in the notion of love at first sight, but I can think of no other words to describe what brought us together.

"Look who's here," I said to Glee, who sat with her back to the room.

"Judging from your doe-eyed grin, I hope it's Neil."

I didn't need to answer, as he had just arrived at the table. Standing, I met him with a hug, a peck on the lips. I told him, "It's great to see you during the workday, just like old times." Back in Chicago, we often met for lunch. Those opportunities were rare in Dumont.

He gently reminded me, "This setup was your idea."

Avoiding that, I told him, "I didn't think you'd mind if Glee joined us today."

"*Mind* it? I love it. Hi, Glee." And he bent to kiss her.

"Hello, treasure. You look smashing, as always."

He answered, "You're looking pretty hot yourself," as we arranged ourselves around the table.

Glee and Neil had struck up an instant friendship when they met shortly after I moved north last winter—in fact, it was New Year's

Eve, a dinner party at the house on Prairie Street. Neil (the big-city architect) and Glee (the small-town cultural authority) discovered common ground in their ability to discuss trends in art, decorating, fashion. Despite Neil's being born nearly two decades later than Glee, they seemed to view each other as contemporaries—due, no doubt, to their mutual interest in the here and now. On matters of style, they shared a mind-set that was purely of the moment.

A waitress arrived with our tea and Neil's iced coffee. She also distributed menus, telling us, "You might want to consider our Tuesday special—chicken potpie with fresh-baked corn bread. It's real good." She winked, implying that she'd sampled it on many a Tuesday.

I'd done so myself, and I had to admit, the Grill had redefined chicken potpie—it bore no resemblance to the frozen, seventeen-cent supermarket brand I'd subsisted on during college, when I'd rented my first apartment and learned to use the oven (that was in the Dark Ages, just before microwave ovens became standard household appliances).

"Thanks," I told the waitress. "We'll need a few minutes to decide."

Mimicking an English matron, Glee quipped, "But we really mustn't dally."

Laughing, I assured the waitress that we weren't rushed, and she left.

Neil watched this exchange quizzically. "I don't get it," he said, licking froth from the edge of his drink. "What's the joke?"

He already knew about the previous day's discovery of the bogus extortion note, framing Pierce. So I brought him up-to-date, explaining, "We had a discussion at the office this morning, regarding the wording of the blackmail note. It referred to Doug and Carrol's fling as a 'dalliance,' which we all found odd."

Neil considered this for a moment, then commented, "It *is* odd—hardly the expected vocabulary of a ruthless killer."

I added, "We had a promising hunch. It seemed that *dalliance* might be a common French word, but it's not."

"It derives from *dally*," said Glee, clarifying her earlier remark. "So Bruno's off the hook—linguistically, at least." She poured her tea, which had been steeping.

"To my mind," I told them, "he's still the suspect with the clearest motive. Call it 'professional rivalry' if you will, but what it really boils down to is greed—money—which tops the list of classic murder motives."

"There was certainly a lot at stake," Glee conceded, sipping.

I told Neil, "Bruno said that Carrol was charging as much as fifteen thousand dollars for one of his—what's it called, Glee?"

She answered, speaking to Neil, "Bruno's miniature cylinder-top desks are absolutely marvelous, and yes, they do fetch top dollar."

Neil's eyes widened with interest—he and Glee were now on their own special turf. He asked, "Which period?"

"Louis Quinze."

"Of *course*." He rolled his eyes. "I'd love to see such a piece."

"He has them at The Nook. It's an extraordinary exhibit."

I'd been squeezing lemon into my iced tea, stirring it, but I stopped with a thought, telling Neil, "Glee and I are going over to The Nook right after lunch. Why don't you join us?"

He considered. "Why not? I have a late-afternoon meeting back at Quatro, but otherwise my time's my own. I'll follow you in my own car."

"Where are you parked?"

"Just up the block, near the *Register*."

Happy to know that I'd be spending some extra time with Neil that day, I opened my menu to ponder lunch. The others did likewise. I mentioned to Neil, "By the way . . ."

He looked up from his menu. "Yes?"

"I noticed a vacant storefront up the street, on the next corner."

"Oh? What about it?"

"It's nice. Handsome. Good location. I'll point it out on the way to the car."

"What for?"

I didn't bother to answer, as he knew very well what I was thinking.

With a grin, his gaze dropped again to the menu.

After lunch, Glee, Neil, and I walked the block or two back to the *Register*'s First Avenue offices. Monday's rainy weather had moved out, and the sunny afternoon had the dry, crisp feel of autumn.

Along the way, we stopped at the intersection to wait for traffic, and I pointed out to Neil the vacant storefront on the opposite corner. He made some noncommittal remark, but I could tell from his long, intent gaze across the street that he liked the place despite his stated indifference. Standing at the stoplight, I studied Neil as he studied the building, hoping to glean from his features some clue as to whether he might actually consider moving his practice to Dumont.

These ruminations were distracted, though, by the tavern that stood near us on the corner. The neon signs flashing in its windows, specifically the one flickering MILLER BEER, reminded me that I had overheard Carrol Cantrell speak of the legal standard by which obscenity is judged. Was it mere coincidence? Did it have any bearing on his murder? Was it linked to the blackmail note?

The light changed, and I dismissed these thoughts as we crossed the street. Passing by the storefront, I noticed that Neil's pace slowed and his head turned. Perhaps he could imagine, hanging near the door, the same tasteful, discreet sign that I had visualized.

A few moments later, we reached Neil's car, and he offered to drive Glee to The Nook with him, saving her the trek to my car. I agreed to meet them.

When I had pulled my own car from the *Register*'s reserved lot, turning onto First Avenue, I wondered whether the street scene in front of Grace Lord's shop would be more active than it had been the previous afternoon, when Pierce met me there to disclose the discovery of the extortion note. Turning off Park Street, heading for The Nook, I found things to be equally quiet now—the only car in sight was Neil's, parked at the curb near the shop. With the rainy spell ended, I also noticed that the trees lining the street were starting to turn golden. Right on cue, a few leaves dropped from high branches and fluttered earthward, a vanguard of the masses that would follow.

Glee and Neil got out of his car, waiting for me on the sidewalk as I parked. They were chatting away about something (dishes, drapes, dresses—who knows?), obviously enjoying each other's company. Leaving my car, crossing the street toward them, I asked, "Everyone ready for a round of hard-hitting journalism?" Saying this, I checked for my notebook and pen.

"Do we have to?" whined Neil. "After that potpie, I'm ready for a nap."

Glee cast him a visual jab. "Come on, kiddo. These tiny interiors will goose your energy level." And she slung an arm through his, marching him toward the entrance to The Nook. I followed, marveling at the apparent silliness of this expedition, but reminding myself that our mission couldn't have been more serious—we were hunting a killer.

Inside the shop, all was quiet, in stark contrast to the near pandemonium of the weekend. The taciturn lady with the clipboard hovered about, checking shelves for inventory. When she saw me, I didn't need to ask about Grace Lord's whereabouts—she simply jerked her head toward the back hall.

Leading the others through the connecting door to the old drugstore, I explained to Neil, "Lord's Rexall was never intended to serve as a convention hall, I'm sure, but the space is surprisingly well suited for the exhibition of miniatures. Just *look* at this"—and I waved my arm as we entered the main room, a gesture that encompassed the aisles of exhibits, the workshop areas, the gallery for the roombox competition.

Clearly, Neil hadn't anticipated such an expansive display of wares. His eyes bugged at the sight of it, unable to take it all in—the kid in a candy shop.

"Ma-aark," a voice singsonged. It was Grace Lord. "Over here."

We turned and saw Grace waving us toward the competition area at the far end of the hall. Walking the main aisle in her direction, I noticed no one else in the room. I called to her, "You haven't been abandoned, have you?"

"Hardly," she said with a laugh as we approached. "The others will be back later in the week for final preparations before opening. Everything's in pretty good shape already."

Glee asked, "Are you putting the finishing touches on your roombox?"

"Exactly," she answered as she began ushering us toward her miniature Rexall, but then she stopped. Eyeing Neil, she said, "I don't believe we've met."

"Sorry," I told both of them. "Grace, this is Neil Waite. We lived together in Chicago, and now Neil's spending some time in Dumont while he's working on the plant expansion out at Quatro Press—he's an architect, and a budding miniatures fan, I suspect."

With a beaming smile, Grace extended her hand, telling him, "Welcome to 'our little world,' Neil. It's a pleasure to meet you."

"Thank you, Grace. The pleasure's mine."

Grace greeted Glee as well, commenting, "You folks always look so spiffed and proper—and me looking like hell again." She laughed while self-consciously primping her hairdo, which looked a bit tired, perhaps, but perfectly presentable. "Care to see the reincarnation of Lord's Rexall?"

"Of course," we gushed. "That's why we're here."

That was not, in fact, the point of our visit—Glee had come to question Grace about the impact of Carrol's death upon the miniatures community—but there was no point in rushing into maudlin territory, which would surely dampen Grace's mood. It was good to see her acting more like her sprightly old self again; it seemed she was beginning to shake the shock of the weekend's tragic events.

"It's almost finished," she told us while fiddling with some electrical cords, plugging one in. As she did so, her model drugstore came to life. Ceiling fans paddled slowly overhead; marquee-style lights raced around a mirror behind the soda fountain; backlit apothecary jars, flanking the prescription desk, glowed green and red; two signs, LORD'S and DRUGS, shone backwards in the display windows on either side of the entrance. And all this was contained in a box about a foot high, some three feet wide.

"It's sensational," Neil told Grace.

"Fabulous," agreed Glee while making notes on her steno pad.

Neil continued, "And the *detail*—just look at all the products on the shelves."

I told him, "Look closer. Everything has authentic labels."

"Jeez." He peered deeply into the roombox, his nose crossing the imaginary fourth wall—Grace had removed the front panel of glass to work on her project. Neil told us, "Even the medicines and the prescription bins are labeled— which is Greek to me, or more likely

Latin." We laughed at this comment as he withdrew from the roombox, saying to Grace, "I assume the medical stuff took lots of research. Or did you just fake it?"

"Heavens, no!" She raised her hands in mock horror, as if flabbergasted by the suggestion. With a laugh, she explained, "No, the drug names are authentic, and I didn't need to look 'em up either." She puffed herself, mocking conceit, a foible unnatural to her. "People forget—I was trained in pharmacy—it's the Lord heritage."

Still eyeing the roombox, Neil concluded, "You've brought it all together beautifully. Congratulations, Grace."

I added, "It looks like a winner to me."

"Tut-tut." Wagging a finger, Grace reminded me, "My entry is 'for show' only, which is sort of a nice position to be in—the *others* can scrap for the prizes."

Glee cleared her throat. "I hate to bring this up, Grace, but now that Carrol Cantrell is . . . out of the picture, who'll judge the competition?"

She wagged her head. "I admit, I was worried about that. It was bad enough, what happened to Carrol, but the thing is, it put *me* in a real pickle." Her features brightened. "As luck would have it—and I apologize for even mentioning luck in a situation like this—Bruno agreed to step in and take over the judging. He *used* to be the second-biggest name in miniatures, you know."

"And now he's number one," I observed wryly.

"That he is. So you see, Mark, I'd be back in a pickle if Sheriff Pierce *arrested* Bruno. Besides, *he* wouldn't kill Carrol. I know, I know—they were serious rivals. But the truth is, they depended on each other for their success."

We all fell quiet while considering Grace's words, and I recognized that she'd made a valid point. Carrol had been responsible for promoting and marketing Bruno's work to the American market, and in turn, Bruno had supplied Carrol with the exquisite miniatures that established Carrol's reputation as retail king of the mini world; their relationship was symbiotic, if not cordial. Nonetheless, I could not forget that Bruno had angrily stated his intentions to sever his dealings with Carrol, whom he called a "parasite"—and two days later, Carrol was dead. So even though Grace could dismiss her suspicions of Bruno, I could not.

She added, "If anything, the stir surrounding all this has only heightened people's interest in the competition."

Glee asked, "May I quote that? It's an interesting aspect of the whole story."

"Sure," Grace replied with a why-not shrug, "anything to promote the show. In fact, you can mention that we've gotten additional entries, due to all the publicity."

I told her, "I *thought* the collection had grown some since yesterday." The roomboxes had now been arranged in two rows, whereas the day before, they were aligned in a single, longer row.

Neil asked, "Can we get a preview tour of the exhibit, Grace?"

Glee added, "We'd really appreciate it."

"Of *course*," replied Grace, already fiddling with a tangle of electrical cords that hung below the double row of roomboxes. The cords were plugged into a power strip, the sort used for computers, and with the flick of a single switch, the collection of shadow boxes was illuminated.

Though the exhibit space itself was not darkened, the little rooms glowed with intensity. Displayed before us was the finest work of many serious amateurs, depicting a variety of rooms that ranged from cutesy to sophisticated, from whimsical flights of fancy to exacting reproductions of historical styles. It was impossible to absorb it all in one eyeful; we three visitors gawked and cooed, spinning our heads in search of a starting point.

Helping us focus, Grace suggested, "I really like this one, a new entry from a man in Kenosha, a relative newcomer to the mini scene. He calls it 'Cabot Cove Summer,' and it's just for fun. It's his idea of what Jessica Fletcher's vacation house would look like—if she had one."

It *was* fun. The miniaturist had constructed the parlor and hallway of a New England summerhouse, all decorated in cool shades of creamy off-white. The parlor also served as work space for television's fictitious mystery writer, with a large desk moved into the light of a cheery bay window. Word processor, coffee mug, dictionary, and a stack of reference books were arrayed close at hand. A fireplace, Windsor chairs, pewter candlesticks, and tieback curtains helped reinforce the room's heritage. Front and center sat a lacquered oriental chest, conveniently coffin-sized, *perfect* for displaying a grim collection of daggers, a mace, noose, and other devices of mayhem, intended for the author's research.

"I *love* it," gushed Glee, recording details of the room in her notes.

"It's certainly no 'dollhouse,' " said Neil. "Everything is perfectly proportioned, obviously the work of a designer's eye."

"You'll like this one too," said Grace, directing our attention to another roombox. "It has a Chicago locale, which I'm sure you'll appreciate. It's called 'East Lake Shore Drive.' "

I told her, "That's the short stretch of the Outer Drive that curves around the Drake Hotel—one of the best addresses in town."

While the first roombox had been infused with a capricious sense of humor, this one was an example of dead-serious decorating. Created in miniature was an elegant double-doored bedroom, big enough to function as a comfortable sitting room as well.

As if thinking aloud, Neil offered Glee a knowledgeable commentary on some of its particulars: "There's an astute mix of furniture styles, including Louis Quinze and Seize, Biedermeier, and contemporary. Above a glazed wainscot, the walls are upholstered in quilted, honey-colored silk—the palette of the entire room is soft and rosy. Framed original paintings glow beneath miniature art lights. And the tabletop accessories are remarkable—antique ivory pieces, bouillotte lamps, mantel clock, desk set, even a perfume-bottle collection." As a finishing touch, a brass telescope, mounted on a mahogany tripod, was aimed out the invisible fourth wall toward the viewer, implying that the room enjoyed an expansive view of Lake Michigan and other high-rises. Neil summed up his judgment in a single word: "Stunning."

"*I'll* say," Glee agreed, making note of Neil's description. She asked Grace, "The furniture—all these flawless pieces—the roombox designer doesn't actually *make* everything, correct?"

"That's right," Grace told her. "The furnishings are collected from many sources. Some are commercially mass-produced; others are individually crafted by artisans like Bruno Hérisson, who's considered the very best."

Neil asked, "Are any of his pieces here?" As he said this, I recalled that his purpose in joining us that afternoon was to see one of Bruno's miniature desks.

"You bet," Grace answered. "Bruno has a large display of his own, like many other exhibitors, but I'm afraid his inventory is locked away right now. It's far too valuable to leave sitting out. However"—she whisked along the row of roomboxes in the competition gallery, stopping at one of them, pointing—"you're in luck. This entry contains several of his pieces."

We gathered round. The roombox, titled "Quai Saint Bernard," depicted an apartment in Paris overlooking the Seine. Through tall French doors, the river could be glimpsed as a backdrop beyond a balcony. The ornate style of decorating contained many visual delights, as well as a lavish assemblage of furniture, but Neil lingered over none of this, zeroing in on the object he'd come to see.

"There it is," he declared, "the cylinder-top desk, Louis Quinze."

The palm-sized piece of furniture matched Glee's earlier description: a rolltop desk, crafted of inlaid hardwood, with an intricate cover that was a solid cylinder instead of slatted. It was lovely, of course, but for the life of me, I couldn't understand all the fuss, let alone the fifteen-thousand-dollar price tag.

"Incredible," said Neil.

"Absolutely nonpareil," Glee whispered, holding her glasses an inch beyond her nose to boost their power.

"Would you like a closer look?" asked Grace. To my amazement, she opened the front glass wall of the roombox, reached inside, and plucked up the desk—seemingly with no more trepidation than if it were a pack of cigarettes, which would be roughly the same size. "Here," she said, offering it to Neil.

Huh? "Hey, Neil," I interjected, "look but don't touch." I cringed to imagine—one false twitch of the fingers, and the desk's delicate toothpick legs could snap.

He looked at me as if I were nuts. "I'll be careful," he assured me while taking the desk from Grace's hand. He, Grace, and Glee leaned in close to examine Bruno's workmanship, commenting on the functioning rolltop, the sliding drawers, the working locks. Huddled over the desk, whispering about it and poking at it, they looked like a team of doctors performing heart surgery on a mouse.

Fearing the worst, I turned away, unable to watch. One slip, and I could find myself with an expensive new hobby—collecting broken miniatures.

"What the—" Neil's voice stopped short. The others fell silent.

Uh-oh.

Neil laughed. "What's this little critter on the bottom?"

"That's Bruno's mark," said Grace, "his trademark. He draws it somewhere inconspicuous on all his pieces."

I breathed again. With my fears allayed and my interest piqued, I joined their circle, peering down at the fuzzy image of an animal on the underside of the desk, straining to focus on it.

"It looks like a . . . porcupine," said Glee.

Aha. I asked her, "May I borrow your glasses?" She lifted the slinky chain over her head and handed me the half-frame spectacles. They were ground to a strong prescription, not intended for my eyes, but by holding them like a magnifying glass, I was able to get a clear look at the trademark. I told the others, "I'll bet it's a hedgehog. Walking to lunch with Roxanne yesterday, she mentioned that *hérisson* literally means 'hedgehog.' "

"Really?" said Neil.

"I never knew that," chimed Glee.

"Well, who'd have thought?" clucked Grace. From the side of her mouth, she added, "Bruno doesn't *look* like a hedgehog."

Laughing with the others, I handed the glasses back to Glee. There was something on my mind, though. The style of the drawn hedgehog, which was slightly abstracted, seemed familiar. Then it clicked. "Glee," I said, "remember Bruno's silk cravat? There was a pattern on it, repeated over and over, like wallpaper, and it—"

She interrupted me with a little gasp. "I do remember the pattern. I couldn't tell what it was. But now I'm sure—it was Bruno's stylized hedgehog."

Now it was Grace's turn to gasp. "My heavens," she told us, "that's the pattern that was on the scarf we found."

"I'm confused," said Neil. "What scarf?"

There was a moment's pause.

I reminded him, "The scarf from the murder scene."

Back at the *Register,* I sat at my desk, transcribing some notes into my computer, when Lucille Haring rushed in from my outer office. Planting herself in a chair across from me, she blurted, "We've dug up some important background on Carrol Cantrell, but first, switch on your radio."

Having been absorbed in my notes, I found it difficult to make sense of her hurried words. "What . . . ?"

"The radio," she commanded. "Turn it on. Denny Diggins."

As instructed, I reached to the credenza along the wall behind my desk and turned on the radio. It was already tuned to the local station, as evinced by the closing lines of a jingle for Dumont Chevrolet, ". . . where we've got just the deal . . . to put *you* behind the wheel."

As Lucy and I shared a silent oh-brother roll of the eyes, the affected tones of a too familiar voice came over the airwaves:

> We're back, friends. You're listening to *Denny Diggins' Dumont Digest.* And *I* . . . am Denny Diggins. As we told you before that noteworthy commercial announcement, our guest this afternoon is Miriam Westerman, founder of Dumont's Feminist Society for the New Age of Cosmological Holism. As many of you know, Miriam has just opened a private New Age day school, called simply A Child's Garden. Welcome to the program, Miriam.
>
> *Thank you, Denny. It's a pleasure to be here.*
>
> Now. We had planned, of course, to discuss the opening of A Child's Garden, but you informed me just before airtime that you'd brought news of rather stunning developments in the Carrol Cantrell murder case.
>
> *That's right, Denny. First let me say that I appreciate the opportunity to tell your listeners about* A Child's Garden*. Conspicuously, the* Dumont Daily Register *has all but ignored our efforts.*
>
> Now *why* doesn't that surprise me? (*Har har.*) Once

again, it only goes to prove that Dumont's only dependable source for unbiased news is right here—with yours truly, Denny Diggins.

So true, so true. But this lapse on the part of the Register *goes far beyond the prejudices of its publisher against my school. Now, it seems, the paper has simply been remiss in not reporting new details crucial to the Cantrell murder case.*

Ooooo, how delicious! Do tell us more.

Well, Denny, as you know, the Register *reported this morning that a routine investigation of the victim's computer files contained a possible new lead. What the* Register *failed to mention was that the computer file was in fact the draft of an extortion note, written by the victim, demanding hush money from a sex partner.*

Ooooo, double delicious!

Hardly. The people of Dumont deserve to know that the other party named in the blackmail note was, first, a man, and, second, a local public official.

My God, you can't be serious. Who was it, Miriam? Please tell us.

None other than . . . Douglas Pierce, sheriff of Dumont County.

Heavens! How shocking—I daresay scandalous. Where did you learn this?

A reliable source, I assure you.

You coy thing, Miriam. Well—I can't thank you enough for breaking this news right here on *Dumont Digest.* It certainly casts the investigation in a whole new light. It also explains why Sheriff Pierce was reported to have turned over the investigation to his chief deputy detective.

Yes, it does. But tell me, Denny—don't you find it strange that this information was withheld by the Register*? Or could it be that the publisher was concealing his own poor judgment in having recently endorsed Pierce for reelection? Hmm?*

Why, Miriam, do I detect a note of cynicism here? I'm sure the *Register* was merely holding back on this story in the name of sound journalistic principles. (*Har har.*) I'm

> sure the *Register*'s editorial stance has in no way infected the paper's reporting of—

Seething, I switched off the radio. "Why, those goddamn, irresponsible, reprehensible . . . If Doug doesn't sue their sorry asses, I certainly ought to! Malice and libel aside, they're sensationalizing the investigation and could jeopardize its outcome. Whoever leaked the information to that bitch ought to be shot."

"That would be Harley Kaiser," Lucy told me nonchalantly, grinning, amused by my outburst. "Think about it: Miriam and the DA are all palsy on the obscenity issue, so they both have an ax to grind with Pierce. Most important, Kaiser was one of the few people privy to the contents of the computer file. Sure, it could have been Deputy Dan, but I'd bet on Kaiser."

"You're right. So would I." Listening to Lucy, I'd calmed down and was relieved to note that her thinking was clearer than mine at that moment. I asked, "What about Cantrell's phone records? Did they reveal any connections that could have been of interest to Kaiser?"

"I'll get to that," she told me, grinning. She opened a file in her lap and ran a hand through her spiky red hair. "I've been on the Internet since our morning meeting, and I've discovered some interesting background on King Carrol. What's more, his probate report was released a few minutes ago, and something is starting to fall together."

Needless to say, she'd captured my attention. Smiling, I again recalled the woman's formidable research and computer skills, which she'd demonstrated back in Chicago at the *Journal*—that's why I'd hired her. "What have you got?"

"Let's start with the California probate report," she said, removing several pages from her folder and spreading them on my desk. "First of all, it shoots holes in the theory we floated this morning that Cantrell may have been having financial problems—in fact, the guy was loaded. Moreover, the report reveals no heirs who would have had a likely motive to kill Cantrell, let alone anyone who'd have the opportunity to strangle the guy here in Dumont. His estate is complicated, but the upshot is, no one's been waiting for him to die."

"Damn," I said, recognizing the morbid ring of my disappointment.

"However"—she paused to twitch her brows—"it was disclosed

that Cantrell's business holdings were somewhat . . . diverse, not limited to the realm of miniatures. In fact, he was involved in a far more profitable venture that actually subsidized his interest in miniatures. Get this: Carrol Cantrell was founder and principal stockholder of Hot Head Video, a producer of gay porn."

"Well now," I said, flumping back in my chair, "that *is* an intriguing angle. It seems my hunch was right—pornography did play some sort of role in the murder. Did Cantrell have organized-crime connections? Was he in trouble with the law?"

"No, no, nothing like that. Hot Head is strictly legit—no kiddie porn, no snuff flicks, just good-ole triple-X adult entertainment. They've actually racked up quite a few awards over the years."

"I'm impressed, Lucy, but what's the point?"

"The point is"—she scattered more pages from her folder on my desk—"I discovered on the Internet that Cantrell was in pretty thick with the ACLU."

"Makes sense. The porn industry has always rallied round the First Amendment—it's the cause célèbre of any civil libertarian."

"*Exactly*." She leaned closer to tell me, "Cantrell wasn't just a card-carrying *member* of the ACLU. He didn't just write them *checks*. No, Mark—he's appeared on their behalf as an expert witness, testifying across the country at numerous obscenity trials."

My hand reflexively rose to my forehead as I absorbed this dizzying bit of information. With the room in a spin, I told Lucy, "I *thought* it was strange that he arrived in town a week early for the miniatures show. His true purpose here must have been related to the trial."

"Uh-huh." She nodded, pulling another page from her folder. "That's where the phone records paid off. Cantrell made a batch of calls from his cell phone to Chicago, all to the same number. It was none other than Aldrich and Associates, a huge law firm hired by a consortium of interested parties to defend the porn shops on the outskirts of Dumont. There's some big money behind pornography, and the industry takes any prosecution—even out here in Podunk—very seriously, as the outcome could saddle them with a dangerous legal precedent. I managed to get through to the head of the defense team, and, yes, he confirmed that Carrol Cantrell was on their witness list."

"Beautiful! Great work, Lucy," I told her, beaming. "This puts our esteemed prosecutor on some very thin ice. Approaching an expert witness without the knowledge or presence of the defense is an ethical breach that—"

"Not so fast. That was *my* first reaction, but here's the catch: The defense team had talked to Cantrell, and they definitely planned to use him as a witness, but they had not yet issued their list. It was to be submitted to the prosecution yesterday morning, Monday, but Cantrell was killed on Sunday."

With a measure of disappointment, I conceded, "Then it's *possible* that Kaiser was leveling with me yesterday at lunch. He claimed to have had no previous knowledge of Cantrell at the time of the Saturday visit with Miriam Westerman. He said the visit was *her* idea. But how would Miriam—"

My words (and the thoughts behind them) were cut short by the sight of Doug Pierce barreling across the newsroom, headed toward my office. Stomping into the room, he blustered, "Did you *hear* it? I didn't—but I sure as hell heard *about* it, and fast!"

Assuming the topic had shifted to Denny Diggins, I told him, "In the next edition, we'll set the record straight as to what is and isn't known about the extortion note. We'll also deliver a firm editorial lecture on the principles of responsible journalism. And I plan to phone Roxanne tonight for an opinion on whether either of us has grounds for legal action. But meanwhile, and this is a big 'meanwhile,' Lucy has dug up something good—something that gives new life to our behind-the-scenes investigation."

Not until I mentioned Lucy's name did Pierce notice her, so focused had he been on his anger. "Oh. Hi, Lucille. Forgive my lousy manners." In one hand he carried a zippered portfolio of paperwork; in the other, an open bag of Chee-Zee Corn Curleez. He set both on my desk.

"Don't mention it, Sheriff. Having a bad day?"

As the answer was self-evident, I added a question of my own: "When did you start eating *those* things? They're fat-bombs, you know."

"I've been . . . nervous," he explained, plucking one of the gnarled, orange-colored snacks from the cellophane bag. Before popping it into his mouth, he asked Lucy, "What'd you find?"

I told him, "You'd better sit down." So he joined Lucy, facing me over the desk. We were cramped there—we would have been far more comfortable in the conference area of my outer office—but the close confines seemed appropriate, lending a secret, conspiratorial edge to our conversation.

Lucy laid it out flatly: "Carrol Cantrell owned Hot Head Video, a producer of gay porn tapes. As a free-speech activist, he also testified effectively on behalf of the ACLU as an expert witness in various porn trials. He planned to testify here in Dumont."

Needlessly, I added, "The implications are staggering." As I said this, my eyes were riveted to the gaping bag of Chee-Zees. Having not tasted one in years (they always reminded me of Styrofoam packing "peanuts" that had been sprayed with that ridiculous fake cheddar color), I took one from the bag and ate it.

Pierce was still absorbing Lucy's revelation. "God," he said, "where do we begin?" He pulled a fistful of Chee-Zees from the bag, eating them from his palm.

I suggested, "Let's talk it through. First, we now know that Cantrell had a track record of helping to defeat porn trials, which was his true purpose in coming to Dumont, where our DA is preparing a must-win obscenity case. Cantrell had a handy pretext for being here—judging a miniatures show—allowing him to get the lay of the land and absorb the local culture, which could have a bearing on his courtroom strategy. This makes sense. But it all hinges on the coincidental timing of the porn trial and the miniatures show. Did the porn defenders just happen to get lucky, asking Cantrell to come here at a time when the trip would have a dual purpose? That doesn't seem likely, does it?" I ate a few of the stray Corn Curleez that now littered my desk.

Lucy answered, "No, Mark, that wouldn't be likely, but you've got it backwards."

"What?" asked Pierce and I, both of us chewing.

"The defense lawyers didn't ask Cantrell to come here. I learned on the phone that Cantrell had proposed it to *them*. He was coming here to judge the miniatures show, and somehow he knew about the trial—he wanted to help."

Mulling this, I wondered, "How would he know about the trial, out there in California? I can't imagine that he—"

"Oh, wow," Pierce interrupted, swallowing a mouthful, clapping the sticky cheese dust from his hands. "It all fits." He unzipped the portfolio of papers he'd brought with him, riffling through it in search of something. "Among the inventory of Carrol's things from the coach house, we found a letter to him from Grace Lord—her initial correspondence inviting him to the convention to judge the show. Ah! Here's the copy."

He positioned it on the desk so that both Lucy and I could read it—the document now bore a big orange thumbprint. Pierce pointed out a particular paragraph, which read:

> *While I am certain, my dear Mr. Cantrell, that Dumont would strike you as something of a quiet little place (perhaps too quiet, at least by Los Angeles standards!), our town is not altogether the backwater that you might presume. We have an active cultural life promoted by our schools and by community orchestra and theater groups. We have an important architectural legacy here as well as a thriving business climate. We even have our share of big-city controversy; a pornography trial, for example, is scheduled to begin soon, attempting to shut down some "adult bookstores" out in Dumont County. My point, Mr. Cantrell, is that Dumont is an energetic, red-blooded Midwestern town with an active, involved citizenry. We're a friendly, outgoing people. Should you decide to honor our community by accepting my invitation, we shall spare no effort in extending to you a royal welcome.*

Pierce told us, "The first time I skimmed through Grace's letter, it struck me as peculiar that she would mention the obscenity trial."

"Yeah," agreed Lucy, "what interest would kindly old Grace Lord have in smut?" She laughed.

I answered, "None, surely. She must have felt that the controversy would impress the jaded, metropolitan King Carrol. It's entirely possible that he accepted Grace's invitation to judge the mini show as an *excuse* to come here." Again distracted by the lure of the snack bag, I succumbed to several of those *dreadful* Curleez.

Pierce returned the letter to his portfolio and zipped it shut.

"When Harley and Miriam visited the coach house, do you suppose that Carrol understood their background with the obscenity trial?"

Lucy leaned close to him. "I hate to bring up a delicate issue, Doug, but of the three of us in this room, you knew him best. Did he ever mention the trial?"

Pierce blushed. "To be perfectly honest, we weren't talking shop." He covered his embarrassment by munching a few more snacks, which were disappearing. Then he added, "I will say this: Carrol had an awful lot of porn magazines lying around, gay porn. I mean, it wouldn't shock me if he traveled with a dirty magazine or two—hell, they can come in handy, especially on the road. But he brought *piles* of the stuff, way more than any one man needs for . . . self-gratification." Again he seemed chagrined by his own words. Again he ate.

Diplomatically, Lucy glided past this, saying, "Videos or magazines—porn is porn. It's all the same business, and Cantrell was *in* the business. His piles of smutty magazines may simply have been 'research.' Maybe he was scouting for video talent—who knows?"

"I'll bet you're right," I told her. With my elbows planted on the desk, I leaned over the Chee-Zees toward both her and Pierce, recounting, "I saw those batches of magazines myself, the morning of the visit with Kaiser and Miriam. I was struck not only by the fact that there were so *many* magazines, but also by Carrol's *indifference* to them—he made no effort to conceal them when we arrived."

Pierce took the last of the whole Curleez from the bag—only broken pieces remained. He asked, "How did they all interact?"

"Cat and mouse, start to finish. I got the impression that they already knew each other—not that they'd actually met, but that they were all *aware* of each other—which makes sense now, even though it then had me confused. It seemed that Cantrell almost *enjoyed* being caught with his porn out. Clearly, he was flaunting it to Kaiser and Miriam, aware of their crusade, daring them to confront him."

Lucy opened her folder and checked her notes. "But we don't really know what Kaiser knew and when he knew it. He told you that the idea for the visit was Miriam's, that she'd essentially dragged him along, unknowing and unwitting."

"And that may be true," I conceded, "but it leaves a big question unanswered: How did addle-headed Miriam figure out Cantrell's background? Doesn't it strike you as far more likely that it was Kaiser himself who somehow found out about Cantrell's plans to testify? I think we should proceed on the assumption that Kaiser instigated the visit."

Pierce was listening with his arms crossed, head bowed in thought, finished eating. He looked up to ask us, "You know what this means, don't you?"

Lucy answered, "We have a new suspect in the murder case."

There was a brief, breathless pause, as no one felt ready to voice the name.

The task fell to me. "Harley Kaiser. The future of his political career as district attorney depends on the outcome of the obscenity case he's preparing for trial. He may have known that Carrol Cantrell had come to Dumont to assure a verdict for civil liberties. There's a motive."

"Did Harley have the means?" asked Pierce rhetorically. "He isn't exactly a hulk of a guy, but he's no weakling either, and I think he could easily have summoned the strength to subdue Carrol and strangle him. As for opportunity—well, *anyone* could have slipped up the coach-house stairs unseen on Sunday morning. I hardly need to add that the attempt to frame me, by planting an extortion note on Carrol's laptop, fits neatly into Harley's agenda—he'd find political life much easier with Dan Kerr as sheriff."

Lucy nodded. "Makes sense. How do we investigate the guy?"

"Good question," I said, picking at the scraps from the snack bag, licking my fingertips. "We're working behind the scenes, remember. We can't very well haul the guy in and question him."

"That reminds me," said Lucy, "I've put a call in to Deputy Dan, asking him to come see us tomorrow morning for that new 'endorsement interview.' "

"Perfect," I told her. "But in the case of Harley Kaiser, I'm afraid we'll need to find a more . . . indirect approach."

We thought for a moment, then Pierce suggested, "Ben Tenelli."

Lucy asked, "The retired doctor who chairs the County Plan Commission?"

"Sure. He knows every politician in town, but he's 'neutral territory,' everyone's best friend."

I quipped, "Like Switzerland?"

Pierce laughed. "Sort of—he's a great old guy. But more to the point, he also authored last week's committee report, calling the adult bookstores an impediment to commercial development. He's in the thick of this issue, and he may have some insights regarding what Harley did or didn't know about Carrol's background. It's worth a shot."

To my mind, the Tenelli angle seemed a long shot at best, but I could offer no better suggestion. What's more, I'd been hearing about the revered old doctor for nearly a week, and we'd never met. Naturally, I was curious about him.

"You offered to introduce us," I reminded Pierce.

He rose, crumpling the cellophane bag. "Busy?"

I rose. "Let's go."

"Gentlemen"—Lucy stopped us as we stepped to the door. She tapped her front teeth with a fingernail. "You'd better brush first."

Pierce directed me as I drove through town to Dr. Benjamin Tenelli's house. As it turned out, he lived in the nicer, older area near the park, in the neighborhood where both Grace Lord and I lived, midway between us, on La Salle Avenue. As I turned off Park Street, Pierce told me, "It's the big house on the next corner."

Driving along the quiet residential street, a street I had not yet explored since my arrival in Dumont, I realized that we were only a block away from Grace Lord's property, but behind it. I could glimpse the roof of the coach house and the treetops that delineated the sprawling backyard—the same backyard where Grace's nephew had once frolicked with his dog.

Ward Lord had been on my mind, off and on, since the previous week when I first saw his picture. I still wondered about him. Where was he? Did he marry and have a family—or not? Would he perhaps return to Dumont from time to time? I wanted information about him, anything at all, but I was reluctant to broach the subject because my motive in asking seemed so transparent—the kid had become the subject of some lustful fantasies. The previous morning, when Doug and I had driven outside of town and found Rambo in the ditch, I had conjectured that Doug and Ward may have grown up together, played with their dogs together. Though tempted to ask about this, I had shied away from the opportunity. Now, since Doug had come out to me, the topic did not seem nearly so troublesome.

So I pulled up to the curb in front of Dr. Tenelli's house and cut my engine. "Hold on a minute, Doug," I told him as he reached to open the car door. "There's something I've been meaning to ask you."

"Yes, Mark?" He smiled.

I paused. "Did you happen to grow up with Ward Lord, Grace's nephew?"

He blinked. "Gee," he said quietly, "talk about a name from the past. He was a few years younger than me, so we never moved in the same circle of friends, but sure, I sort of knew him. Why do you ask?"

I knew *that* was coming. So I explained how I happened to see the photo. "I have to level with you, Doug. I can't get the kid out of my thoughts. And I confess that these thoughts have been disarmingly . . . lecherous."

Pierce laughed. "God, he *was* a looker, wasn't he?"

I shared the laugh. "*That's* an understatement." Then, seriously: "But what happened to him?"

Pierce thought for a moment, shrugged. "Left town. Sorry, I don't know the details. I went away for college, then *he* went away for college, and I guess he never came back."

"You never heard any follow-up—where he went, what he's doing?"

Mulling these queries, he shook his head gently. "No, sorry. I think the family moved West—Grace's brother's family—and Ward must have gone to school out there. We just . . . lost touch. Good question, though. I wonder what Ward *is* up to these days." After a pause, Pierce added, "I wouldn't mind getting another look at him myself."

Though Pierce's recollections were less than illuminating (a phone number would have been illuminating), I had the scant satisfaction of knowing there was simply nothing to be known. Life would go on, and I could nurture scenarios about Ward at will, unfettered by facts.

As there was nothing left to discuss, I told Pierce, "Let's meet the good doctor," and we got out of the car.

I saw that the Tenelli residence was easily the most lavish on La Salle Avenue, which came as no surprise—he was a doctor, after all, whose career had prospered for decades in Dumont. The two-story house was built of red brick with a high-pitched roof. In size and stature, it was not unlike my own home, only a couple of blocks away on Prairie Street, but the styles of the two bore no resemblance. The graceful Taliesin design of my house made it unique in Dumont, while Tenelli's house was of the Germanic "burgher" style that was so popular among old money in Wisconsin. Though this heavy aesthetic had little appeal for me, the house was beautifully landscaped and immaculately maintained. Glancing back at my car, I noted that the Bavarian V-8 looked especially stately in front of Tenelli's mini-mansion.

Late-afternoon sun angled through the old elms that arched the street, painting the front of the house with a random, shifting pattern of yellow light. Windows were flung open; curtains wagged in the breeze. Next to the house, set a few yards away from it, the matching red-brick garage sat with its door gaping open to a dark void within. I said to Pierce, "Maybe no one's home."

"One way to find out," he told me. As we climbed the stairs of the front porch together, approached the door, and rang the bell, it became apparent that someone was indeed home. The inner door was open and the dissonant strains of an opera recording (something modern) could be heard playing within.

"Coming," called a man's voice. Then his figure appeared in the shadows behind the screen. Recognizing Pierce, he swung the screen door open, bellowing above the music, "What a pleasant surprise, Sheriff! Do come in." He wiped his hands on a dish towel that was tucked through his belt.

Pierce and I entered, and while my eyes adjusted to the dimmer light of the interior, the doctor excused himself momentarily to turn down the music. We stood in a center hall between the parlor and the library—tasteful old rooms trimmed with dark, varnished hardwood, nicely furnished with plump chairs, tasseled curtains, and huge Oriental rugs. A hall clock ticked loudly enough to be heard above the music, then chimed four.

The music plunged to background level, and the doctor reappeared, apologizing, "Opera's no good unless it's loud, and I have a particular affection for Benjamin Britten."

"That's *Peter Grimes*, isn't it?" I asked, recognizing a theme.

"Indeed it is, Mr. Manning," he told me, shaking my hand, "indeed it is."

As he seemed to know me, I asked, "We've met?"

"We have *now*." He smiled. "Actually, I've seen your picture, in the *Journal* as well as the *Register*. Both are home-delivered every day."

I instantly liked the man. He was not only a reader, but a subscriber.

He added, "And I've seen you about town in your car—a magnificent vehicle."

I was liking the guy more and more.

Pierce said, "Speaking of cars, Ben, do you know your garage door is open?"

"Mary's out running a few errands before supper," he explained. "Now, Douglas, what can I do for you?"

"I was wondering if you could spare a few minutes. It's about time that you and Mark got to know each other—both of you being such prominent citizens." Pierce was laying it on a little thick, I thought. "But also, Ben, we'd like to talk a bit about the County Plan Commission."

He chuckled. "I don't suppose this relates to the obscenity issue?"

Pierce and I looked at each other. With a laugh, I admitted, "In fact, it does."

Dr. Tenelli nodded. "I've been expecting a phone call from you, Mark. But face-to-face is better yet. If you don't mind, let's talk in the kitchen—I've been puttering with something. Come on, fellas." And with sure, robust strides, he led us through the hall toward the back of the house.

Along the way, I recalled that Dr. Tenelli was some seventy years old. He didn't look it—or act it. Not that I had a preconceived picture of some feeble, doddering geezer, but I simply hadn't expected a man of such vigor, alertness, and easygoing humor. With his full head of hair (silver and thick) and still-handsome features, he could have passed for fifty-five or sixty. I was further impressed by his varied tastes and interests—the retired Italian doctor in the big German house with the loud English opera. Already, I could well appreciate Pierce's description of Tenelli as a beloved and respected figure.

Entering the kitchen, I saw at once that it had recently been modernized. It appeared that interior walls had been removed from other rooms, leaving a large, open space intended for casual entertaining, where guests might pitch in with their hosts in the preparation of a late meal. That afternoon, something was simmering on the restaurant-style stove, and its rich, spicy smell produced in me an instant hunger pang (even though I still felt bloated by Chee-Zees). Obviously, Tenelli took his cooking seriously, as neat piles of ingredients, mostly vegetables, were stacked on various work surfaces, awaiting his surgical skills. An open bottle of red wine, meant for drinking as well as cooking, stood on the counter near the stove with a nearly empty glass at its side. Tenelli hoisted the bottle—"Join me?"

Pierce and I looked at each other. It was after four. We wouldn't be returning to our offices that afternoon. "Sure," we answered. "Thanks."

Tenelli opened a cupboard, plucked two fresh wineglasses from a shelf, and set them with his own on the table in an oversize breakfast nook nestled in the curve of a bay window. Pouring, he said, "Have a seat, fellas," then joined us, sliding into the upholstered booth, sitting across the table from Pierce and me. He lifted his glass in a silent toast, and as we drank, I took a close look at the bottle. I presumed he was serving Italian wine, maybe Californian, but it was French—another manifestation of his international tastes.

I told him, "That's a wonderful Bordeaux, Doctor." I was amazed by his extravagance in cooking with such a wine—it surely cost more than the entire meal.

He smiled and, leaning toward me with his forearms on the table, said, "Two things, Mark. First, my name is Ben. And second, I'm glad you appreciate the exceptional character of this *grand cru* Pauillac." He swirled the glass. "When it comes to wine, no one holds a candle to the French."

Thinking he'd appreciate the comment, I told him, "Some of the Italian vintners have been making great strides in recent years."

"Bah!" He roared with laughter. "That stuff tastes like coal."

His humor was infectious, and we laughed with him. I said, "In truth, Ben, I've never quite developed a palate for Italian wine myself, but somehow, I presumed you would have."

"Why?" he asked with feigned resentment. "Because my last name ends with an *i*?" He winked at Pierce.

Ashamed, I admitted, "Something like that, yes."

"Look, Mark." He leaned toward me again. "I'm American, period. My parents were Italian, born there, and I certainly respect their heritage—to say nothing of their food. But they came to this country to start over. I was born here, and they raised me as an American. They named me Benjamin, after Mr. Franklin, you know. They spoke some Italian around the house, and I can understand a few phrases, but I never learned the language. I spent my early years on a farm out in the county, but when I was old enough for high school, they moved the family into town—just to make sure I grew up like any other American kid. It was all part of their dream. They wanted a doctor as a son, an American doctor."

Pierce told him quietly, "I'm sure they were very, very proud of you."

"Sure they were." Tenelli sat back, recalling, "I never thought twice about establishing my practice anywhere but here—just to make sure that everyone they knew would never forget that they were 'the doctor's parents.' I know they appreciated that."

"*Everyone* appreciated the fact that you were here," Pierce assured him. "Virtually every baby born in Dumont since the midfifties had you to thank for their first breath—including me. Why'd you retire, Ben?"

"I'm *old!*" He laughed, as if the answer should be self-evident.

"Hardly," I told him. "Age can't be measured in years alone."

"Thank you, both of you. But the truth is, medicine has changed a *lot* since I was young. Hell, when I first hung my shingle, it was the height of the baby boom. We'd won another world war, the economy was spinning like a top, and folks were poppin' out kids left and right—it was a golden age of unbridled optimism. But I don't need to tell you, things got ugly. Assassinations, Vietnam, recession, you name it—and along with this general demoralizing of society, lawyers got greedy and medicine became a popular target. There was a dramatic rise in malpractice suits, and obstetrics became a particularly vulnerable field. It got to the point where I was working not for myself or for my patients, but for the malpractice-insurance guys. Who needs it? By the time I reached sixty-five, I felt more than ready to hand it all over to the next generation." He paused, then smiled. "And I'm enjoying myself immensely."

"Well," said Pierce, "you certainly deserve it." He raised his glass to Dr. Tenelli. I did likewise, and we all tasted more of the wine.

The doctor told us, "The day will come when you guys will be more than ready to hang it up—trust me. Of course, it seems that you, Douglas, are already neck-deep with this murder case." He grunted a short burst of a laugh.

I wasn't sure whether Tenelli was referring to the murder investigation in general or to Pierce's being implicated in it, as revealed only an hour earlier on the radio. How quickly had word traveled? Had he heard that Pierce had shared the victim's bed on the morning of the murder? Was he aware that Pierce had officially stepped out of the investigation? Steering the conversation away from these points, I told Tenelli, "Doug can handle it. In fact, we were brainstorming a new lead just this afternoon, which is really the purpose of this visit."

"Oh?" said the doctor. "I'll help any way I can, naturally."

"Thanks, Ben," Pierce told him. "There's only so much I can tell you, of course, but we're dealing with some new information suggesting that Carrol Cantrell's murder may have some connection to the upcoming obscenity trial."

Tenelli set down his glass and moved it aside. "Good Lord, that sounds terribly . . . involved . . . and sinister."

"We don't know much," said Pierce, evading the need to elaborate, "but I'm wondering if you could tell us anything of your experience with the County Plan Commission. Specifically, how did the committee reach the conclusions that were filed in last Friday's report?"

Tenelli lifted the wine bottle, topping up Pierce's glass, then mine, but not his own, as the bottle was now empty. "I was hoping," he told us, "for the chance to explain that. I'm truly sorry that we find ourselves on opposite sides of the issue."

"It's a free country," Pierce told him. "That's the purpose of public debate."

"Yes, yes, of course. What I'm trying to say, though, is that in my heart of hearts, I *agree* with you both, at least on the fundamentals. Like most educated, rational, freethinking Americans, I deplore the very notion of censorship. When the content of reading and viewing material becomes a matter of public policy, we're *all* in trouble. When that policy is shaped to reflect moralistic or religious standards, as is often the case in this debate, the situation is all the worse, having veered very far indeed from the enlightened intent of our Founding Fathers."

Gosh, I thought, I couldn't have said it better myself. I asked, "Then why did your report take the direction it did?" I wondered, Was he pressured? Was the name Harley Kaiser about to pop up?

No. Tenelli explained, "The committee was charged with addressing a very narrow issue—commercial development of the highway between the city line and the interstate. In our studied opinion, it was an inescapable conclusion that a strip of porn shops on the edge of town simply presents the wrong image to new businesses that may consider relocating to an industrial park being planned for the area. Many on the committee shared my serious reservations about the free-speech implications of the obscenity ordinance, but we ultimately felt that such objections could be judiciously overridden for the sake of Dumont's economic development—which is precisely the issue we were charged with assessing."

Pierce said, "I noticed that the report stopped short of specifically recommending beefed-up enforcement of the ordinance."

"Exactly. There are those who will infer what they will from the report, and that bothers me greatly. Our *intent*, though, was merely to address the desirability of commercial development along the highway, not the means of achieving it."

He'd stated his position well. Fingering the rim of my wineglass, I wondered if I myself would have the intellectual flexibility to endorse the same findings if I'd sat on the County Plan Commission. Would I be able to focus on the committee's stated purpose and draw a pragmatic conclusion, or would I be a slave to my journalistic principles, deciding that the march of commerce was secondary to the rights of a handful of smut peddlers? Tough call.

Pierce told him, "I really appreciate these insights, Ben. I was worried that there might—"

"*Who's here?*" lilted a friendly voice, a woman's voice, interrupting Pierce as the back door swung open. "Why, *Sheriff,* what a surprise," she said, entering the kitchen with a single bag of groceries, setting it on a counter near the refrigerator. She wriggled out of her tweedy autumn topcoat, flung it over the back of a barstool, and approached the table.

We all rose. Tenelli kissed her. Pierce kissed her. She waited—I was next—but I didn't even know the woman. I assumed, of course, that this was Mary Tenelli, the doctor's wife.

She said, "Okay, Mark—your turn."

I obliged with a peck. "My pleasure, Mary. How'd you know my name?"

She jerked her head toward the front of the house. "That car—everybody knows *that* car." She winked at her husband, who laughed.

Was that a joke? What was I missing? I found it odd that both the doctor and his wife, within moments of meeting me, had mentioned my car. Was it simply too conspicuous for the streets of Dumont? Was I thought pretentious for driving it? Surely the Tenellis, with all their affluence and their worldly tastes, would not begrudge me the delights of an overengineered automobile.

Tenelli asked her, "Care for some wine, Mary? I can open another bottle."

"Too early for me"—she flicked her hands—"I'd sleep through dinner." She thought of something: "Did you invite the boys to stay for supper, Ben?"

"Not yet. But I was about to." He turned to us. "How 'bout it?"

"Thanks, but no," said Pierce. "There's a lot going on right now."

I seconded his thanks, telling the doctor, "That's awfully kind of you, but I'm expected at home. Perhaps some other time? I'd enjoy it, and I think you'd enjoy meeting my 'better half,' Neil Waite."

"*Any*time," Tenelli told me, clapping an arm over my shoulder.

"We'd *love* to meet Neil," echoed Mary. "We've heard so much about him."

I'll bet.

"Say," said Tenelli. "You fellas like a good beer now and then, don't you?"

"Sure," said Pierce, "but not now, I'm afraid. We really ought to go."

"Yes, I understand," the doctor said while sidestepping to a door near the hall. "This'll be for later. I want you both to take home something special." He opened the door, switched on a light, and descended the stairs to the basement, calling up to us, "I won't be a minute."

Mary fluttered toward the bag of groceries she'd brought home, telling us over her shoulder, "Lord only knows what he'll find for you down there—he keeps an overstocked kitchen."

Her statement confused me. We were *in* the kitchen, weren't we?

Pierce must have read my puzzled expression, as he explained, "It's sort of a traditional setup among Italian-American households in this area. They have a second kitchen in the basement, used for *serious* cooking, for big family events. More often than not, it's the husband's domain."

"That it is," Mary assured us while arranging on the counter the contents of her shopping bag—bunches of fresh basil and cilantro, fist-size bulbs of garlic, and of course tomatoes—the most gorgeous I'd ever seen. Where had she gotten them? Was there an Italian market in town? While she fussed with all this, we could hear the doctor fussing in the basement. There was a clatter of bottles, then the distinct latching sound of a refrigerator door. As his footsteps creaked up the stairs, Mary told us, "It really *must* be something special if it came from that fridge. He won't let me near it—claims it's his own private stash." She laughed off this territorial eccentricity, doubtless one of many whimsical details that had lent color to their decades of marriage.

"Here we are," he said, huffing up to the top step, nudging the door closed behind him with his hip. In each hand he carried a six-pack of beer. The odd-size bottles and unfamiliar packaging made it clear that the brew he'd fetched was an exotic import, which I figured would be some boutique German brand—after all, he was snobbishly loyal to French *vin*, so I assumed his beer would be *Bier*.

But no. "Chinese," he said, plunking both six-packs before us on the kitchen's center island. "I think you'll really enjoy this. Care to try one now?"

"I'm afraid we—" Pierce started to answer.

"Now, Ben," Mary scolded without rancor, "the boys can't dally here, drinking with you. *They're* not retired."

We all laughed—they were such an easy, likable couple. It was twice now that she had referred to Pierce and me as "boys," and I was surprised to find this diminutive term curiously comforting, perhaps mothering. I didn't know if the Tenellis had children (who would be about my age), but Mary certainly fit the maternal role, which was underscored by her name as well as by her words.

Mary had also spoken the word *dally*, which of course had a resonance that was neither comforting nor mothering, not after our protracted discussion of the etymology of *dalliance*, the word that had flagged our attention in the bogus extortion note, presumably written by Carrol Cantrell's killer. I had to remind myself that the word was nothing more or less than standard English, available for anyone to use on a moment's notice. Yes, the term was a tad unusual, a bit outdated, but there was surely no reason to suspect that sweet Mary Tenelli might be the Dumont strangler, a homicidal psychopath. The notion was absurd.

"Thanks a million, Ben," Pierce was saying as I mulled my rambling thoughts. Hefting his six-pack, he told the doctor, "I'll put this to good use later tonight."

Lifting mine, I thanked Tenelli, adding, "I'll share this with Neil, and we'll toast you and Mary." Checking my watch, I told Pierce, "We'd better run."

"It's such a pleasant afternoon," said Tenelli, "I'll walk you out to the car."

Mary piped in, "Me too," and the four of us headed through the house toward the front door. It was a peculiar little procession, not required by etiquette and in fact rather awkward. I couldn't imagine why the Tenellis seemed so eager to escort us to the car—the weather wasn't *that* nice, and they were both in the midst of preparing their evening meal.

Arriving at the curb, Pierce and I stowed our bottled booty on the floor of the backseat, then got into the car. Starting the engine, I lowered my window to bid farewell, expecting the doctor and his wife to retreat into the house. But they just stood there on the parkway, arm in arm, waving at us—you'd have thought we were embarking for Mars. Pulling away from the curb, I returned their wave, feeling downright foolish, and drove a few yards toward the corner. As I passed their driveway, I glanced at the garage. Then I braked.

The garage door was still open, and parked there was a big Bavarian V-8, just like mine, but green.

I looked back at the Tenellis, who were now laughing. The doctor called to me, "Told you we liked it! Ours is brand-new—picked it up yesterday."

"Enjoy it," I called back to them. And I drove away. Raising my window, I told Pierce with a laugh, "I guess that explains why they kept yapping about my car."

"It does," he agreed. "But it leaves something else *un*explained."

I finished the thought for him: "What was that car doing out at Star-Spangled Video yesterday morning?"

Pierce suggested, "Maybe the good doctor has a taste for smut."

"Maybe. But then why would he issue a report aimed at shutting down the porn shops?"

Pierce thought for a moment. "It doesn't add up."

"No. It doesn't."

Wednesday, September 20

Working at my desk the next morning, I glanced up from a proof of the *Register*'s editorial page and noticed Lucille Haring, my managing editor, walking across the newsroom with a willowy, athletic-looking man. He was younger than I, nicely dressed, and they were headed in my direction. Rising from the desk, I met them at the doorway to my outer office.

"Mark," said Lucy, "I'd like you to meet Lieutenant Daniel Kerr of the sheriff's department. He was kind enough to agree to meet with me this morning regarding our election endorsement."

I shook his hand. "Nice to meet you, Lieutenant. Mark Manning."

"Thank you, Mr. Manning. I appreciate the opportunity to talk, actually."

His tone was not what I expected. After all, this was the detective who was trying to unseat Sheriff Pierce—his own mentor and one of my best friends. I'd presumed that Deputy Dan would come across as a cocky little guy, but neither his manner nor appearance fit that notion. I wanted to study him a bit more, so I asked Lucy, "Where did you plan to conduct your interview?"

She jerked her head—"Conference room down the hall."

I suggested, "Why not use my outer office? It's much more comfortable."

"Great. You're the boss." Reading my intentions, she added, "If you have a few minutes, why don't you join us?"

I checked my watch and surveyed the activity in the newsroom.

"Well," I hemmed, "I suppose I could sit in for a while." With a sweep of my arm, I waved them into the room.

They entered, and the three of us arranged ourselves around the low table. Lucy carried a thick folder of notes, her pen and pad, and a small, black tape recorder. She arrayed these items in front of her and cued up a cassette. Neither Kerr nor I carried anything. I didn't even have my pen and was tempted to go get it, but resisted, as any note-taking would be inconsistent with my role as the "casual observer." Kerr did not dress as a cop, but as a businessman, like the sheriff. The deputy's deep blue suit looked good on him that morning, nicely setting off a thick mop of straight, dark hair, but the outfit was basically workaday; Kerr may have aspired to the sheriff's sense of style, but he hadn't yet attained it. As for me, I'd been caught in my shirtsleeves, cuffs rolled up. I offered, "Coffee, Lieutenant?"

"No, thank you, sir. And please, sir, call me Dan."

I winced—*sir* twice. At forty-two, I was barely comfortable with the concept of middle age, and I still stumbled on *sir.* From a child, fine—but from a thirty-five-year-old detective? Please. "Thanks, Dan. And do call me Mark."

Lucy got down to business. "As you know, Deputy, the *Register* endorsed Sheriff Pierce for reelection in last Saturday's edition. As for our reasoning, that was spelled out clearly enough in the column, which I'm sure you've read. However, circumstances have changed considerably since Saturday, and the paper now finds itself in the embarrassing position of needing to reconsider its endorsement."

As she spoke, I watched Kerr, trying to read his reaction to her words. Granted, we'd called him to this meeting on a false pretext—I had no intention of retracting my endorsement of Pierce, and our real purpose in talking to Kerr was to explore our suspicions that he'd had a hand in planting the extortion note. Unless he was extremely clever, though, he had no reason to doubt Lucy's words, so I assumed he'd hear her message with a measure of glee—he was getting a second crack at securing the town's only meaningful endorsement in his bid for local election. But he didn't appear to gloat in the least. Rather, he listened soberly, hands in his lap, picking at a nasty hangnail that glowed red.

Lucy continued, "Sheriff Pierce has now been implicated in the very murder he was attempting to solve, and as a result, he's turned over the investigation to you. There's an irony here, of course, that I'm sure has not escaped you, namely—"

"I know, ma'am," he interrupted. "It strikes you as fishy that *I* found the note. I'm Doug's opponent in the election, and the note has serious implications for the outcome of the election. Look, ma'am, I want to win it—that's why I'm running—but I want to win it fair and square. I realize that the note looks like high jinks. It slurs Doug, and it makes *me* look like an opportunist—or worse." He paused, gathering his thoughts.

The man was far more perceptive than I'd anticipated. Was he cunning as well, attempting to cover his tracks and win our confidence? Or was he simply being candid? Though I had little to go on, I was inclined to take him at his word.

Leaning toward us, elbows on knees, he continued, "Doug and I are very different people, but we've always respected each other. Without him, I wouldn't have gotten as far as I have in the department. I really *like* the guy—so does my wife, so do my kids. The note makes public a sensitive issue that's been the topic of lots of speculation for years, and I can imagine how rough this is on him. If Doug is gay, that's his business. It doesn't matter. What does matter is this: he's a great cop, and he would never stoop to murder, not even to salvage his career."

His words had a familiar ring. With a soft laugh, I told him, "Doug says the same about you." I hadn't intended to participate in this discussion, but it had taken an unexpected turn. We could drop the pretense that this was an endorsement interview.

"I'm flattered," said Kerr, "but I'm also worried. After all, the note casts suspicion on *both* Doug and me. If the note is genuine, Doug would have a clear motive for murder; if the note is bogus, I'd have the clear motive to plant it."

Lucy nodded, recognizing his succinct appraisal of the situation. "We have a dilemma, then," she told him. "Would you be willing to help us sort it out?"

"What I can tell you is limited, naturally. But go ahead and ask."

"What's your own assessment of the note—fake or real?"

He leaned back in his chair, exhaling loudly. "There's very little to go on. I suppose you've heard that I neglected to check the laptop for fingerprints before I went to work on it."

"We have." Lucy underlined some detail of her notes. "This may seem like an obvious question, but did you happen to notice the time-and-date stamp of the computer file that contained the note?"

"Certainly. The note was written Sunday morning at one minute past seven."

Lucy frowned. "That puts it *before* the murder—the coroner estimates that Cantrell died around nine, so maybe he *did* write the note."

I told her, "Not if the computer was set to California time, two hours earlier."

"I hadn't thought of that," said Kerr. "People reset their watches when traveling between time zones, but I doubt if they bother with their computers."

"Yeah," said Lucy. Taking this line of thought further, she added, "And have you ever noticed how computer clocks never seem to be set correctly? They're always off by a few minutes."

"Right," agreed Kerr. "So if the seven-o'clock note was really written at nine o'clock central time that morning, give or take a few minutes, that puts it very near the time of death."

Thinking aloud, I told them, "That's consistent with my theory that the note was planted by the killer shortly after the murder. Consider the alternative: it seems highly improbable that Cantrell would write the note one minute and get murdered the next."

Kerr nodded. "By that reasoning, Doug is probably off the hook."

"So are you," Lucy told him. "Mark didn't discover the body till around eleven-thirty, so it must have been nearly noon before you arrived on the scene."

Kerr's features brightened. "And the laptop wasn't in my possession till several hours later. I can't recall even glancing at its clock. I'll check it first thing when I get back to the department. I'll bet it *is* on California time, which would mean the note was written by the killer at the crime scene."

There was a moment's silence while we all pondered this. On the one hand, it was heartening to approach the conclusion that neither

Pierce nor his deputy was guilty of the crime; on the other, it threw the investigation back to square one.

Then I thought of a wrinkle. Standing, I paced the office while telling them, "Sorry, Dan, but these circumstances don't completely exonerate you. There are two possibilities that we haven't considered. First, even though you arrived at the crime scene around noon, that doesn't negate the possibility that you slipped up to the coach house earlier—for whatever purpose. Second, even if you had not been there before noon and you didn't have possession of the laptop till later, you could still have reset the computer clock, planted the note to look as if it had been written earlier, then set the clock back to the correct California time."

Lucy arched her brows, impressed that I'd suggested these scenarios. She was drawing a grid on her notepad, organizing her thoughts graphically.

Kerr had listened intently, without taking offense—he understood that my intention was not to accuse him, but merely to raise issues that would have to be addressed. He told me, "The first possibility—that I sneaked up there earlier—is easily dismissed. At nine Sunday morning, I was at church with my family, and there were hundreds of God-fearing witnesses who saw me."

Lucy drew a big X over one of the squares on her grid.

Kerr continued, "The second possibility—that I rigged the computer clock—is tougher to disprove, and frankly, I'm not sure that I can. Truth is, I'm not all that familiar with laptops. I don't own one, and I don't think I'd be clever enough to rig its clock." He asked anyone, "Is it difficult?"

Lucy wagged her head. "Not at all." She was speaking, of course, from the perspective of a computer wiz, a true-blue techie, but I tended to agree with her—Kerr doubtless had sufficient wits to figure out the clock on Cantrell's laptop.

Strolling behind Lucy, I glanced over her shoulder at her notes. She had scrawled a snaky question mark over one of the squares on her grid. Looking across the table toward Kerr, I said, "For purposes of this discussion, Dan, I'm assuming that the extortion note was bogus—Cantrell didn't write it, and Doug didn't kill him. I'm also willing to assume *your* noncomplicity in writing and planting the note. But if you didn't do it, who could have, and why?"

He shrugged. "There weren't that many people who even had access to the computer. If we assume that the clock was *not* tampered with, the note was probably planted by the killer, right there in the coach house at the time of the murder—it could have been anyone—anyone, that is, with a motive. On the other hand, if we assume that the clock *was* tampered with, the note was probably planted after the computer was in police custody."

Lucy asked, "Who had access to it besides you?" She started marking off the rectangles of a new grid on her notepad.

Ticking off possibilities on his fingers, Kerr answered, "Doug had access, as did a handful of department clerks and technicians, and of course the DA's office."

The pen in Lucy's hand froze. "The DA? Did you ever see Harley Kaiser in direct contact with the computer?"

"Yes," Kerr answered, hesitating, "I think so. Well, maybe. There was a lot going on down at the department later that afternoon and into the evening. Harley was around the bull room when I started my search of the victim's files, but I didn't pay much attention to him—I was focused on the files."

While Lucy embellished one of her grid squares with curlicues, I asked Kerr, "Was Kaiser ever alone with the computer?"

"Hard to say. I left my desk from time to time, and he may have been hanging around. He *was* there when I went home Sunday night—he'd asked to use the phone on my desk, and he was still talking when I left."

I sat down next to Lucy and looked Kerr in the eye. "Could you tell who was on the other end of the phone?"

"Sure," he said without a moment's thought, "it was Ben Tenelli. Harley addressed him as 'Doctor' and asked about Mary. So?"

"*Dan*," I said, amazed that he saw no significance to this detail, "aren't you aware that Kaiser and Tenelli are buddies on the porn-shop issue? Kaiser is preparing to bring a must-win obscenity case to trial, and Tenelli has just issued a report from the County Plan Commission that strongly supports Kaiser's case."

Kerr repeated, "So? I support the obscenity ordinance myself—it's one of the few real issues in this election. Plenty of folks are just plain sick of having that trashy element at the edge of town."

"Fine," I said, growing frustrated, "but for the moment, that's not the issue. Consider this: only yesterday afternoon, a probate investigation revealed that Carrol Cantrell owned the controlling interest in a porn-video production company."

"Yes"—Kerr nodded slowly—"I saw that report."

"Also yesterday, Lucy's own research on behalf of the *Register* revealed that Cantrell was in thick with the ACLU, having successfully testified as an expert witness at various smut trials. We also know that Cantrell's true purpose in coming to Dumont was to thwart Kaiser's big case. We suspect that Kaiser may have been aware of Cantrell's background. The stakes are extremely high for Kaiser—the *last* thing he needed was Cantrell encamped here."

"You're not suggesting—?" Kerr couldn't bring himself to voice the thought.

"I'm suggesting that there may be a conspiracy of interested parties, attempting to influence the outcome of that trial. I'm suggesting that your political stand on this single issue—obscenity—makes you an attractive candidate to those with an agenda. Dan, have you considered that you may have become a pawn in something rather sinister?"

Kerr weighed my words, then stood. From his blank expression, I could read neither humiliation nor outrage—either emotion was justified by the circumstances. He paced the length of the room, then turned to me. "Mark"—his voice was calm, inflection flat—"I simply can't believe that there's anything of that sort going on. I understand that Harley has an awful lot riding on this trial, but he wouldn't *kill* to assure its outcome. And as for Doc Tenelli, well, my God, the man is beyond reproach."

"Then what was he doing out at Star-Spangled Video on Monday morning?"

"*What?*" asked Lucy and Kerr in unison.

"Doug and I were out near the edge of town Monday, checking another lead, when we saw Tenelli's new car at Star-Spangled. Apparently he'd just picked it up—maybe he thought no one would recognize it. We didn't know it was *his* till late yesterday, when Doug and I saw it at his house."

Kerr shook his head. "You must be mistaken. Tenelli wouldn't—"

"Dan, I'm *positive*. I recognized the tape marks from the window sticker—it was the same car."

Lucy's grid now had a few new squares on it. "I think I'll run some routine record checks, Mark. Taxes and such. There must be some connection we're not aware of."

"Good idea," I told her.

Kerr insisted, "You're looking for boogeymen under the bed, but there's nothing there." He paused before adding, "Something is troubling me, though."

I stood and stepped a few paces toward him, waiting to hear it.

From where she sat, Lucy asked, "What is it, Deputy?"

He collected his thoughts, as if checking facts against his memory, before telling us, "When I found the extortion note on the laptop on Monday, it was of course a breakthrough clue, and a highly sensitive one at that—the political implications for both Doug and me were obvious. But instead of congratulating myself on a job well done, a mission accomplished, I was embarrassed by the fact that I hadn't found it during my initial search on Sunday. The file containing the note was in a directory that I was sure I'd already gone over—how could I have missed it?"

I suggested, "Maybe you were overtired on Sunday."

"I was. Still, the whole thing struck me as . . . funny."

Lucy said, "It strikes me as 'funny' too."

Glancing back at her, I saw that one of the squares on her grid had been blackened by doodles.

Thad was in a hurry that night, but he wanted to share the events of his school day with us. So Neil and I hustled to get dinner on the table by six-thirty, forgoing the ritual of our cocktail hour, intent on enjoying some quiet time together after Thad left the house.

"What time are callbacks?" Neil asked Thad while heaping a second mound of butter-streaked mashed potatoes on his plate.

"Seven-thirty." He looked over his shoulder at the wall clock.

"Eat," Neil commanded through a grin. "There's plenty of time."

I grinned too. During the weeks Neil had spent in Dumont working on the Quatro project, he'd proven himself a natural at parenting. Though I'd known all along that he possessed many sterling qualities (after all, I "married" the guy), this particular talent came as a surprise to me. Neil was one of the most urbane men I'd ever met; he skillfully wore his intellect and his sophisticated tastes without pretense. I'd seen him adapt his life to mine before, but I would never have guessed that he could so seamlessly slide into the role of "Thad's other dad"—or whatever term best fit this unexpected relationship. In truth, he'd adapted to our offbeat family better than I had, without fretting over the names for our new roles. While I studiously analyzed every niggling situation, attempting to weigh consequences and predict outcomes, Neil simply "went with it."

That Wednesday evening, he'd arrived home from work, learned that Thad had been called back for final auditions for the school play, and was determined to get a square meal on the table in time to let the three of us share some "quality time" before Thad would rush back to school. It wasn't elegant—we were seated in the kitchen—but it was a real dinner, nothing from a bag fetched at a drive-through. Neil had broiled chicken, creating a mysterious but wonderful sauce with whatever was at hand. I took charge of the salad. Thad mashed potatoes. A green vegetable managed to appear. And now we were eating dinner together like three adults—an amazing accomplishment, considering that one of us was only sixteen.

"I couldn't believe it," Thad was saying, "when I saw my name on the callback list. I think I've actually got a *chance*."

"There are only so many roles," Neil reminded him. "But even if you don't end up being cast, it's an honor to be called back."

Clearly, Neil was trying to soften the possible blow of disappointment, but Thad didn't hear it—he was hyped. Swallowing a gulp of milk, he said, "And now I've been called back *twice*."

I was confused. Since I'd never been in a play, this process was foreign to me, and with the murder on my mind since the weekend, I hadn't paid adequate attention to Thad's quest to be cast in *Arsenic and Old Lace*. Wiping my lips with my napkin, I asked him, "You've already auditioned twice?"

"Yeah. General tryouts were after school on Monday. I was nervous, but I must have done okay—Mrs. Osborne called me back with a bunch of others yesterday after school. She said that final callbacks would be tonight, and I made the list. There aren't that many of us."

"That's great," I told him, cuffing his shoulder. "You made the final cut."

"I'm glad I took the time to read the script first. It really helped." He turned to Neil. "Thanks for telling me to do that. Nobody else even bothered—I could tell." Thad ate more of his chicken. "This is good. What's in it?"

Neil laughed. "Beats me. I was sort of rushed."

"Gosh," I said wistfully, "this recipe will never be duplicated. Enjoy it while you can. It *is* good, kiddo."

Brushing off our compliments, Neil feigned demure modesty, telling us, "I'm not accustomed to such flattery." He said it with a Southern accent, like some fragile Tennessee Williams heroine.

Thad found this hilarious, repeating the line, embellishing the accent. My God, I thought, maybe he *does* have a knack for theater.

Neil asked him, "Does Mrs. Osborne have a particular role in mind for you? By this stage, you can usually tell."

"She had me reading lots of parts at first, but last night, she kept asking me to read the part of Dr. Einstein—he's pretty cool."

"Dr. Einstein?" I asked, not remembering that character, at least not by name.

Neil said, "He's Jonathan's sidekick, the plastic surgeon who made the evil brother look like Boris Karloff."

"Of course," I remembered, "the Peter Lorre role in the movie. You'd have a lot of fun with that one, Thad."

Neil asked him, "Have you been reading it with the accent?"

Thad's face went blank. "What accent?"

Neil had to think about it. With a laugh, he admitted, "I'm not exactly sure *what* the accent was—I don't remember if the script spells out where Einstein is from. But Peter Lorre played it sort of German, sort of Eastern European, sort of weaselly. Like: 'But, Chonnie, vee got a hot shtiff in the rrrumble seat.' "

Neil's mimicking was more than passable—it was surprisingly good—and both Thad and I broke into laughter and applause.

Thad said, "Let me try it." And he did. After several tries, with Neil coaching him, Thad had it nailed, and he began practicing the accent on new sentences. He really had an ear for it.

Neil cautioned him, "Your director may not care for the accent, and she's the boss. So when Mrs. Osborne asks you to read the role for the first time tonight, tell her you'd like to try something new with it, then do the accent *once*. If she likes it, keep it up, but if she's cool toward it, drop it and read the role straight."

"Right," said Thad, nodding that he understood the plan. There was such energy in his eyes, though, I got the distinct feeling we'd be hearing a lot of that accent for weeks to come.

Within a few minutes, we'd finished the chicken. As there hadn't been time to fuss with dessert (which Thad wouldn't have had time to eat anyway), our meal was over. Thad offered, "I've got to run, but I can help clear this stuff first."

I was stunned—when did *he* get so agreeable?

Neil told him, "That's okay; we'll take care of it. But go brush your teeth first. And use mouthwash. Respect your instrument."

Oh, brother. I laughed as Thad bounded out of the kitchen and up the stairs. Eyeing Neil, I asked skeptically, " 'Respect your *instrument'?*"

"Theater talk."

Enough said.

Half an hour later, Thad had left for his audition. The night had turned brisk, cold actually, and Neil managed to convince Thad to wear a coat and scarf—out of respect for his instrument, I guess. This all transpired while Neil and I cleaned up the kitchen, carping about the need to replace long-gone Hazel. Though our complaints were lighthearted, they reflected a fact that was increasingly apparent: we did need help.

"Once this murder investigation is comfortably behind us," I told Neil while wiping down the countertop, "we need to have a serious talk, the three of us. We need a housekeeper, probably live-in. Money's not the issue."

"No," Neil agreed, wrapping a few leftovers, stowing them in the refrigerator, "the *issue* is having our home invaded by a stranger, an employee. Those of us not 'to the manner born' find such a setup pretty weird."

"I hear you." Dampening the towel, I wiped out the sink. "But from all accounts, adjusting to domestic help is a hurdle worth jumping. They say it's an easily acquired taste—like champagne or limousines."

Neil nodded while punching the button, starting the dishwasher. "We'll talk about it."

Something else along these lines needed discussion as well—that vacant corner storefront on First Avenue. I was tempted to remind Neil of it, and in fact I opened my mouth to do so. But the words stuck in my throat. Not only was I unsure of how to broach the possibility of moving Neil's architectural practice to Dumont, but I was afraid that if I did, I would not get the response I hoped for. If I pushed too hard, too early, he might reject the idea out of hand. This would have to wait.

Finding much safer ground, I asked, "Ready for a drink? We missed cocktails."

"Sure." He breathed a relaxed sigh. "That sounds great."

With a flash of inspiration, I suggested, "Why don't we have them in the den? The night's turned cold—I can light a fire, the first of the season."

Neil stepped to me and slung his arms around my waist. "That sounds rather cozy, Mr. Manning. I daresay romantic."

"I daresay," I agreed, kissing him. "Tell you what: I'll get the fire ready. You bring the hooch."

He laughed. "Deal."

The den in the house on Prairie Street was originally my uncle Edwin Quatrain's home office. Located on the first floor adjacent to the front hall, it occupied a corner, with tall windows facing prime views in two directions. Though I now claimed this generous space as my own private domain, I had changed little of the already handsome quarters.

The room was dominated by my uncle's massive partners desk, a beautiful old piece of furniture that bore no resemblance to Bruno Hérisson's delicate cylinder-top desks. Not intended for milady's letter-writing, but for work, the two-sided mahogany desk was covered by an oversize suede blotter. Matching leather chairs faced each other from identical arched kneeholes.

Away from the desk, a tidy chesterfield suite—a studded leather love seat with two matching armchairs—surrounded a coffee table, facing the fireplace. The oak mantel and brick surround had been custom-designed by the Taliesin architect, so the style could be described as neither traditional nor modern, but artfully geometric, somewhat sculptural, vaguely Oriental. Between the gunmetal andirons stood logs and kindling, arranged there since spring, ready for the match. Opening the flue, I checked the draft, flicked a lighter, and touched the flame to the crumpled old copies of the *Register* that were stuffed beneath the grate. Within seconds, the burning newspapers filled the room with their yellow glow.

Neil rattled through the doorway with a tray and shuffled to the coffee table, setting down his load. The tray held an ice bucket, two heavy crystal glasses, strips of orange peel on a saucer, and the bottle of Japanese vodka, just plucked from the freezer. The frost-covered bottle, now placed within inches of the flames, was already streaked with tears that formed a pool at its base. "Fire and ice," Neil cooed. "I love that."

"And I love *you*," I reminded him, patting his knee as we sat together on the sofa. Leaning forward to the table, I plunked ice into the glasses, uncapped the bottle (it was still cold enough to burn my fingertips), and poured. Neil twisted the orange peel over both drinks; backlit by the fire, tiny droplets of citrus oil could be seen exploding in midair, instantly filling the room—and our nostrils—with their piquant scent.

Neil handed me one of the glasses, then touched his own to it. "To saner times," he told me. And we sipped the icy vodka.

Settling back into the sofa with our drinks, I rested my free arm around Neil's shoulders, cuddling. A minute or two passed in silence as we watched the fire.

I took a fresh sip from my glass. "We haven't done this enough lately. I hope you don't feel that I've come to take your presence here for granted."

"I would *never* feel that," he joshed.

"I mean, our situation right now, the Quatro assignment—it feels as if we're living together again, but we both know it's sort of 'borrowed time.' "

He touched a finger to my lips. "Don't go there, not now. Let's just enjoy the time we *do* have together. As to the future—who knows?"

What did *that* mean? Was he saying that we'd just have to adjust to our future separation, or was he hinting that it was time to review our alternating-weekend "arrangement"? If we did review the arrangement, which way was he leaning? Did I have reason to hope that he might join me in Dumont permanently? I was tempted to ask, but once again feared that his response would disappoint me. So I heeded his advice and let the issue rest.

He interrupted my thoughts, saying, "I hesitate to ask, but what's new with King Carrol's case?"

"Quite a bit, actually." Plenty had transpired in the last two days, but the previous evening had kept Neil late at the Quatro plant, and we'd had no relaxed time together when I could bring him up to speed. He already knew about Monday's bombshell—the bogus extortion note "outing" Pierce and implicating him in the murder—but Neil had heard nothing yet about what we'd learned of Cantrell's background.

Collecting my thoughts, I downed a hefty slug of vodka, then told Neil, "The plot has thickened considerably. First, probate revealed that Cantrell owned controlling interest in a highly profitable gay-porn video company—it essentially subsidized his miniatures museum. Second, Lucy discovered that he had connections with the ACLU and frequently testified as a free-speech advocate at porn trials—he was planning to appear for the defense in the case now being mounted in Dumont by Harley Kaiser. Third, while Deputy Dan is the obvious suspect for having planted the bogus extortion note, I think he may simply be a pawn in some conspiracy to shut down the porn shops—suggesting the possible complicity of the DA himself."

"Wow." Neil had gotten an earful, and he needed a moment to sort through it. He chomped an ice cube, swallowing it. "Which video company did Cantrell own?"

I laughed. Aware of Neil's long-standing interest in erotic videos, I'd had a hunch he'd zero in on that detail of my revelations. "I knew you'd ask, but I can't quite remember the name of the company—those porn studios all sound so much alike. It was something like . . ." Then it clicked. "I've got it. It was Hot Head Video."

Neil pulled a leg up onto the sofa, turning to face me. "Cantrell owned Hot Head? No way!"

"You've heard of it?"

"Well *sure*." His tone suggested I was completely out of it. "Hot Head is one of the biggest names in the business—has been for years."

"Are they . . . 'good'?" My question sounded stupid, but Neil understood what I was trying to ask: Did Hot Head simply grind out sleaze, or did they measure up to Neil's finicky, somewhat cerebral, porn standards?

"Good? They're great. Hot Head redefined the gay video when they burst onto the scene back in the seventies. Their production values have always been first-rate, and their scripts always have a *plot*, a real story that goes beyond the hard-core action—though there's plenty of that too, of course."

"Lucy mentioned that the studio is strictly legit—no kiddie porn, for instance."

"Absolutely. In the world of porn, Hot Head is a class act."

It was an odd compliment, but there was nothing facetious about Neil's tone, and I trusted his judgment in this arena. I thought aloud, "If Hot Head has enjoyed such a respected reputation, I suppose that's a credit to Cantrell—he was the founder and guiding force."

"I suppose," Neil conceded, hesitating. "Cantrell must have stayed in the background, though, because I don't recall anything in the press about him. If you ask me, Hot Head Video owes its success to one man—Rascal Tyner."

The name had a familiar ring, but I couldn't place it. "Who?"

"*You* remember," said Neil, gently shaking my shoulder as if to jog my memory. "Rascal Tyner. He was the gorgeous young headliner who took the porn world by storm during Hot Head's early days.

Overnight, he catapulted Hot Head to the status of a major player in the gay video business."

"I *do* remember that." Though Neil was speaking of gay-porn history that was made more than twenty years earlier—long before I would recognize that I myself was gay—I could indeed recall the name, even the face, of Rascal Tyner. He was a phenomenon, a true star, whose sheer sexual magnetism garnered ample attention in the mainstream press. I remembered, "He was widely rumored to be straight."

"Right," said Neil. "That might have been PR—he might have been eyeing a career shift to the larger straight audience—but who cares? Even if he wasn't gay, he was more than convincing onscreen. He turned out an astounding oeuvre of flicks for legions of hungry gay fans who couldn't get enough of him. He enjoyed a meteoric career in the late seventies, when home VCRs were first introduced. It wasn't just his obvious physical attributes that secured his porn stardom, though. The guy could really *act,* which set him far apart from his hunky colleagues who had never uttered a line in the silent days of eight-millimeter porn." Neil shook his head wistfully, adding, "It was even said that Rascal Tyner never needed a fluffer—not once in all that taping."

Just when I thought I was following all this, I was lost. "What's a 'fluffer'?"

Neil grinned, sliding his hand between my legs. "A fluffer is an off-camera stagehand. His sole duty is to keep the star aroused between takes."

"Tough duty." I laughed, imagining the creative means I might employ to keep Rascal Tyner camera-ready. I let my head fall back, enjoying the feel of Neil's hand on my crotch—his attentions were having the predictable effect. But then I thought of something. Something bothersome. Turning my head toward Neil, I asked, "Something happened, right? What happened to Rascal Tyner?"

Neil withdrew his hand from my legs, sipped his vodka, and set down the glass. "AIDS happened. Rascal Tyner's career ended in 1983, when he was felled by AIDS during the early days of the epidemic. Condoms were not yet standard equipment in porn videos, and his death taught the industry a painful lesson."

"Now I remember," I said, sipping from my own glass, which had turned sweaty in my hands. "The story was widely reported during the onset of the 'gay plague.' It made sensational headlines for a month. All the newsweeklies did cover stories. I wasn't 'out' yet—it would be many years before you helped me find myself—but the story sure caught my attention. It made me curious."

"I'll *bet* it did."

"I *mean*, it made me curious about Rascal Tyner. I recognized that his death was tragic, but I couldn't imagine all the hoo-ha over his videos. There was a colleague at the paper whom I knew to be gay, so I asked him why these particular videos were considered so special. The next day, he left a cassette on my desk with a note: 'A picture's worth a thousand words. See for yourself.' I took it home, and that night I got my first glimpse of gay porn—and Rascal Tyner."

"*Well* now," said Neil with a grin, having never heard this story before, "I guess you *were* curious. You got a first-class initiation. What'd you think of it?"

Evasively, I answered, "It was . . . interesting. I could appreciate that he'd developed a following." In truth, I'd found the tape mesmerizing. Alone in my apartment, I watched it through several times that night. And I now realized that ever since, I had carried with me erotic visions of the long-gone porn star named Rascal Tyner.

"Which tape did you see?"

I shook my head—I couldn't possibly remember the title after so many years. "Some commemorative anthology, lots of scenes spliced together."

"My God, that must have been *Rascal Tyner's Hottest Hits*. It was released in the early eighties, rushed out within weeks of his death. It was the very first tape in my collection, the one Roxanne bought for me in college. I've been a fan of Hot Head Video ever since. And you know what? Even though that compilation of clips is umpteen years old, I still consider it the best."

Offhandedly I asked, "Do you still have it?" I swirled the remnants of my drink and drained the glass.

"Of course. It's back at the loft with the rest of the collection."

We fell quiet, watching the dance of the fire for a few moments.

Then Neil had an idea—one that I could have predicted. "Hey," he said, sitting upright on the edge of the sofa, "Roxanne is driving up this weekend. She checks the loft for us now and then. Why don't I ask her to bring up the *Hottest Hits* tape? It'd be a hoot—a trip down memory lane, so to speak."

"If you want. I don't care."

Truth is, after so many years, I couldn't wait to get another look at it.

Thursday, September 21

Call it mistrust. Call it a skeptical hunch. Go ahead, call it paranoia. Whatever name best labels it, a nagging suspicion kept telling me that Dumont's district attorney was somehow involved in the Carrol Cantrell case—if not in the murder itself, then possibly in planting the extortion note that had thwarted the investigation, "outed" Doug Pierce, and threatened to influence the outcome of an important local election. After all, the impending obscenity trial gave Harley Kaiser a clear conflict of interest in all this. What's more, Roxanne Exner, a shrewd judge of character with an insider's view of the law biz, had derided Kaiser's hot-dog tactics before she'd even met him. So . . . I invited the man to lunch.

My purpose, of course, was not to break bread with Kaiser, but to sound him out. Perhaps over a meal, one-on-one, he would let slip a detail or two that could shed light on his true role in this. When I phoned him that Thursday morning to extend the invitation, I needed some pretext (chummy we weren't), so I told him that I felt the need to atone for interrupting his lunch with Pierce on Monday when Roxanne and I joined them at their table.

"I appreciate the thought, Manning," he told me dryly on the phone, "but no harm was done. No payback is required or expected."

He was ready to hang up, so I fudged, "Actually, Harley, there's a matter of some importance—and delicacy—that I'd like to discuss with you. It regards the *Register*'s endorsement of Doug Pierce."

"Oh?" His voice now carried the distinct ring of interest. "When would you like to meet, Mark?"

"How about high noon? First Avenue Grill."

"I'll be there."

And he was. I arrived a minute or two past the hour to find him waiting near the door. Dumont had weathered the season's first hard frost overnight—a few weeks early—and the dawn had broken bright but cold. So we both wore topcoats that day. Meeting inside the entrance to the Grill, we greeted each other and shook hands while shrugging out of our coats, an awkward little duet that would become better-practiced as the season grew colder. The hostess took our coats while ushering us to my table between the fireplace and the window. A shaft of noontide sunlight angled through the plate glass, confirming that the earth's axis had tipped.

Our waitress appeared with menus, offering drinks. I ordered a Lillet, hoping that Kaiser might also opt for alcohol (the better to loosen his lips), but he ordered coffee instead, "black and hot." He emphasized these instructions to the waitress with a nod of dismissal, which wagged his mound of poodle hair.

Unfolding my napkin and dropping it to my lap, I asked, "Did Deputy Kerr mention that he came into the office for an interview yesterday?"

"He did," confirmed Kaiser, unfurling his own napkin with a snap. "Rather, he mentioned that he was *going* to. I haven't spoken to him since the meeting." Kaiser leaned forward, no more than an inch. Through the faintest of smiles, he said, "I understand that the paper was reevaluating its endorsement. What happened?"

I needed to weigh my response. Both the meeting with Kerr and the present lunch with Kaiser had been called under the same false pretext. Kerr now knew that the real purpose of yesterday's meeting was to evaluate the authenticity and origin of the extortion note, which he himself assumed to be spurious. Kerr was also aware that he had raised my own suspicions of Kaiser. Had any of this been conveyed to Kaiser? Or was Kaiser on the level just now when he told me he hadn't spoken to Kerr since the meeting? It was possible, even likely, that Kerr had been avoiding contact with Kaiser, not wishing to report what we'd discussed.

Waffling, I told Kaiser, "Our meeting was inconclusive. If the *Register* is to retract its endorsement of Doug Pierce, we have to feel certain that his implication in the Cantrell murder wasn't a setup. If Doug has committed a crime, he's obviously unfit for office. But short of that, I'm still reluctant to switch our endorsement to Dan Kerr. As you know, we have some serious philosophical differences."

Kaiser nodded. "Obscenity."

"Some call it censorship."

"I'm not here to dither over semantics," he told me, sitting back in his chair, pointedly putting some distance between us. "The law is clear. The sheriff's job is to enforce it; mine is to prosecute violators. If the current sheriff has a problem with that, he should be replaced. If, far worse, he's a criminal, he should be behind bars."

"You're getting ahead of yourself, aren't you, Harley? Don't you presume Doug innocent? He has that right, you know. Stay objective."

Kaiser snorted a short, derisive laugh. "Doug's got a serious problem, Manning, and you know it. I like the guy—we grew up together—and I'm giving him every benefit of the doubt. But I can't simply look the other way when I'm faced with a compelling piece of evidence. What's happened to *your* objectivity? Is it out the window because you and Doug are friends, because you're . . . 'alike'?"

"Hot coffee, black," said the waitress—a fortuitous interruption. "And your Lillet, Mr. Manning. Need some more time with the menus?"

"We haven't looked yet," I told her with a wan smile, and she disappeared.

Kaiser sipped his coffee. Returning the cup to the saucer, he huffed a long breath through puckered lips, blowing off steam—the coffee was indeed hot. Oddly, this process seemed to calm him. "Look," he told me, "contention serves no purpose here. There's a riddle to be solved: Who killed Carrol Cantrell? You have your suspicions, and I have mine, but ultimately there's only one answer. It's safe to say, all concerned are in search of that answer—the one answer, the truth."

"Of course." I nodded my assent—his reasonable words left little room for argument. Tasting my Lillet, I reviewed the whole riddle as the soothing, velvety liquor wrapped my tongue. After swallowing, I told him, "Our hunches may differ, Harley, but we can at least agree on the known facts. Consider: Cantrell came to Dumont with the stated purpose of judging a miniatures show. He arrived here early, as did Bruno Hérisson, with whom he shared a long-standing and bitter professional rivalry. On Sunday morning at eleven-thirty, I found Cantrell dead, apparently the victim of a strangulation that occurred around nine that morning. On Monday, Deputy Kerr found the draft of an extortion note in the victim's computer, implying that there'd been sexual relations with the sheriff and attempting to extort unspecified 'considerations' from the sheriff, presumably hush money. Now, *if* there's any truth to the assertion that Doug and Cantrell had been—"

"It's true." Kaiser wasn't gloating, merely stating a fact. "As you know, Doug turned the whole investigation over to Deputy Kerr late Monday, after the note was found. Since then, Doug decided to clear the air, I guess, and to spare the investigation the unseemly grunt work of digging into the dirty details. He provided Kerr with a statement, acknowledging that he and Carrol Cantrell had spent several nights together. He insists, however, that when he left the coach house at around seven Sunday morning, Cantrell was alive and well, and no threats of blackmail had ever been made."

This was news to me. I took a quick sip from my glass and swallowed without tasting it. "When did Doug provide this statement?"

"Wednesday—yesterday."

I thought aloud, "He didn't mention it to me. Was it late in the day?"

"In fact, it was. It may have been in the evening."

I sat back, mulling the implications of Pierce's statement to his deputy. First, it meant that he had taken an enormous, difficult step forward in acknowledging his sexual identity. Dumont County now had a self-declared gay sheriff. In terms of the murder investigation, he'd proven his integrity—and I couldn't have felt prouder of him for risking such honesty. In terms of the election, however, he'd wandered onto thin ice.

This alone gave me plenty to ponder, but I also recognized a further, more insidious, implication to what Kaiser had just told me. I now knew that Kaiser and Deputy Kerr had in fact spoken to each other since my Wednesday-morning meeting with Kerr at the *Regis-*

ter. Kaiser had baldly told me otherwise not five minutes earlier; he had lied to me. While recognizing that the DA did not "owe" me the truth—the official murder investigation was frankly none of my business—he had committed this lie in the guise of fellowship and cooperation. So I knew that he was not trustworthy. Was there reason to assume, then, that he was capable of complicity in the very crime he now sought to prosecute? And what of Deputy Dan? Were he and Kaiser possibly involved in this together?

Picking up our discussion, I told Kaiser, "Logically, then, we're faced with two possibilities. Either Doug lied in his statement about not being blackmailed by Cantrell, or Doug left the guy happy as a clam on Sunday morning, which suggests that the extortion note was planted by someone other than the victim, most likely the killer himself." I arched my brows as if to ask, Have I overlooked anything?

Kaiser gulped from his coffee cup—it had cooled some. He agreed, "Those would seem to be the two possibilities. If Pierce did it, his motive was clear enough. If someone else did it, the only one with a known motive was Bruno, but he appears to have a strong alibi. I know of no one else who had a 'problem' with Cantrell." He looked me straight in the eye. "Do you?"

Of course I did. Kaiser himself had a major problem with Cantrell, as did anyone else with an interest in the outcome of the pending obscenity trial. By his question, he implied that he still knew nothing of Cantrell's links to the ACLU, that he had no idea that Cantrell's purpose in Dumont was to thwart Kaiser's efforts in court. I knew this background only because Lucille Haring's own research had revealed it. I strongly suspected that Kaiser had known it all along, as suggested by his strange visit to the coach house with Miriam Westerman on Saturday morning. For whatever reason, Kaiser was choosing to play dumb on this point, and I saw no reason to challenge him on the issue—not yet—so I decided to play the same game. I told him, "Maybe we need to look at this more . . . broadly."

"What does *that* mean?" He asked the question with a smirk, as if I were a half-wit, and a meddling one at that. Clearly, he did not appreciate my interest in this case. He wanted me to simply go away.

He could bet I wouldn't, though, so his only choice was to follow my discussion down this new path.

I leaned forward, elbows on the table, explaining, as if these were fresh ideas, "What if we've *missed* something—something obvious?"

"Like what?" Sarcastically, he suggested, "A suicide note? Maybe Cantrell strangled *himself*."

I wanted to slap Kaiser's smug poodle-puss. Instead, I laughed off his comment, telling him, "No, of course not. But what if Cantrell was not, in fact, strangled? Maybe the killer contrived the crime scene to make it *look* that way." I was grasping for possibilities, however remote.

Kaiser shook his head. "Vernon issued his initial findings no more than an hour ago." Kaiser was referring to Dumont County's coroner, Vernon Formhals. "He estimates the time of death to be very near nine o'clock that morning, as we'd already guessed, and he confirms that Carrol Cantrell was indeed strangled. Vernon's final report, though, will not be issued until results of routine toxicology tests are received."

"That can take weeks," I thought aloud.

"Yes, sometimes."

So I ventured into stickier territory, conceding, "Okay, let's assume Cantrell died of strangulation. We know the method. But we're not sure of the motive."

"We've got two strong possibilities," Kaiser reminded me.

"But maybe there's a third."

"I can't imagine what. Probate revealed no heirs or business associates who stood to profit from the crime."

There. He'd opened the door. So I played my hand, telling him, "You're well aware, then, that probate also revealed Cantrell's business dealings in the porn industry. Further, the *Register*'s own investigation revealed Cantrell's reputation as a free-speech crusader. And a simple phone call to Aldrich and Associates confirmed that he had a purpose in Dumont not related to the miniatures show. He was here to fight you in court on the obscenity issue—and there's plenty to suggest that you knew this."

Fingering his saucer, Kaiser leaned forward, as if to suggest that we should both lower our voices. "All right. That's a factor."

"When did you know this background, Harley?"

With a quiet laugh (sort of a breathy sneer), he told me, "I'm not accountable to *you*, Manning."

"But I'm accountable to my readers," I reminded him without flinching. "The people of Dumont County deserve to know if their elected district attorney has engaged in unethical behavior—for the purpose of swaying the outcome of a politically sensitive trial. The issue is witness tampering. It's a serious matter, and to my way of thinking, it might warrant a page-one editorial. If so, tomorrow morning's headline will ask a simple, direct question: WHAT DID HARLEY KAISER KNOW, AND WHEN DID HE KNOW IT?" Sitting back comfortably, I concluded, "Or would you prefer to clear the air right now?"

Again he laughed quietly, but this time it was no sneer—he was squirming. "Well, I don't suppose there's any need to make a public hoo-ha over this, is there? Especially when your suspicions—which are quite understandable, Mark—can be dispatched so easily. What exactly would you like to know?" He stretched his lips into a false, toothy smile, the very picture of accommodation.

Before restating my question, I slipped my pen and steno pad onto the table, readying both for note-taking. He knew that his words were for public consumption when I asked, "What was your purpose in visiting Carrol Cantrell at the coach house last Saturday?"

Mechanically, like a witness on the stand, he recited, "My only purpose in being there was to accompany Miriam Westerman. As I told you before, the visit was her idea. When we overheard Cantrell on the phone and he mentioned the Miller standard, I was stunned. I suddenly realized that I may have put myself in an ethically questionable position that could compromise the pending trial. On Monday, when Aldrich and Associates issued their witness list for the defense, I learned that Cantrell had in fact been slated to testify. On Tuesday, with the release of the California probate report, I learned of his interest in the pornographic video industry. But none of that background was known to me on Saturday when I met him."

Looking up from the notes I was writing, I asked, "When Miriam suggested the visit, didn't you ask its purpose?"

"Of course. It all seemed so . . . lamebrained."

"That's Miriam," I muttered.

Gliding past this, he continued, "She simply told me that the visit was important. She told me coyly that I'd understand later."

"When you left the coach house, did you ask her to explain?"

"*No*—at that point I didn't *want* to know. I suspected that Cantrell might somehow be linked to the trial, so I deliberately put my blinders on. I wanted no direct knowledge of his purpose here."

"Did you assume at that point that Miriam knew why he was here?"

He shrugged. "She must have, right?"

Rhetorically, I wondered aloud, "But how could she possibly . . . ?"

"Ask her yourself," he told me, mustering a bit of his old spunk.

"My point, Harley, is this: Carrol Cantrell came to Dumont to testify at an obscenity trial, and now he's dead. Doesn't it seem at least feasible that there's some connection? Why haven't you brought this possibility to the attention of the sheriff's investigation? Why haven't you explored this angle yourself?"

He glanced at my pad. "I'd appreciate it if you'd put away your notes now."

I did so, then repeated, "Why haven't you officially explored these matters?"

Quietly but firmly, he answered, "Because there's nothing *to* explore. If Cantrell's death is related to the obscenity case, it points directly to me—obviously. But good Lord, *I* didn't kill the guy. So what the hell would I investigate?"

Barely above a whisper, I suggested, "Conspiracy," leaning close.

He seemed astounded. Collecting his thoughts, he whispered fiercely, "Are you insane? Who—just for the sake of argument, please—who could conceivably populate the cast of characters in this imaginary conspiracy? Who, besides me, has a vested interest in the outcome of that obscenity trial?"

Dryly, I ticked off, "Deputy Kerr. Miriam Westerman. Dr. Tenelli."

He rolled his eyes. He didn't bother whispering when he lectured, "I won't even address the absurdity of your suggestion that either Dan Kerr or Miriam Westerman could be a party to murder. But if you seriously believe that I'll tolerate your audacity in even *hinting* that there could be collusion with Benjamin Tenelli, you're sadly mistaken. You're still a newcomer to Dumont, Manning, but in case you haven't heard, you'd better learn that Ben Tenelli is probably the finest man who's ever served this community. His name is not to be invoked lightly—and I'm frankly appalled that you would stoop to use him in such a manner."

I took a moment to set my glass aside, a deliberate movement that allowed me to lean within inches of Kaiser over the table. "Harley, I'm equally appalled that *you* would stoop to use him."

"I *beg* your pardon?"

"Do you actually think that I'm willing to assume sheer coincidence in the timing of the County Plan Commission's call for a crackdown on porn? Doesn't it strike you as a tad suspicious that the revered doctor's report, which stops just short of demanding the forced closure of Dumont's porn shops, was issued virtually on the eve of an obscenity trial that, politically, you *must* win? Harley, face it: it looks for all the world as if you exerted some behind-the-scenes influence on Tenelli and his committee."

As I spoke, Kaiser's expression of dismay transformed itself to a look of confusion, then amusement. He now broke into laughter—loud, gut-forced laughter that quelled conversation throughout the dining room and fetched an audience of quizzical stares. As his laughter waned, he made a show of dabbing tears from his eyes with his napkin as he turned to apologize to nearby tables for the outburst.

When the others had returned their attention to their lunch, when the noise of the room swelled to its previous level, Kaiser's expression turned dead serious. He fixed me in his stare and told me, "You've got it backwards. If there's been any pressure exerted between Tenelli and me, it hasn't been from me—but from *him*."

Thinking this through, I couldn't imagine what Kaiser meant.

Reading the confusion in my face, he explained, "Ben Tenelli has spent a lot of time on the phone with me in recent months, and he's shown a lot of interest in the impending trial. He's expressed concern about the timing of the case, and at times I've felt that he was rushing me. He called it 'good strategy' for the trial to open in conjunction with his committee's report."

" 'Strategy'? Why the plan? What's the goal?"

"The good of the community, I'm sure. Ben feels strongly that the porn shops have a negative impact on Dumont's economic development."

"So I've heard."

"The man's above reproach, Mark. He's as good as they get, a model of altruism."

"So I've heard."

Returning to the office after lunch, I was pondering the several new angles I'd gleaned from Kaiser, when Connie called to me from her lobby window, "Mr. Manning—the sheriff's upstairs with Miss Haring. They both need to see you."

Waving my thanks for the message, I climbed the flight of stairs to the newsroom, looked about for Doug Pierce and Lucille Haring, then noticed that they were huddled at the table in my outer office. Crossing through the maze of news desks, I could see through the glass wall of my office that the table was spread with a mess of paperwork. As I entered the room, I closed the door behind me, asking, "What's up?"

They both stood. Lucy pointed to the pile of papers on the table. "Today's mail brought an inordinate number of letters to the editor, and—guess what—they're all on the same topic."

Doug explained, "They all demand my resignation."

With a wry laugh, I conjectured, "And their wording is uncannily similar."

" 'Uncanny' hardly describes it," said Lucy, sitting, picking a handful of the letters at random. "Listen: 'Dumont County's chief law-enforcement officer has committed an abomination against Mother Nature.' And another: 'Sheriff Pierce has used his penis as a weapon to intimidate Dumont's citizens and to disgust Mother Nature.' And still another: 'Mother Nature herself has decreed this flagrant penis cultist unfit for public office.' "

"I've got the idea," I told Lucy before she could read more. Sitting at the table, I sifted through a stack of the letters, confirming that they were all alike. Not only was their wording similar, but they were all handwritten, all lacking return addresses, all signed with jerky pseudonyms like *Watching and Waiting*, *A Friend of the Family*, and the highly original *A Concerned Citizen*. One was even signed by *Mother Nature* herself. Turning to Pierce, I said, "Considering the source, I wouldn't let these bother you. Rest assured—they'll never see print."

He sat next to me. "Thanks, Mark. Things are starting to move pretty fast now. Frankly, my future *is* feeling uncertain. The last thing I need is a hostile letter-writing campaign from a bunch of crazed feminists." Turning to Lucy, he added, "No offense, Miss Haring."

"None taken," she assured him, sitting with us at the table. "I've always supported equality of the sexes in the workplace and in society at large, but Miriam Westerman and her group take the notion to another plane entirely."

"The cosmological plane," I suggested with a derisive laugh. "What's the group's full name? I always have trouble with it."

Lucy scratched her scalp. "Beats me. I'll look it up."

"That won't be necessary," said Pierce, whose history with Westerman traced back to their high-school days. "FSNACH, or Fem-Snach, stands for the Feminist Society for the New Age of Cosmological Holism. Catchy, huh?"

Lucy shook her head in dismay. "And to think: Miriam Westerman is now headmistress of a school that indoctrinates *kids* with such crap."

"She belongs in a loony bin," I told them, never passing up a chance to defame the woman. Tossing my handful of letters back onto the pile like so much garbage, I reminded them, "When I first moved to Dumont last December, Miriam and her coven of crones used the same tactic on *me*, hoping to drive me out of town with their hate mail. I had no idea who was behind it, of course, so it made for a rather frightening welcome. I called the cops."

"If I'm not mistaken," said Pierce, "that was when you and I first met—Christmas morning, as I recall."

"Exactly. It was good of you to come to the house on such short notice, on a holiday, no less. You calmed me down, Doug, and gave me the lowdown on Miriam." I leaned toward him. "I've thought of you as a friend since that first meeting, and I'm happy to return the favor now by assuring you that Miriam's hateful antics, while annoying, don't mean squat."

As I said this, I extended a comforting hand and patted his knee, letting my fingers rest there. Though I'd felt fondness for the man since the day we'd met, though I'd had vibes from the beginning that he might be gay, I'd always felt uneasy about showing any physical signs of my affection. For some nine months, he'd allowed me his friendship but had deprived me of the very nuggets of knowledge upon which true friendship is built—he hadn't "let me in." Now, only three days ago, he'd finally come out to me, and though the circumstances were not of his choosing, the effect of his disclosure was nonetheless liberating. I now felt no qualms whatever about touching the man, and I didn't have to disguise such a gesture as a ritualized handshake or an "accidental" brushing of shoulders. I simply put my hand on his leg, and I left it there.

To my utter amazement, he placed his hand over mine, telling me, "Thanks, Mark. I was just doing my job last Christmas. Now, you've really gone out on a limb for me."

I laughed. "This is one hell of a story. When this is all over, I plan to sell a few papers."

Lucy cleared her throat. "I hate to interrupt the schmaltz, gentlemen, but if we're going to sell papers, we need to meet deadlines." Her admonishment, though mild and good-natured, was pointed—we had work to do. Focusing our discussion, she cleared a space on the table for her folder of notes, asking, "Where are we?"

Sitting back in my chair, I told them, "I just had lunch with the DA. He told me flatly that he had no knowledge of Cantrell's porn-related background when he met him at the coach house on Saturday. He insists that the visit was Miriam's idea—and if it was, we're faced with some intriguing new questions. Meanwhile, though, Kaiser is up to something, I'm sure. I don't trust him."

Pierce looked at me skeptically. "I don't much *like* him either, Mark, but I can't believe Harley Kaiser is covering up any actual involvement with this case."

I raised a hand, a note of caution, repeating, "He's *up* to something. I don't know if Kaiser actually strangled Carrol Cantrell. I don't know if he actually planted the fake blackmail note on the victim's computer. But I do know this: he's been heavily involved with the sainted Dr. Tenelli in planning a 'strategy' to shut down the porn shops on the edge of town. Some might call that 'politics as usual,' but I call it 'conspiracy.' The true purpose of their plotting? I don't know yet. But I cannot dismiss as coincidence the fact that their unknown purpose has been served by Cantrell's death."

Pierce listened, slowly shaking his head while considering my words. He was clearly uncomfortable hearing that my suspicions ran in this direction.

Lucy scratched at her notes, looking up at me. "You say that Kaiser and Tenelli have been 'involved.' What do you mean?"

"They've been spending a lot of time on the phone together. Deputy Dan noted this during our meeting yesterday, then Kaiser himself confirmed it at lunch. And *here's* an interesting twist: I don't know whether to believe Kaiser, but he claims Tenelli has been pressuring *him*, not vice versa."

"Huh?" asked Pierce. "That makes no sense. I might be willing to believe that Harley pressured the doctor regarding the report of the County Plan Commission—its findings and its timing could help assure Harley a victory in the obscenity trial. But what conceivable purpose could Tenelli have in pressuring the DA?"

"Good question. And here's another: What conceivable purpose could Tenelli have had out at Star-Spangled Video on Monday morning, when we spotted his new car?" Turning to Lucy, I asked, "Any luck with that little research project?"

"Not yet," she told me dryly, flipping a page of her notebook. "Tenelli's tax records pointed to nothing suspicious. Now, I presume, you want a complete background check, right?"

"Right—association memberships, financial interests, that sort of thing. When Doug and I talked to him on Tuesday, he mentioned malpractice suits. Maybe that's worth exploring."

Lucy nodded, checking over her notes. "It'll take me a day or so to get to this. The digging is slow when you don't know what you're looking for."

"Whenever you can get to it—just let me know if you find anything."

Pierce said, "I think you're barking up the wrong tree. Ben Tenelli already explained to us his position on the porn shops—it was a carefully weighed decision in which he allowed the pragmatic concerns of commercial development to overrule his own philosophical objections. You may not agree with his conclusion, Mark, but I think you'll have to admit that he was honest in arriving at it. Ben has no 'agenda'—all he wants is what's best for the town."

I stood, needing to pace. "Doug, you keep telling me that. *Everyone* keeps telling me that. Maybe I should just take your word and lay off the guy. But I'm new here, and I don't share the town's emotional history with him. As far as I'm concerned, he's clearly a piece of this puzzle. Maybe he's done nothing wrong—maybe his motives are indeed altruistic—but he *is* part of the porn issue, and everything tells me that the porn issue killed Cantrell."

Pierce stood, facing me. "That's a reasonable theory," he conceded, "the best one we've got. But Ben Tenelli just *couldn't* have strangled Carrol."

"Why not? He's a big guy, plenty vigorous for his age."

Pierce shook his head. "Ben might be physically capable of the murder, but not emotionally, not philosophically. He's a good, decent man. He's a doctor."

"Fine. Let's say Tenelli didn't do it. Let's say he had no motive whatever to want Cantrell dead. Let's even say he has no ulterior interest in the obscenity issue. If all those assumptions are true, though, what sense can we make of Harley Kaiser's assertion that Tenelli has been a driving force behind the obscenity trial?"

"None," Pierce answered with a shake of his head. "It makes no sense."

"Exactly. It suggests that Kaiser was lying about his relationship with Tenelli—which drives *my* suspicions right back to Kaiser himself."

Pierce sat down again and gestured that I should do likewise. With a tone of forced patience, he explained, "Mark, Harley Kaiser is simply not capable of murder, for political gain or otherwise. Period."

"Then who did it, Doug? You'll have a tough time proving it was Bruno—his alibi appears to be tight. Who else had a motive? Deputy Dan Kerr, DA Harley Kaiser, and possibly Dr. Benjamin Tenelli. I hardly need to add that some of those suspects would be delighted to move *your* name to the top of the list. What's more, any one of you would have sufficient physical stature to subdue Carrol Cantrell and strangle him. Don't you see that—"

Lucy interrupted, "*Was* he strangled? Has that been shown conclusively?"

"Kaiser told me at lunch that the coroner issued his preliminary findings late this morning—it should be on the city newswire by now. The upshot is this: Vernon Formhals found that (a) the victim died very near nine o'clock on Sunday morning and (b) he was indeed strangled. The findings, as I said, are preliminary. The final report is contingent on the results of toxicology tests."

"Toxicology?" asked Lucy. "Why bother if it's obvious Cantrell was strangled?"

Pierce explained, "A complete forensic autopsy, including toxicology, is routine procedure in the case of homicides or any suspicious deaths."

I told him, "Test results could take weeks though, right?"

"Two weeks is fairly standard, although sometimes they can speed it up if the investigation warrants it. I wonder if Formhals has requested a rush from the lab. Mind if I use your phone, Mark?" Pierce was already on his feet.

"Be my guest," I told him, gesturing toward the desk in my inner office. "Punch any line that's not lit; dial nine first."

He nodded, stepped to my desk, lifted the receiver, and dialed. When his call was answered by a switchboard, he identified himself and asked to speak to Formhals. After a brief wait, he said into the phone, "Good afternoon, Vernon. Doug Pierce. I was wondering, Vernon, if—"

But he was cut short by the coroner, who apparently had something important to say. A few moments later, Pierce said, "Yes, Dan? When did you arrive?"

Lucy and I exchanged a quizzical look—was Pierce now speaking to Deputy Dan Kerr? Pierce's end of the conversation consisted of short questions that did nothing to enlighten us. At last Pierce said, "I'll be right over," and then he hung up.

Lucy and I both stood as he returned from my desk. I asked, "Well . . . ?"

He explained, "When I reached Formhals, he immediately told me that Deputy Kerr was with him there at the morgue, then he handed the phone over to him. Kerr told me that Formhals had called him over because he'd just discovered something that may be pertinent to the investigation."

"*What?*" blurted Lucy.

Pierce laughed. "Kerr wouldn't tell me, but he assured me that it was significant. He asked me to get over there and see for myself." And with that, Pierce moved toward the door, ready to rush out through the newsroom. In the doorway, he turned back to ask me through a grin, "Well? Are you coming?"

The phone on my desk rang as I answered Pierce, "I didn't know I was invited. After all, I'm 'press'—will they let me in?"

Lucy stepped to the desk to answer my phone as Pierce assured me, "They'll let you in if you're with *me*. Come on."

He didn't need to ask me twice. Patting my pockets, I confirmed that I had my pen and notebook. I wouldn't bother with a topcoat—Pierce was ready to roll. I had just about stepped out the door with him when Lucy called to me, "It's your nephew. He's at school. Says it's important."

I wagged my head from Pierce, to the phone, and back to Pierce. I was torn.

Pierce nodded, smiled. "Go ahead and take it."

"I'll keep it short," I assured him while crossing to my desk. Taking the phone from Lucy, I said into it, "Hey, Thad. I'm kind of busy right now. What's wrong?"

"Nothin'!" There was a lot of background noise—he must have called from the hall between classes.

"Well . . . good," I said awkwardly. "But I don't usually hear from you during the day. What's going on?"

"I got it, Mark! The part in the play—I'm Dr. Einstein!"

"What? Really? No kidding? That's wonderful, Thad. I'm proud of you."

"I've already got the script, and Mrs. Osborne told me to go ahead and underline my lines, and now I have to start memorizing everything—scary, huh?" He didn't sound the least bit scared by the challenge.

"You're going to love every minute of this. Have you told Neil yet?"

"Not yet. I'll call him next. I've got a few minutes before the next class."

"Congratulations, kiddo. I'll see you at home tonight. Bye, now."

"Bye, Mark."

Riding over to the morgue with Pierce, I explained, "Thad really needed *something*. I'm glad he got the part. In the time I've known him, he's never shown such enthusiasm."

"What's the play again?" asked Pierce, eyes on the road.

"*Arsenic and Old Lace*. Don't tell me you've never heard of it."

"I've *heard* of it, sure, but I've never seen it. What's it about?"

"Two little old ladies who poison old men and bury them in their basement."

Pierce looked at me. "This is a comedy, right? Sounds kind of ghoulish."

With a laugh, I conceded, "I guess it *is* kind of ghoulish. The play's villain, Jonathan Brewster, is a sadistic killer, while his sidekick—Thad's role—is a drunken plastic surgeon who disguises his friend by repeatedly cutting up his face."

Pierce turned to me with a look of dismay.

"Kids love it," I assured him.

Glancing through the windshield, he announced, "Next stop: county morgue."

Pierce laughed at the irony in the timing of our arrival, but my own lighthearted mood was squelched by his words, which reminded me of the purpose of our mission. It was sobering to ponder the emotional chasm that separated, on the one hand, the melodramatic chills of a three-act comic thriller from, on the other hand, the grim reality of a four-day-old corpse that had methodically been dissected in search of clues to its demise.

During my career, I'd seen enough victims of murder, suicide, and accidents that I could stay analytical when faced with the aftermath of tragedy. I'd visited morgues before, as well, and I'd witnessed procedures that most laymen would find unspeakably repulsive. Rarely, however, had I known the victim, and never had I been invited to view the autopsied cadaver of a man who'd expressed interest in me sexually, as Carrol Cantrell had. I suddenly wondered why I'd so eagerly agreed to accompany Pierce. Certainly, the prospect of learning enticing new details on a major story had proved more than sufficient to whet my reporter's curiosity, but professional considerations were now outweighed by a gut emotion that resembled, for lack of a better word, dread. I didn't want to be here. I didn't want to do this. Short of simply confessing my cowardice to Pierce, though, I knew of no way to back out.

As Pierce pulled into a parking space marked with his name, I realized that the morgue was located within the county's sprawling Public Safety Building, which also housed the sheriff's department and emergency offices. His was one of many tan cars bearing "Official" plates in the assigned lot behind the building, and his parking spot was among those closest to the door, an unassuming back entrance with restricted access. He got out of the car, and I followed as he stepped up to the metal door and swiped a card through its lock. When the door clicked open, he swung it wide for me and followed me inside.

We found ourselves in the heart of a dispatch area, where several officers staffed a switchboard. A wide hallway broke off in four directions. The floors were gray terrazzo; the walls were white; the ceiling was a suspended grid of diffused fluorescent lighting. Someone behind a counter said, "No messages, Sheriff." Pierce nodded his thanks while leading me down one of the hallways at a brisk clip. Our heels snapped on the hard, shiny floor.

"Have you met Vernon yet?" he asked me.

"No, but his name has come up in various stories since I took over the *Register*. He's an MD, right?"

"Right. He's both coroner and chief medical examiner, a trained forensic pathologist. In a town this size, we're lucky to have him."

Pierce turned down another short hallway and stepped to a door that bore a simple engraved-plastic sign: CORONER. "Let's introduce you," said Pierce, opening the door.

We entered a small office. A clerk worked at a desk. There were a few extra chairs. A faded print of a bucolic cow-dotted landscape hung in a plastic frame, slightly askew, on an otherwise blank, windowless wall. Pierce asked the clerk, "Is Vernon in his office?"

"Go right in, Sheriff. Deputy Kerr is with him."

Pierce led me around a corner, into a larger office where Dan Kerr stood talking to an imposing figure of a black man in a white lab coat. I assumed that this was Vernon Formhals, though I hadn't known that he was black. As coroner, he was often quoted in the paper, but he hadn't been pictured on the *Register*'s pages during my tenure there as publisher.

Pierce, Formhals, and Kerr exchanged perfunctory greetings, using first names, no titles. Then Pierce said, "Vernon, I'd like you to meet Mark Manning, publisher of the *Register*. He's been lending me some brainpower on this case."

Shaking hands, I told him, "It's a pleasure, Dr. Formhals. The sheriff speaks highly of you." As I spoke, I studied his face and found it impossible to peg his age. Whether he was mature-looking for thirty or young-looking for sixty, I honestly couldn't tell.

"The pleasure's mine, Mark." The coroner's manner was cordial but predictably dry—I'd hardly expect a bubbly personality in his line of work. "Do call me Vernon. We needn't stand on ceremony." He allowed himself a friendly chortle.

"Doug," said Deputy Kerr, getting right to the point, "Vernon called me a few minutes ago because he noticed something on the body that he'd previously overlooked. It opens new possibilities in the investigation."

"Doug," said Vernon, jumping in, "I hope I've not committed a breech of protocol. It was my understanding that you'd turned the investigation over to Dan."

"You're absolutely right," Pierce assured him.

"Look," said Kerr, "I realize that I was assigned to this case under iffy circumstances. There's no turf to be defended—there's simply a murder to be solved. I want Doug's input, and if Doug wants Mark's input as well, so be it. Let's put our heads together and get to the bottom of this."

"Well said," Vernon told Kerr, his tone rather stiff and academic.

I marveled at the professed spirit of cooperation I'd just witnessed. Back in the big city, this would never have happened between ranks and departments. As for the welcome participation of a journalist—that was simply unthinkable. While there are doubtless those who would judge this approach highly unprofessional, I found it, in a word, refreshing, not only because it allowed me a firsthand role in the investigation of a top story, but also because it brought a measure of common sense to police procedures.

Now that we were all working from the same page, Pierce asked Formhals, "What did you find?"

"This way, gentlemen." And Formhals led us out of his office, through a set of swinging double doors—the sort designed to accommodate a gurney.

At this point, my momentary enthusiasm, inspired by office chat of mutual cooperation, waned. Back at the coroner's desk, the issues we discussed were theoretical; passing through the doors to the morgue complex, we entered the realm of the highly tangible. And once again, I dreaded the notion of seeing Carrol Cantrell's autopsied remains.

Formhals gabbed with the sheriff and his deputy as we made our way through several rooms—labs for blood work and photography; the examination room with its stainless-steel dissection table, its drains, pumps, and lights; and finally, the cold, quiet confines of the morgue proper, a file room for the deceased.

The equipment, the smells of disinfectant, the hum of compressors, the background trickle of water—it was all familiar—other morgues in larger cities served the same purpose. Dumont's facility was much like the others, only smaller. This final room contained only a few of the refrigerated drawers in which corpses could be stored, not the rows of anonymous crypts found in crime-embattled urban counties. Owing to my work at the paper, I knew that only one suspicious death was currently under investigation. Only one of these drawers was occupied.

While gripping the handle of the pertinent drawer, Formhals told us, "I'm embarrassed to admit, gentlemen, that during my initial examination of the subject, I failed to notice a small detail that could, just possibly, have an enormous impact on your investigation. The cause of death, which we have all assumed to be strangulation, may in fact have been otherwise. Stand back, please."

As instructed, we backed away as the drawer slid open. There lay a long, lean corpse, chilled and fully shrouded, presumably Carrol Cantrell. Pierce stood along one side of the drawer with Formhals; Kerr and I faced them from the other side. I knew what had been done to the body, and I didn't want to see it. Sensing my uneasiness, the coroner lifted the sheet near the head so that only Pierce could see the face as well as most of the body to confirm the identity of the victim.

Regardless of how routine such experiences may be in police work, I can't imagine how Pierce managed to view the corpse with such complete lack of emotion. I knew that the scalp had been cut back and the skull sawed open so that the brain could be removed. I knew that a giant Y-shaped incision had been cut across the chest and down the abdomen so that everything else could be removed, examined, bagged, tagged, and replaced. I also knew that this defiled specimen had, in life, made love to Pierce three nights running. With a sober nod, Pierce confirmed, "Yes, that's Cantrell."

"Now then," said Formhals, tucking the shroud back in place, "I'd like for you all to have a look at the victim's right thigh." Exposing a section of the leg below the hip, he arranged the sheet so that only the flesh of Cantrell's outer thigh could be seen. "Don't be shy, Mr. Manning. Please step over here and take a close look." He offered me a magnifying glass.

My curiosity was sufficient to outweigh my instinctive reluctance, so I stepped around the feet of the corpse and took hold of the magnifying glass, positioning myself between the coroner and the sheriff. Squatting, I peered at Cantrell's leg, mere inches from my face. The skin had lost its fleshy color, of course, and now appeared distinctly gray and lifeless. Otherwise, there was little abhorrent about the experience of nearing this framed section of a man's leg—the rotting had been arrested by refrigeration, and if there was a putrid smell at all, it was well masked by other odors that carried the sting of chemicals. Lifting the lens in front of my eyes, I saw nothing unusual on the skin—a random pattern of short, fuzzy hairs; their follicles; a few blemishes, including a blackhead and a pimple or two. I told Formhals, "I don't know what I'm looking for."

He pointed to the pimples, a few inches apart. Examining them more closely, I saw that these two tiny red patches did not have lumps at their centers, as pimples would, but rather craters, darkened presumably by blood.

Pierce conjectured, "Needle marks?"

"Yes, indeed," said Formhals. "Unmistakable. Two of them."

Standing, I handed the magnifier back to Formhals, asking, "Was Cantrell doing drugs?"

"There was some residual evidence of previous drug use, but that's not what killed him, and that's not what made those marks." Covering the section of leg, he slid the corpse back into the wall. The drawer closed with a clank.

Deputy Kerr suggested, "Poisoning? Injected poison?"

Formhals shook his head. "I doubt it. Gentleman, all of you saw the victim at the crime scene on Sunday. Do you recall that he wore a Medic Alert bracelet?"

"I *do* recall that," I told the group. "I noticed it when Cantrell arrived last Thursday—the bracelet's design was conspicuously different from his other jewelry. Then, when I accompanied Harley Kaiser and Miriam Westerman to the coach house on Saturday morning, the bracelet came up in conversation. Cantrell said he was allergic to nuts."

"Indeed he was," confirmed Formhals. "The bracelet gave clear warning of Cantrell's nut allergy, which was severe enough to cause anaphylactic shock. The bracelet also gave instructions for use of the antidote."

Pierce asked, "The EpiPen? I saw it—Carrol always had it nearby."

"You've lost me," I told the others while slipping my notebook out of my pocket and uncapping my Montblanc. "What's an EpiPen?"

Formhals explained, "An EpiPen resembles an ordinary fountain pen, which has been described by some as 'a fat pen.' It—"

"Of *course*," I said. "When I first saw Cantrell's pen, I wondered why he'd chosen one of such ungainly design. Then, on Saturday morning, after Harley and Miriam left the coach house, Cantrell tried to tidy up the place, and it struck me as odd that he left the pen near the bed instead of placing it on the desk."

"That's the point," said Formhals. "An EpiPen is not a writing instrument, but a syringe designed for emergency use. It contains a premeasured dose of epinephrine, a synthetic version of the hormone adrenaline. At the onset of an anaphylactic reaction, the patient removes the pen's cap and pushes its tip against his outer thigh, injecting the antidote directly into a muscle or vein. If delivered in time, it goes to work on the cardiovascular and respiratory systems, causing rapid constriction of blood vessels. It reverses throat swelling and prevents cardiovascular collapse."

Deputy Kerr asked, "Can we back up a minute? What's anaphylactic shock?"

"It's an acute allergic reaction that, in sensitive subjects, can be triggered by just about anything—shellfish, bee stings, and pointedly, nuts. The reaction causes rapid swelling of the breathing passage, loss of consciousness, and sometimes death. If fatal, the symptoms are identical to those of asphyxiation. The most evident symptom is cyanosis—the victim's face and extremities turn blue."

I told Formhals, "That's consistent with Cantrell's condition when I found him. Pardon an obvious question: Had the EpiPen been discharged?"

The coroner breathed a short, exasperated sigh. "We don't know."

Pierce explained, "At the crime scene on Sunday, the EpiPen was not in plain view. In fact, it was on the floor under the rumpled bedding. While removing the body, one of the investigators stepped on the pen and crushed it. By the time we identified it, it was of course empty—and thoroughly contaminated."

Sheepishly, Kerr said, "I think *I'm* the one who stepped on it—we're not sure."

Formhals added, "If the victim *did* inject the hormone to stave off shock, it's unlikely to show up in lab tests. In other words, we have no direct evidence as to whether the pen was used—just the needle marks. Our best bet is to await analysis of his stomach contents to see if he'd ingested nuts."

Reviewing the notes I'd been writing, I asked, "In your opinion, then, what's the bottom line? Was the cause of death strangulation or anaphylactic shock?"

"At this point, we can conclusively state only that the *mechanism* of death was asphyxiation. The *cause* of death may have been either strangulation or an allergic reaction to nuts."

Pierce suggested, "If he ate nuts, the death may have been accidental."

"Unless," I said, "someone knowingly slipped him the nuts in something else."

"But wait," said Kerr. "If he died from eating nuts, how do we explain the red abrasions around his neck? It sure *looked* as if he'd been strangled—we even found that wrinkled scarf at the scene."

Formhals nodded, telling us, "Yes, the abrasions were real. Unless they were self-inflicted, which seems highly improbable, I suggest this scenario:

"Carrol Cantrell ate nuts, probably unknowingly, and went into anaphylactic shock. He attempted to inject himself with epinephrine, but the antidote, for whatever reason, failed. Then, when he was at or very near the point of death, someone garroted him with the scarf. The abrasions on his neck, coupled with the blue pallor of cyanosis, created a convincing case for death by strangulation."

I summarized, "What you're saying, then, is that he may have been poisoned—with nuts."

"In the broadest sense, yes, that would be poisoning."

"My God," I said, capping my pen, "that implies that whoever garroted Cantrell with the scarf didn't need to physically overpower him. The victim was already in his death throes when the killer scarred his neck. The killer didn't need brawn to subdue him—the poison did the dirty work."

After a moment's consideration, Formhals agreed, "Certainly.

Anyone could have done it—anyone, that is, with knowledge of the allergy."

"Anyone," I repeated. "Even a woman."

"Miriam Westerman would stoop to anything—the hateful witch."

"Isn't that a touch strong?" Pierce asked me through a grin. We were in his car again; he was driving me back to the *Register* from the morgue.

"She *is* hateful," I insisted. "She is literally 'full of hate.' She hates pornography. She hates homosexuals—"

"Homosexual *men*."

"Precisely. The point is, in her twisted view, Carrol Cantrell was about as low as they get. You'll recall that Miriam was the driving force behind Dumont's obscenity ordinance in the first place. She looks forward to the impending porn trial as her finest hour. And if Harley Kaiser's story is true—that it was Miriam's idea to visit the coach house on Saturday—we can assume that she'd somehow found out that Cantrell had come to Dumont to thwart their efforts. Add to that the fact that Cantrell was so obviously gay, and it's easy to imagine that Miriam might see him as not only a threat, but a target."

Pierce nodded, eyes on the road. "She's nutty enough."

I turned on the seat to face him. "And speaking of nuts, she *knew* about Cantrell's allergy. She was at the coach house Saturday morning with Kaiser and me when Cantrell told us about his Medic Alert bracelet."

"I don't know. Miriam's been goofy for years. Do you actually think she'd try to *kill* someone?"

"She's vicious. I've had my share of run-ins with the woman, and believe me, I'd put nothing past her."

Reluctantly, Pierce acknowledged, "Maybe we'd better question her."

"That won't be easy. The moment she knows she's under suspicion, she'll start yapping about harassment and restraining orders and God knows what. Plus, she's in so thick with the DA, she could probably outmaneuver us. She'll be a tough subject to interrogate."

Stopping at an intersection to wait for a light, Pierce turned to ask me, "Any better suggestions?"

"Actually"—I grinned—"yes. Miriam's been bleating that the *Register* hasn't given her new school the publicity it deserves, so why don't I send Glee Savage over to talk to her? We'll tell her we're planning a big photo feature. Glee is fully briefed on the Cantrell story. I trust her instincts—she'll know what to dig for."

"Not bad," said Pierce, impressed with the plan. "But even if Miriam is dumb enough, or arrogant enough, to admit that she had an ax to grind with Carrol, you can bet she isn't going to come right out and say, 'Yeah, I slipped him the nuts.' " Pierce laughed, then added, "How *would* someone get an allergic person to unknowingly eat nuts?"

I shrugged. "Grind 'em up, I guess. Put them *in* something."

Pierce pulled the car through the intersection. "Something," he asked slowly, "like a cake?"

We looked at each other in silence for a moment, amazed at our stupidity. There'd been a partially eaten homemade cake at the crime scene Sunday morning. I'd seen it; so had Pierce. For all I knew, he may have helped Cantrell eat it for breakfast that morning.

"Where is it?" I asked.

"In evidence—along with the computer and the silk scarf and the bracelet and the broken EpiPen and everything else."

I breathed a sigh of relief. "Good. Do you know where it came from?"

"Not a clue. It was there late Saturday when I arrived for the night."

I got out my pen and was making more notes. "Can you have it analyzed?"

"I'll talk to Vernon as soon as I get back to the department. He'll handle it. The stomach contents are out for analysis as part of routine toxicology—those results may take a while. But analyzing the cake should be much faster—that's easy."

"A piece of cake," I quipped.

Pierce rolled his eyes as he pulled the car to the curb in front of the *Register*.

Before opening the door, I checked over my notes. "Any chance of my getting a photo of the gold-colored scarf that was found at the scene?"

"Sure. What for?"

I capped my pen and returned my notes to my pocket. "Just a hunch."

Shifting into park, Pierce thought aloud, "I assumed the investigation had taken a new direction."

"It has," I assured him while getting out of the car. Before thumping the door closed, I told him, "The hunt is on—we're looking for nuts."

That afternoon, I left my office at the *Register* early, claiming the need to spend some time at my desk at home. It's not that I owed anyone an excuse—I owned the paper, after all, and could work any hours that pleased me. No, this white lie regarding my intentions was meant more to assuage my own conscience. During the midst of a major story, on a day that had been marked by the discovery of important new details, leads, and suspicions, I couldn't honestly convince myself that a responsible publisher would go home early to take a run through the park—but that's precisely what I did.

At times a person needs to step back from a grueling situation, to focus elsewhere, to clear the mind. Besides, seeing Carrol Cantrell's four-day-old corpse at the morgue that afternoon had proven unexpectedly disturbing, leaving me in a weird, introspective mood. I wanted to shake the memory of that experience; the smell of disinfectant still clung to my clothes. Simply put, I needed some fresh air.

Throughout my life, at least since high school, to run has triggered a powerful, inexplicable response somewhere in my psyche. Don't get me wrong—I'm not a particularly avid, committed runner—I'm no fanatic. I've simply come to understand that running is good for me. They say that it strengthens the heart, and I know that it's kept me thin. Vanity alone would be an adequate explanation for enduring these physical rigors, but my interest in this pastime runs deeper. It's about goal-setting. It's about competing with yourself. It's about staving off the paunch and sag of middle age. And it's also . . . well, *erotic.*

This aspect of running is admittedly idiosyncratic—I assume few of my fellow runners get quite the same charge from it that I often feel. I can't quite trace the root of these feelings; perhaps they stem from vague locker-room fantasies that may have tickled my subconscious during the early years of puberty. Who knows? And who cares? If it is essentially my libido that has kept me running all these years, I feel lucky to have been so driven.

That Thursday afternoon in early autumn was reminiscent of my cross-country days in high school, when we practiced in a park in the town where I grew up in Illinois. I'd never been outdoorsy, and I was downright miserable at competitive sports—team sports—but I found both the setting and the challenge of cross-country oddly to my liking. Crisp, blue-skyed fall weather has always marked my favorite time of year, and to spend those late afternoons with a group of other guys who weren't out to "beat" me, but rather to cheer me on, helping me boost *my* endurance, *my* distance—the whole experience was nothing short of revelatory. Not only had I found an athletic activity that I could actually *do*, but I discovered, all the more to my surprise, that I was pretty good at it.

Autumn had entered Dumont exactly on cue that week, and the season's first hard frost had worked its magic upon the town's trees, adorning them overnight in fresh new hues of gold, accented with crimson. The lure of the afternoon was irresistible, so when I arrived home early from the office (to "spend some time at my desk"), I didn't even pause in the front hall as I passed by the door to the den and climbed the stairs to my uncle's old bedroom, which I now shared with Neil.

The house on Prairie Street was quiet. Thad was still at school, Neil at work. In this silence the creak of the closet door seemed magnified as I opened it and quickly undressed. Donning faded yellow cotton shorts and a roomy gray T-shirt, I then perched on the edge of the bed to lace up a worn pair of Reeboks over rumpled white crew socks. Standing again, I lingered for a moment to inspect myself in the long mirror mounted on the closet door. Though my attire hardly qualified as a fashion statement, I found it oddly pleasing—so basic, so right for its purpose, and yes, in a word, so butch. Perhaps because I had never aspired to hypermasculinity in my manner, appearance, or mind-set, it was something of a turn-on to glimpse the reflection of this athletic-looking figure and to realize that it was none other than me. A tingle in my groin alerted me to the initial stage of arousal, a warm chubbiness between my legs that was not yet visible but certainly felt. If I tarried there much longer, I would be apt to forget my purpose (running) and indulge instead in an impromptu bout of mutual masturbation with my macho twin behind the glass—a tempting thought. But no. I shut the closet door, swinging the mirror to reflect its own darkness. After a few quick warm-up stretches there on the bedroom carpet, I bounded down the stairs and out the front door.

Trotting down the walk from the porch to the street, I felt the chill of autumn air as it whorled past my bare legs. In my mind's eye, I could see each hair springing erect in its follicle—my skin's natural defense against the cold. This brought to mind the section of Carrol Cantrell's leg that I'd examined just a few hours earlier—its natural defenses as well as its color were four days gone. Pondering this, I gained new appreciation for a phenomenon that I'd long dismissed as involuntary and therefore unworthy of thought: goose bumps.

Turning off Prairie Street onto Park Street, I whisked past the terminus of Durkee Avenue on my left, then La Salle, skirting the park itself on my right. Ahead lay an entrance to the park, a narrow path ideal for runners, which I'd discovered last winter shortly after my move to Dumont—it had become my habitual route. Scooting over the curb, my feet left the asphalt, crossed a plot of grass, then crunched the gravel of the pathway.

Entering the park, I was struck again by its pervasive silence, as if this slice of nature had been frozen in time for my sole appreciation. The moraine, with its enormous boulders and steep ravines, had been carved there by a glacier during a long-ago age of perpetual winter. Now, the ice was gone, and the scarred earth had patched itself with a blanket of green. Trees had sprouted in the fertile silt; their roots now burrowed the craggy terrain; their branches reached high toward the patchy light of a perfect September sky.

All this history, all this geological tumult so benignly resolved, and there ran I.

Me—this polite, awed intruder, prancing through nature in gym shorts and Reeboks, out for a jog, in need of fresh air.

The path, which wound and sloped sharply from the street, now settled onto an easier course, straight and level, through an expanse of turf that formed a valley floor within the park's rugged confines. A stream flowed cold in the distance. The perimeter of trees cast their broad blue shadows across the grassy field. The gravel path stretched long and flat before me, inviting me to find my pace, to up my speed, to burn the calories that would cause me to sweat in spite of the chilled landscape through which I ran.

Finding my second wind, settling into the cruising pace that would propel the duration of my run, I was at last able to clear my mind of recent stresses, entering that zone of suspended consciousness that is the runner's compensation for tedium, a reward for the discipline of ignoring pain. The tap of my feet, the beat of my pulse, the rate of my breathing, all these rhythms became fixed and juxtaposed, like the syncopated clatter of the parts of some complex, precise machine.

As earth and sky blurred past me, I thought of nothing. And yet, I thought of everything. Vague remnants of my workaday life, my waking worries, flicked through my brain like the disjointed scenes of an unwanted dream.

These half-thoughts were dominated, of course, by the murder of Carrol Cantrell. That very afternoon, his shrouded, iced body had served as a powerful and tangible reminder that a heinous crime had darkened my newly adopted community. In a purely philosophical sense, a wrong had been committed, and righting it was a matter of simple justice—that alone was ample motivation to solve the mystery and unmask Cantrell's killer.

But more was at stake than rectitude. Douglas Pierce—the sheriff, my friend—had been implicated in the crime and "outed." At worst, if he was formally accused and convicted of the murder, he would lose his life's freedom, not to mention his career, reputation, and every shred of respect. At best, if he managed to debunk the accusations arising from the extortion note, he would still remain at the center of a sex scandal that could seriously jeopardize his chances for reelection. Though his political opponent, Dan Kerr, seemed surprisingly sympathetic to Pierce's difficulties, he was the one man with the most to gain from Pierce's possible downfall, and I felt strongly that the town would be ill-served by a voters' backlash that could whisk Kerr into office.

Which brought to mind that there was more at stake than Pierce's future. My own reputation was on the line as well. I'd already published my endorsement of Pierce for reelection, and I was loath to retract it. Not only would such backpedaling humiliate me in the eyes of the *Register*'s fickle readership, but it would also shift the paper's support to Kerr, whom I still opposed on philosophical grounds.

My reputation was on the line in another sense too. On the Monday afternoon when Pierce had told me about the discovery of the extortion note, he had asked me to help him. A friend in need, he called upon my past skills as an investigative reporter to help solve the mystery and save his neck. I readily agreed. Since then, however, I'd merely littered the investigation with a growing throng of suspects, only one of whom, at this point, could convincingly be argued to have had the motive, means, and opportunity to commit the crime: Pierce himself.

In a more abstract sense, the whole "gay thing" was also at stake. The victim, we now knew, had been a gay pornographer. A publicly named suspect, Pierce, the closeted gay sheriff, had slept with Cantrell the night before he died. Wouldn't it be just ducky if, in the public's mind, the whole sordid mess were dismissed as gay infighting? They'd conclude that the murder simply didn't matter.

But it did matter. Someone had blood on his hands—and I couldn't consider for a moment that it might actually be Pierce. Was I too trusting? Was I blinded by friendship, or possibly by gay unity, or even by my underlying, unspoken attraction to Pierce? Could he have, in fact, killed Cantrell?

I had to believe that it was someone else. Bruno Hérisson, Dan Kerr, Harley Kaiser, and even the seraphic Dr. Ben Tenelli all raised varying levels of suspicion within me. And now a new possibility, an extremely promising suspect, had reared her ugly head. Miriam Westerman had the clear *motive* of hate. Her knowledge of Cantrell's allergy gave her the *means* to kill him. But did she have the *opportunity* to mix motive and means—with nuts—in a deadly cake? Lab reports were pending on the cake itself. If it proved to contain nuts, could I prove that she'd concocted it?

These thoughts were not the purpose of my run—far from it. I'd taken to this trail in hopes of escaping such vexing questions, if only for half an hour. Without missing a step, I shook my head, clearing my brain. I again focused on my surroundings and was quickly lost in the late-afternoon splendors of the park. The path had looped around the valley floor and now began its gradual ascent through the tree-thick slopes on the far side of the ravine.

Running on this incline, I had to work harder to maintain my pace. My breathing quickened, and with the extra gulps of oxygen came a familiar light-headedness—the gentle, pleasing "high" of hyperventilation that some runners equate with meditative, trance-like bliss. Preferring to enjoy this phenomenon simply as a physiological oddity, I was nonetheless struck by the vivid impressions, the flashes of insight, that it inspired.

The run up the hill reminded me of a morning some three years earlier. It was Christmas, bright and warm, on a mountainside in Phoenix. I'd met Neil a few months before while he was visiting his friend Roxanne in Chicago. There was an immediate spark between us, but that was during my repressed, closeted days, and I failed to act upon my feelings for Neil during his visit. Later, when he suggested that I spend the holiday with him in the desert, I went. Arriving late on Christmas Eve, I slept the sound sleep of exhaustion that night, then awoke to his coffee and his invitation to join him for a shirtless morning run through his mountainside neighborhood.

Unaccustomed to running on hills, I followed him up the street, mesmerized by the sight of his body in motion, by the trickle of sweat down the lumps of his spine, forming a damp V in the crack of his shorts. When he turned at the top of a hill, I realized that he was as thoroughly aroused by our workout as I was. Sprinting back to the house in perfect unison, we instinctively, wordlessly made love outdoors that morning at the edge of a secluded pool. It was not only our first intimacy, but also the first time I'd had sex with another man. It marked the beginning of a whole new life for me, one that seemed so suddenly right and natural that I have never looked back, never regretted it. Indeed, the only question it raised was, What took me so long?

Recalling all this during my run through the park, I'd become aroused again, just as I had on that first morning with Neil. Running with an erection—an erection cramped by a pair of shorts—was not altogether comfortable. Perversely, this confusion of pleasure and pain did not diminish the pleasure, but rather intensified it. Before long, my mind was in the throes of a full-blown fantasy, indulging in erotic scenarios triggered by nothing more than my stream of consciousness.

Ahead of me now on the hilly pathway was not Neil, but the long-gone porn star Rascal Tyner. He wore only his white leather running shoes, and he turned now and then to egg me on, urging me to follow to some secret clearing. Then he stopped on the path, facing me. He stroked his penis, not yet fully erect, telling me, "I could use some help with this."

Stopping, watching his hands, I told him, "But you never need a fluffer."

He laughed. "I don't *need* anything. But I do want *you*."

Not inclined to argue, I stepped forward and hunkered down in front of him, indulging for a moment in the sight of him so near, the smell of his sweat, the warmth of his panting breath. Wrapping my arms around him, I cupped his buttocks in my hands while nuzzling his cock. My hands slid down his legs, feeling the long tendons of his thighs, the fine mat of hair, the plump bulge of his calves, and then his shins. My fingers slipped inside his socks to explore the bony knobs of his ankles, then traced the contours of his feet, feeling the cracked, soft leather of his running shoes, the web of their laces, the jagged tread of their soles. I'd lost all interest in his penis and was focused instead on the guy's *shoes*.

Wait a minute. This seemed not only goofy, but familiar. For as long as I could remember, I'd had fantasies of those feet, those shoes. In recent years, with Neil, I'd learned to simply indulge this harmless fetish and not question its roots. But now, running alone in the park that afternoon, I suddenly became aware of how and when I'd acquired my overenthusiasm for sneakers. It wasn't something I was born with. It wasn't a locker-room experience that had stuck with me since high school. No, it happened much later.

In the early eighties, when Rascal Tyner was felled by AIDS, I'd borrowed that videotape from a fellow reporter at the *Chicago Journal*. The compilation of clips was titled *Rascal Tyner's Hottest Hits*. In one of the scenes, the porn superstar was out for a run, leading the camera and the viewer deep into a woods. He wore only his running shoes—*those* white leather running shoes—and the video provided loving close-ups of those shoes as Rascal brought himself to orgasm.

On the pretext of journalistic curiosity, I watched the tape several times that night, masturbating (more than once) to the shoe scene. The next day, I returned the tape to my colleague, assuring both him and myself that my curiosity had been satisfied. Years passed, and the tape was forgotten.

Or so I'd thought. Clearly, that shoe scene had stuck with me—it had just replayed itself in rich detail before my mind's eye. Why had I repressed the memory of something that had so deeply intrigued me? Was I too embarrassed to admit, even to myself, that the sight of a guy's sneakers was sufficient to pop my load? Embarrassed? I was probably mortified.

That was nearly twenty years ago, back in my heterosexual days, when I wouldn't dare admit that I was attracted to men—let alone shoes. Now, of course, my perspective had shifted dramatically, but I still felt unprepared to confront the psychology of this private, squelched fantasy. Did I fear that by acknowledging it, I might lose it?

The wooded path had circled back to the valley floor, and the level terrain eased the strain of my run. Similarly, my muddlement ebbed, and I dismissed the issue of Rascal Tyner's track shoes as little more than a blip in my psychosexual makeup. Besides—I reminded myself—if demons were lurking in that old video, I would soon have my chance to vanquish them. Roxanne was driving up to Dumont that weekend, and at Neil's bidding, she would bring along a copy of the very tape in question. While the prospect of seeing that tape again inspired me with trepidation, that emotion was far outweighed by my eagerness to see, once again, Rascal Tyner shooting semen on those shoes.

This whole line of thought, I realized, had grown a little weird. Here I was—a responsible, mature adult, a businessman to boot, committed to a loving relationship with another man—pondering a worn-out fantasy of some college guy on tape, a Hollywood creation who simply wasn't real. He was, after all, long dead, and even in life he wasn't really gay—that was just an act that assured him a niche audience. Why waste any thought, any emotional energy, on a memory that was essentially false and manufactured? Why allow myself to be manipulated? If I needed prurient fantasies (and I was sufficiently self-aware to admit that I did enjoy them), I was creative enough to concoct my own.

Not to say that I don't recognize the value of a healthy balance between the real world and the imagined. In the investigation and reporting of news, for instance, I have trained myself to tread only in the realm of the objective—if I can't see it, hear it, or measure it, I don't write about it. While this rigorous standard can be applied to all aspects of life, I have come to appreciate that it signals no loss of intellectual integrity to indulge occasionally in the more emotional realm of the subjective. Our creative growth—whether as artists, as dreamers, as sexual beings, or simply as *people*—depends, to some extent, on our ability to let loose. Though there is a reality that is fixed and external, a reality that can't be changed by wishing or by prayer, there is another environment that exists solely within us, and it would be folly to deny or to thwart this spirit that makes us each uniquely human. Our challenge is to develop the insight to distinguish between these two natures, while cultivating the discipline to disregard external reality only when appropriate. In other words, there's a time and a place for everything.

Which is precisely why I now felt a measure of guilt for the whims I'd allowed myself that afternoon. It was hardly the time (in the midst of a vexing murder investigation) or the place (a public park) to be flexing my libido in daydreams of encounters with a young porn god. After all, I was happily committed to Neil. While I saw scant danger in indulging in sporadic fantasies of other men, particularly this "unreal" man who existed only in old videotapes, I was still wary that too much pining over imaginary men might dull my appreciation for the real one I had.

Even more disturbing was the fact (still not comfortably entrenched as part of my fixed, external reality) that I was now a "father." Thad was sixteen, only a few years younger than the fantasy hunk Rascal Tyner, who'd just invited me to fluff him in the park. Thad had barely begun to *shave*. And though I had never *ever* thought of Thad in any way but the paternal, I knew that I was veering near the edge of dangerous territory.

Don't go there, I warned myself. Don't even think about it. Forget that his sixteen gangly years will blossom into eighteen strapping ones. You do *not* find the kid attractive—not that way. The very notion fills you with a revulsion that's been hardwired into your psyche by society, by law, and by nature itself.

My run had slowed to a sloppy jog, barely a brisk walk. So I stopped, alone on the trail in the middle of the park. Breathing deeply, I assured myself that this angst was unwarranted. I had weighed the fear routinely promoted by homophobes—that I was unfit to serve as Thad's father, that I was somehow out to recruit the boy. And in weighing this fear, I was able to dismiss it. I knew myself well enough to understand that Thad did not live at risk under my roof. I had made a commitment to his mother, my cousin, that I would raise him in her absence. Granted, when I made that promise, I felt certain that I'd never be called upon to fulfill it, but circumstances had decreed otherwise, and I was determined to prove myself the boy's best possible father—for my own sake as well as Thad's. Within such a mind-set, any sort of leering thoughts, to say nothing of abuse, were simply unthinkable.

With that resolved, I continued along the path, walking at a comfortable pace, heading back up the hillside that would take me home.

Home. The house on Prairie Street had in fact become a home for me, but it still lacked Neil's permanent presence, and I fretted again over whether he would eventually feel drawn to join me there. He took so naturally to the task of parenting Thad, and he enjoyed it too. While I had initially feared that my responsibilities toward Thad might make Neil feel distanced from me, the effect was the opposite—emotionally, Neil was closer to me now than ever before, a partner in the unlikely duties of raising an orphaned adolescent. For Thad, the house on Prairie Street was now the only home he knew; he had no other options.

It was humbling to realize that I now played such an important role in this kid's life. We hadn't *asked* for this arrangement, but then, kids never do get to choose their parents, and similarly, the babies dealt to even the most willing parents are a bit of a genetic crapshoot. So my relationship to Thad, while unconventional, had at least one advantage—we both knew what we were getting.

Even so, the whole setup was still new and unnatural to me. I wasn't Thad's father—not really. I wasn't even his uncle—Roxanne had explained, with lawyerly precision, that we were cousins once removed. And now I realized that I was profoundly (perhaps irrationally) bothered by the lack of a clear label for my relationship with Thad.

I also realized that I'd been playing these name games all my life, most recently with Neil, back when we met. Though instantly attracted to him, it took me months to act upon my desires simply because I dreaded losing the label that described my former life—and I mortally feared the names that would apply to the new life I was entering. Then, when it finally happened, the transition was painless, indeed joyful. Though much had changed around me, I was still "myself."

Perhaps I would still achieve that comfort level with Thad. Perhaps it didn't matter if I was his father or guardian or uncle or foster parent. The names didn't seem to perplex Thad; he simply called me Mark. And Neil never cared whether I was his lover or roommate or husband or friend; he simply called me Mark.

Lighten up, Mark, I told myself as I reached the edge of the park. Go home. Start supper.

Friday, September 22

Glee Savage had phoned Miriam Westerman to pitch our idea for a photo feature on her New Age school, and predictably, Westerman snapped at the bait, inviting Glee to visit the new facility on Friday, shortly after the opening of school.

Wanting to see Westerman in action with my own eyes, I offered to pick up Glee at her apartment before work that morning and drive her to the school; she readily accepted, happy to have me along. What I didn't understand when making this offer, though, was that Westerman's school operated on two calendars—a lunar calendar to determine which weeks classes were held, and a solar calendar to govern the school day. "What the hell does *that* mean?" I asked Glee.

"It means that the schedule shifts every day to get the kids in sync with their planet. Classes start at sunrise."

"Christ. These days, that's about . . . when, six-thirty?"

"About." She grinned. "Miriam insisted I arrive well before seven—in order to fully appreciate the day's birth energy."

So Friday morning, at the crack of dawn, I drove from the house on Prairie Street toward Glee's downtown apartment building. My dashboard thermometer said the outdoor temperature was forty-two, forcing me to wonder why I'd been foolhardy enough to leave the house without a topcoat. The windshield defroster switched on automatically, and the rush of dry, heated air against my face served as a reminder that summer was truly gone.

Glee's building lay ahead, on the corner of Third Avenue and

Park. Lights burned yellow in many of its windows as residents arose to prepare for the day. Under the portico, between a pair of ornate lanterns that had been left on all night, stood the *Register*'s veteran features editor, ready to roll.

Dressed for fall in a deep-hued wool skirt and jacket, Glee also sported a tidy waist-length cape, its collar trimmed with dark fur—that touch of mink. She always wore a hat—today's brown velvet pillbox was spiffed with an enameled pin representing a cluster of leaves in bright autumn colors. And she always carried a purse—today's portfolio-size carpetbag was pumpkin orange, overlaid with a darker pattern of fallen leaves.

Strutting toward my car as I circled into the driveway, she grabbed the door handle, swung it open, and hopped in. "It's been a while since I've seen the sunrise," she told me dryly. Brightly, she added, "Morning, boss."

"Good morning, Glee. Ready to take on Dragon Woman?"

"Bring 'er on," she said boldly, peeping inside her purse to check for her notebook. Satisfied, she snapped the bag shut.

Pulling out of the driveway, I asked, "Where is this place—what's it called?"

"A Child's Garden," she reminded me.

I snorted. "Pretty sappy."

"It's on some converted farm outside of town."

Glancing at her with raised brows, I asked, "Not out there by the porn shops?"

"No!" She laughed. "Other side of town. Scoot out on First Avenue."

And we did. Breezing through downtown (there was no traffic yet), I recapped, "Now the plan is, I'll stay in the background. The interview is all yours. Miriam won't like the fact that I'm there at all, so you do the schmoozing."

"Right. She'll be expecting a photographer, though. What'll I tell her?"

I thought for a moment. "Say that we'll be sending one to follow up later."

"Maybe we *should* send one. This joint sounds weird. It might be worth a feature—though I doubt if Miriam would appreciate the tack we'd take."

I grinned. "I do like the way you think. Have you prepared enough 'intelligent' questions to flesh out a real story?"

"Of *course*," she mocked offense that I would ask. "Miriam won't have a clue that our true purpose this morning is to ferret out any connection she might have to the Cantrell case."

"We assume that she had ample reason to hate Cantrell. So remember, we need answers to two questions: First, how could she possibly have been clued to the fact that Cantrell was here to testify for the porn industry? And second, was it Miriam who made that cake?"

Glee nodded patiently—she was fully aware of the plan.

As we zipped past the city line, the sun slid through a bank of clouds that clung to the horizon like distant gray mountains. The clear sky overhead instantly grew blue. Responding to something in the air, my car's defroster shut off, and the cabin now seemed eerily quiet, as if awed by the solemn moment of daybreak.

"The school's just ahead," Glee told me, pointing, "on the far left."

"That's appropriate," I muttered while slowing the car.

A rough-hewn sign at the edge of the road announced A CHILD'S GARDEN, its letters woven from tortured twigs. Beneath, a second sign, crudely painted on barn boards, explained, PRIVATE DAY SCHOOL, K–12, MIRIAM WESTERMAN, HEADMISTRESS. Amazed, I asked, "All twelve grades?"

"Plus kindergarten."

Pulling into the crushed-limestone driveway, I saw that the grounds were clearly those of a farm. The house, barn, and its old outbuildings still dotted the property, as did several new buildings of spare, featureless design—all freshly painted a goofy shade of park-bench green, the color of the eco-movement. The driveway opened to an irregular-shaped gravel parking lot, where a dozen or so vehicles were scattered without order.

Near the door of the largest of the new buildings, a gold-trimmed Jeep idled, its muffler sputtering exhaust into the cold morning air.

The woman behind the wheel wore a bathrobe, and her hair was a mess—she'd obviously overslept and had torn out of the house to get her kid to school. When the youngster leaped out and ran inside the building, the mom pulled away, meeting my car in a tight squeeze. I opened my window to apologize. She opened hers, telling me, "This shifting sunrise schedule—I don't know." Peeved, she blew a shock of hair from her face.

When our paths had cleared, I parked wherever space allowed, and both Glee and I got out of the car. All was quiet. Looking around, we weren't sure where to go, so we moved toward the building that we'd seen the child enter. A sign at the door listed SCHOOL OFFICES, FSNACH OFFICE, CLASSROOMS. Glee and I exchanged a quizzical glance—this was apparently the school's all-purpose building. Opening the door, we stepped into a hall.

". . . and if you don't agree, you can damn well get *out!*" screamed a shrewish voice, Miriam Westerman's—I'd know it anywhere. She was ranting at someone inside an office, its open doorway just a few yards from where we stood.

Another woman's voice, far quieter, near tears, responded, "But don't you think you should at least take into account the views of some of your faculty?"

"*Views?*" asked Westerman, crowing sarcastically. "There are no 'views' that matter here other than those expressed in the founding principles of the Society."

"But some of the *boys* in the school—"

Westerman cracked something on a desk or a table—it sounded like a bullwhip. When the other woman had stopped speaking and started crying, Westerman hissed, "I think I know what's best for the chill-dren." She pronounced the word with slow, exaggerated precision. "Now get back to your class—they're late for leaf-gathering."

The young teacher skittered from the office into the hall. Seeing us, she found her anguish compounded by embarrassment and buried her face in her hands, stumbling off in the opposite direction.

Jerking my head toward Westerman's office, I told Glee under my breath, "I guess the headmistress is in."

Behave yourself, she told me silently with a smirk. Then she stepped to the open doorway, rapped on the jamb, and asked, "Miriam, is this a bad time?"

Westerman gasped. A chair scraped the floor as she stood. Her voice dripped sweetness as she said from within, "Why, Ms. Savage, I didn't hear you arrive."

Of course you didn't, I wanted to say. You were practicing your banshee act.

"It's *Miss* Savage," Glee corrected her. "But do call me Glee."

"*Glee*," Westerman said the word with delight, as if hearing it newly coined. "Such a fine, spirited name, it sounds as if it sprang kicking from the womb of Mother Earth herself." She tittered while clomping toward the door and into the hall, reaching to shake hands. "It's indeed a pleasure, Glee, to welcome such an esteemed writer to A Child's—" Westerman stopped short, features falling as she saw me. Brusquely, she asked, "What's *he* doing here?"

"Mark's just along for the ride," Glee assured her blithely. "You know *men*—nosy but harmless."

"Hello, Miriam," I told her through an innocuous smile.

Glee continued, her tone girl-to-girl, "He signs my check, Miriam, so I thought I'd better let him come—but I made him promise to keep his mitts off my story."

I smiled benignly.

"Well"—this was clearly against Westerman's better judgment—"all right." She swirled her head away from me, returning her attentions to Glee, as if I ceased to exist. What she failed to understand was that her insulting behavior suited me fine. As she stood there in the hall, engaging in sister chat with Glee, I had the opportunity to study the woman unnoticed, as a fly on the wall might.

She wore her usual formless gray cloak, which hung to the knees. A pair of snagged green tights slithered down to those lumpish, muddy clogs. In addition to the primitive necklace (the one that looked like painted bones and teeth) that always rattled against her chest, she'd strung a crude, childish chain of still damp leaves around her neck. Flecks of these leaves, bark, and other debris clung to her cloak like dirty scabs. Her lifeless hair was an oily tangle, knotted with a leather thong into a halfhearted ponytail—apparently her "office do." I knew she was forty-five (the same as Doug Pierce and Harley Kaiser, who were all contemporaries), but she looked far older than Glee Savage, who was in her early fifties. In fact, compared to my stylish features editor, Westerman looked like an absolute hellhag—but then, my view was a tad tainted.

Glee had fished the notebook out of her bag and was asking, "And your enrollment is what, Miriam?"

"We opened two weeks ago with a charter enrollment of seventeen chill-dren."

Glee noted the number. "That's about . . . two students per class."

"On average, yes. But the lower grades are the largest. In fact, we have only one student in ninth grade, and none above that—yet. The lower grades will 'feed' the upper school, of course, and we continue to recruit new enrollment from the ranks of our FSNACH membership."

"With such small classes," said Glee, "you must be able to lavish considerable attention on each student. I assume your curriculum is highly progressive—computers from day one?"

Westerman looked aghast, clapping a palm to her flat chest. "Heavens *no*, Glee. No electronics whatever. We rely solely on traditional methods and a natural geo-based curriculum."

"Which would be . . . ?" asked Glee, suppressing a laugh with a dainty cough.

"We instruct our chill-dren, from kindergarten on, to respect the generative force of Mother Earth and to absorb the celestial harmony that governs the life cycle of the seasons." Westerman paused in thought, then summed up, "Basic holism."

With perfect composure, Glee queried, "The school is of course accredited? And the teachers certified?"

Westerman tisked. "None of that is necessary, and in fact, such bureaucratic meddling only serves to frustrate the learning process. According to Wisconsin state law, we need only demonstrate that a sequential curriculum—"

Two shrill noises interrupted Westerman's lecture, noises like the call of some huge predatory bird. Glee froze wide-eyed. I nearly wet my pants. With a wild expression, Westerman grabbed Glee by the shoulders and yanked her inside the office. I slipped in with them.

"What *is* it?" asked Glee, quavering.

In a matter-of-fact tone, Westerman explained, "Ms. Avery signals the change of class periods with birdcalls. We waste no opportunity to educate the chill-dren in nature's own native vocabulary. There's a quiz at the end of the day. If I'm not mistaken, that was the red-tailed hawk." As she spoke, the hustle of little feet could be heard pattering through the hall.

"But why," Glee sputtered, "did you pull me into the office?"

Westerman paused. "I must apologize, Glee. But I didn't want the chill-dren to see you—not like that. They might be frightened by your pelt." She wagged a naughty-naughty finger at Glee's mink collar.

I bit my tongue. The woman was not only ludicrous, but hypocritical. I wanted to ask, How about that collection of bones and teeth hanging around your own neck, sister? *That* carnage is enough to frighten anyone.

Westerman delicately suggested, "Perhaps if we could just hang that up . . . ?" And she beckoned to remove the pert little cape from Glee's shoulders. Eyeing me askance for a moment, Glee obliged by doffing the garment and offering it to Westerman, who handled it gingerly, so as not to touch its fur trim. Draping it over the back of a chair, she said wistfully, "Man has inflicted such violence on the world, there's no point in exposing chill-dren to the sadistic butchery of trappers."

I hoped Glee would lay into the harpy, but she remained focused on her mission. Glossing over the implied insult, she commiserated, "And to think that such wanton violence has now visited our own community . . ."

Westerman didn't follow. "Trappers?"

"No," Glee explained patiently, "murder. Carrol Cantrell was victimized within our town's very borders. And to think that I'd actually interviewed the man before he was strangled. I've never met anyone who later died so horribly."

"I met him too, but I can't say he left a very favorable impression."

Glee and I both waited, hoping Westerman would expound on this, but she wasn't going to make our job that easy.

"Now then," she said, her manner again cloyingly sweet, "would you like to see the compound?"

"That's why we're here," Glee reminded her.

"This way then," Westerman singsonged, whisking past me to lead Glee toward the door. I turned, pausing long enough to take a good look at the office. I was still wondering what had been the source of that slapping noise we'd heard earlier while Westerman was berating the tearful teacher. It took me only a moment to spot it amidst the mess on her desk—not a bullwhip, but an old-fashioned hickory pointer, the type used by schoolmarms to whack errant pupils.

Also on the desk was a computer, up and running, with a Web site displayed on its monitor. Colorful graphics jerked and flashed, coarsely animated. Unable to discern the nature of the site that Westerman had been visiting, I cleared my throat, catching Glee's eye, directing it toward the screen.

"Oh," she said, "just a moment, Miriam."

Westerman turned from the hallway, looking back into the room. "Yes?"

Glancing up from her notepad, Glee asked with a confused laugh, "Didn't you say there were no computers in the school?" She gestured toward the desk.

Echoing Glee's laugh, the headmistress explained, "Electronics play no role in educating the chill-dren, but I myself have found the computer to be highly useful as a communications tool. Our worldwide sisterhood is wired!" she assured us. "We *know* how to network." And she whisked us out of the room.

So then—Earth Woman had gone techie. Suddenly, there was a plausible explanation as to how she might have learned Cantrell's true purpose in Dumont. Linked by the Internet to a network of antiporn crusaders, she could have picked up a leaked list of defense witnesses from just about anywhere. Further, I now knew that she had the wits to plant a file in Cantrell's laptop and rig its clock. Still, the hanging question remained: Did she make that cake?

Out in the hall, Westerman was explaining, "Our curriculum is ideally suited to the open-classroom approach, and I like to think of A Child's Garden as an entire school without walls." She yammered on while leading us through the building, which did indeed have walls—lots of them. Some of the "classrooms" were little more than closets, where two or three kids would labor at a card table on projects ranging from mud pies to macramé. In spite of Westerman's professed allegiance to traditional teaching methods, I saw no activity that could be described as even remotely academic. Indeed, the whole setup struck me as something of a nursery school for kids of all ages—even the older ones engaged in nothing more mental than the chanting of wicca lore.

Leaving the main building, we followed Westerman through the compound, listening to her prattle about earthbound religions, the Great Goddess, and holistic feminism, confirming my assumption that the true purpose of her school was not education, but indoctrination. We toured the barn (where a child was instructed in the finer points of milking a cow), an activities building (where another student attempted to contort herself into the lotus position), and finally the dining hall (where a woeful child labored at husking corn, dutifully laying out the silk to dry for some unknown purpose). Encountering each of her students, the headmistress would warble, "Brightest blessings, child!" To which each would respond dully, mechanically, "Brightest blessings, Ms. Westerman."

Standing there in the lunchroom, listening to her lecture Glee on the importance of strict adherence to the principles of organic nutrition (everything was natural, herbal, and of course vegetarian), I was concluding that our mission had failed. Though I was more convinced than ever that Westerman's drug-addled hippie days had left her brain permanently impaired, and while Glee had accumulated more than sufficient material for a jaw-dropper of a story, we had not managed to glean from this wacky character any evidence of involvement in Carrol Cantrell's murder. The mere presence of a computer on her desk was not sufficient to implicate her—we needed to know if she had baked that suspicious cake. Then I realized that we stood not ten feet from the dining hall's kitchen, its swinging door propped open. Catching Glee's attention, I discreetly led her glance to the door. With equal discretion, she nodded that she understood.

"Can I assume then," she asked Westerman while adjusting her glasses to read her notes, "that you also serve as the school's dietitian?"

"Indeed," Westerman puffed. "I pride myself as a holistic chef and have developed every aspect of the chill-dren's menu."

Poor kids, I thought, imagining the dreary grub forced on them.

"*Really?*" With mock astonishment, Glee removed her glasses. "I had no idea, Miriam—you're something of a jack-of-all-trades."

Westerman beamed. "Actually, more of a Jill," she corrected Glee with a wink.

If this was a joke, it was a lame one, so Glee let it pass without comment. Instead she asked, as if she'd just thought of it, "May we see your kitchen? I'd love to see where all this wholesome culinary magic is conjured."

"Of *course*," Westerman gushed. "I'm flattered that you'd ask." And she led us through the doorway.

I half expected to find a fat black cauldron bubbling on a crumbling brick hearth, but the kitchen was new and unremarkable, of utilitarian design, doubtless up to code. There was a big commercial cooktop and ovens, a long stainless-steel sink, and a double-doored refrigerator with windows, its contents lit. Aluminum pots hung from ceiling hooks. Rows of shelving hung from wall brackets. These shelves contained books and dishes, as well as bags of pantry staples like flour and cornmeal. Also displayed there were large clear-glass jars containing . . . well, weird brown stuff, the type of stuff collected in the woods, like twigs and herbs and dried berries and buds. One of the jars contained leafy things that looked for all the world like bat wings.

Then I noticed that Glee's eyes had settled on another row of jars on the room's opposite wall. Their contents were not the least bit mysterious or unconventional. These jars contained a wide assortment of readily recognizable nuts: walnuts, chestnuts, acorns, pecans, Brazil nuts, hazelnuts, peanuts, cashews, and a smaller jar of precious pine nuts.

Glee asked, "Do you bake?"

"It's a bit of a challenge," lamented Westerman, "without refined sugar, as nothing really turns out *white,* but I do my best, and the chill-dren always seem to enjoy my treats."

She blabbered on, bestowing baking tips on Glee, who dutifully recorded them in her notes. I was mulling the comment about recipes not turning out white, when I recalled that the cake I'd seen at the crime scene had looked homemade because it seemed so inelegant and unappetizing—and its bland appearance stemmed from its being so *brown.* No icing, no color, no sheen. If not for its shape, the cake could have passed for a loaf of pumpernickel. Its coarse texture could easily have disguised all manner of nuts, which were stockpiled in potentially lethal quantities right here in Westerman's kitchen.

Glee and she had moved to the refrigerator and were peering through its glass doors. I sidled up behind them and nosed over their shoulders. Westerman was crowing about the organic lettuce stored there: "Our greens are fertilized with our own manure." I made a mental note to steer clear of her salads. "And it would be *criminal* to pasteurize our milk." I hoped, for the sake of the kids, that the fridge was cranked to the max.

Glee tapped her pen on the window. "What's that, Miriam?"

"Hmm?"

"Back there in the corner—it looks like a strongbox."

Sure enough, at the bottom of the refrigerator, nestled beneath a clump of grotesque vegetables (rutabaga or something—nothing *I'd* eat) was a drab green strongbox, which appeared to be locked.

Westerman responded coyly, "Secret recipes."

Glee fished, "Like what?"

"If I told you, they wouldn't be secret."

That afternoon, I decided to pay Grace Lord a visit. Though she'd been questioned at length about what and whom she'd seen in the environs of the coach house on Sunday, the morning of the murder, I would now try to jog her memory regarding Saturday. Perhaps she could recall something of the arrival of the cake.

Driving from the *Register,* I heard the hourly beep of my dashboard clock and recalled that it was time for Denny Diggins. Since his Tuesday show with Miriam Westerman, I'd made a habit of listening daily, wondering if Doug Pierce or I would again be publicly trashed. So I switched on the radio, tapping the button for the local station in time to hear the end of the Chevrolet jingle.

> We're back, friends. You're listening to *Denny Diggins' Dumont Digest*. And *I* . . . am Denny Diggins. As we told you before that important commercial break, our guest this Friday afternoon is none other than Harley Kaiser, Dumont County's distinguished district attorney. Welcome to the program, Harley. So good of you to take time out of your busy schedule.
>
> *Thanks, Denny. Glad to be here.*
>
> Now, Harley. We all know that the Carrol Cantrell murder investigation has reached something of a critical stage. We're also aware that you're limited in your ability to speak of these matters, in light of your esteemed position. I wonder, though, if you could share your *feelings* about the investigation.
>
> *I'm, uh, not quite sure what you mean, Denny.*
>
> I'm referring to the—shall we say?—more "sensational" aspects of this story. And there are indeed many: the murder itself, the now acknowledged sexual liaison between the victim and Sheriff Pierce, the sheriff's possible implication in the murder, the reassignment of the investigation to Deputy Kerr. The list goes on and on. Have these many—shall we say?—"wrinkles" been an obstacle to your pursuit of justice?
>
> *Of course. An investigation of this nature is never easy, but I must say, this particular go-round has proven particularly vexing. Are you aware that there's new evidence to suggest that the victim may not have died of strangulation after all?*
>
> Ooooo! Really? Why no, I'm not aware of that development. But then, where would I learn of it, Harley, if not from you? The *Register* has certainly been mum on all this.
>
> *The press has its own agenda, Denny.*
>
> By "the press," I assume you refer only to the *Register*,

Harley. *Dumont Digest* has no agenda beyond the education of an informed citizenry, which—

Yeah, Denny, whatever.

So tell us: What are these new developments regarding the cause of death?

It would be premature of me to speak publicly on that issue, but information should be available very soon. In fact, when I leave the studio today, I'm going directly to meet with Vernon Formhals.

Ooooo, the coroner—how delicious! Then what?

Then things should start to move fairly fast. Sheriff Pierce may well have cause to worry. That's all I can say right now.

You're *such* a tease, Harley. Well then, since we still have plenty of airtime to fill, would you care to talk a bit about . . . obscenity?

Denny, I thought you'd never ask.

As our listeners know, this is a nasty issue that just won't seem to go away. In spite of the county board's finest efforts to stamp out trash at our doorstep, mounting a worthy crusade that reflects the good, decent values of a smut-weary populace, next week's obscenity trial has been maligned . . .

I'd heard enough—besides, I'd arrived at Grace Lord's miniatures store, The Nook. So I pulled to the curb and cut the engine, silencing Denny Diggins.

The normally quiet side street was busy that afternoon, as the convention of the Midwest Miniatures Society was scheduled to open there the next morning. Exhibitors had returned to put finishing touches on their booths in the converted Rexall store adjacent to The Nook, so the bustle of activity outside both stores had reached a fever pitch. Getting out of the car and crossing the street toward the hubbub, I realized I'd picked a bad time for a chat with Grace—her mind was surely far from the murder right now.

Even as I thought this, I saw her emerge from the front door of the shop, carrying some supplies, answering questions asked by others who were headed in. Though I could not hear her, her mood seemed chipper—if she felt any jitters about the impending opening of the show she was hosting, she hid them well. I noticed too that she was headed in the direction of her house, so as luck would have it, I might be able to spend a few minutes alone with her.

Quickening my pace, I approached her from behind, calling, "Need some help with that, Grace?"

She stopped, turned, and broke into her usual impish smile, surprised to see me. "It seems you're always around to lend a hand when I need it," she said, handing me some of her things—a box containing markers and tape, and several big sheets of bristol board. She'd been lettering posters to guide visitors around the exhibit hall, and these were leftover supplies.

"Going home?"

"Just for a while. Need to put my feet up a bit." She began walking toward the house again. "But there's plenty left to do before tomorrow."

"Could you use some company?" I was already following her. "I'd like to talk to you about something."

"Sure, Mark—always time for you."

A few minutes later, we were settled on her back porch, sitting in yellow canvas chairs drinking coffee from white ceramic mugs. She apologized for the strong brew—it had been reheated and was in fact pretty bad—but the warmth of the cup felt good on my hands. It was another chilly day, and it seemed odd to be sitting outdoors. Why not go inside?

As if reading my mind, she answered, "Not many decent days left now—looks like we might have an early winter. It's good to enjoy the sunny weather while we can." She was right, of course, and I felt mildly ashamed—while I'd focused on the cold, she saw the sunshine. From that perspective, it *was* a beautiful day, and the setting was nearly idyllic. That rolling backyard, the huge old trees freshly brushed with autumn color, the quaint charm of the coach house just a few yards down the red-brick path—it didn't look like a murder scene.

But it was, and that's why I was there. "Grace," I began with a touch of reticence, "I know you've been over this again and again—what you saw on the morning of the murder—but I thought of a new angle and wonder if you'd humor me by answering a few more questions."

She didn't need coaxing. "Look, Mark. Sheriff Pierce is in trouble, and we need to help him—I know that's your main concern. If you need me, I'm happy to help. What would you like to know?"

Grateful for her cooperation, I gave her a warm smile, leaned forward, and reached to pat her hand. She grasped my fingers and gave them a solid shake, as if to assure me that everything was going to be all right. Settling back into my chair, I sipped the coffee (it tasted better now) and then said, "You've told us a lot about the activity in and around the coach house last weekend, but so far, these discussions have centered on Sunday morning."

She nodded. "The day of the murder."

"Right. But we're working with a new theory now: Maybe Mr. Cantrell wasn't strangled. He may have been poisoned."

"Oh, dear," Grace gasped, sloshing a bit of coffee over the edge of her mug, then brushing the few drops from her jeans with the back of her free hand.

"If our theory is correct, the killer didn't visit the coach house on Sunday morning, but earlier, probably Saturday. And we haven't yet detailed what you saw or heard that day."

"Oh, Lord," she said, wagging her head slowly. "I've been concentrating so hard on Sunday, I'm not sure I can even *remember* any details about Saturday. Things were busy all weekend with the setup and all—and Carrol had *lots* of visitors."

"I know, Grace. Let me see if I can refresh your memory. I myself dropped by on Saturday morning and went upstairs. I hadn't planned to, but I did. Did you happen to see me?"

She thought, but not long, before turning to ask through a quizzical expression, "You weren't alone, though, were you? You were with Harley Kaiser and that Miriam woman."

Big smile. "That's absolutely right. The only reason I went up to the coach house at all is because I ran into them on the street and they told me they'd come to see Carrol. I couldn't imagine what they wanted with him, so I tagged along."

"What *did* they want?"

"I *still* don't know, or at least I'm not sure." I didn't want to tip Grace off regarding my suspicions, as that could color her memory of the day's events. So I simply said, "Now that you have a frame of reference for Saturday morning, I wonder if you can specifically recall any other visitors who came to the coach house later that day."

Without hesitation, she asked, "You mean visitors other than Miriam?"

My breathing stopped for a moment. I asked, "When you say 'other than Miriam,' are you referring to her morning visit, along with Harley Kaiser and me?"

"No!" Grace laughed as if I were dense. "I'm talking about later that afternoon, when she came back with that cake."

Kettle drums. Fanfares. The heavens resounded with angelic choirs. "You *saw* her? You saw her bring the *cake?*"

"Sure." Grace shrugged. "It was in a box. I heard her clomping up the stairs with it. That's why I happened to look out from the kitchen window. Carrol wasn't upstairs then—he was probably over at the hall—so Miriam just left it there on the porch. So what?"

I sputtered, "Why . . . why didn't you mention this before?"

"No one *asked* about Saturday. No one seemed to think it was important."

Laughing at the gravity of this overlooked detail, I stood, pacing the porch. I wasn't sure how much to tell Grace, assuming she wouldn't understand the whole business of the nut allergy, the possibility of anaphylactic shock. Then it clicked—she was a trained pharmacist. Grace surely had greater background knowledge of Cantrell's condition than I did.

I crossed to her chair and rested a hand on her shoulder, explaining, "Carrol may have died from anaphylactic shock. The symptoms would be indistinguishable from those of asphyxiation."

Grace stared blankly into space, then raised her fingers to her mouth, stunned. "Good God," she said softly, her tone analytical and unemotional. "The nut allergy, the bracelet, the EpiPen. Carrol and I discussed his condition thoroughly before I cooked anything for him. When the cake appeared, I cautioned him not to eat it—there was no way to be sure what was in it. But when I told him it had come from Miriam, he decided it was safe. He ate some of it, and he gave me some too. He assured me that he'd already mentioned his allergy to Miriam."

"Indeed he did," I recalled.

Grace looked up at me. "But why? She had no reason . . ."

"It's complicated, but she had her reasons."

"I'll tell you something else." The perplexity in Grace's features vanished as her face wrinkled with disgust. "That woman bakes a damn lousy cake."

Tearing back downtown, I used my car phone to call Doug Pierce at the sheriff's department, but learned from the dispatcher that he'd just gone over to see me at the *Register*. I was eager to tell him what I'd just learned, but it could wait till I arrived at my office—we could brainstorm the situation with Lucille Haring and Glee Savage as well.

Turning onto Park Street, whisking past the succession of avenues that led to downtown, I glimpsed my reflection in the rearview mirror and was surprised to note that a wide grin had contorted my features. I was actually gloating. We now had an eyewitness who'd seen someone deliver to the victim a cake that could have been concocted to kill him. And that "someone" was none other than Miriam Westerman. Too bad, I mused, that Wisconsin had no death penalty. Though philosophically opposed to capital punishment, in this instance I'd be happy to set aside my reservations and volunteer for switch duty.

Arriving at First Avenue, I saw that Pierce's tan, unmarked car was parked at the curb near the *Register*'s front door. I swung into my reserved space behind the building, dashed inside, and raced through the lobby toward the stairs.

"Yoo-hoo, Mr. Manning," Connie warbled at me from her window.

I turned long enough to tell her, "I know, Connie—the sheriff's waiting for me. Thanks." And I bounded up the stairs into the newsroom.

The pace upstairs was brisk. Not only were there two big local stories (the murder investigation and next week's obscenity trial) being followed by the staff, but it was the middle of Friday afternoon, with a slew of weekly sections being wrapped up for the thick Sunday edition. The ring of phones seemed magnified. The milling of staff looked chaotic. But to anyone accustomed to the approach of a "bulldog" deadline, the scene in the city room was merely business as usual.

Across the maze of desks, behind the glass wall of my outer office,

I could see Pierce huddled around the low table with Lucy and Glee. Whatever it was he'd come for, they were already at it. Rushing to join them, I entered the room, closing the door behind me. "What's up?"

They all turned from where they sat.

"Hi, Mark."

"Hey, boss."

"Grab a chair."

Joining them at the table, I saw that Pierce had brought photos of the scarf found at the crime scene, as I had asked him to do the previous afternoon. But it wasn't the pictures that occupied their attention at that moment. Rather, it was the half-eaten bag of Chee-Zee Corn Curleez that Pierce had torn open and planted in the middle of the table. The sheriff, my managing editor, and my features editor all had sticky orange fingertips. My mouth immediately watered.

Without commenting on the Chee-Zees, I grabbed a few and, before eating them, asked everyone, "What do you make of the pictures?"

Pierce wiped his hands on a handkerchief before picking up the two large glossy photos and displaying them squarely before me. One pictured the whole silk scarf; the other was an enlarged detail of its pattern. Pointing to the detail, he said, "This little figure is repeated all over the scarf."

"No question," said Glee, dabbing the corners of her lips with her fingers, "it's Bruno's stylized hedgehog. It matches the trademark we found on his miniature furniture."

"Which means," said Lucy, sitting back while crossing her legs, "that the scarf surely came from Bruno—at least originally. He probably had a number of them custom-made, not only for his own use, but as gifts. In light of his long history of business dealings with Carrol Cantrell, it's likely that Cantrell already had one, and in fact, Grace Lord mentioned in her police statement that she'd seen a collection of silk scarves while cleaning the victim's quarters."

I swallowed a mouthful of Curleez. "So the scarf might have been Bruno's, or it might have been Carrol's—or anyone else's, for that matter."

"Right," said Pierce. "Bruno is still having trouble producing evidence that he was actually in Milwaukee at the exact time of the murder—no parking stubs—but frankly, I'm inclined to believe him. I don't think he'd be dumb enough to strangle a business rival with his own cravat and then conveniently leave such an obvious, incriminating murder weapon right there at the crime scene."

"I don't either," said Lucy, scratching the bristly red hair behind an ear. "It's *plausible*, but not probable. Besides, with this new angle that Cantrell could have died from anaphylactic shock, it's arguable that the scarf was not the actual weapon, but was merely planted to suggest strangulation and to disguise the real cause of death."

"Which brings us back to the possibility of a nut-tainted cake," said Glee, "which in turn could have been baked by Miriam Westerman."

I leaned forward. "Okay, gang. Get this. I've just come from Grace Lord's house. While chatting on her back porch, sipping coffee, she dropped a real bombshell—a stunning bit of information that could help us nail Cantrell's killer." I paused for effect, popping a Chee-Zee into my mouth and munching loudly.

Lucy drummed her fingers on the arm of her chair. "For Christ's sake, Mark. What'd she tell you?"

I smiled. "As you know, on Saturday morning, the day before the murder, I visited the coach house with Harley Kaiser and Miriam Westerman. Grace saw us. Later, that afternoon, she saw Miriam return—*leaving a cake on the porch*."

Receiving the round of gasps I'd hoped to elicit, I continued, "Aware of Cantrell's allergic condition, Grace cautioned him not to eat the cake, but he specifically assured her that it was safe because he'd already informed Miriam of his condition. Grace saw him eat it."

Glee slid a perfectly manicured red nail between her front teeth, dislodging an orange crumb. She wondered aloud, "If Carrol was so severely allergic to nuts, and he ate the cake on Saturday afternoon, why did he die on Sunday morning? Wouldn't he react faster than that?"

Pierce assured us, "He was healthy Saturday *night*."

"The timing does seem strange," I admitted, "but everything else fits. Consider: Miriam had a *motive*—her hate of Cantrell as a male homosexual who also threatened her antiporn crusade. She had the *means* to kill him—lacing a cake with nuts after learning of his allergy. And now we know she had the *opportunity*—an eyewitness saw her deliver the cake." Rewarding myself for such a neat summation, I grabbed another fistful of Curleez.

As I ate, the others silently weighed all this, nodding their assent that we were closing in on a killer. Pierce said, "All we need now for an airtight conviction is some physical evidence that Carrol ingested nuts. If testing reveals nuts in either the cake or the stomach contents—better yet, both—this mystery is solved."

"And Miriam Westerman," I added through a facetious pout, "goes bye-bye."

"Before you pack her bags," Lucy reminded me, "we need to at least *consider* the possibility that both test results could come up negative. Then what?"

With my spirits dampened by the prospects of such a scenario, I soberly admitted, "Then the focus of the investigation would shift to the only other suspect who had motive, means, and opportunity to kill Cantrell."

There was a pause. Pierce said, "Me—right?"

"It'll never come to that. There's not a reason in the—"

"Don't sugarcoat it, Mark. If testing doesn't reveal nuts in either the cake or the stomach, I'm screwed. After all, I had the motive—silencing a sex scandal that could threaten my chances for reelection. I had the means—sufficient physical stature to subdue and strangle Carrol. And I had the opportunity—I'd spent the night with the man in the very bed where his body was found."

We all recognized that his summation was as neat as mine had been. Lamely, Glee pointed out, "But there *are* other suspects."

Pierce said, "If we dismiss Bruno, there are only three other possibilities that have even been discussed: Dan Kerr, Harley Kaiser, and Ben Tenelli. Of those, Dr. Tenelli is found suspicious only by Mark. Aside from the fact that the County Plan Commission, chaired by Tenelli, issued a report opposing the porn shops, I see no reason to suspect his involvement in any of this—plus the fact that he's demonstrated, by a lifelong career, that he's a healer, not a killer.

"Which leaves us with my deputy, Dan Kerr, and our district attorney, Harley Kaiser. Yes, I agree that they both have a lot at stake politically here, so it's arguable that they each had a motive to kill Carrol—for Dan, the murder could serve to neatly frame me and get me out of the way for his election, and for Harley, the murder removes a strong foe who sought to deny him victory in his must-win obscenity trial. Even if I were willing to concede—and I'm not—that either Dan or Harley could stoop to murder, we've shown only that these guys had a *motive*. As to whether either of them also had both the *means* and the *opportunity* to kill Carrol, that's pure speculation—we've established no further evidence to link either one of them to this crime."

Pierce didn't need to add the logistical hurdle: Dan Kerr was in charge of investigating the murder, and Harley Kaiser's job was to prosecute it. If either one of them was actually guilty of the crime, he was in an excellent position to assure that justice would *not* be served.

I'd lost my appetite for the snacks, as had Pierce. Both Lucy and Glee had also abandoned the Curleez, which lay scattered there on the torn cellophane bag like so many sad little question marks. All four of us glumly eyed the Chee-Zees, pondering in silence what options for action we might have, thinking of none.

These ruminations were interrupted by the phone on my desk—a startling noise that snapped us back to the moment. "That's Connie," I said, recognizing the receptionist's short double-rings. Leaning to Lucy, who sat nearest the door to my inner office, I asked, "Could you see what she wants?"

My editor nodded, rose from her chair, and stepped inside to answer the phone. "Yes, Connie?" We all listened. "Thank you. I'll tell him." And she hung up. Returning to the table where we sat, she said, "The DA and the coroner are downstairs. They want to see the sheriff."

I recalled that Harley Kaiser had told Denny Diggins on that afternoon's radio show that he planned to meet the coroner right after the program. Something of substance must have arisen from their meeting—they'd tracked down the sheriff.

"Now what?" said Pierce. Rising, he stepped to the door, leaving to meet them in the lobby.

"Doug," I said, "wait. Can we bring them up here? Whatever it is, we may all be able to help. Lucy can see them up."

"Sure. Why not?" He returned to the table as Lucy left the room.

Pierce, Glee, and I spent a minute or two in idle speculation as to the purpose of this visit, till we saw Lucy returning through the newsroom with Harley Kaiser and Vernon Formhals. Even from a distance, I could see that Kaiser wore his usual smirky, tight-lipped expression—the poodle with an attitude. Formhals, by contrast, carried himself with dignity but good humor, nodding to staffers and exchanging pleasantries as they made their way to my office.

When they all entered, I realized that the room wasn't big enough to accommodate six of us comfortably—the space felt instantly cramped and hot. Glee already knew the district attorney, but she had never met the county coroner, so I introduced them. As soon as this courtesy was dispatched, Kaiser snapped, "We need to talk *alone*, Pierce."

The sheriff answered, "If this relates to the murder investigation, my deputy's in charge—you know that."

"Look," I told the DA, "I know you're reluctant to discuss the case in front of me. But if you want this discussion off-the-record, I'll honor that. I'm a man of my word, Harley."

He paused. Again the smirk. "You wouldn't print this anyway, Manning. It doesn't fit your agenda."

Though I felt like throttling the weasel, I was in no mood to argue with him.

Pierce asked flatly, "What have you got?"

With a flip of his hand, Kaiser turned the discussion over to Formhals.

The coroner came forward a step, tightening our circle. Clearing his throat, he told us, "I've just received the report analyzing the cake's contents. It contained substantial swirls of peanut butter."

As his words sank in, Glee and Lucy sighed audibly. Pierce and I exchanged a relieved smile. I couldn't imagine why Kaiser had said that this news would not "fit my agenda"—it exonerated Pierce, didn't it?

Pierce fished his car keys out of a pocket. "Time to pay Miriam a visit." And he began moving toward the door.

"*Why?*" asked Kaiser, as if Pierce were an idiot.

As if Kaiser himself were an idiot, Pierce turned and told him,

"The cake came from Miriam, who knew of the victim's severe nut allergy. The cake was laced with peanut butter. That wraps it up."

"Hardly," said Formhals. All heads turned as the coroner explained, "The victim's bracelet specified that he was allergic to 'nuts,' but the cake contained peanuts, which are technically legumes, distinct from tree nuts. The cake may have had no effect on the victim whatever. Only the still-awaited toxicology report will reveal whether he died from peanut poisoning or if perhaps he was slipped a dose of 'real' nuts by some other means. Frankly, I now find those possibilities doubtful. My strongest theory is our initial theory, that the victim was strangled to death."

Now, of course, I understood Kaiser's assumption that I would be disappointed by these findings. Still, Formhals's explanation left me fuddled. I told him, "I've read *many* accounts of deadly reactions to peanuts—there's even been talk of banning them as airplane snacks."

"Yes, yes," he lectured, "but there's widespread confusion on this topic. About one percent of the population is allergic to nuts. Of those, about half are allergic only to peanuts. Of the rest, some react only to tree nuts, others to both. Common sense would advise anyone in any of these groups to avoid *all* nuts. Our problem here is that we just don't know which allergy group Cantrell fell into. His Medic Alert bracelet specified only 'nuts.' If he was known to be allergic to peanuts, the bracelet should have said so. In short, unless toxicology proves otherwise, Cantrell didn't die from eating that cake."

Glee muttered, "That let's Miriam off the hook."

The coroner's findings did more than that; they shifted the brunt of the prosecutor's suspicions right back to Pierce. Curiously, though, Kaiser didn't pounce on these implications. Instead, he asked anyone, "Why do I keep hearing Miriam's name in this discussion?"

The question reminded me that Kaiser himself had never considered Westerman a suspect—that was *our* theory, behind the scenes, developed only a day earlier. What's more, Kaiser and Westerman were allies in their battle against porn. Something warned me that it was strategically unsound to share with Kaiser any hunches we had about Westerman.

Fishing for something—anything—to drive the conversation in a fresh direction, I said to Formhals, "The event that sent us down this new path of investigation—the possibility of anaphylactic shock—was your discovery yesterday of the two needle marks on Cantrell's thigh. Because the EpiPen was crushed underfoot at the crime scene, we can't be sure if it was actually discharged by the victim in an attempt to stave off an allergic reaction. It's reasonable to speculate, though, that he made two attempts to inject himself with the antidote, hence the two needle marks."

"Yes . . . ?" said Formhals patiently, unsure of where I was headed.

In truth, I myself didn't know, but I forged onward, "Since there were two needle marks, there are logically three possibilities: both came from the EpiPen, or both came from something else, or one came from the EpiPen while the other came from something else."

Kaiser butted in, "Something else? Like what?"

"Like . . . *poison*," I suggested, bluffing, as if the answer were obvious. Even as I said it, though, I realized that I had raised a sensible possibility that had not yet been explored. "I'm curious," I told Formhals. "Is it conceivable that Cantrell was injected with something other than the EpiPen's epinephrine, some fatal solution that could go undetected?"

Kaiser blurted, "For God's sake, Manning, you're grasping at straws."

"Hold on, now," said Formhals with the calm voice of medical authority. His black fingers straightened the white tips of his perfectly pressed collar. Pinching a fresh dimple in the knot of his tie, he told us, "Mr. Manning poses an interesting question, if only from an academic standpoint. Consider the neurotoxins."

Reaching inside my jacket, I extracted my pen and notebook, preparing for a lesson that was out of my field. Both Lucy and Glee were already taking notes.

Formhals continued, "Some of these metabolic poisons, which limit their action to the nervous system, could produce symptoms quite similar to those observed in the victim. Well-known examples include strychnine and curare, as well as an assortment of nerve gases developed for chemical warfare. Even such familiar substances as caffeine and nicotine are, in sufficient doses, powerful poisons that can cause the lethal stimulation, then depression, of the central nervous system."

Lucy told him, "I assume, though, that any of these substances would eventually show up in toxicology tests."

"Exactly." Formhals nodded. "Another class of potential poisons would be alkaline elements like potassium and calcium, available in many injectable drugs. Overdoses of these body elements can cause rapid respiratory failure and death, with asphyxiation symptoms identical to those observed in Mr. Cantrell. The use of these poisons too would be easily revealed by toxicology."

I breathed a frustrated sigh. "I guess that's the nature of poison. It always leaves its telltale marks—right?"

Formhals hesitated. "No, Mr. Manning. Not always." He arched a brow.

The rest of us exchanged a round of wondering glances, then returned our attention to the coroner.

His manner now distinctly sheepish, he explained, "I can think of at least one neat exception. I have some direct experience with an injectable lethal drug that could *not* be detected by testing. It's well-known within the medical community." He turned to the DA. "Mr. Kaiser, to be perfectly blunt, I'm not entirely certain of the legality of the experience I'd like to relate."

Kaiser flapped his hands, shooing the coroner's concerns, assuring him, "We're all off-the-record here. We just want to get to the bottom of this."

"Very well." Formhals paused, collecting his thoughts. "After leaving medical school back East, I did my residency at an inner-city hospital. Since I lived only a couple of blocks away, it was too short to drive, so I walked to and from home, often at odd hours. It was a terribly dangerous neighborhood. Purely in self-defense, mind you, I always carried with me a syringe loaded with succinylcholine."

Lucy, Glee, and I looked up from our note-taking, needing help.

Formhals spelled the word for us, adding, "For short, call it succinyl, or just sux. It's a surgical anesthetic, a muscle relaxant that's been in wide use for many years. A twenty-milligram injection 'stabbed' anywhere fleshy—a thigh will do nicely—would fell an attacker within mere seconds. Within five minutes, he'd be dead of asphyxiation." Formhals turned to the DA, pointedly adding, "Thank God, I never had to use it."

Glee wondered aloud, "Something that lethal—wouldn't it show up in toxicology tests?"

"*No,*" Formhals assured her. "That's the 'beauty' of sux. Upon injection, it's rapidly metabolized by the body as a natural substance, leaving nothing to be traced by toxicology."

"Good Lord," said Glee, "it's frightening to think such stuff exists."

"Succinylcholine is indispensable," he reminded her, "for its intended use. Fortunately, this powerful drug has no prescribed use outside of anesthesia, so only a doctor would have access to it."

Pierce asked him, "Then what's the likelihood that it could have been responsible for Cantrell's death."

"Very remote," replied Formhals, shaking his head, "practically nil. Succinyl poisoning is a long shot at best. And even if it *was* responsible for Mr. Cantrell's death, there'd be no way to prove it."

We all fell silent. I capped my pen.

Doug Pierce, who had listened silently to this whole discussion, now said, "So we're back to square one."

"Actually," said Kaiser, "we're not. We've very nearly wrapped this up. All we need now is the final toxicology report, and Vernon has requested a rush on it. We'll have the results within thirty-six hours. By Sunday morning, no later, we'll know whether the victim had ingested nuts—*real* nuts, tree nuts, the kind that could kill him. Meanwhile, Doug, let me offer you a word of friendly advice."

I didn't like the sound of that. Neither did Glee or Lucy, who exchanged an apprehensive glance, then returned their attention to Kaiser.

He concluded, "Get a lawyer, Doug. You'd be well advised to begin preparing a defense. If those tests fail to reveal the presence of nuts in the victim's belly, Dan Kerr and I will take steps to arrest you. You'll be charged with the murder of Carrol Cantrell."

PART FOUR

Prurient Interests

PORN TRIAL SLATED

Jury selection begins Monday in crucial test of county's smut law

---

by CHARLES OAKLAND
Staff Reporter, Dumont Daily Register

Sept. 23, DUMONT WI—Dumont County district attorney Harley Kaiser announced in a prepared statement late Friday that jury selection will begin Monday in a controversial obscenity case that is seen by many as a "must-win" test of the county's local obscenity ordinance. In previous cases prosecuted by Kaiser, juries stunned moralists by finding adult bookstores on the edge of town "not guilty" of violating the county ordinance, which is patterned after state law.

When Kaiser first attempted to shut down the porn shops some two years ago, he told the press, "Our county board put limits on this kind of expression because some expressions are intrinsically harmful to society and they should be banned."

After viewing *Rectal Rampage*, a tape procured by sheriff's deputies at a county bookstore, a local jury surprised pundits by finding the video not obscene. Responding to this first of several defeats, Kaiser told reporters, "Maybe I should have spent more time explaining to the jury that normal sex could be displayed in a patently offensive way."

The new case seeks to convict Star-Spangled Video, another county porn shop, of pandering to prurient interests through the sale of such tapes. Dogged by civil-liberties groups claiming that both the local ordinance and the state law violate First Amendment freedoms, the prosecutor has recruited a series of expert witnesses to bolster his case. They represent the interests of feminist and Religious Right groups.

In yesterday's statement, Kaiser averred, "This time, we're prepared. Dumont County will at last score a resounding victory for family values."

Dr. Benjamin Tenelli, a retired obstetrician and new ally of the district attorney in his campaign to rid Dumont of smut, cautioned the public, "Our county stands at a crossroads. Nothing less than our prospects for future development are at stake." ❑

Saturday, September 23

Pornography had been on my mind for over a week—in more ways than one. On a philosophical level, smut was an issue that had raised virulent community debate, pitting free-speech advocates, such as Carrol Cantrell and me, against self-appointed defenders of public morals, such as Harley Kaiser and Miriam Westerman. On a prurient level, however, smut was simply smut, and for several days, its erotic power had taken hold of my imagination, producing rich fantasies that were fired by discussion and memories of a fallen gay-porn hero, Rascal Tyner.

It came as no surprise, then, that pornography—as both a political issue and an erotic escape—worked its way into my subconscious and surfaced in another dream.

I'm in a large barnlike room, which is dark, except for an area at one end that is flooded with light. There's a buzz of activity near the light, with perhaps a dozen men fussing with various tasks. The tone is fast-paced and businesslike. Approaching the activity, I see that the bright light comes from overhead fixtures that are focused on a group of furniture—it looks like a living room. But there's also equipment scattered about that doesn't belong in a living room. Thick black cables connect all this gear. They are video cameras. The room containing all this is a soundstage, and the crew is preparing to tape a pornographic video.

A tall figure silhouetted against the light claps his hands, silencing the others. "Let's get going," he calls. "Where's Rascal?"

"Here," says a voice. "All set." And Rascal Tyner himself emerges from the shadows. He's fully dressed—shorts, knit shirt, and those white leather running shoes. The scene will begin with some semblance of a plot, a setup that will quickly motivate Rascal to lose his clothes. He's ready, picture-perfect, primped and buffed. The crew is hushed and still, starstruck by his presence.

This will be one of Rascal's legendary solo scenes—no man on film has ever found his own heated company more gratifying. The scene has never been rehearsed. Everyone already knows how it will end, but getting there, that's the fun. Rascal asks to review a script, so the tall guy, the man in charge, steps into the light and offers Rascal a look at his clipboard. The star says, "Thanks, Carrol."

And I realize that Carrol Cantrell has been present throughout—he's alive and well. Hot Head Video is his own production company, and he's here to direct the young discovery who shot to stardom, taking the studio with him. Carrol Cantrell, the man behind the scenes, and Rascal Tyner, the porn god, owe their success to each other. I wonder if Rascal is Carrol's lover. Then I recall that Rascal is straight, acting a role. This is business, nothing more.

"There's music throughout," explains Carrol, "but we'll dub it in later. In the early part of the scene, we'll be recording your half of the phone call, so keep it all in character. Once you've got your clothes off, though, only the dubbed music will be heard on the finished tape. During the jackoff, I'll give you directions, and you be sure to tell us when you're ready to come, so we can zoom in for it . . ."

As Carrol reviews this plan, I'm getting aroused just hearing about it. Stepping closer, I get a better look at Rascal. His subtly pumped physique shows just enough edge to remind us that he's not a boy anymore. Otherwise, he projects a softness suggesting he has not lost touch with his youthful vulnerability. He's a boyman, a living apparition of a best-of-both-worlds ideal, a dream come true.

Without hesitation, I slip out of my clothes and stroke myself to full erection. Then I notice that I'm not the only one inclined to get comfortable. Most everyone on the crew has kicked out of his clothes. Some wear jockstraps. Some wear biker's boots or other bits of leather. But most are totally naked, all fully aroused.

All, that is, except Rascal and Carrol. Rascal is still clothed because the script begins that way. Carrol remains clothed by choice. He wears a beautiful gray silk suit (probably Armani) with a T-shirt (very California), similar to the outfit he wore on the morning when he arrived in Dumont. In a pair of soft leather loafers (no socks), he glides about the set, adjusting furniture, tidying props.

"There!" he says, surveying his work. "Places, everyone." Rascal leaves the set and stands outside the door to the fake living room. The crew members take their positions. Backing off the set, Carrol says, "Whenever we're ready—action."

The onstage phone rings. A key rattles in the lock, the door flings open, and Rascal bounds into the room. Cameras swing to focus on him. He drops a stack of books on the coffee table and stretches across the sofa to grab the phone. "Hello?" Banal, perhaps, but the mere sight of the guy sets an intensely erotic mood.

Rascal converses with his imagined phone buddy. "Hi, Aaron. Just got in from class. Glad I caught your call." Pause. "I've been thinking about *you* too!" With a laugh, he slips out of his shirt, managing not to tangle it with the phone cord.

He continues to talk, but I don't hear his words. I'm focused instead on the sight of him, chest bared. Idly, he traces a finger across the ridge of his pectorals, plays with a nipple. I mimic his actions, imagining that my hands are his. Moving closer to the set for a better view, I park next to a console where a naked but jackbooted technician sits on a stool, watching a set of meters. I name him Jack.

By now, Rascal has stepped out of his shorts—the shoes will stay on. With one foot on the coffee table, he continues to yack on the phone while using his free hand to tickle his testicles. He watches, amused by the bobbing of his penis.

Mesmerized by this, I haven't noticed Jack, who's stepped over from the console and now brushes up behind me. He traces a fingertip down my spine, slipping it between the crack of my buttocks. "Squat," he commands quietly.

Eyes on Rascal, I obey Jack's order. He hunkers down with me, squeaking his boots. Feeling my anus, he taps the perimeter, teasing with the threat of entry. "Not yet," I tell him. I'm masturbating in earnest, enjoying the ride.

Ditto for Rascal. "There's something I need to take care of," he tells Aaron, hanging up the phone, spreading himself on the sofa.

With both hands free now, he can really go at it, fingering himself from behind while pumping.

Carrol calls over the action, "Take it home, Rascal. The scene's all yours now. Somebody, give him some music—he needs to hear the beat."

One of the stagehands clicks on a tinny boom box, which blasts some cheesy disco hit, all percussion and brass. This isn't the music that will be heard on the finished tape—it's only being played to give Rascal a background thump for his jackoff finale. He captures the beat with fervor.

"*Other* hand," Carrol calls to him. "Everyone wants to *see* that, Rascal."

Lying there, grooving, Rascal laughs with abandon, switching hands.

Rascal's not the only one working his way toward orgasm. Jack has slid beneath me on the floor to slurp at my groin. Other stagehands are grinding away as well, alone or in pairs. Everyone's getting into it. Everyone's getting close. Everyone, that is, except Carrol Cantrell, who continues to coach Rascal, asking him to prolong the frenzy for another minute—just another minute. And the beat goes on.

Pound-pound-pound-pound-POUND.

What was *that?* It wasn't the disco tape—same rhythm, but out of sync, way louder, from the far side of the room. Rascal heard it too. Distracted, he's lost the beat. Muttering an apology, he redoubles his efforts and attempts to save the scene—without a good come shot, the whole day's work is lost.

Pound-pound-pound-pound-POUND.

"Jee-sus *Christ!*" shrills Carrol. "What the hell's going on?"

"There's someone at the door, Mr. Cantrell," a stagehand shouts to him.

"Fuck! Keep shooting. Rascal, keep it up—bring it home. Let's get this wrapped!" Carrol bounds away from the set to the other end of the soundstage, where the pounding reverberates from a huge metal door. He yells, "We're working!"

Muffled voices bellow something from the other side. The whole crew has turned to watch this encounter as Rascal dutifully tries to regain his momentum.

"Not now!" Carrol howls to the intruders. "Go away!"

"Mr. Cantrell!" cries Jack, who has returned to his console. Tapping one of the meters, he announces, "Rascal has lost his erection!"

There's a collective gasp from the crew. (Do they have the kid's *dick* wired?)

Carrol roars, "*What!?*" Pacing a few steps in front of the door, he tells everyone, "That's fabulous—simply peachy. Well, damn it all, where's Rascal's fluffer?"

All heads turn to me. Jack grins. "You're on, Mark. Have fun, buddy."

Huh? "Carrol," I call across the room, "I was just visiting. Really, I don't—"

"This is no time to quibble—Rascal lost his hard-on. Get busy!"

The music is still thumping, the door is still pounding, but the room seems to fall silent for a moment. I turn from Carrol at the door to Rascal on the set. Sprawled on the sofa, legs spread wide, he glances at his crotch. "Actually," he tells me, chagrined, "I could use some help with this."

Duty calls. Without further protest, I stride onto the set. Kneeling at the feet of the porn god, I tell him, "I can't make any promises, but I'll sure as hell try."

And I do—to the applause of the crew. Carrol has resumed his shouting match at the door, but I'm not listening. I'm focused on the job of fluffing Rascal Tyner. His problem seems to warrant oral stimulation, so I attempt that remedy first (it goes without saying that I myself need no fluffing whatever). Then the shouting grows louder. The door rolls open on its track, admitting a blast of daylight.

There's a shriek from the crew—"It's a raid!"

Rascal goes limp in my mouth as I glance to the open door to see two figures hustling toward the set, followed by Carrol. He tells anyone, "Turn off that damn music." The disco throb is squelched mid-measure. Carrol yammers, "I know my rights. You've exceeded your authority. You have no warrant—"

"We don't need a warrant," barks one of the intruders. "We have a law." And who should prance into the light of the fake living room but Harley Kaiser, intrepid prosecutor, poodle on a leash, walking on all fours. "Our county board put limits on this kind of expression because some expressions are intrinsically harmful to society and they should be banned."

"Heel!" bleats his cloaked companion, snapping the leash like a whip. It is his antiporn cohort, Miriam Westerman. She's on a mission, and she's mad. Rattling her necklace of bones, she stomps onto the set, telling the world, "This is perverted. This is disgusting. Pack a room full of penis cultists, and this is what—"

"Hello, Miriam," I tell her innocently, rising from my task.

She eyes me aghast, her hateful gaze drifting from my face to my still-bloated penis. I wag it at her. She recoils, lifting crossed arms.

Harley yips at Carrol, "You'll answer to the law for this!"

Carrol tells him dryly, "You'll need to convince a jury first." Laughing, Carrol adds, "Your record's abysmal."

Kaiser crouches on his haunches, whimpering, "Maybe I should have spent more time explaining to those juries that normal sex could be displayed in a patently offensive way." He rests his snout on the floor.

"There now," Westerman consoles Kaiser. Squatting, she pats his fluffy head and unhooks his leash. Rising again, she confronts Carrol. "This is *your* doing." Menacingly, she loops the leash around her fist. "You should be disciplined."

Carrol laughs. "Hey, lady, don't blame me." He reminds her, "I'm dead."

Stepping forward, I tell her, "And there's a good chance, *Mizz* Westerman, that he'd still be alive if someone hadn't laced his cake with nuts."

Spinning toward me, cloak furling, she raises her fist and snaps the leather leash at my groin. "I'll lace *your* nuts!" she cackles.

As the whip smacks its target, I scream.

And I awoke.

Normally the weekend breakfast scene in the house on Prairie Street was relaxed and unstructured, but this Saturday morning was hardly the start of a normal weekend. Neil and Thad were busy setting out the boxes and bags that would provide our "continental" breakfast. Doug Pierce had already arrived, fresh from the health club, hair still wet. Also present were my two editors, Lucille Haring and Glee Savage—I'd asked them to come over that morning so we could have a brainstorming session there in the kitchen.

The pressure was on. Toxicology results and the coroner's final report were due by the following morning. If the tests provided no new evidence that Carrol Cantrell had died from an allergic reaction to nuts, Sheriff Pierce would in all probability be unjustly accused of the crime. He stood to lose everything—freedom, career, dignity. As a friend (and also as a journalist on the scent of a great story), I'd agreed to help him solve the mystery of Cantrell's death. During the early days of our behind-the-scenes investigation, the puzzle had gripped me as an intellectual challenge. Now, with only a day remaining to prove Pierce's innocence, the same challenge took on an urgency that was deeply emotional—was I up to the task?

Thad was buttering toast, piling it on a plate. When he finished, he took two or three slices for himself and spread a thick layer of peanut butter over the transparent sheen of the melted butter. Clanging his knife in the jar, he said, "We need more peanut butter."

"Already?" I asked. Neil had bought some a week ago.

"It's on the list," Neil told Thad.

I mentioned, "As long as we're taking inventory, put Chee-Zees on the list."

The room fell dead silent. "*What?*" asked Neil, who'd never seen me eat such a thing—and clearly didn't approve.

"Actually," I tried to explain, "they're not bad."

"They're pretty good," agreed Glee.

Lucy shook her head, unwilling to admit her own acquired taste for them.

Pierce broke into laughter.

Thad brought the plate of toast and a glass of milk to the table, pulling up a chair, wedging himself between Pierce and me. The table was designed for four, but all six of us had now managed to crowd around it. Coffee and juice were already poured. On his way from the gym, Pierce had picked up a chocolate-slathered kringle—a large horseshoe-shaped pastry, something of a Wisconsin specialty (so much for Pierce's workout). Glee had brought doughnuts; Lucy, a bag of beautiful cantaloupes and honeydews. All this bounty was spread before us, combined with the usual cereals and pastry from our own cupboard, creating an impressive selection for a household not prone to cook breakfast.

The table was further ladened with newspapers—there were at least four copies of that morning's edition of the *Register* with its front-page story about jury selection for the obscenity trial, a story that carried the Charles Oakland byline. Also displayed there was Glee's follow-up on the miniatures show, due to open that morning. The remainder of the front page was devoted to the murder.

Swallowing half a wedge of toast, Thad asked, "So the guy who got strangled—he might have been *poisoned?*" His eager tone suggested that this development was way beyond cool.

It made me uncomfortable that he seemed to dwell on the murder, though who could blame him? I'd assembled a mob in our home for breakfast, and our purpose was obvious—we hoped to snare a killer. Still, I didn't want to discuss our hunches in unvarnished detail in front of Thad. So I shifted the topic, saying to everyone, "Speaking of poisoning, does everyone know that Thad landed a role in his school play?"

Lucy leaned to ask me under her breath, "What's that got to do with poison?"

I laughed, acknowledging my non sequitur. "Sorry. The play is *Arsenic and Old Lace*. It's about little old ladies who—"

"—who poison little old men," Lucy finished my sentence with a chuckle, remembering the play. "Which role, Thad?"

"Dr. Einstein, the plastic surgeon who drinks a lot." Then Thad hammed a line or two, demonstrating the accent Neil had taught him.

"Congratulations," Glee and Lucy told him. "That's marvelous." Lucy had been in my office with Pierce on Thursday afternoon when Thad called with the news, but Pierce and I were just then rushing out to visit the coroner, so she never got the full story.

Thad told us, "We're having a read-through of the script tonight. Mrs. Osborne says it's very important—it's the first time the whole cast gets to hear the whole play." He slurped some milk.

"That's right," Neil told him, having nibbled a bit of kringle. "Once rehearsals start, you won't get to hear the whole play again till weeks later. The read-through is lots of fun—you get to know the rest of the cast, and there isn't much pressure yet." Neil must have liked the pastry because he now sliced off a palm-size chunk of it and slid it onto his plate.

Thad quavered, "I *am* a little nervous about learning all the lines, though. I've never done it before."

"Here's a tip," said Neil, after swallowing. "Count the pages on which you have lines to learn, then count the days you have till lines are due. Divide the pages by the days, and you'll know exactly how much you need to learn each day—every day, without fail. Then you *know* you'll be ready."

"Yeah . . ." Thad seemed surprised by the simplicity of this surefire plan. "Thanks, Neil. I'll get to work right after breakfast."

"When you get further along," Neil offered, "I'll help you run your lines."

The discussion continued in this vein for a while, all of us encouraging Thad and predicting that he'd be great in the role. Though our intention was to calm his nerves and to assure him there was no need to worry, our words revved him up even further. Not that he seemed frightened by the uncertain prospects of the production—on the contrary, he was chomping at the bit, barely able to remain seated. You'd have thought that that evening's read-through was not a first rehearsal, but opening night.

After managing to down several pieces of toast, half a melon, and a quart of milk, he excused himself from the table, took his dishes to the sink, and darted from the kitchen, telling us, "I'll be in my room working on lines."

We couldn't help laughing as he left. Pierce told me, "If you were worried that he needed some 'involvement,' I think he's found it! He's a great kid, Mark."

"Thanks, Doug." Responding to this compliment, I was surprised to realize that the emotion I felt was pride—*parental* pride. I realized too that I'd done little that seemed worthy of credit. For less than a year, I'd sheltered the kid, encouraged him, tried to understand his problems and to nurture his interests. Was that, in essence, the nature of parenting? Was it really that simple?

"Meanwhile," said Lucy, ending my wistful thoughts, "who killed

Carrol Cantrell?" Her four-word question brought abrupt focus to our purpose that morning. Stacking a few dishes aside, she pulled a folder from the briefcase propped near her chair and opened it on the table. "I've done a bit of research on succinylcholine, the drug that Coroner Formhals told us about yesterday."

Glee shivered, stabbing a piece of melon with her fork, slicing it from the rind. "Such a gruesome prospect—to think that the mere prick of a needle could fell someone so robust as Carrol Cantrell without leaving a trace of evidence."

"Any evidence would be indirect then, right?" asked Neil. The night before, I'd told him all about Dr. Formhals's experience with succinyl during his residency at an Eastern hospital in a dangerous neighborhood.

"Right," answered Pierce. "It's a long shot at best, but if Carrol was injected with a lethal dose of succinyl, the drug itself would be fully metabolized and therefore undetectable. To make the case for this scenario, we'd have to establish credible circumstantial evidence. In short, we'd need to show that someone with a motive to kill Carrol had access to the drug and an opportunity to use it."

I turned to Lucy. "What have you learned about the drug?"

She leaned over her notes. "Succinylcholine is technically classified as a depolarizing neuromuscular blocker. Its fast onset and short duration make it a drug of choice for such procedures as terminating laryngospasm, endotracheal intubation, and electroconvulsive shock therapy . . ."

"Meaning," I said, "it's essentially a surgical anesthetic."

"Essentially, yes. Sux has been widely used in anesthesia for some fifty years. It's very stable, with an indefinitely long shelf life under refrigeration. It has its share of adverse reactions, including hypotension and allergic reaction. Its contraindications and drug interactions include . . ." Lucy prattled on, teaching us more than we wanted to learn about the history and uses of succinylcholine.

In the midst of all this numbing detail, a thought managed to grab me. "Wait a minute," I stopped Lucy. "The drug has been around forever and it'll keep forever—if refrigerated."

"Yes." She sat back, taking a breather from her notes. "So?"

"This may sound nutty, but during the course of this story, which began a week ago Thursday, I've encountered no less than three suspicious refrigerators."

Neil grinned. "What, pray tell, is a 'suspicious refrigerator'?"

I also grinned, aware that my statement sounded absurd. Pushing my chair back a few inches, I explained to everyone, "On the day Cantrell arrived, Glee and I helped Grace Lord move some things from the coach house to the garage below. Among all the stuff stored there, mostly remnants of the Lord's Rexall store, was a refrigerator, an old Kelvinator, with a padlock on its handle. Grace said she kept it locked 'so little kids won't play in it,' shuddering at the thought.

"Then, a few days later, this past Tuesday, Doug took me over to Dr. Tenelli's house and introduced us. When the doctor went to the basement to fetch us some imported beer, his wife Mary mentioned that he never let her near that downstairs refrigerator, claiming it contained 'his own private stash.'

"Finally, yesterday morning, Glee and I visited Miriam Westerman at her goofy New Age School. In the kitchen was a glass-doored refrigerator containing, among other things, a strongbox hidden under a bunch of vegetables. Miriam told us it held her 'secret recipes.' "

Without further comment, I crossed my arms, allowing my listeners to consider this tale of three suspicious refrigerators.

"*Mark*," blurted Neil, suppressing a laugh, "there are *thousands* of refrigerators in Dumont, any one of which could be used to store succinylcholine."

From the side of her mouth, Glee told me, "He's got a point, boss."

I was feeling a bit deflated when Pierce said, "Now hold on. Remember our formula for suspicion: motive, means, and opportunity. All three of Mark's refrigerators relate well to this formula. Unfortunately, there isn't one of them that fits all the criteria."

The rest of us glanced at each other, confused—Pierce was a step ahead of us in analyzing the riddle of the three refrigerators.

Leaning forward, he elaborated, "First, consider Grace Lord's locked Kelvinator. She was trained as a pharmacist, so we can assume she has knowledge of succinyl and its uses. The fridge is there in the garage with lots of other stuff from the Rexall store, so it could conceivably be used to store drugs. If we assume, for the sake of argument, that Grace had access to both succinyl and hypodermics, then she had the *means* to kill Carrol."

Neil nodded. "And by the same line of reasoning, she also had the *opportunity*."

"Right," said Lucy, starting to draw the familiar grid on her notepad, "Grace had constant access to the coach house."

"However"—Glee raised a finger—"what she did not have was a *motive*."

We all weighed this statement for a moment, then nodded our agreement. I spoke what we were all thinking: "Grace had no reason to want Cantrell dead. She stood to gain nothing from it. To the contrary, she had every reason to want him *alive* today for the opening of her show. That's why she invited him here—for professional esteem. If anything, his death has blackened her reputation among the miniatures crowd."

"On top of which," added Neil with a tone of heavy understatement, "Grace doesn't quite fit the homicidal profile."

Lucy wryly pointed out, "Neither did the sweet aunties in Thad's play."

We all shared a good laugh, needing to lighten the moment.

"Refrigerator number two," said Pierce, refocusing our conversation. "Ben Tenelli is a retired doctor, so he certainly had knowledge of succinyl and access to it. Yes, he could have stored it with the Chinese beer in his basement. Like Grace, then, he may have had the *means* to kill Carrol. But while Grace had ample *opportunity*, I have no reason to think that the good doctor ever had access to the victim at the coach house."

I reminded Pierce, "People came and went for three days. Cantrell had many visitors, and Grace was often busy in the exhibit hall—she didn't see *everyone*. Tenelli could easily have slipped up there."

"All right," Pierce conceded, "that's arguable. But we're still left with the fact that Dr. Tenelli had no *motive* to kill Carrol. They didn't even know each other."

I corrected Pierce's statement: "Tenelli had no *known* motive to kill Carrol. But I'm still not convinced that Tenelli's hands are clean. I still suspect some sort of conspiracy between him and the

DA with regard to the obscenity case, so it's very likely that both Tenelli *and* Kaiser viewed the victim as an enemy." Turning to Lucy, I asked, "Were you able to dig up any background on the doctor?"

"Sorry"—she shook her head, tapping her notes—"still nothing. I expect to be at the office all weekend. I'll keep digging."

Pierce chuckled. He told both Lucy and me, "You're *not* going to find anything, but go ahead, satisfy your curiosity. You're wasting your time though."

I reminded him, "We're doing this for *you*, Doug."

He smiled. "I know that. And believe me, I'm grateful. So then: door number three, Miriam Westerman's refrigerator."

Under my breath, I told the group, "Here's a suspect we'd *all* like to nail." I crossed my legs—the memory of my dream was still achingly vivid.

"Absolutely," agreed Glee, stabbing another piece of melon. "That woman is capable of anything—her snap mood-shifts are downright frightening. Even if she didn't commit the murder, she has no business working with children, running a school. One way or the other, we ought to run her out of town." With fork and knife, she delicately butchered the fruit on her plate.

Neil said, "Clearly, the woman had a *motive* to want Cantrell dead—he was a threat to her feminist porn battle. And yes, she kept a locked box in her fridge, which could be used to store succinyl. But the rest doesn't fit. Where would she *get* the succinyl? How would she even *know* about it? She has no medical background."

I tossed my palms in the air, conceding that Neil's questions were hard to answer. Summing up, I told them, "What we're left with, then, is this: Grace Lord and Ben Tenelli both had access to the drug, but neither had an apparent motive. Miriam, on the other hand, had a motive, but no apparent access to the drug."

The five of us fell silent—we were stumped. What's more, I reminded myself, the succinyl theory was little more than a far-fetched hunch. Were we merely "grasping at straws," as Harley Kaiser had said? Was I merely fishing for any feasible explanation of Cantrell's death that would offer an alternative to the case being built against Pierce? Had friendship clouded my objectivity? Might Pierce have in fact strangled his paramour to silence him? Such a conclusion was unthinkable, but then, our other theories (succinyl poisoning or a lethal reaction to nuts) simply were not panning out. Our Saturday-morning brainstorming session had raised more questions than answers.

"All right, then," I told my two editors, exhaling a frustrated sigh, "I know you both need to be going. Sorry to take so much of your time on a weekend."

"No problem," said Lucy, rising, gathering her notes. "I'd planned to spend the day on research anyway."

"I'm on duty too," said Glee, also rising. "The miniatures convention opens later this morning—I've got to be there."

"I'd nearly forgotten about that," I told her, wagging my head. "With everything else going on . . ."

Standing, Neil told Glee, "We'll see you later at The Nook. Mark and I both want to check out the action. Our friend Roxanne will be with us."

"God," I said, rising with the others, "I forgot about that too."

Neil reminded me, "She's coming up for the weekend." Checking his watch, he added, "She's on the road even as we speak."

Pierce, last to rise from the table, told Glee and Lucy, "Thanks, gals. I appreciate all your efforts."

Hefting her big flat purse, Glee assured him, "We're on your side, Doug. I only hope we can help." She pinched her oily red lower lip between her teeth.

Lucy, the less effusive, more pragmatic of the two, told us, "We'd better be going. My computer terminal awaits."

I thanked them again, and we said our good-byes. Having parked in the driveway next to the house, both women left the kitchen by the back door.

Pierce said, "Let me help you clear the table."

Gazing down at our breakfast debris, I wondered aloud, "How'd we make such a mess? Sure, Doug, we'd appreciate a hand." Then he, Neil, and I set about cleaning the table, rinsing dishes, bagging uneaten pastry. "Don't clear the coffee," I suggested. "I haven't had a chance to look at the paper yet."

So a few minutes later, we were seated again with our coffee and the pile of newspapers. Tapping the front page with a finger, Neil said,

"This obscenity business is really heating up. Kaiser is sounding awfully aggressive: 'Dumont County will at last score a resounding victory for family values.' What a flake."

I laughed at Neil's tame epithet for Kaiser—I'd have been far less charitable.

Neil continued, "It's a pretty good article though. Well written."

"Yeah," I agreed, "Charlie did a good job with it. It's a complicated story—the history of the dispute, the legal angles—difficult to report concisely, on deadline." I raised my coffee mug to my mouth, hiding a grin.

Neil lifted the paper and peered at the byline. "Just who *is* Charles Oakland?"

I reached to refill his coffee, asking, "Back in college, in the dorm, didn't you ever play that name game? It was good for a laugh or two at dinner."

He stared at me blankly, as though I'd lost it.

I turned to Pierce and filled his cup. "How about you, Doug—remember?"

He watched the coffee swirling in his cup, then his head bobbed up as he asked, "Something to do with your mom's maiden name?"

"That's it. You'd ask someone his middle name, then his mother's maiden name. Put those two together, and you'd invented that person's new pen name. Sometimes, the results were pretty funny, but most of the time, you'd end up with something sounding credibly 'literary.' "

Pierce laughed. "I *do* remember that. If I myself should ever attempt to scribe the great American novel, I'll write it as Lewis Swan."

" 'Lewis Swan' "—I roared with laughter—"I *love* it. How about you, Neil?" I knew his middle name, naturally, but he'd never told me much about his mother's family. Both parents had died before we met.

He thought a moment, grinned. "I'd be Michael Ellison."

"That works," I told him. "I like it."

Pierce said, "How about you, Mark?"

I hesitated. Neil chuckled, asking, "That doesn't quite make it, does it?"

"No." I explained to Pierce, "Mom was a Quatrain, so I was named Mark Quatrain Manning, which I've always liked. As a nom de plume, though, Quatrain Quatrain just wouldn't fly." We all laughed.

Pierce thought of something. Scratching his head, he asked, "Wasn't there a second part to the name game?"

"You bet—and that's where it gets truly interesting. After everyone's decided on their pen names, you move on to *stage* names."

"Of *course*," said Pierce, pounding the table. "Pets!"

"Right. First you ask someone the name of a childhood pet, then you ask the name of the street where he grew up. Put *those* together, and you usually end up with something that sounds like a stage name."

"Or a stripper," said Pierce, again on the verge of laughter. "Girls with cats were especially prone to embarrassing monikers, like Boots Astor or Fluffy Center."

"There was a demure young lady in our crowd," I remembered, "who had a dog. Her unfortunate new handle: Gypsy Jupiter. She never lived it down."

Pierce told Neil, "If you get enough people around a table, you're bound to come up with some doozies. Of course, if a person's hometown streets were *numbered*, the game's out the window."

We continued to amuse ourselves by concocting more ridiculous examples (the gals all sounded like hookers, the guys like brainless beefcake), when Neil stopped short. "Hey," he asked me, "what's *your* stage name?"

"Well, I had a cat named Charlie—"

"Yeah!" Pierce interrupted. "Charlie the cat. You told me about him."

"And I grew up on Oakland Avenue."

There was a moment's silence.

"I'll be damned," said Pierce. "Charles Oakland."

Neil asked me, "*You're* Charles Oakland?"

"Yup. You see, when I bought the *Register* a year ago, I knew I'd never be content to settle into the role of an administrator, writing a few editorials. Reporting is in my blood, and I saw no reason to resist the occasional lure of a strong story. Unfortunately, there's always a certain amount of prejudice that runs against a paper's publisher, especially in small towns. I felt that readers here might question my objectivity as a reporter, since I also own the paper. So I needed another name. Turning to the old name game, I knew that the pen-name formula wouldn't work. Not only would Quatrain Quatrain look ridiculous in print, but also, I wanted anonymity, and the Quatrain name is too well known here because of Quatro Press. I turned, therefore, to the stage-name formula and have been writing contentedly as Charles Oakland ever since." I paused, then grinned, offering, "More coffee?"

Pierce stood. "Not for me, thanks. I need to put in some time down at the department—watching for that toxicology report—and hoping for a lucky break."

We stood with him. Tentatively, Neil asked, "Have you done any . . . contingency planning?"

Pierce frowned. "Like what?" He stepped toward the door.

Neil was reluctant to say it, so I did: "Maybe you should talk to a lawyer."

"Roxanne will be here soon," said Neil. "I'm sure she'd help."

Pierce rubbed his neck. "Think so?"

"Sure," I told him. "She likes you. And she's one of the best."

With his hand on the doorknob, Pierce nodded. "Could you ask her to phone me when she gets here? I'll be at the office."

And he left.

Later that morning, Roxanne roared into town from Chicago, intending to stay till her Monday meeting with Neil and some Quatro bigwigs—they had routine legal matters to discuss regarding the massive expansion of the printing plant. Though she'd be staying at the house for only two nights, she brought enough luggage for a week. This came as no surprise, as Neil and I were accustomed to her visits, which we always enjoyed. So we happily unloaded her car and got her settled in the upstairs guest room. The jolly mood surrounding her arrival was tempered, though, by our concern for Doug Pierce and the impending toxicology report. We explained the worsening situation to her as she unpacked.

"The bottom line," I told her, lolling on the bed with Neil, "is that Doug may need a good defense attorney. By this time tomorrow, he may be under arrest, booked for murder."

She turned from the closet, where she was hanging some things from a garment bag. "Good Lord," she said, "things have certainly deteriorated since our lunch last Monday. We shared a table with Doug and Harley Kaiser—there was no hint then that Doug himself was under suspicion. When did *that* develop?"

"Right after lunch that day." I told her about the extortion note found by Doug's deputy, Dan Kerr, on Carrol Cantrell's laptop. I voiced my varied suspicions of Kerr, Kaiser, Westerman, and Dr. Tenelli. I brought her up-to-date on everything—the nut theory, the succinylcholine theory, and my persistent hunch that Tenelli's involvement in the obscenity issue ran deeper than we understood. "He'd be my prime suspect," I concluded, "if I could just pin him with a clear motive."

Roxanne zipped up the empty garment bag, asking, "If Tenelli's not your prime suspect, who is?"

I exchanged an uncertain glance with Neil before answering, "Miriam Westerman. The woman's insane; she's capable of anything. I recognize that it's difficult for me to deal with her impartially—she's the one suspect I'd *enjoy* nailing. Unfortunately, all the pieces don't fit."

Roxanne paced the bedroom. "Last time we talked, your prime suspect was the Frenchman. What happened to *him?*"

"We've sort of lost interest in Bruno. Though he has no airtight proof of his whereabouts at the *exact* time of the murder, there's ample evidence that he went to Milwaukee that weekend. We'd have a tough time proving that he slipped into and out of Dumont to do the deed on Sunday morning—and the burden of proof would rest, of course, with the prosecution."

"Toxicology is due when—tomorrow?"

Neil got up from the bed, confirming, "The results could be issued anytime between now and tomorrow morning. It's a waiting game, Rox."

Standing, I added, "Kaiser was blunt—unless the tests conclude that Cantrell had ingested tree nuts, Doug will be charged with the murder."

"Where's Doug now?"

"At his office downtown."
"Do you know his number?"
"Of course."

Roxanne spoke to Pierce, reviewing his situation, concluding there was nothing to be done until toxicology results were known—in Neil's words, it was a "waiting game." She further assured Pierce that she'd defend him if she was needed. Trying to lighten the conversation, she added, "I don't think it'll come to that, but if it does, I can stay on in Dumont awhile—I brought a few extra things."

I was now glad that she had not traveled light. My instincts told me that her two-night stay at the house would be considerably extended.

After Roxanne hung up with Pierce, Neil said, "If there's nothing we can do for Doug right now, why don't we head over to The Nook? The convention began this morning, and the exhibits should be open to the public by now. It might be fun."

"Good idea," I told him. "Glee is covering the opening, but I'd like to see it for myself. Besides, I'm sure Grace would be glad to see us. This has to be a difficult day for her, with Carrol Cantrell so conspicuously absent. If nothing else, we can offer a bit of moral support."

"Fine," said Roxanne. "How does one dress?"

Despite our assurances that there was no particular dress code for the miniatures show, Roxanne fussed with a new outfit before leaving the house. As always, she looked spectacular, choosing a tweedy gray suit with pants, perfect for the crisp fall morning. Slinging the gold chain of a large, handsome purse over her shoulder, she announced, "I'm ready now."

As it was only a few blocks to The Nook, we decided to walk, enjoying the weather as we strolled down Prairie Street together. Turning onto Park, it became apparent that our decision not to drive was wise—the side streets were clogged with parked cars. "Wow," said Neil. "I had no idea the show would draw such a crowd. Grace will be thrilled."

Several minutes later, we were waiting in line in front of The

Nook, preparing to buy tickets. Over the past week, I'd learned that the world of miniatures had many enthusiasts and that these shows were always well attended. But the scene in front of The Nook that morning was downright chaotic. The publicity surrounding Carrol Cantrell's death had undoubtedly heightened the interest in this convention. An esoteric hobby had been spiced by murder, drawing the curious as well as the committed.

While paying a lady at the door a few dollars for our tickets, I noticed a sign posted there: KEEP ALL RECEIPTS. BAGS SUBJECT TO SEARCH WHEN LEAVING. The lady selling the tickets saw me read this, apologizing, "We *hate* to make our guests feel like criminals, but with such expensive merchandise, and all of it so small . . ."

Neil eyed Roxanne's big purse.

With unconcerned innocence, she told us, "I've nothing to hide," patting the purse. Then, feeling something inside, she frowned. Opening the purse, she looked within and laughed. "Actually, I *do* have something to hide." And she whisked out a videocassette, holding it high—it was *Rascal Tyner's Hottest Hits*. She explained to Neil, "I stopped at the loft last night, as requested."

"For God's sake," I told her, grabbing the tape out of her hand. The cassette label featured a large color photo of the porn idol in his aroused, naked glory, wearing only those running shoes that had become my secret fixation. Several people waiting nearby in the crowd were staring at the video, aghast. Roxanne's tearful laughter drew all the more gapes. I fumbled to hide the tape, sliding it into one of my blazer's patch pockets. The pocket wasn't quite big enough to conceal the cassette entirely, and Rascal's shoes peaked up over the flap. "Now behave yourself," I whispered loudly, grasping her elbow and yanking her inside the shop.

If the scene outdoors was chaotic, the scene within was mayhem. Roxanne, Neil, and I could barely move. Any notion of browsing or shopping was out of the question. Our best bet was to reach the rear doorway that connected to the exhibit hall, hoping the larger space beyond would be less jammed. "This way," I told them while sidling through the crowd.

My hunch proved correct. The exhibit hall in the converted drugstore was considerably more welcoming; though crowded, there was at least room to move. Neil had visited the hall with me on Tuesday afternoon, when Grace showed us her finished roombox, so the exhibits held few surprises for him. Roxanne, on the other hand, was setting foot in the convention hall for the first time. What's more, she was entering with no background knowledge of the miniatures world; she surely felt the same skepticism I had felt, nine days prior, when reading the announcement that the Midwest Miniatures Society was preparing to convene in Dumont. So Neil and I both did our best to fill her in, giving her a crash course that included such topics as roomboxes, one-twelfth scale, and celebrity artisans within the field.

As we strolled the aisles, Roxanne came to feel more at home in this strange little world, and predictably, her interest grew. Her comments lost their cynical edge, and her questions revealed an underlying appreciation for the exhibitors' passion for perfection. Glancing up from a tiny set of barware that she was examining at one of the booths, she noticed a buzz of activity at the far end of the hall and wondered aloud, "What's going on?"

"Let's find out," I said, and the three of us jostled toward the end of the aisle, where a clump of onlookers had gathered in the competition area. A set of television lights blinked on, adding to the excitement.

Approaching the crowd, I realized that a press conference was in progress. At the center of the action was Grace Lord with Bruno Hérisson, fielding questions from several reporters. Glee Savage was among them, with a *Register* photographer. There were other reporters from out-of-town papers and the trade press, including *Nutshell Digest*, and I recognized the crew from a Green Bay television station.

Grace was saying, ". . . and I'm told that this morning's attendance has broken all first-day records for any convention of the Midwest Miniatures Society." She beamed proudly into the TV lights. "It's so very gratifying, in spite of the tragic circumstances."

"I'm sure," said the toothy airhead from Green Bay—he looked like an aging frat boy in a bad suit. Swinging his microphone to Bruno, he said, "Those same 'tragic circumstances' have left you, Mr. Harrison, in the winner's circle." Big fake smile. "From the scoop I've heard around the hall, *you* are now the reigning king of miniatures. What's it feel like, Mr. Harrison?"

Bruno looked utterly bewildered by the reporter, his manner, and his question. He answered tentatively, "Very nice, I suppose."

"I suppose!" echoed the reporter, slapping Bruno's back.

Glee Savage butted in, "Mr. Hérisson?" She pronounced it correctly, of course. "You've not yet commented publicly on the death of Carrol Cantrell. It's widely known within the miniatures world that the two of you developed something of a bitter rivalry over the years. Is there anything you'd care to say regarding Mr. Cantrell's passing?"

"*Chère* Glee," he answered, "I mourn his passing. I shall deeply miss Cantrell as a lost friend. Thank you for allowing me to express my sympathies to all those who loved him."

What was *that* all about? Bruno's kind words went beyond shallow diplomacy—their delivery had the ring of sincere grief. In the week since Cantrell's murder, had his archrival's attitudes mellowed so markedly that he now felt moved to deliver spot eulogies to the press? Or was Bruno merely acting, playing the role that would serve his business best? Perhaps he was cunning enough to fear that his ascension to Cantrell's throne could backfire if his new subjects came to see him as a usurper.

As I pondered this, the interviews continued, and I realized that the focus of this attention was the roombox competition. Bruno had stepped in for his fallen rival as celebrity judge, and Grace was introducing him to the press as he prepared to announce the winners and award the ribbons. One of the reporters asked Grace about her own entry, the miniature reproduction of Lord's Rexall. Blushing as the cameras swung to her roombox, she told the history of the family drugstore and explained some of the intricacies of building the miniature, but emphasized that this entry was for exhibition only. She concluded, "I built it for the joy of doing it, as a tribute to the Lord family and their contributions to life here in Dumont. That's reward enough—I don't expect any ribbons." And all present applauded her.

It was a sentimental moment as Roxanne, Neil, and I paused with the others, clapping, honoring the woman whose efforts had mounted this event. Against all odds, she'd succeeded in bringing the world of miniatures to our little town in central Wisconsin.

Most who applauded Grace didn't even know her; they were miniaturists from afar who were simply expressing their gratitude for a job well done. Others who applauded Grace had known her for years; they were the locals who cherished the nostalgia of Lord's Rexall and had grown up with the family that once filled the big clapboard house next door. As I myself applauded, I realized that I fit neither of these two groups. Yes, I did know Grace, but I had not grown up with her family in Dumont.

Thinking of the Lord family, I allowed my mind to drift once more to the image of Grace's nephew. Ward Lord, whom I'd glimpsed but once in the old photograph that I'd carried down the stairs from the coach house, romped again with his collie on the rolling lawn behind the Lord family home. He flashed his perfect smile, flexed his perfect body, and was gone.

My doting was interrupted by the jab of Neil's elbow. "Hey," he told me, "Grace is waving at you—she's trying to catch your eye."

Sure enough, she'd spotted me in the crowd and waved happily, looking at least a foot taller than the prim little lady who'd struggled through such difficult times of late. Her tight silver curls were again beauty-parlor fresh, her features looked relaxed and radiant, and her smart autumn outfit required no self-effacing apologies—no jeans today. I waved back, then shot her a thumbs-up, offering silent congratulations on the whole affair. She returned my thumbs-up, sharing my assessment of the morning, then turned her attention to a photographer from *Nutshell Digest*, who snapped a picture of her with Bruno.

I would have liked to spend some time talking with Grace, but she was busy and the logistics of the crowd were difficult, so I decided not to try—our chitchat could wait. I told Neil and Roxanne, "There are some workshop sessions at the other end of the hall that might be interesting. Care to have a look?"

"Sure," they agreed. "Why not?" And we retreated from the crowd.

Three or four workshops were in session along the far wall, where eager students gleaned "tricks that click" from the masters. More than lectures, these were hands-on classes, working on actual projects with real materials. Advance enrollment, prepaid, was required for these sessions, which filled quickly. Still, anyone could watch, and a milling crowd of curious spectators observed the participants, who labored at tables.

One of these workshops, dedicated to techniques of curtain-making (in miniature, of course), caught Neil's attention, so Roxanne and I waited in the aisle with him as he craned over shoulders to observe the action. The basic tool used by the class was a ridged rubber form. The parallel ridges, perhaps a pencil-width apart, served to align the folds of draw drapes being constructed. The fabric or paper, chosen for both its pattern and its pliability, was forced into the form and set with polymer, shellac, or just plain steam or water, depending on the material used and the effect desired. The result was a stiff set of drapes with perfect pleats that could then be installed as part of a larger roombox project. Even this small detail, which would doubtless go unnoticed by a casual observer of the finished room, required time, patience, and the acquired skill of the miniaturist.

The students, both men and women, all middle-aged, worked quietly under the tutelage of the expert, a plump older woman in a jumpsuit who leaned in close to demonstrate technique or to offer words of advice. Those of us watching barely spoke, as the intensity of the workshop seemed to demand silence. Collectively, we tuned out the bustle of the hall behind us, reducing the distant hubbub to a muffled din.

Placing my hands on my hips, attempting to lean closer for a better look, I knocked the Rascal Tyner video out of my jacket pocket. The plastic cassette clattered loudly as it hit the tile floor, evoking a group gasp from the entire workshop. "Sorry," I muttered lamely as I stooped to retrieve the video. The disturbance I'd created was now compounded by Roxanne's laughter, which she attempted—unsuccessfully—to stifle. Neil inched a step or two away from us, pretending not to know us.

Down on the floor, I glanced at the cassette label, pausing for a moment to enjoy the sight of Rascal Tyner in his running shoes. With a sigh of longing, I returned the tape to my blazer's patch pocket. Just as I was about to stand, my field of vision was filled with someone else's shoes—a pair of clogs—and my lusty little fantasy was instantly washed over by sheer revulsion.

"I *thought* I'd find you here," yapped Miriam Westerman. Her voice was loud enough to draw the attention of several bystanders.

As I rose to my feet, my eyes passed her wrinkled green tights, her wicked-witch cloak, her necklace of carnage. Meeting her face-to-face, I told her dryly, "Brightest blessings, Miriam."

"You scurvy penis cultist!" she blared at me, drawing the attention of everyone else within earshot. "I'll teach you to defame *my* character—I'll sue your sorry cock-whipped ass!"

Before I could think of a response, both Neil and Roxanne had closed ranks on either side of me. Shocked by the woman's outburst, Roxanne told her, "Watch it, babe." Her tone was strictly business. "Unless you're prepared to tangle with *me* in a court of law, you'd better shut your mouth."

Westerman puffed herself up and literally hissed—like a big snake with hair. "Ssssisters shouldn't turn on sisterssss," she warned Roxanne.

Now Roxanne was speechless, which took some doing.

But Neil was undaunted. "What's this about, Miriam? This is hardly the—"

She hollered, "This is *about* the death of Carrol Cantrell. This is *about* the slanderous accusations that I was in any way involved in that crime."

Now at least I understood the point of this confrontation. Obviously, Harley Kaiser had tattled to Westerman the suspicions we had clumsily voiced in his presence at my office the previous afternoon. Obviously, she'd figured out that the *Register*'s only interest in visiting her loony school was to sniff her out as a murder suspect. With a small army of wide-eyed witnesses now hanging on every word of this unorthodox debate, I told her, "You've been accused of nothing, Miriam. We'd be remiss in our investigation if we failed to follow up on suspicious circumstances."

Seething, she snapped back, "The only 'suspicious circumstance' in this crime is that our homosexual sheriff happened to sodomize the victim mere hours before his strangled body was discovered. I also find it suspicious that you, Mr. Manning, have spared no effort to convince the public that our homosexual sheriff's scandalous behavior is irrelevant to both the murder and the election. Could it be that your prurient interest in a fellow sodomite has tainted your precious objectivity?" She glared at me in silence, raising an inquisitive brow.

I'd managed to control my emotions throughout this assault, but now she'd pushed too far. It was time to lash back—not with a temperamental outburst, but with the one question that could truly hurt her. "Miriam," I asked point-blank before the scores of onlookers, "why would anyone lace a cake with peanut butter, then feed it to a man who was known to be severely allergic to nuts?"

I wasn't sure what sort of reaction to expect from her, but I was not prepared for what followed. She became suddenly calm, as though she had expected my question and had wanted me to ask it. Her cracked lips parted, forming a smirk. A whiff of her warm, foul breath hung between us. A look of victory flashed in her eyes as she told me dryly, rotely, "The peanut is a legume, Mr. Manning, not a nut. What's your point?"

Her comeback produced its intended effect—it left me wordless.

With an air of triumph, she spun on one clog, twirling her cape. Perhaps it was my imagination, but I'd swear she cackled—wickedly, of course—as she clomped down the aisle, headed for the exit.

Crowds parted, letting her pass.

They gave her wide berth.

Was Miriam Westerman aware of the distinction between peanuts and tree nuts when she laced Cantrell's cake with peanut butter? I would never know the answer to this question—Harley Kaiser had tipped her off regarding things that were said during our Friday-afternoon meeting with the coroner. She had learned that I suspected her of the murder, and she had learned of the coroner's contention that peanuts are not necessarily deadly to someone with a nut allergy.

I couldn't prove, of course, that Kaiser had armed her with this information. More important, I could now never prove that her intent was murderous when she laced the cake. In the exhibit hall that morning, before a throng of witnesses, she had proved her knowledge that peanuts are legumes, implying that this is common knowledge rather than botanical trivia. If the toxicology tests proved that Cantrell had indeed died from peanuts, Westerman now had a plausible defense—she had known only of his allergy to "nuts" and assumed peanuts were harmless to him. Alternately, if the tests proved that Cantrell did not die from an allergic reaction, Westerman would be off the hook entirely—and Douglas Pierce would find himself charged with the murder of his flamboyant gay sex partner.

These were the thoughts, the circular worries, that nettled me all day Saturday. Returning from the miniatures show, Neil, Roxanne, and I had a casual lunch at the house on Prairie Street, attempting to limit our banter to the convention's various curiosities, but we invariably digressed, rehashing irksome details of the murder mystery—the allergy, the needle marks, the extortion note, the silk scarf. Each of these clues pointed the investigation in a different direction, arousing new suspicions, but none of these clues had led us to name Cantrell's unknown killer.

Frustrated, we went our separate ways that afternoon. I went to the *Register* to check on Lucy and her research of Dr. Tenelli (no promising leads). Roxanne went to visit Pierce at the sheriff's department to review details of his involvement with Cantrell. Neil went grocery shopping. And Thad stayed home memorizing his role.

Converging back at the house, no one felt sufficiently motivated to cook, and we again voiced our growing need to replace Hazel, the Quatrain family's retired housekeeper. So we decided to go out—an early dinner at First Avenue Grill might lighten our spirits, and Thad would be finished in time to rush off to his first rehearsal, the read-through of *Arsenic and Old Lace*.

Thad was so psyched about the play, it dominated our conversation at table that evening—a welcome breather from our obsessive analysis of clues and suspects. It was the first time Roxanne had heard details of Thad's budding interest in theater, and sure enough, "I was *in* that play!" she told us.

"I never knew that," said Neil, laughing.

It was the first I'd heard of it too. "You weren't one of the kindly old aunties, were you?" I recalled that the large cast had few female roles, and I couldn't quite envision Roxanne hobbling around in black bombazine and a mourning veil.

"*No*," she assured us. "I was Elaine, the ingenue from next door."

"The *minister's* daughter?" cracked Neil. "Not exactly typecasting, was it?"

"It was *high* school," she reminded us. "I was innocent—once."

Thad loved hearing about all this, and by seven o'clock, he excused himself, offering a round of hugs before tearing out of the restaurant with his script.

Neil, Roxanne, and I lingered over dessert and coffee awhile, but soon it was time for us to leave as well. It was Saturday evening, and it was still early, but there was really nothing to "do," so the three of us returned to the house. In truth, we weren't in the mood for a night out. We knew that with each passing hour, Doug Pierce's waiting game with the coroner was drawing to a close. By morning, Vernon Formhals would have Cantrell's toxicology report. For all we knew, Pierce's fate was already sealed—in an envelope headed for Dumont by express messenger.

"Anything on TV?" asked Neil as we entered the house, switching on lights.

"Is there ever?" I replied with a sarcastic edge, having no taste for those second-run action movies that dominate the tube on Saturday night.

Roxanne said, "You have a VCR, don't you?" Her tone had a wry, suggestive quality that puzzled me. Then she explained glibly, "The kid's out of the house for the evening. Why don't we take a look at that old tape you had me deliver?"

Her suggestion caught me off guard, and I wasn't sure how to react to it. On the one hand, I'd been yearning for days to get another look at the video of Rascal Tyner that had made such an erotic impression on me years earlier during my closeted past. On the other hand, the images on that tape depicted so many of my *private* fantasies, I was uncomfortable with the notion of viewing it again in Neil's presence—let alone Roxanne's.

But the two of them had no qualms at all. "Do you realize," Neil asked Roxanne, "that this is the same tape you bought for me back in college?"

Laughing, she reminisced, "It seems I've always been procuring for you." She didn't need to explain that she still took credit for introducing me to Neil.

He turned, asking, "How about it, Mark? Up for a bit of historic eroticism?"

"I don't care," I lied. "Whatever."

"Then it's show time," said Roxanne, rubbing her hands gleefully.

Laughing, I asked her, "What's *your* interest in gay pornography?"

She paused, eyeing me skeptically. "Mark, I'm a mature heterosexual woman. I enjoy watching horny naked men as much as you do. Kicks is kicks."

Duly chastised for my lack of insight, I felt compelled to ask, "We won't have to lock you in your room tonight, will we?"

"I'll behave. Promise."

Neil was already setting up for our evening of video nostalgia, deciding on the television in the cozy confines of my den, plumping pillows on the leather sofa, asking me, "Where's the tape?"

"In my desk, top drawer." Getting into the spirit of things, I offered, "Drinks, everyone?"

"Sure," they answered. Neil added, "I picked up a bag of those orange things for you. They're in the cupboard with the cereal."

Chee-Zees? This evening was shaping up better than anticipated. Retreating to the kitchen, I found the snacks, opened the bag, and dumped them into a big yellow Fiesta bowl. Then I poured a round of drinks—I didn't need to ask the specifics. Neil and I would have our usual vodka on ice, while Roxanne, three years on the wagon, would indulge in nothing stronger than mineral water. With the three glasses garnished, I loaded them on a tray with the Chee-Zees and met the others in the den.

Neil hunkered near the fireplace, opening a cabinet that housed the VCR, loading the cassette. Roxanne flitted from lamp to lamp, dimming lights. In the semidarkened room, a shaft of light from the porch angled in through the front window and zigzagged across my desk to the floor. Setting my tray on the coffee table, I sat in the middle of the love seat. Neil and Roxanne joined me, squeezing in on either side. They had already removed their shoes, and I now kicked mine off as well. On an unspoken but mutually understood cue, we reached for our drinks, removing them from the tray.

"To the future," said Roxanne, lifting her glass.

"To the present," I said, skoaling both of my companions.

"To the past," said Neil, saluting the blank TV screen. With his finger poised over the remote control, he added, "To Rascal Tyner." And he pushed the button.

As we sipped from our glasses, the screen flickered to life. Neil zapped through the dead leader, the obligatory "FBI Warning," the scrolling text about free speech, the glittering Hot Head Video logo, then finally the main title: *Rascal Tyner's Hottest Hits*. As Neil removed his finger from the button, the tape began playing at normal speed, and we now heard the sound—the same dated, nameless disco hit that had thumped into my dreams.

And then, there he was. Rascal Tyner appeared on the screen, dancing naked to the disco beat. The program was clearly old—its technical finesse seemed ancient—but it had been shot directly on videotape, not film, so the moving image of the dead porn idol had an uncanny immediacy. The close shots of his face made it instantly apparent why he'd captured such an adoring audience. Roxanne growled hungrily. Neil squeezed my thigh. I felt the warm lump of arousal in my pants and wondered if this group viewing was such a good idea—things could get embarrassing. But I couldn't take my eyes off the screen. The camera drifted over various sections of Rascal's body as he danced, while the superimposed title paraded past in a continuous ribbon: *Rascal Tyner's Hottest Hits . . . Rascal Tyner's Hottest Hits . . . Rascal Tyner's Hottest Hits . . .*

At last the camera showed his entire body. Yes! He wore those shoes, those same white leather running shoes that had captured my imagination, fueled my fantasies, and spiced my dreams. The title continued to roll past the screen, flashing psychedelic colors to the disco beat: *Rascal Tyner's Hottest Hits . . . Rascal Tyner's Hottest Hits . . . Rascal Tyner's Hottest Hits . . .*

The music continued, but now the image of Rascal's dancing body was interrupted by stills from the various "solo" scenes to be featured on the tape. We got quick peeks, teasers, of the hunky porn star masturbating—on a pool table, in the shower, in an open field, on a bulldozer—each scene progressively more fevered. Throughout, the main title continued to roll: *Rascal Tyner's Hottest Hits . . . Rascal Tyner's Hottest Hits . . . Rascal Tyner's Hottest Hits . . .*

I was getting every bit as aroused as the man I saw on the screen, and I'd ceased to care whether Neil or Roxanne noticed. After all, this was *their* idea—if the video produced its intended effect on me, so what? We were all of age. We were well within the bounds of propriety. We were enjoying a bit of adult entertainment in the privacy of our own home.

Dingdong.

Huh? Roxanne, Neil, and I froze guiltily where we sat, then wagged our heads at each other, asking silently, Was that the doorbell? *Now?*

Dingdong.

"Jeez," I muttered. "Can you see who that is, Neil?"

He was on the end of the sofa nearest the window, where a shadow now fell from the porch light. He stepped over to the curtain and glimpsed out. "Hey, Mark, it's your editor, Lucille Haring."

I stood reluctantly (I'd lost my fearless attitude about my erection more quickly than I was able to lose the erection itself), telling them, "This could be important." Stepping out of the den into the front hall, I called back to Roxanne, "Can you take care of that, please?" meaning, Turn off the television.

When the disco stopped thumping, I opened the front door. Lucy rushed in, telling me, "Mark, I found something." Not normally one to show much emotion, tonight she was effusive, explaining, "I had to tell you to your face." She grinned.

By now Neil and Roxanne had emerged from the den, their curiosity piqued. When Lucy saw them, she acknowledged them offhandedly. Since she normally went gaga at the sight of Roxanne, I knew she must have found something big.

She told me, "You said you needed a piece of the puzzle to link Dr. Tenelli to the obscenity trial. I think I've dug it up."

I smiled broadly. "Oh, really?" Stepping closer to Lucy in the front hall, I saw through the den doorway that Roxanne had not turned off the television, but had merely paused the VCR. There was Rascal Tyner, frozen in the middle of a dance step, strutting his manhood in those sexy shoes—I could just see the tops of them. His ankles were barely covered by sagging white athletic socks.

Focus, I ordered myself. "Let's have it, Lucy. What did you find?" Though I would hang on her every word, I could not prevent my gaze from drifting back to the image on the screen as she spoke.

"I've been at it all day, and I was coming up dry. I checked out everything we have on Tenelli—the *Register*'s morgue has bulging files on the guy—he's been such a conspicuous figure in Dumont all these years. But there was nothing to arouse the slightest suspicion. So then I got busy with public documents, logging into court records to see if there was anything fishy with regard to malpractice—but nothing. Then I retraced my earlier research of the county assessor's office, and there was nothing with regard to taxes, real estate, or any other business dealings that would even raise an eyebrow—nothing overdue, nothing contested, nothing audited." She paused for a breath.

I laughed. "Very thorough, Lucy. But what's the point?" Having asked the question, I allowed my gaze to return to the television, where it lingered on the electronic image of Rascal frozen in a midair leap, flashing that perfect smile, flexing that perfect body. The title was still emblazoned across the screen: *Rascal Tyner's Hottest Hits . . . Rascal Tyner's Hottest Hits . . . Rascal Tyner's Hottest Hits . . .*

"The *point*," said Lucy, "is that Ben Tenelli's tax and real-estate records show no impropriety whatever. They did, however, get me curious about Tenelli's family history, which in turn sheds light on . . . everything. Are you aware that Tenelli grew up on a farm?"

"Yeah. He mentioned that. Lots of people around here grew up on farms. His family moved into town when he entered high school. That was fifty-some years ago." I was beginning to think that Lucy's research had led her down a dead-end path. At that moment, the image on the screen was far more intriguing—Rascal Tyner, frozen in time.

"Eventually," continued Lucy, "when the parents were growing older, they put the property in a trust that was set up by a Milwaukee bank. For several years, a succession of tenant farmers leased the land, with the bank handling all payments, taxes, and any other bookwork. When the parents died, Ben inherited the farm, which is out along the highway, near the interstate. Long ago, he was approached by a business that wanted to set up shop on the property, but before granting the lease, Ben created a shell corporation in Minnesota. Privately held, its sole stockholder was Ben himself, and its sole purpose was to hold the new lease and to transfer payments back into the trust at the Wisconsin bank."

Neil shook his head. "Is it just me? I can't follow that."

"I'm a lawyer," Roxanne noted, "and even *I* find the setup confusing."

"It was *meant* to be confusing," Lucy assured us. "With the various tenant farmers, the trust in Milwaukee, and finally the shell corporation in Minnesota, Ben created the illusion that the property had changed hands several times over the years—but he still owns that farm. The barn is now painted pink. It's Star-Spangled Video."

"*What?*" Neil, Roxanne, and I asked in unison.

Needing to verify what I'd heard, I asked, "Tenelli owns Star-Spangled Video?" As I spoke, I turned again to glimpse the video image of Rascal Tyner in the next room.

"The land," confirmed Lucy, "not the business. In fact, the business itself changed hands some years ago, bought out by a larger outfit based in New York. The new owners assumed the cheap, ironclad long-term lease from the Minnesota corporation. They had no way of knowing who the actual owner of the land was, and Tenelli had no way of knowing that there were any serious prospects of development along the highway. Now, everything's changed, and the land would be worth a fortune if he could get rid of the porn shop."

"Suddenly," said Roxanne, "it seems that the revered Dr. Tenelli had a very strong motive indeed for making sure that Carrol Cantrell would not defend the First Amendment at the upcoming obscenity trial."

"Amazing," said Neil, shaking his head. "This really explains a lot. Mark saw Tenelli's car parked at the porn shop this week. I wonder what game he's playing."

Was a game being played? Thinking through Lucy's revelations, following them to their logical conclusion, I again drank in the sight of the beautiful young man frozen, leaping, on the screen. *Rascal Tyner's Hottest Hits . . . Rascal Tyner's Hottest Hits . . . Rascal Tyner's Hottest Hits . . .*

Then I gasped. "My God, that's it!"

"Well, duh," said Roxanne. "Of *course* 'that's it.' "

"What now?" asked Lucy, ready for action.

I thought quickly. "I need to tell Doug. Then he can call Tenelli and ask him to meet us on some pretext—anything. Does Glee happen to be at the office?"

Lucy answered, "That's where I left her. She was working late on her report of the opening of the miniatures convention."

"Perfect," I said. "Swing back and get her—and ask her to phone Grace Lord. She can open the coach house for us. That's where I want all of us to meet, there at the crime scene."

"Let me guess," Roxanne said playfully. "We're all going to try to establish whether Dr. Tenelli had the opportunity to visit Carrol Cantrell on the morning of his murder."

I paused, smiled. "Perhaps."

Minutes later, I pulled into Grace Lord's driveway. Getting out of the car with Neil and Roxanne, I noticed that Sheriff Pierce had already arrived. He stood near the back door of the house, talking with Grace under the porch light.

"Wait here," I suggested to Neil and Roxanne as I stepped from the driveway up to the porch.

Pierce turned from his conversation with Grace to tell me, "Dr. Tenelli was just finishing dinner. I asked him to meet us 'at the crime scene,' as you asked, and he said he'd come right over." Pierce's words were weighted with the exhaustion of the past week. Though I'd speculated on the phone that this evening's meeting would exonerate Pierce, he was still skeptical that the good doctor could have any involvement with the crime, and he was clearly bothered that I'd asked him to summon Tenelli.

"What *is* it?" Grace asked either of us, her voice wrought with confusion. "Why is Dr. Tenelli coming over?" She too looked exhausted. With the opening day of the convention behind her, she'd obviously planned on a quiet evening at home alone, kicking back—she was wearing jeans again, with a heavy flannel shirt to ward off the evening chill. She told us, "I'll be happy to unlock the coach house for you, but why tonight?"

For Pierce's benefit as well as Grace's, I answered, "Because we now know who killed Carrol Cantrell." My statement was unequivocal—no speculating, no waffling—and the surety of my words registered on both of their faces.

Grace studied me for a moment, glanced at Pierce, then turned back to tell me, "I just can't believe that Ben would . . ." She left the thought unfinished, drew a hefty breath of night air, then said, her tone resolved, "Come what may, we have to get to the bottom of this. We have to *know*. I've got my key—let's go." And she led us from the porch.

The cool night air was still and dry. A fat orange moon, not quite full, hung low in a clear sky peppered with stars—beyond them gaped a blackened universe. Silhouetted by moonlight, trees drifted like tall ships with billowing sails on the rolling waves of the expansive lawn behind the house.

Walking from the driveway to the coach house, we were joined by Roxanne and Neil, who greeted Pierce and Grace in subdued tones, everyone aware of the gravity of our visit. As we spoke, a pair of headlights pulled in next to the house—it was Lucille Haring and Glee Savage, arrived from the *Register*. They too knew the purpose of our assembly, joining the group with mumbled good-evenings.

With the seven of us gathered at the foot of the stairs, I told the others, "Everyone's here but Tenelli. Why don't we go on up? He'll find us."

Roxanne leaned and whispered into my ear, "I'm sure he knows the way."

Grace took the lead, pinching the key in her fingers as she started up the stairs. We filed behind her in twos—Pierce and I, Roxanne and Neil, Glee and Lucy. Our quiet procession rose tread by tread with the grim stateliness of a funeral march. As we turned the stairway's landing, I peered out across the lawn to the tree that sheltered a grave. There lay the collie that once romped with Ward Lord, the nephew Grace doted on. The pointed shaft of the dog's stone obelisk was dappled with moonbeams filtered by leaves.

Arriving on the covered porch, we clustered behind Grace as she fiddled with the key in the lock. "I haven't been up here since the police left," she told us. "You'll have to excuse my housekeeping if things aren't quite up to snuff."

With a soft laugh, I assured her that there would be no white-glove test.

She swung the door open, switched on a light, and led us inside.

The guest quarters had been closed up for a few days, smelling stale, feeling warm. We left the door open, Grace raised a window on the far wall, and fresh air swept through the room. Otherwise, everything appeared normal and neat—nothing suggested that a murder had been committed here.

We settled into the room, Pierce and I at the table, Grace in a comfortable maple rocker. Lucy and Glee pulled chairs to the cramped writing desk, spreading out their notes. Roxanne and Neil, who had never before set foot in the coach house, perched on the edge of the bed, where the rest of us had seen Cantrell's body sprawled. Silence fell over us. The chatter of crickets drifted in on the night air.

Pierce cleared his throat. "Well, Mark? You called this meeting."

Self-consciously I stood, feeling a bit professorial. I began, "I think you all know Lucille Haring, my managing editor." (I was fully aware that everyone in the room was by now well acquainted, but I needed to open with *something*, and the statement had a preambular ring.) "Lucy has spent the day doing some background research on Dr. Benjamin Tenelli, and her digging has yielded some troubling information. It seems that Dr. Tenelli has some real-estate holdings that point to a vested interest in the outcome of next week's obscenity trial."

A car could be heard pulling into the driveway and parking behind the others. As the driver cut the engine and opened the door, I raised a finger to my lips, commanding silence. We listened as the car door closed. Shoes ground the gravel, walking in our direction. The walking slowed, hesitated, then stopped. After a few moments, we heard the feet climbing stairs—only three. The new arrival was on the back porch of the house. A fist rapped at the screen door. "*Grace? Douglas?*" called Tenelli's voice. He laughed. "Where *is* everyone?"

I stepped out to the porch of the coach house and leaned on the banister. "Ben!" I called to him. "Mark Manning—up here."

He looked up at me, shielding his eyes from the glare of the porch light. "Evening, Mark. Where's the party?"

"Up here," I repeated. Clearly, he had no idea why Pierce had phoned him. Also, it seemed, he had no idea how to get up to the porch where I stood. I explained, "The stairway is along the side of the garage. Careful—it's not well lit."

Peering into the moon shadows behind the house, Tenelli acknowledged that he now saw the stairs. Leaving the house, he crossed the path toward the garage, gripped the green railing, and started up. "Sorry to keep everyone waiting," he told me as he climbed. For a man of seventy, he was remarkably vigorous—the steep stairway didn't daunt him in the least. Arriving at the top, he asked, "What's up? Douglas certainly sounded *mysterious* on the phone." He laughed with gusto.

I simply told him, "Come on in, Ben. Glad you could make it."

Swinging the door open for him, I followed him inside and quickly introduced him to Neil, Roxanne, and Lucy. No introductions were needed for Pierce, Grace, or Glee—they'd known Tenelli all their lives. I suggested that he take the chair in which I'd been sitting, at the table with Pierce. As the doctor settled in, everyone fell mum. In a jocular tone, he asked, "What on earth's the *matter?*"

"Ben," Grace said flatly, trying not to protract this encounter, "Mark has just told us that you own some real estate that relates to the obscenity trial. What's he talking about?"

Tenelli's smile fell. He hawed, "I own quite a bit of property, Grace. There's no safer investment than land, and I've been lucky."

"Specifically," I butted in, "we've learned that you own Star-Spangled Video."

"Huh?" said Pierce.

Grace gasped so forcefully, her rocker shook.

Tenelli sputtered defensively.

I qualified my statement, "You don't own the business, just the land—and the hot-pink barn. But now you have a vested interest in getting the porn shop *off* your property. Due to your civic-minded efforts on the County Plan Commission, that land is now worth a fortune."

"Ben," said Pierce, crestfallen, "is any of this true?"

Tenelli paused. Then he admitted, "Yes, all of it." He knew there was no point in denying these facts, as they were a matter of public record—if anyone bothered digging deep enough. "How'd you figure it out, Mark?"

I gestured toward Lucy. "My managing editor's research savvy reaped the particulars just this evening, but my suspicions were first aroused last Monday morning, when Doug and I spotted a car like mine out at Star-Spangled. The next afternoon, we learned that it was yours. You said you had picked it up on Monday."

With a slow, frustrated shake of his head, he explained, "The Commission's study had raised some technical questions regarding zoning setbacks, and I wanted to confirm the exact property line with my own eyes. So I went out there to nose around for the original surveyor's stakes—I presumed the new car was a perfect cover." He sighed. "Guess not . . ."

Pierce raised a stickier issue. "Harley Kaiser claims that you've been pressuring him to speed up his obscenity prosecutions."

"Gentlemen," Tenelli told us matter-of-factly, "that's the way of the world. That's business."

"That's *hypocrisy*," Grace corrected him, rising from the rocker and confronting him nose to nose. "I'm ashamed of you, Ben—collecting rent from those filthy smut peddlers all these years, then turning on *them* when it suits your needs."

"Sorry, Grace. I never claimed to be a saint."

Everyone *else* had claimed the doctor was a saint, though, and I felt calmly vindicated for my skepticism. Hoping this point was not lost on Pierce, I reminded him, "I had a theory all along, Doug, that Dr. Tenelli's interest in the porn issue was less than altruistic." Pointedly, I added, "Now we know that he also had an interest in silencing Carrol Cantrell, whose true purpose in Dumont was to scuttle next week's porn trial."

Grace looked confused. "What are you talking about, Mark? Carrol came here to judge the roombox competition—at *my* invitation."

Before I could respond, Tenelli piped in, "Now see here, Manning, if you're implying that I had anything to do with that man's murder, I . . . I'll . . ."

"Look, Mark," said Pierce, rising, placing a hand on my shoulder, "these developments are troublesome, I admit. Yes, I think Ben has some explaining to do regarding his chairmanship of County Plan, but I *don't* think he's connected to the murder. Remember, you instructed me to phone him tonight and ask him to meet us 'at the crime scene.' When he arrived, we all heard him—he didn't know where we were, and you had to direct him to the stairs."

From the writing desk, Glee concurred, "He's right, boss." It was the first time Glee, Lucy, Neil, or Roxanne had spoken since Tenelli's arrival. All heads turned, surprised by the sound from the perimeter of the room. Glee responded with a sheepish shrug.

I smiled. "I know, Glee. Doug is correct. Dr. Tenelli's interest in the pornography issue had nothing to do with Cantrell's murder. The murder, however, had *everything* to do with pornography."

I paused, letting this riddle settle on the ears of my listeners. Everyone turned to one another, whispering, twisting their features. Everyone wondered what I meant. Everyone, that is, except Grace Lord, who stood near me in the middle of the room.

Turning to her, I said, "The murder was *about* pornography, wasn't it, Grace?"

She shook her head, as if clearing her thoughts, as if she didn't hear me.

I told her, "The porn star Rascal Tyner, who died of AIDS in the early years of the epidemic, was your nephew, Ward Lord."

"What . . . ?" She looked at me with a dull lack of comprehension, searching for words. Then her legs went limp, and she looked as if she might collapse. Pierce and I grabbed her by the arms and walked her to the rocker. As she sat, everyone else rose, forming a circle around the chair. The faces surrounding her bore expressions ranging from concern to astonishment. She swallowed, then told me weakly, "I don't know what you're talking about, Mark."

Standing directly in front of her, I explained, "The morning I met you, the Thursday morning when you were preparing for Cantrell's arrival, Glee and I helped you move some things out of the coach house. I carried a picture of a young man playing with a dog, a collie. You told me, 'That's Ward and Rascal.' "

Neil mumbled, "Oh, my God," raising a hand to his mouth.

I continued, "A few days later, on Sunday morning, just before we found Cantrell's body, I asked you about that obelisk under the tree, and you told me, 'That's Rascal's grave,' referring to Ward's collie."

Roxanne leaned to Neil, asking, "So what? I don't get it."

I told everyone, "There was a name game we used to play in college. You'd combine the name of a childhood pet with the name of the street where you grew up, and that would become your new stage name. Ward Lord had a collie named Rascal, and he grew up right here on Tyner Avenue."

Grace sat speechless as the others voiced expressions of dismay. I silently chided myself for not having earlier decoded the porn star's name. After all, Grace had told me the collie's name at least twice. As for Tyner Avenue, I saw the street sign every day, driving from home to the office and back. The street was specifically mentioned in Glee's article announcing Cantrell's "royal" visit. When I drove Glee to The Nook that morning to meet Cantrell, I needed directions, and she pointed out the turn. Subsequently, I drove there myself, often noting the street. But it wasn't until that very evening, minutes earlier, when Lucy had interrupted our video-viewing at the house, that I finally recognized the freeze-frame image of Rascal Tyner leaping in midair. He flashed a perfect smile, flexed a perfect body, exactly as Ward Lord had done in the old snapshot. And superimposed over that image was the name Rascal Tyner.

"Mark," said Grace, mustering some energy, "I loved Ward like a son, but after he went away to college in California, I didn't see him much. I haven't heard from him in many years." A tear slipped down her cheek. "I don't know what happened to him."

Dr. Tenelli told us softly, "My God, I haven't thought about Ward Lord in ages. What a beautiful baby he was—I delivered him some forty years ago, during the early years of my practice."

I dropped to one knee, resting an arm on Grace's chair, looking into her face. "Now, Grace," I told her, "I've seen Ward's picture—he *looked* like Rascal Tyner. And we can easily find out what Rascal Tyner's real name was—it's a matter of simple research. But that's not necessary. We *know* that Ward and Rascal were the same person, don't we, Grace?"

Leaning back her head, she glimpsed the circle of faces looking down at her. Then, with just a trace of defensiveness, she asked me, "What if they *were* the same person? What does that prove?"

It had to be said: "It proves that you killed Carrol Cantrell."

"Mark! What? I . . . I," she sputtered.

Pierce quietly cautioned me, "Hey, Mark. Easy now."

Roxanne asked me, "That's a bit of a leap, isn't it?"

"No," I told everyone, "it isn't a leap. It's a logical conclusion. Everything else fits." Rising, I stepped away from the group around Grace's chair, gathering my thoughts. From the middle of the room, I told them, "Consider this scenario:

"Grace doted on her nephew. She never married or had her own kids, and she just now told us that she loved Ward like a son. He went away to college in California, where his astounding good looks led to a career as porn star Rascal Tyner. Grace did not lose touch with Ward, but knew exactly what he was doing and expressed her disapproval. Their conversations revealed that a man named Carrol Cantrell was responsible for Ward's unseemly video career.

"Then Grace's worst fears were realized: Ward died of AIDS contracted from the unsafe sex practices he performed in Cantrell's videos. Grace held Cantrell responsible for the death of her beloved nephew. Vengeance was an appealing notion, but she knew the possibility was remote, since she and the porn producer moved in such different circles, two thousand miles apart.

"Years passed. Grace's career plans changed from pharmacy to miniatures, and she eventually discovered that a man named Carrol Cantrell had established himself as a big name in her little world. Along the way, she had gotten computer literate; she mentioned to Glee and me that she used the Internet to locate the inventory of miniature products for her Rexall roombox. Tapping this research knowledge, she easily determined that Carrol Cantrell was the same man who had produced Ward's videos, and she further learned that Cantrell had become something of a free-speech crusader in pornography battles—the very same sort of legal battle that was shaping up here in Dumont. So she hatched a plan.

"She decided to host a convention of the Midwest Miniatures Society at The Nook, inviting Cantrell to judge the roombox competition—she even offered to lodge him here in the coach house. Her letter of invitation, which was found among Cantrell's things, made specific mention of the porn trial that was looming. She guessed correctly that this 'coincidence' would lure him to Dumont. Once he was here, under her own roof, the rest was easy." Needing a breather, I paused.

Grace had listened silently, shaking her head lamely, sniffling.

The others heard my scenario with less emotion, judging its plausibility. Tenelli, who had not been privy to the many turns of the investigation, told the group, "This is all just speculation. I've heard little that would actually link Grace to the crime." He patted her shoulder.

I explained to him, "The known facts of the case fit together with unerring precision. We have, I'm afraid, ample evidence to accuse Grace of murder."

Her sniffling mushroomed into a single loud sob, then subsided.

"Let's review the rest of it," I told the group. "Last Sunday morning, in this room, we found Carrol Cantrell's body, apparently strangled. His extremities were blue; his neck was marked with abrasion wounds. A wrinkled silk scarf, the apparent murder weapon, was found snagged on the wooden banister outside. This pointed to Bruno Hérisson as the obvious suspect.

"Then, on Monday, a file was discovered on the victim's laptop, an extortion note intended to cast suspicion on Doug Pierce. Since Doug *knew* that he didn't kill Cantrell, we could assume the note was bogus—somebody planted it there. This development led us to suspect both Dan Kerr and Harley Kaiser.

"On Thursday, the coroner raised a new possibility—the victim may not have died from strangulation, but from anaphylactic shock triggered by an allergic reaction to nuts. Miriam Westerman shot to the top of our list.

"Finally, on Friday, the coroner raised the further possibility of poisoning by succinylcholine, which raised my suspicions of you, Dr. Tenelli."

"*Me?*" said the doctor, astounded. "You've gone goofy, Manning. You're running in circles like a dog chasing its tail."

"Sorry, Ben. Not to cast aspersions on you, but everything fit. What's more, the only other person we knew of who might have access to the drug was Grace, but we assumed she had no motive to kill Cantrell. Now we know otherwise. She was bent on avenging the death of her nephew. And here's how she did it:

"A trained pharmacist, Grace was devastated decades ago when her family-owned drugstore succumbed to competition from the Walgreens chain and closed its doors. She helped oversee the dismantling of Lord's Rexall, storing a garageful of paraphernalia directly beneath this room, where there's a locked refrigerator, an old Kelvinator. Stowed within it, I'm sure, is a supply of succinyl, kept potent all these years.

"Enter Carrol Cantrell. His days were numbered when he arrived in Dumont on that Thursday morning. Within three days, Grace had had ample time to observe her intended victim and to fabricate an intricate web of confusion that would mask his true cause of death.

"So on Sunday morning, she entered the coach house on some pretext—perhaps to tidy up her guest's room—and in the process, she pricked his thigh with a syringe she had loaded with a deadly dose of succinyl, downing him within seconds. When he was debilitated, helpless, and dying, she garroted him with a silk scarf from his collection, recognizing the scarf as a gift from his business rival, Bruno Hérisson. Producing Cantrell's neck wounds when he was at the point of death, she created a set of symptoms that convincingly suggested strangulation.

"But Grace wasn't through. She then injected him with his own EpiPen, casting double confusion on the cause of death and leading the investigation on another stray tangent.

"Finally, creating a third red herring, she called upon her computer skills to add a bogus extortion note to the files on Cantrell's laptop, implicating Doug, whom she'd seen at the coach house several times. The document was oddly worded, referring to a 'dalliance' between Doug and the victim, a term that struck us as highly peculiar. I *knew* I'd recently heard someone use it, or a variant of it, and now I recall the incident vividly. On the Thursday morning when I first met Grace, she told Glee and me about the miniature drugstore she was building, and we asked to see it. 'There's no time to dally, not now,' she told us, because Cantrell was due to arrive any minute.

"Even though we concluded from the beginning that the extortion note was a fake, a plant, it accomplished its purpose, deflecting suspicion from the real killer by attempting to frame Doug. More important, it wrenched the investigation itself, as Doug felt obligated to withdraw from it."

I fell silent, having stated my case exhaustively and, to my mind, conclusively. While I spoke, the group of listeners had drifted from the rocking chair, seating themselves about the room, pondering the facts. Only Ben Tenelli remained with Grace, whose tears had dried on an expressionless face. Tenelli told her, "Don't worry, Grace. Manning tells a good story, but remember, he's a writer. He may have crafted a clever plot, but what he still lacks is evidence. He has *nothing* to link you to this crime."

Stepping toward them, I said flatly, "Doug can obtain a warrant—tonight—to examine the contents of the locked refrigerator downstairs in the garage. If that search reveals possession of succinylcholine, any featherweight prosecutor could build a winning case on the basis of strong circumstantial evidence."

Grace looked at me, then at Tenelli, then her gaze fell to her lap. Tenelli retreated from the rocking chair, flumping into a seat at the table.

Again I dropped to one knee, leaning in close to her. She looked especially tiny and shrunken, surrounded by the maple spindles of the rocker. Taking her hands in mine, I said, "It might have worked, Grace, if we'd failed to fathom your motive. You hid your pain well all these years. Maybe it was just dumb luck that I crossed paths again with Rascal Tyner this week, but even if I hadn't, the connection would have clicked eventually."

She raised her head and asked, with genuine curiosity, "Why?"

"Something has been troubling me for days, and I just now figured it out. On the morning I met you, you were cleaning some things out of the coach house, getting ready for Cantrell's visit. You explained that you didn't think the king of miniatures would be interested in pondering 'the Lord family's sentimental old bric-a-brac.' So Glee and I helped you carry these things down to the garage—I carried the photo of Ward. Otherwise, though, the boxes contained what I'd call 'junk,' nothing of sentimental value.

"Two days later, when I visited Cantrell up here with Miriam Westerman and Harley Kaiser, I noticed the dresser—that one." I pointed. Everyone in the room turned to look as I continued, "I noticed right away that something seemed to be missing, something that had been hanging on the wall above it. Naturally, I presumed that it was the photo of Ward that was gone. Still, the whole tableau bothered me, and now I know why.

"First, the dresser is cluttered with knickknacks, snapshots, and other memorabilia—stuff that certainly qualifies as 'sentimental old bric-a-brac,' which would have been removed if you'd been speaking truthfully on Thursday. In fact, though, the only item of sentimental value that had been taken from the room was the enlarged picture of Ward—because Cantrell would have recognized it.

"Second, the missing photo of Ward had hung there between candles, as if enshrined on an altar. It should have struck me then and there that your devotion to the boy had a passionate edge. And I'll tell you this, Grace: though what you've done is wrong, I most certainly understand your passion."

In the silence of the room, I smiled, trying to coax one in return.

Grace sniffled, flicking the crust of a dried tear from her lashes. "Thank you, Mark," she told me, patting my hand, returning the smile. "All right," she added with a wan little chuckle, "you got me."

Roxanne rolled her eyes.

I stood. My knees were killing me.

As for Grace, the crisis had passed, and she now appeared serene—shot, but serenely so. She told everyone, "Yes, Mark got it right, the whole dismal story. I did indeed love Ward. I still do. With a passion—I guess that's the right word. When Ward moved to California with my brother's family, I grieved that I'd lost him. Little did I know how prophetic that grief would prove to be. Losing Ward was the worst chapter of my life, far worse than losing the drugstore. Because of the circumstances of Ward's death—the AIDS, the pornography—the whole tragedy was never acknowledged by the family. My God, there wasn't even a *funeral*. The wound just festered. There was no 'closure.' Well, there's certainly 'closure' now—I killed Carrol Cantrell with an injection of succinylcholine, just as Mark said. I went too far. I know that. But what's done is done." She paused, then added, "For whatever it's worth, I'm sorry."

Both of my editors, Lucy and Glee, were engaged in some frantic note-taking at the desk, preparing tomorrow's headline story.

Neil sat with Roxanne on the edge of the bed, his comforting arm slung over her shoulder as they listened to Grace's confession.

Tenelli remained seated at the table, shaking his head in somber disbelief.

I reminded the little woman in the rocking chair, "You've cast suspicion on a number of people, Grace. But the person you've truly hurt is Doug."

"Mark"—Pierce stepped toward me—"don't."

"No, Mark is right," said Grace, rising from the chair, stepping a single pace toward us. "Douglas, I am so very sorry. I've always been fond of you, and I was reluctant to implicate you in the crime, but I needed *someone* to be the object of the extortion note I planted, and well, I'd actually seen you visit the coach house at night. But believe me, Doug, I had no idea that you and Carrol were in fact having a dalliance. I assumed you would easily clear yourself, but instead, it seems I've actually hurt your chances in the election. I didn't mean to—what?—push you out of the closet. I didn't even know you were in a closet." She covered her mouth with her fingertips.

"Grace," said Pierce, heaving a sigh, "you may have done me a favor. I can handle the 'outing'—not that I appreciate being accused of murder."

Stepping toward him, she said, "Well, Douglas—do your duty."

He hesitated. "Grace, I can't tell you how difficult—"

"Posh now. You know what needs to be done, Sheriff. How does it go? 'You have the right to remain silent'?"

Roxanne rolled her eyes again.

And Pierce recited Grace's rights.

EPILOGUE

Six Weeks Later

IT'S A SQUEAKER!

Local voters return Douglas Pierce to office by a razor-thin margin

---

Election results compiled by the *Register*'s staff
Dumont Daily Register

Nov. 8, DUMONT WI—In Dumont County's most closely watched local election, Douglas Pierce appeared headed for a narrow victory in his bid to secure reelection as sheriff. As the *Register* went to press in Wednesday's early-morning hours, Pierce maintained a slim lead over his opponent, Lieutenant Daniel Kerr. They were separated by a margin of less than one-half of one percent.

Pierce overcame a flood of negative publicity tainting his campaign when he was falsely implicated in the September 17 murder of Carrol Cantrell. Though the allegations proved groundless, circumstances led Pierce to a public acknowledgment of his homosexuality.

The *Register* endorsed Pierce early in the campaign, maintaining its endorsement throughout the scandal. Public opinion, however, has shifted radically since the murder, first swinging against Pierce when the news broke, then favoring him with a sympathetic backlash when the crime was resolved. In the weeks since, debate has focused on whether Dumont County is willing to reelect an openly gay sheriff.

"It's in the hands of the voters now," Pierce said at an election-night gathering of supporters. "I'm confident that the people of Dumont will prove themselves tolerant and fair-minded, ignoring personal issues that simply have no bearing on county government."

In Dumont County, city voters have traditionally taken a more liberal stand at the polls, while the county's rural voters tend to be more conservative. Pierce garnered a comfortable lead in the city, with all precincts counted. His opponent led slightly in outlying areas, where some communities still use paper ballots and are slow to report.

Though a final count in the close race may not be available till after daybreak, the *Register* is sufficiently confident in Pierce's lead to declare him the winner. ❑

Wednesday, November 8

What's in a name?

That's the question that keeps popping to mind as I look back at events that marked the last couple of months. Names—their meaning, their power, their hidden allusions—names played an unexpected role in the story that began that Thursday morning in mid-September.

Nine days later, when the mystery of Carrol Cantrell's death was solved, some of those name games ended. We named Cantrell's killer. We named the hypocrisy of Dr. Tenelli's maneuvers to rid Dumont County of porn. And I discovered that the beautiful boyman pictured playing with his dog, enshrined in a gilt frame, had not one name, but two: Ward Lord and Rascal Tyner.

The events of that week in September left other riddles, other name games, that could not be resolved so neatly. I still wondered about my fatherly role toward Thad, unsure that I was fit for it and even less certain what to name it. I still fretted over Neil's temporary residence in the house on Prairie Street—his project at Quatro Press would wrap up before winter, and by plan, he would return to his architectural firm in Chicago. Is there a name for such a relationship, a "marriage" restricted to alternating weekend visits? And I wondered, along with every other voter in Dumont County, whether an openly gay sheriff named Douglas Pierce, facing reelection, could overcome the latent prejudices of Middle America and find victory in the common sense of ordinary people.

Now, at least, I knew the answer to that last question. It was around seven o'clock on the Wednesday morning after the election. The November dawn was predictably cold and bleak— the sun had not yet risen, and a cloud-clogged sky would hold back the daylight for another hour. Indoors, lamps burned as if at night, day's end, but in fact we three were coursing headlong into a new day, one that Thad, Neil, and I each greeted with special enthusiasm.

Gathered in the kitchen, we clucked about the election, giddy and a bit groggy in the wake of Pierce's narrow victory—his "mandate" of barely a hundred votes was now official. Thad, not yet dressed but wearing a long, loose pair of knit shorts that reminded me of bloomers, was busy spreading his usual peanut butter on toast. Neil stood at the counter in his robe, adding a few things to the shopping list. "Don't worry," he told me. "Chee-Zees have graduated to the top of the list, along with bread and milk." Seated at the table, I laughed while studying page one, drinking coffee, fully dressed for the office. It had been a long night, both in the newsroom and at Pierce's campaign party, but I needed to get back to the *Register* early—it would be a hectic day, with follow-up stories on winners and losers alike.

The morning after an election always brings with it a sense of relief. Regardless of outcome, the tension and hype are over. That Wednesday morning, my sense of relief was tempered by an undercurrent of letdown. Though my friend had won his election, the adrenaline-rushed days of fighting the good fight were now past.

By contrast, Thad was still on an emotional upswing. His energies had yet to peak, as his school play was now in the final week of production—*Arsenic and Old Lace* would open in two days, on Friday night. "So, you're like *coming*, aren't you?" he asked while scooting to the table with his toast and milk. "I can't *wait* for you to see this—it's great!"

Though both Neil and I had seen *Arsenic* several times over, we'd never seen it with Thad as Dr. Einstein. I assured him, "We wouldn't miss it."

Neil joined us at the table, asking Thad, "We won't make you nervous, will we? If you'd prefer, we can skip opening night and come on Saturday."

Thad gulped some milk. "*Nervous?* Are you kidding? I *want* you in the audience. I've told the whole cast, 'Mark and Neil will be there.' I want them to meet you after the show." He paused. Dead serious and a bit sheepish, he added, "I want to show you off."

Neil and I glanced at each other, astounded. There I was, still fretting over which label to apply to my relationship with this sixteen-year-old, still perplexed by the odd makeup of our household, when Thad suddenly taught me that he *needed* me. Not only that, he valued *us*, Neil and me. And he had no problem whatever in describing us to his friends—we were simply Mark and Neil. Period. I realized in that same instant that I not only felt duty-bound to rear and protect Thad. I now understood something far more profound: I loved him.

"Of course," we told him. "We'll be there."

Neil added, "You're obviously enthused about the show. You must be ready."

"Mrs. Osborne says we are. Tonight is our last rehearsal—full final dress—complete with costumes, makeup, lights, and sound. She plans to give us Thursday night off, says the rest will do us good. Then Friday night, curtain up!"

Wryly, I looked past Thad to tell Neil, "It seems the theater bug has truly bit."

"Big time," Neil concurred.

Thad asked him, "Will you run lines with me again tonight before rehearsal?"

"You bet—that's my job. I'd be offended if you asked anyone else."

The back door cracked open. "Any coffee left?" asked Pierce, stepping in. He'd been up all night, awaiting the final vote tally, then went directly from his victory party to the gym for his early-morning workout. He'd shaved and changed there, looking fresh for the day—his hair was still wet from the shower. Wearing that olive-colored, calf-length duster, he had the rugged look of an outback lawman. The bagged kringle he carried was so fresh, he must have waited for the bakery to ice it.

We rose from our chairs with a chorus of congratulations. Neil gave Pierce a victory hug as Thad took the pastry and opened it on the table—its cream-cheese topping was still warm and glistening. Thad reacted to the sight of the big Danish as if it were covered with slime; though he'd matured in many ways during the months since I'd first met him, his adolescent tastes still found cream cheese repugnant.

Laughing, I helped Pierce out of his coat and hung it in the back hall. Then the four of us settled around the table, one on each side of it.

Reaching to pour coffee for Pierce, I told him, "Well, Doug, it was an uphill battle, but you did it."

"*We* did it," he emphasized, "and I'll never be able to thank you guys."

"Don't thank us," Neil told him. "Just keep doing a great job, as always."

With a pensive chuckle, Pierce said, "I knew the election would be close—but ninety-six votes? It seems I still have a bit of work to do in winning back the confidence of my constituents. There are plenty of them still uncomfortable with the idea of a gay sheriff."

"The point is," said Neil, "you won. You proved yourself innocent of Carrol Cantrell's murder, and in the process, you arrested the true killer."

Thad asked, "The old lady, right?" Inching from his chair with excitement, he told us, "It's so cool—everyone says it's just like our play, like Aunt Martha and Aunt Abby, who poison everybody. There's been so much in the paper about it, Mrs. Osborne says we can expect sellout crowds. Are you coming, Sheriff? I'll make sure you have a ticket."

I suggested, "Why don't you come with us, Doug? Neil and I are going to the opening, Friday night."

Without a moment's hesitation, Pierce said, "Sure. Sounds great." As he yakked with Thad about the play, I marveled at the progress Pierce had made with his coming out. Though he'd befriended me during the week of my arrival in Dumont, he'd always seemed uneasy about socializing with Neil and me—he'd even turned down invitations to parties at our home. Now, of course, people had no reason to speculate about his sexual orientation, which was a matter of public record. Though Pierce had been outed in a particularly ugly way, he quickly concluded that he'd been not shamed, but liberated. So he didn't think twice about making a date with Neil and me to attend the opening of our kid's school play.

"Gosh," Thad told us, glancing at the clock, "I'd better get dressed." Carrying his dishes from the table, he turned to tell Pierce, "Congratulations again, Sheriff." Then he raced from the kitchen to the front hall, bounding up the stairs.

"Imagine that," said Pierce with a laugh. "They're selling tickets like hotcakes because the play bears a resemblance to a local murder story."

"Hey," said Neil, ever the practical philosopher, "whatever works."

I observed, "Unfortunately for Grace Lord, the future's not nearly so rosy as it was for the dear aunties, who committed themselves to Happydale Sanitarium."

"No," said Pierce, shaking his head, "life in prison will be no Happydale for Grace. She'll be treated well, of course, and with any luck, she could be eligible for parole in a few years. But at her age—who knows? She may never see the outside world again."

Neil said, "Her 'little world' just got a lot smaller. Poor Grace."

"She murdered a man in cold blood," I reminded him, "and the crime was premeditated, planned in exacting detail. She almost got away with it, and if she had, Doug wouldn't be pothering over ninety-six votes this morning. Justice has been served." Even so, I felt no joy in the situation. Neil was right. Poor Grace.

Pierce cut a couple of slices from the kringle, serving Neil and me. He told us, "It was hard enough *arresting* Grace. Harley Kaiser had to *prosecute* the case against her, a task he didn't relish. It didn't set well with a lot of people."

I smiled. "The DA seems adrift in a public-relations crisis, doesn't he?"

Neil chomped the corner of his pastry. After wiping cream cheese from his lips, he told us, "Kaiser sure looked like a fool when he lost his must-win porn case. At considerable expense to county taxpayers, he shipped in that army of expert witnesses, and he *still* couldn't get a local jury to agree on what's obscene. Maybe he's finally learned a lesson."

"Regardless," said Pierce, "the county board will now be loath to renew funding for the assistant prosecutor hired by Kaiser to handle these cases. Their moral indignation over the presence of the porn shops has been overshadowed by an unshakable political reality—after all is said and done, the people of Dumont are *not* book burners. They simply don't appreciate the efforts of those who seek to force their own private morality on the public at large. This is an issue to be fought from the pulpit, not city hall."

"Amen," said Neil with a smirk.

Listening, nodding, I was in complete agreement with the sentiments expressed by both Pierce and Neil. "But it's ironic," I told them, "that Kaiser didn't lose this case on moralistic grounds. From the beginning, the prosecution was tainted by the whiff of witness tampering, a direct result of Kaiser's ill-advised visit to Cantrell on the morning before the murder. Ultimately, though, what scuttled Kaiser's chances of wooing a jury was the public outrage over Dr. Tenelli's financial interest in the trial."

From the side of his mouth, Pierce told me, "You wasted no time getting *that* story out."

I grinned. "Just doing my job, Doug—it was a natural for a page-one exposé. If the sainted doctor happened to be disgraced in the process, that was *his* doing, not mine. At least he had the decency not to deny anything. He resigned from the County Plan Commission the morning the story broke."

Pierce's tone turned philosophical. "Miriam Westerman also suffered a setback with the defeat of that obscenity case. Her ax-grinding wasn't based on moral grounds or financial interests, but on purely sexist motives. And she sought to elect my opponent, Deputy Dan, because his family-values platform fit her own agenda. Now that she's been slapped down, maybe she'll keep quiet for a while."

"I *doubt* it!" said Neil with a single burst of laughter.

I told them, "I'll bet she's just lying dormant—but she could blow any day, without warning."

Now Pierce laughed. "Your take on Miriam is a bit slanted, isn't it, Mark?"

"Okay. It's no secret that I don't like the woman. It goes beyond that, though. I think she's truly dangerous—not just her wacky views, not just her influence over innocent children, but also her stridency, her conviction. I believe she would stoop to *anything*, and I believe she *did* try to kill Carrol Cantrell. We know she laced that cake with peanut butter; what we'll never know, because Kaiser tipped her off, is whether she understood that the peanuts would not be lethal to Cantrell. In a morbid sense, Miriam simply got lucky—someone else poisoned Cantrell, finishing the job she set out to do."

Pierce cautioned me gently, "Reserve your judgment on that, Mark. As you say, we'll just never know what Miriam was up to. Whether she was 'lucky' or not, that's for her to decide. Tragedies like this rarely have a silver lining. Fortune smiled on no one."

Fingering the rim of my coffee mug, I nodded. Pierce was right. "There *weren't* any winners, were there? Carrol Cantrell, Grace Lord, Ben Tenelli—they're all worse off than they were two months ago."

"Not so fast," said Neil. "Don't forget Bruno Hérisson. He's now the reigning king of miniatures. His principal rival is out of the picture. Bruno even abandoned plans to open his own miniatures gallery—he simply bought out Cantrell's business and moved right in."

"And don't forget *me*," said Pierce, leaning on his elbows, which brought him a few inches closer to both Neil and me. "I may have been falsely implicated in a murder. I may have been unceremoniously outed in the process. But now that it's done, I *am* better off. I've discovered the depth of your friendship, I'm living my life openly, and I even managed to get reelected—by ninety-six votes. What more could a man ask?"

"Ninety-seven?" quipped Neil.

"Doug," I told him, resting a hand on his sleeve, "friendship works both ways. Neil and I are equally privileged to know *you*. From day one, you've made us feel welcome in this town. If you ever need us, we're here for you."

We all paused for a moment, sharing a smile, feeling a bit soppy. I tried to cover a grin by slurping some coffee, but it had gone cold, and the pot was empty.

"Shall I make some more?" offered Neil.

"Not for me," said Pierce, rising. "I'd better get down to the department. When I left yesterday, there was an element of uncertainty as to whether I'd be back this morning." He laughed, checking his watch. "Time to prove the point."

We stood with him, agreeing that we too needed to launch our day. I was eager to get downtown to the *Register;* Neil wasn't even dressed yet. So we thanked Pierce for the kringle, congratulated him again with a hug or two, got him into his coat, and watched as he left through the back door, admitting a nippy gust of November dawn.

Neil told me, "You need to get going. I'll clean up here."

"No rush. I'll help." And we set about clearing the table, loading the dishwasher, scrubbing down the sink and countertops. Stowing the leftover pastry in the refrigerator, thumping the door closed, I turned to tell Neil, "I've made a decision."

"Oh?" he said, looking up from the coffeemaker, wiping it clean.

"We need a housekeeper. It's time. I'll place a classified as soon as I get downtown. We can start interviewing applicants this weekend."

"You're right," he said, folding a dish towel. "It *is* time. You'll really need the extra help, now that the Quatro project is wrapping up." With a laugh, he added, "You guys will be losing your 'housewife.' "

I didn't want to hear that, not this morning. But it was now or never—I finally had to broach the topic I'd been brooding over.

"Except," he continued, interrupting my thoughts, "I've come to a decision of my own." He grinned. It was that handsome grin I'd first fallen in love with. It was the face, the smile, that had changed my life.

The sight of it only reinforced my dread of the day when Neil would return to his Chicago job. I must have been nuts, proposing our alternating-weekend "arrangement" in the first place. Warily, I asked, "A decision about what?"

He answered with a question of his own: "Free for lunch today?"

I answered with yet another question: "For you? Any day. *Every* day."

"What if I meet you at the Grill? I'd like to show you something."

I paused, afraid to ask. Could he possibly—?

"That corner storefront. I've signed a lease. I've got the key. I mean, how could I leave Dumont now? Thad needs us—*us*. We have so little time with him until college, it would be crazy to miss these years together. So I'll just have to take the plunge and try to reestablish my practice up here. Anyway, I want to show you the space and pick your brain about—"

Stepping to him, I interrupted his discourse with a full-body hug—an engulfing, passionate, splat-against-the-wall embrace, replete with a deep coffee-flavored, tongue-wagging kiss. This wasn't foreplay. This wasn't fooling around. This was the real item—a kiss of love and thanks and adoration. That kind of rapture, that kind of happiness, doesn't come along often. Some poor devils go to the grave without knowing it even once. Yet, there it was, right there in the kitchen on Prairie Street.

"You're . . . *crying*," Neil told me as he held my face in his hands. "What's wrong, Mark?"

"Nothing. Absolutely nothing."

Tracing a finger across his lips, I counted myself a lucky man. ❑